MW01223514

Neighbours On the Green by Margaret Oliphant

Margaret Oliphant Wilson was born on April 4th, 1828 to Francis W. Wilson, a clerk, and Margaret Oliphant, at Wallyford, near Musselburgh, East Lothian.

Her youth was spent in establishing a writing style and by 1849 she had her first novel published: Passages in the Life of Mrs. Margaret Maitland.

Two years later, in 1851 Caleb Field was published and also an invitation to contribute to Blackwood's Magazine; the beginning of a life time business relationship.

In May 1852, Margaret married her cousin, Frank Wilson Oliphant. Their marriage produced six children but, tragically, three died in infancy. When her husband developed signs of the dreaded consumption (tuberculosis) they moved to Florence, and then to Rome where, sadly, he died.

Margaret was naturally devastated but was also now left without support and only her income from writing to support the family. She returned to England and took up the burden of supporting her three remaining children by her literary activity.

Her incredible and prolific work rate increased both her commercial reputation and the size of her reading audience. Tragedy struck again in January 1864 when her only remaining daughter Maggie died.

In 1866 she settled at Windsor to be closer to her sons, who were being educated at near-by Eton School.

For more than thirty years she pursued a varied literary career but family life continued to bring problems. Cyril Francis, her eldest son, died in 1890. The younger son, Francis, who she nicknamed 'Cecco', died in 1894.

With the last of her children now lost to her, she had little further interest in life. Her health steadily and inexorably declined.

Margaret Oliphant Wilson Oliphant died at the age of 69 in Wimbledon on 20th June 1897. She is buried in Eton beside her sons.

Index of Contents

MARGARET OLIPHANT – A SHORT BIOGRAPHY
MARGARET OLIPHANT - A CONCISE BIBLIOGRAPHY

MY NEIGHBOUR NELLY

CHAPTER I

They were both my neighbours, of course: but to apportion one's heart's love in equal shares according to the claims of justice is a very different matter. I saw as much of one sister as the other. And Martha was an excellent girl, quite honest and friendly and good; but as for Ellen, there never could be any question about her. One did not even think of discriminating which were her special good qualities. She was Ellen, that was enough; or Nelly, which I prefer, for my part. We all lived at Dinglefield Green in these old days. It is a model of a village, in one sense of the word; not the kind of place, it is true, to which the name is generally applied, but a village orné, as there are cottages ornés. The real little hamlet, where the poor people lived, was at a little distance, and gave us plenty of occupation and trouble. But for Dinglefield Green proper, it was such a village as exists chiefly in novels. The Green was the central point, a great triangular breadth of soft grass, more like a small common than a village green, with the prettiest houses round—houses inclosed in their own grounds,—houses at the very least embosomed in pretty gardens, peeping out from among the trees. None of us were very rich; nor was there anything that could be called a 'place' in the circle of dwellings. But I believe there was as much good blood and good connection among us as are rarely to be found even in a much larger community. The great house opposite, which was separated from the green by a ha-ha, and opened to us only a pretty sweep of lawn, looking almost like a park, belonged to Sir Thomas Denzil, whose pedigree, as everybody knows, is longer than the Queen's. Next to him was Mrs. Stoke's pretty cottage who was— one of the Stokes who have given their name to places all over the country: the son is now General Stoke, a C.B., and I don't know what besides: and her daughter married Lord Leamington. Next to that— but it is needless to give a directory of the place: probably our neighbours, in their different habitations, may appear in their proper persons before my story is done.

The sisters lived next to me; my house lay, as their father said, athwart their bows. The Admiral was too much a gentleman to talk ship, or shop, as the gentlemen call it, in ordinary conversation; but he did say that my cottage lay athwart his bows; and the girls admitted that it would have been unpleasant had it been anybody but me. I was then a rather young widow, and having no children, did not want much of a house. My cottage was very pretty. I think myself that there was not so pretty a room in all the green as my drawing-room; but it was small. My house stood with its gable-end to the green, and fronted the hedge which was the boundary of Admiral Fortis' grounds. His big gate and my small one were close together. If the hedge had been cut down, I should have commanded a full view of the lawn before his house, and the door; and nobody could have gone out or come in without my inspection. They were so friendly, that it was once proposed to cut it down, and give me and my flowers more air; but we both reflected that we were mortal; circumstances might change with both of us; I might die, and some one else come to the cottage whose inspection might not be desirable; or the Admiral might die, and his girls marry, and strangers come. In short, the end of it was that the hedge remained; but instead of being a thick holly wall, like the rest of my inclosure, it was a picturesque hedge of hawthorn, which was very sweet in spring and a perfect mass of convolvulus in autumn; and it had gaps in it and openings. Nelly herself made a round cutting just opposite my window, and twined the honeysuckle into a frame for it. I could see them through it as I sat at work. I could see them at their croquet, and mounting their horses at the door, and going out for their walks, and doing their capricious gardening. Indeed it was Nelly only who ever attempted to work in the garden; the other was afraid of her hands and her complexion, and a hundred things. Nelly was not afraid of anything—not even of Mr. Nicholson, the gardener, who filled me with awe and trembling. Perhaps you may say that there was not much fear of her complexion. She was brown, to begin with; but the prettiest brown—clear, with crimson flushes that went and came, and changed her aspect every moment. Her eyes were the softest dark eyes I ever saw; they did not penetrate or flash or sparkle, but glowed on you with a warm lambent light. In winter, with her red cloak on, she was the prettiest little figure; and the cold suited her, and made her glow and bound about like a creature of air. As for Martha, she was a great deal larger and whiter than her sister. I suppose, on the whole, she was the prettier of the two, though she did not please me so well. They were their father's only children, and he was very fond of them. Their mother had been dead so long that they had no recollection of her; and the girls were not without those defects which girls brought up by a man are so apt to have. They were rather disposed to think that anything could be had for a little coaxing. Perhaps they had more confidence in their own blandishments than is common with girls, and were more ready to use them, knowing how powerless papa was against their arts. They were badly educated, for the same reason. The Admiral was too fond of them to part with them; and he was one of the men who fear reports and rumours, and would not have a lady, not even a middle-aged governess, in his house. He had expensive masters for his girls, and the girls did what they pleased with those excellent gentlemen, and grew up with the very smallest amount of education compatible with civilization. I rather liked it, I confess, in Nelly, who was very bright, and asked about everything, and jumped at an understanding of most things she heard of. But it did not answer in Martha's case, who was not bright, and was the sort of girl who wanted to be taught music, for instance, properly, and to practise six hours a day. Without being taught, and without practising, the good girl (for Nelly, as she explained, had no taste for music) thought it her duty to play to amuse her friends; and the result was a trial to the temper of Dinglefield Green. We had some very good musicians among us, and Martha heard them continually, but never was enlightened as to the nature of her own performance; whereas Nelly knew and grew crimson every time her sister approached the piano. But Nelly was my favourite, as everybody knew; and perhaps, as a natural consequence, I did her sister less than justice.

We led a very pleasant, neighbourly life in those days. Some of us were richer, and some poorer; but we all visited each other. The bigger houses asked the smaller ones to dinner, and did not disdain to pay a return visit to tea. In the summer afternoons, if you crossed the Green (and could hear anything for the noise the cricketers made) you would be sure to hear, in one quarter or another, the click of the croquet balls, and find all the young people of the place assembled over their game, not without groups of the elder ones sitting round on the edge of the well-mown lawns. When I settled there first, I was neither young nor old, and there was a difficulty which party to class me with; but by degrees I found my place among the mothers, or aunts, or general guardians of the society; and by degrees my young neighbours came to be appropriated to me as my particular charge. We walked home together, and we went to parties together; and, of course, a little gossip got up about the Admiral—gossip which was entirely without foundation, for I detest second marriages, and indeed have had quite enough of it for my part. But Nelly took a clinging to me—I don't say a fancy, which would be too light a word. She had never known a woman intimately before—never one older than herself, to whom she was half a child and half a companion. And she liked it, and so did I.

There was one absurd peculiarity about the two girls, which I shall always think was the foundation of all the mischief. They never called each other, nor were called, by their names. They were 'the Sisters' to everybody. I suppose it was a fancy of their father's—he called them 'the Sisters' always. They called each other Sister when they spoke to or of each other. It annoyed me at first, and I made an attempt to change the custom. But Martha disliked her name. She had been called after her grandmother, and she thought it was a shame. 'Martha and Ellen!' she said indignantly. 'What could papa be thinking of? It sounds like two old women in the alms-houses. And other girls have such pretty names. If you call me Martha, Mrs. Mulgrave, I will never speak to you again.' When one thought of it, it was a hard case. I felt for her, for my own name is Sarah, and I remember the trouble it was to me when I was a girl; and the general use and wont of course overcame me at last. They were called 'the Sisters' everywhere on the Green. I believe some of us did not even know their proper names. I said mischief might come of it, and they laughed at me; but there came a time when Nelly, at least, laughed at me no more.

It was in the early summer that young Llewellyn came to stay with the Denzils at their great house opposite. He was a distant cousin of theirs, which was a warrant that his family was all that could be desired. And he had a nice little property in Wales, which had come to him unexpectedly on the death of an elder brother. And, to crown all, he was a sailor, having gone into the navy when he was a second son. Of course, being a naval man, it was but natural that he should be brought to the Admiral first of all. And he very soon got to be very intimate in the house; and indeed, for that matter, in every house on the Green. I believe it is natural to sailors to have that hearty, cordial way. He came to see me, though I had no particular attraction for him, as cheerfully as if I had been a girl, or alas! had girls of my own. Perhaps it was the opening in the hedge that pleased him. He would sit and look—but he did not speak to me of the sisters, more's the pity. He was shy of that subject. I could see he was in real earnest, as the children say, by his shyness about the girls. He would begin to say something, and then rush on to another subject, and come back again half an hour after to the identical point he had started from. But I suppose it never occurred to him that I had any skill to fathom that. He went with them on all their picnics, and was at all their parties; and he rode with them, riding very well for a sailor. The rides are beautiful round Dinglefield. There is a royal park close at hand, where you can lose yourself in grassy glades and alleys without number. I had even been tempted to put myself on my old pony, and wander about with them on the springy turf under the trees; though, as for their canterings and gallopings, and the way in which Nelly's horse kicked its heels about when it got excited, they were always alarming to me. But it was a pleasant life. There is something in that moment of existence when the two who are to go together through life see each other first, and are mysteriously attracted towards each other, and forswear their own ideal and all their dreams, and mate themselves, under some secret compulsion which they do not understand—I say there is something in such a moment which throws a charm over life to all their surroundings. Though it be all over for us; though perhaps we may have been in our own persons thoroughly disenchanted, or may even have grown bitter in our sense of the difference between reality and romance, still the progress of an incipient wooing gives a zest to our pleasure. There is something in the air, some magical influence, some glamour, radiating from the hero and the heroine. When everything is settled, and the wedding looms in sight, fairyland melts away, and the lovers are no more interesting than any other pair. It is perhaps the uncertainty, the chance of disaster; the sense that one may take flight or offence, or that some rival may come in, or a hundred things happen to dissipate the rising tenderness. There is the excitement of a drama about it—a drama subject to the curious contradictions of actual existence, and utterly regardless of all the unities. I thought I could see the little sister, who was my pet and favourite, gradually grouping thus with young Llewellyn. They got together somehow, whatever the arrangements of the party might be. They might drive to the Dingle, which was our favourite spot, in different carriages, with different parties, and at different times; but they were always to be found together under the trees when everybody had arrived. Perhaps they did not yet know it themselves; but other people began to smile, and Lady Denzil, I could see, was watching Nelly. She had other views, I imagine, for her young cousin since he came to the estate. Nelly, too, once had very different views. I knew what her ideal was. It, or rather he, was a blonde young giant, six feet tall at least, with blue eyes, and curling golden hair. He was to farm his own land, and live a country life, and be of no profession; and he was to be pure Saxon, to counterbalance a little defect in Nelly's race, or rather, as she supposed, in her complexion, occasioned by the fact that her mother was of Spanish blood. Such was her ideal, as she had often confided to me. It was funny to see how this gigantic and glorious vision melted out of her mind. Llewellyn was not very tall; he was almost as dark as Nelly; he was a sailor, and he was a Welshman. What did it matter? One can change one's ideal so easily when one is under twenty. Perhaps in his imagination he had loved a milk-white maiden too.

Lady Denzil however watched, having, as I shall always believe, other intentions in her mind for Llewellyn, though she had no daughter of her own; and I am sure it was her influence which hurried him away the last day, without taking leave of any of us. She kept back the telegram which summoned him to join his ship, until there was just time to get the train. And so he had to rush away, taking off his hat to us, and almost getting out of the window of the carriage in his eagerness, when he saw us at the Admiral's door, as he dashed past to the station.

'Good-bye, for the moment,' he shouted; 'I hope I am coming back.' And I could see, by the colour in Nelly's cheek, that their eyes had met, and understood each other. Her sister bowed and smiled very graciously, and chattered about a hundred things.

'I wonder why he is going in such a hurry? I wonder what he means about coming back?' said Martha. 'I am sure I am very sorry he is gone. He was very nice, and always ready for anything. What a bore a ship is! I remember when papa was like that—always rushing away. Don't you, Sister?—but you were too young.'

'I remember hearing people talk of it,' said Nelly with a sigh.

She was rêveuse, clouded over, everything that it was natural to be under the circumstances. She would not trust herself to say he was nice. It was I who had to answer, and keep up the conversation for her. For my own part, I confess I was vexed that he had gone so soon—that he had gone without an explanation. These things are far better to be settled out of hand. A man has to go away when his duty calls; but nobody can make sure when he may come back, or what he may find when he comes back. I was sorry, for I knew a hundred things might happen to detain, or keep him silent; and Nelly's heart was caught, I could see. She had been quite unsuspecting, unfearing; and it was gone ere she understood what she was doing. My heart quaked a little for her; not with any fear of the result, but only with a certain throbbing of experience and anxiety that springs therefrom. Experience does not produce hope in the things of this world. It lays one's heart open to suspicions and fears which never trouble the innocent. It was not because of anything I had seen in Llewellyn; but because I had seen a great deal of the world, and things in general. This was why I kissed her with a little extra meaning, and told her to lie down on the sofa when she got home.

'You have not been looking your best for some days,' I said. 'You are not a giantess, nor so robust as you pretend to be. You must take care of yourself.' And Nelly, though she made no reply, kissed me in her clinging way in return.

Some weeks passed after that without any particular incident. Things went on in their usual way, and though we were all sorry that Llewellyn was gone, we made no particular moan over him after the first. It was very rarely that a day passed on which I did not see the sisters; but the weather was beginning to get cold, and one Friday there was a fog which prevented me from going out. Ours is a low country, with a great many trees, and the river is not far off; and when there is a fog, it is very dreary and overwhelming. It closes in over the Green, so that you cannot see an inch before you; and the damp creeps into your very bones: though it was only the end of October, the trees hung invisible over our heads in heavy masses, now and then dropping a faded leaf out of the fog in a ghostly, silent way: and the chill went to one's heart. I had a new book, for which I was very thankful, and my fire burned brightly, and I did not stir out of doors all day. I confess it surprised me a little that the girls did not come in to me in the evening, as they had a way of doing, with their red cloaks round them, and the hoods over their heads, like Red Riding Hood. But I took it for granted they had some friends from town, or something pleasant on hand; though I had not heard any carriage driving up. As for seeing, that was impossible. Next morning, by a pleasant change, was bright, sunny, and frosty. For the first time that season, the hedges and gardens, and even the Green itself, was crisp and white with hoar-frost, which, of course, did not last, but gave us warning of winter. When I went out, I met Nelly just leaving her own door. She was in her red cloak, with her dress tucked up, and the little black hat with the red feather, which was always so becoming to her. But either it was not becoming that day, or there was something the matter with the child. I don't remember whether I have said that she had large eyes—eyes that, when she was thinner than usual, or ill, looked out of proportion to the size of her face. They had this effect upon me that day. One did not seem to see Nelly at all; but only a big pair of wistful, soft eyes looking at one, with shadowy lines round them. I was alarmed, to tell the truth, whenever I saw her. Either something had happened, or the child was ill.

'Good morning, my dear,' I said, 'I did not see you all yesterday, and it feels like a year. Were you coming to me now?'

'No,' said Nelly—and even in the sound of her voice there was something changed—'it is so long since I have been in the village. I had settled to go down there this morning, and take poor Mary Jackson some warm socks we have been knitting for the babies. It is so cold to-day.'

'I thought you never felt the cold,' said I, as one does without thinking. 'You are always as merry as a cricket in the winter weather, when we are all shivering. You know you never feel the cold.'

'No,' said Nelly again. 'I suppose it is only the first chill'—and she gave me a strange little sick smile, and suddenly looked down and stooped to pick up something. I saw in a moment there was nothing to pick up. Could it be that there were tears in her eyes, which she wanted to hide? 'But I must go now,' she went on hurriedly. 'Oh, no, don't think of coming with me; it is too cold, and I shall have to walk fast, I am in such a hurry. Good-bye.'

I could do nothing but stand and stare after her when she had gone on. What did it mean? Nelly was not given to taking fancies, or losing her temper—at least not in this way. She walked away so rapidly that she seemed to vanish out of my sight, and never once looked round or turned aside for anything. The surprise was so great that I actually forgot where I was going. It could not be for nothing that she had changed like this. I went back to my own door, and then I came out again and opened the Admiral's gate. Probably Martha was at home, and would know what was the matter. As I was going in, Martha met me coming out. She was in her red cloak, like Nelly, and she had a letter in her hand. When she saw me she laughed, and blushed a little. 'Will you come with me to the post, Mrs. Mulgrave?' she said. 'Sister would not wait for me; and when one has an important letter to post—' Martha went on, holding it up to me, and laughing and blushing again.

'What makes it so very important?' said I; and I confess that I tried very hard to make out the address.

'Oh, didn't she tell you?' said Martha. 'What a funny girl she is! If it had been me I should have rushed all over the Green, and told everybody. It is—can't you guess?'

And she held out to me the letter in her hand. It was addressed to 'Captain Llewellyn, H.M.S. Spitfire, Portsmouth.' I looked at it, and I looked at her, and wonder took possession of me. The address was in Martha's handwriting. It was she who was going to post it; it was she who, conscious and triumphant, giggling a little and blushing a little, stood waiting for my congratulations. I looked at her aghast, and my tongue failed me. 'I don't know what it means,' I said, gasping. 'I can't guess. Is it you who have been writing to Captain Llewellyn, or is it Nelly, or who is it? Can there have been any mistake?'

Martha was offended, as indeed she had reason to be. 'There is no mistake,' she said indignantly. 'It is a very strange sort of thing to say, when any friend, any acquaintance even, would have congratulated me. And you who know us so well! Captain Llewellyn has asked me to marry him—that is all. I thought you might have found out what was coming. But you have no eyes for anybody but Sister. You never think of me.'

'I beg your pardon,' said I, faltering; 'I was so much taken by surprise. I am sure I wish you every happiness, Martha. Nobody can be more anxious for your welfare than I am—' and here I stopped short in my confusion, choked by the words, and not knowing what to say.

'Yes, I am sure of that,' said Martha affectionately, stopping at the gate to give me a kiss. 'I said so to Sister this morning. I said I am sure Mrs. Mulgrave will be pleased. But are you really so much surprised? Did you never think this was how it was to be?'

'No,' I said, trembling in spite of myself; 'I never thought of it. I thought indeed—but that makes no difference now.'

'What did you think?' said Martha; and then her private sense of pride and pleasure surmounted everything else. 'Well, you see it is so,' she said, with a beaming smile. 'He kept his own counsel, you see. I should not have thought he was so sly—should you? I dare say he thinks he showed it more than he did; for he says I must have seen how it was from the first day.'

And she stood before me so beaming, so dimpling over with smiles and pleasure, that my heart sank within me. Could it be a mistake, or was it I—ah! how little it mattered for me—was it my poor Nelly who had been deceived?

'And did you?' I said, looking into her face, 'did you see it from the first day?'

'Well, n-no,' said Martha, hesitating; and then she resumed with a laugh, 'That shows you how sly he must have been. I don't think I ever suspected such a thing; but then, to be sure, I never thought much about him, you know.'

A little gleam of comfort came into my heart as she spoke. 'Oh, then,' I said, relieved, 'there is no occasion for congratulations after all.'

'Why is there no occasion for congratulations?' said Martha. 'Of course there is occasion. I wanted Sister to run in and tell you last night, but she wouldn't; and I rather wanted you to tell me what I should say, or, rather, how I should say it; but I managed it after all by myself. I suppose one always can if one tries.'

It comes by nature, people say.' And Martha laughed again, and blushed, and cast a proud glance on the letter she held in her hand.

'But if you never had thought of him yesterday,' said I, 'you can't have accepted him to-day.'

'Why not?' said Martha, with a toss of her pretty head—and she was pretty, especially in that moment of excitement. I could not refuse to see it. It was a mere piece of pink-and-white prettiness, instead of my little nut-brown maid, with her soft eyes, and her bright varied gleams of feeling and intelligence. But then you can never calculate on what a man may think in respect to a girl. Men are such fools; I mean where women are concerned.

'Why not?' said Martha, with a laugh. 'I don't mean I am frantically in love with him, you know. How could I be, when I never knew he cared for me? But I always said he was very nice; and then it is so suitable. And I don't care for anybody else. It would be very foolish of me to refuse him without any reason. Of course,' said Martha, looking down upon her letter, 'I shall think of him very differently now.'

What could I say? I was at my wits' end. I walked on by her side to the post-office in a maze of confusion and doubt. I could have snatched the letter out of her hand, and torn it into a hundred pieces; but that would have done little good; and how could I tell if it was a mistake after all? He might have sought Nelly for her sister's sake. He might have been such a fool, such a dolt, as to prefer Martha. All this time he might but have been making his advances to her covertly—under shield as it were of the gay bright creature who was too young and too simple-hearted to understand such devices. Oh, my little nut-brown maid! no wonder her eyes were so large and shadowy, her pretty cheeks so colourless! I could have cried with vexation and despair as I went along step for step with the other on the quiet country road. Though she was so far from being bright, Martha at last was struck by my silence. It took her a considerable time to find it out, for naturally her own thoughts were many, and her mind was fully pre-occupied; but she did perceive it at last.

'I don't think you seem to like it, Mrs. Mulgrave,' she said; 'not so much as I thought you would. You were the very first person I thought of; I was coming to tell you when I met you. And I thought you would sympathize with me and be so pleased to hear—'

'My dear,' said I, 'I am pleased to hear—anything that is for your happiness; but then I am so much surprised. It was not what I looked for. And then, good heavens! if it should turn out to be some mistake—'

'Mrs. Mulgrave,' said Martha angrily, 'I don't know what you can mean. This is the second time you have talked of a mistake. What mistake could there be? I suppose Captain Llewellyn knows what he is doing: unless you want to be unkind and cross. And what have I done that you should be so disagreeable to me?'

'Oh, my dear child!' I cried in despair, 'I don't know what I mean; I thought once—there was Major Frost, you know—'

'Oh, is it that?' said Martha, restored to perfect good-humour; 'poor Major Frost! But of course if he did not choose to come forward in time, he could not expect me to wait for him. You may make your mind quite easy if that is all.'

'And then,' I said, taking a little courage, 'Captain Llewellyn paid Nelly a good deal of attention. He might have thought—'

'Yes,' said Martha, 'to be sure; and I never once suspected that he meant it for me all the time.'

I ask anybody who is competent to judge, could I have said any more? I walked to the post-office with her, and I saw the letter put in. And an hour afterwards I saw the mail-cart rattling past with the bags, and knew it had set out to its destination. He would get it next morning, and the two lives would be bound for ever and ever. The wrong two?—or was it only we, Nelly and I, who had made the mistake? Had it been Martha he sought all the time?

CHAPTER II

The news soon became known to everybody on the Green, and great surprise was excited by it. Everybody, I think, spoke to me on the subject. They said, 'If it had been the other sister!' Even Lady Denzil went so far as to say this, when, after having called at the Admiral's to offer her congratulations, she came in to see me. 'I do not pretend that I like the marriage,' she said, with a little solemnity. 'There were claims upon him nearer home. It is not every man that is at liberty to choose for himself; but if it had been the little one I could have understood it.' I hope nobody spoke like this to Nelly; she kept up a great deal too well to satisfy me. She was in the very centre of all the flutter that such an event makes in a small society like ours, and she knew people were watching her; but she never betrayed herself. She had lost her colour somehow—everybody remarked that; and the proud little girl got up a succession of maladies, and said she had influenza and indigestion, and I know not what, that nobody might suspect any other cause. Sometimes I caught her for one instant off her guard, but it was a thing that happened very rarely. Two or three times I met her going off by herself for a long walk, and she would not have my company when I offered to go with her. 'I walk so fast,' she said, 'and then it is too far for you.' Once I even saw her in the spot to which all our walks tended—the Dingle, which was our favourite haunt. It was a glorious autumn, and the fine weather lasted long—much longer than usual. Up to the middle of November there were still masses of gorgeous foliage on the trees, and the sky was as blue—not as Italy, for Italy is soft and languorous and melting—but as an English sky without clouds, full of sunshine, yet clear, with a premonitory touch of frost, can be. The trees in the Dingle are no common trees; they are giant beeches, big-boled, heavily-clothed giants, that redden and crisp and hold their own until the latest moment; and that mount up upon heights, and descend into hollows, and open up here and there into gleams of the fair plain around, growing misty in the distance as if it were sea. The great point in the landscape is a royal castle, the noblest dwelling-place I ever saw. We who live so near are learned in the different points of view; we know where to catch it shining like a fairy stronghold in the white hazy country, or stretching out in gray profile upon its height, or setting itself—here the great donjon, there a flanking tower—in frames of leafy branches. I had left my little carriage and my stout old pony on the road, and had wandered up alone to have my last peep before winter set in, when suddenly I saw Nelly before me. She was walking up and down on the soft yielding mossy grass, carpeted with beech-mast and pine-needles; sometimes stopping to gaze blankly at the view—at the great plain whitening off to the horizon, and the castle rising in the midst. I knew what the view was, but I saw also that she did not see it. Her face was all drawn together, small and shrunken up. There were deep shadowy lines round her eyes; and as for the eyes themselves, it was them and not Nelly that I saw. They were dilated, almost exaggerated, unlike anything I ever saw before. She had come out here to be alone, poor child! I crept away as best I could through the brown crackling ferns. If she heard anything probably she thought it was some woodland creature that could not spy upon her. But I don't believe she heard anything, nor saw anything; and I was no spy upon her, dear heart!

The nearest we ever came to conversation on the subject was once when I was telling her about a girl I once knew, whose story had been a very sad one. She had pledged her heart and her life to a foolish young fellow, who was very fond of her, and then was very fond of somebody else; and would have been fond of her again, periodically, to any number of times. She had borne it as long as she could, and then she had broken down; and it had been a relief to her, poor girl, to come and cry her heart out to me.

'It has never been my way, Nelly,' I said, 'but it seems to ease the heart when it can speak. I don't think that I could have spoken to any one, had it been me.'

'And as for me,' cried Nelly, 'if I should ever be like that—and if any one, even you, were so much as to look at me as if you knew, I think I should die!'

This was before the lamp was lighted; and in the dark, I think she put up a hand to wipe off something from her eyelash. But you may be sure I took care not to look. I tried to put all speculation out of my eyes whenever I looked at her afterwards. My poor Nelly! in the very extravagance of her pride was there not an appeal, and piteous throwing of herself upon my forbearance? I thought there was, and it went to my heart.

The next thing, of course, was that Llewellyn announced himself as coming to visit his betrothed. He was to come at Christmas, not being able to leave his ship before. And then it was to be settled when the marriage should take place. I confess that I listened to all this with a very bad grace. Any reference to the marriage put me out of temper. He wrote to her regularly and very often, and Martha used to read his letters complacently before us all, and communicate little bits out of them, and spend half her mornings writing her replies. She was not a ready writer, and it really was hard work to her, and improved her education—at least in the mechanical matters of writing and spelling. But I wonder what sort of rubbish it was she wrote to him, and what he thought of it. Was it possible he could suppose it was my Nelly who wrote all those commonplaces, or was the mistake on my part, not on his? As time went on, I came to think, more and more, that the latter was the case. We had been deceived, Nelly and I. And Martha and Llewellyn were two lovers worthy of each other. I fear I was not very charitable to him in my thoughts.

But I could not help being very nervous the day of his arrival. It was a bleak wintry day, Christmas Eve, but not what people call Christmas weather. It rarely is Christmas weather at Christmas. The sky hung low and leaden over our bare trees, and of course there were no cricketers now on the Green, nor sound of croquet balls, to enliven the stillness. I could not rest at home. We had not been informed what train Captain Llewellyn was to come by, and my mind was in such a disturbed state, that I kept coming and going, all day long, on one errand or another, lingering about the road. I don't myself know what I meant by it; nor could I have explained it to anybody. Sometimes I thought, if I should meet him first, I would speak and make sure. Sometimes I fancied that I could read in his face, at the first look, what it all meant. But, anyhow, I did not meet him. I thought all the trains were in when I went to the Admiral's in the afternoon, at five o'clock—that is, all the trains that could arrive before dinner, for we were two miles from the station. Martha and her father were in the drawing-room when I entered. There was a bright fire, but the candles were not lighted; I suppose, out of reluctance to shut up the house, and close all the windows, before the visitor came. Martha was sitting by the fire looking very gay and bright, and a little excited. She told me Nelly had been all day in the church, helping with the decorations, and that she was to stay at the rectory to dinner, as there was a Christmas-tree for the school-children to be got ready. 'I dare say she thought we should not want her this first evening,' Martha said with a little laugh; and such was the bitterness and unreasonableness of my heart that I was speechless with exasperation; which was nonsense, for of course she had a right to the society of her betrothed. While we were sitting thus over the fire, all at once there came a sound of wheels, and the dog-cart from the little inn at Dinglefield Station came rattling up. Martha gave a little cry, and ran to the drawing-room door. I know I should have gone away, but I did not. I stood behind in the ruddy gloom, and saw her rush into Llewellyn's arms. And he kissed her. And the next moment they were back in the room beside us, she chatting about his journey, and looking up in his face, and showing her satisfaction and delight, as it was quite natural she should do. It seemed to me that he did not make very much reply; but the room was dark, and his arrival was sudden, and there was a certain confusion about everything. The Admiral came forward, and shook hands with him, and so did I; and instead of looking as if he wished us a hundred miles off, Llewellyn kept peering into the corners, as if he wanted another greeting. Then he came to the fire, and stood before it, making the room all the darker with his shadow; and after we had all asked him if he had felt the cold on his journey, there did not seem very much to say. I don't know how the others felt, but I know my heart began to beat wildly. Martha was in an unnatural state of excitement. She drew a great comfortable easy-chair to the fire for him. 'Dear Ellis, sit down,' she said, laying her hand softly on his arm. The touch seemed to wake him up out of a kind of reverie. He took her hand, and held it for a moment, and then let it fall.

'You are far too kind,' he said, 'to take so much trouble for me. A thousand thanks. Where is—your sister? She knew I was to come by this train.'

'No, I don't think Sister knew,' said Martha; 'that was my little secret. I would not tell them what train you were coming by. She is helping with the church decorations. She will see you to-morrow, you know. I wish they would bring the tea: papa, will you ring?—Oh, papa has gone away. Wait a minute, Ellis dear, and I will run and make them bring it immediately. It will warm you better than anything else. I sha'n't be a moment gone.'

The moment she had left us poor Llewellyn turned to me. Notwithstanding the ruddy firelight, I could see he was quite haggard with the awful suspicion that must have flashed upon him. 'Mrs. Mulgrave!' he cried hurriedly, holding out his hands, 'for God's sake, tell me, what does this mean?'

'It means that you have come to see your betrothed, Captain Llewellyn,' said I; 'she has just gone out of the room. You made your choice, and I hope you did not expect to have both the sisters. Martha stayed to receive you, as was right and natural. You could not expect the same from Nelly. She thought neither of you would want a third to-night.'

I was so angry that I said all this in a breath. I know I ought to be ashamed of myself, but I did it; I don't think however that he heard half. He covered his face with his hands and gave a groan, which seemed to me to echo all through the house; and I had to add on to what I was saying, 'Oh, for heaven's sake, restrain yourself,' I cried, without even taking breath; 'now it is too late!'

And then Martha came in, excited and joyous, half dancing with high spirits. I could have groaned too and hid my face from the light as he did, poor fellow! but she went up to him and drew down his hands playfully and said, 'I am here, Ellis, you needn't cover your eyes.' He did not answer her with a compliment or a caress, as perhaps she expected; and Martha looked at me where I was standing by the side of the fire. I knew she thought I was the restraining influence that closed his mouth and subdued his joy—and what could I do?—I went away: I could be of no use to him, poor boy! He must face it now as best he could. I went away, and as soon as I got safely into my own house sat down and cried. Not that crying would do any good; but when everything is going wrong, and everybody is on the way to ruin and you see how it is, and know how to mend it, and yet cannot, dare not, put forth a hand, what can any one do but sit down and cry?

But I could not rest in my quiet, comfortable, lonely house, and know that those poor young hearts were being wrung, and keep still and take no notice. I had my cup of tea, and I put on my warm cloak and hood and went across the Green, though it was wet and slippery, to the school-room, where I knew Nelly would be. She was in the midst of a heap of toys and paper-flags and little tapers, dressing up the Christmas-tree. There were three or four girls altogether, and Nelly was the busiest of all. Her little hands were pricked and scratched with the points of the holly and the sharp needles of the little fir-tree on which she was working. Poor child! I wish it had been her hands only that were wounded. The others had gloves on, but Nelly had taken hers off, either because she found the pain of the pricks good for her, or because of some emblematical meaning in it. 'I can't work in gloves,' she said carelessly, 'and it doesn't hurt so much when you are used to it.' When I saw her I could not but think of the pictures of Indians tied to the stake, with arrows flying at them from all quarters. I am aware St. Sebastian was killed in the same way—but I did not think of him.

'I wish you would come with me, Nelly,' I said; 'you know Christmas Eve is never very merry to me. There is no dinner, but you shall have something with your tea.'

'I am going to the rectory,' said Nelly. She did not venture to look at me, and she spoke very quick, with a kind of catch in her breath. 'I promised—and there is a great deal to do yet. When Christmas is not merry it is best to try and forget it is Christmas. If I were to go with you, you would talk to me, and that would make you feel everything the more.'

'I would not talk—you may trust me, Nelly,' I said eagerly. In my excitement I was for one minute off my guard.

She gave me one look and then turned away, and began arranging the flags and pricking her poor little soft fingers. 'Talking does not matter to me,' she said in her careless way. Her pride was something that filled me with consternation. She would not yield, not if she had been cut in little pieces. Her heart was being torn out of her very breast, and she was ready to look her executioners in the face and cheer them on.

I don't know how they all got through that evening. Nelly, I know, went home late and went to her own room at once, as being tired. It was poor Llewellyn that was the most to be pitied. I could not get him out of my mind. I sat and thought and thought over it till I could scarcely rest. Would he have the courage to emancipate himself and tell the truth? Or would the dreadful coil of circumstances in which he had got involved overcome him and subdue his spirit? I asked myself this question till it made me sick and faint. How was he to turn upon the girl who was hanging on him so proud and pleased and confident, and say that he had never cared for her and never sought her? There are men who would have the nerve to do that; but my poor simple, tender-hearted sailor—who would not hurt a fly, and who had no warning nor preparation for the fate that was coming on him—I could not hope that he would be so brave.

I saw by my first glance next morning at church that he had not been brave. He was seated by Martha's side, looking pale and haggard and stern; such a contrast to her lively and demonstrative happiness. Nelly was at the other end of the pew under her father's shadow. I don't know what she had done to herself—either it was excitement, or in her pride she had had recourse to artificial aids. She had recovered her colour as if by a miracle. I am afraid that I did not pay so much attention to the service as I ought to have done. My whole thoughts were bent upon the Admiral's seat, where there were two people quite serene and comfortable, and two in the depths of misery and despair. There were moments when I felt as if I could have got up in church and protested against it in the sight of God. One feels as if one could do that: but one keeps still and does nothing all the same.

In the afternoon Llewellyn came to see me. He would have done it anyhow, I feel sure, for he had a good heart. But there was a stronger reason still that Christmas Day. He did not say much to me when he came. He walked about my drawing-room and looked at all the ornaments on the tables, and opened the books, and examined my Christmas presents. Then he came and sat down beside me before the fire. He tried to talk, and then he broke off and leant his face between his hands. It was again a gray, dark, sunless day; and it was all the darker in my room because of the verandah over the windows, which makes it so pleasant in summer. I could see his profile darkly before me as he made an attempt at conversation, not looking at me, but staring into the fire; and then, all at once, his shoulders went up, and his face disappeared in the shadow of his hands. He stared into the fire still, under that shelter; but he felt himself safe from my inspection, poor fellow!

'I ought to beg your pardon,' he said, suddenly, concentrating all his attention upon the glowing embers, 'for speaking as I did—last night—'

'There was nothing to pardon,' said I. And then we came to an embarrassed pause, for I did not know which was best—to speak, or to be silent.

'I know I was very abrupt,' he said, 'I was rude. I hope you will forgive me. It was the surprise.' And then he gave vent to something between a cry and a groan. 'What is to become of us all, good God!' he muttered. It was all I could do to hear him, and the exclamation did not sound to me profane.

'Captain Llewellyn,' I said, 'I don't know whether I ought to say anything, or whether I should hold my tongue. I understand it all; and I feel for you with all my heart.'

'It doesn't matter,' he said; 'it doesn't matter. Feeling is of no use. But there is one thing you could tell me. She—you know—I can't call her by any name—I don't seem to know her name—Just tell me one thing, and I'll try and bear it. Did she mind? Does she think me—? Good heavens! what does it matter what any one thinks? If you are sure it did not hurt her, I—don't mind.'

'N—no,' said I; but I don't think he got any comfort from my tone. 'You may be sure it will not hurt her,' I went on, summoning up all my pride. 'She is not the sort of girl to let it hurt her.' I spoke indignantly, for I did not know what was coming. He seized my hand, poor boy, and wrung it till I could have screamed; and then he broke down, as a man does when he has come to the last point of wretchedness: two or three hoarse sobs burst from him. 'God bless her!' he cried.

I was wound up to such a pitch that I could not sit still. I got up and grasped his shoulder. In my excitement I did not know what I was doing.

'Are you going to bear it?' I said. 'Do you mean to let it go on? It is a lie; and are you going to set it up for the truth? Oh, Captain Llewellyn! is it possible that you mean to let it go on?'

Then he gave me one sorrowful look, and shook his head. 'I have accepted it,' he said. 'It is too late. You said so last night.'

I knew I had said so; but things somehow looked different now. 'I would speak to Martha herself,' said I. And I saw he shuddered at her name. 'I would speak to her father. The Admiral is sensible and kind. He will know what to do.'

'He will think I mean to insult them,' said Llewellyn, shaking his head. 'I have done harm enough. How was I to know? But never mind—never mind. It is my own doing, and I must bear it.' Then he rose up suddenly, and turned to me with a wan kind of smile. 'I cannot afford to indulge myself with talk,' he said. 'Good-bye, and thanks. I don't feel as if I cared much now what happened. The only thing is, I can't stay here.'

'But you must stay a week—you must stay over Christmas,' I cried, as he stood holding my hand.

'Yes,' he said with a sigh. 'I must get through to-night. If you'd keep her out of the way, Mrs. Mulgrave, it would be the kindest thing you could do. I can't look at her. It kills me. But I'll be summoned by telegram to-morrow,' he added, with a kind of desperate satisfaction. 'I wrote this morning.' And then he shook hands with me hurriedly, and went away.

I had very little trouble to keep Nelly—poor Nelly!—out of his way. She made me go up-stairs with her after dinner (I always dined there on Christmas) to show me the presents she had got, and the things she had prepared for her pensioners in the village. We made a great pet of the village, we people who lived on the Green, and, I fear, rather spoiled it. There were things for the babies, and things for the old women, which were to be bestowed next day when they all came to the school-room for the Christmas-tree. She never mentioned Llewellyn to me, nor Martha, nor referred to the domestic event which, in other circumstances, would have occupied her mind above all. I almost wonder it did not occur to her that to speak of, and show an interest in, her sister's engagement was quite a necessary part of her own self-defence. Either it was too much, and she could not, or it did not enter into her mind. She never took any notice of it, at least to me. She never so much as mentioned his name. They never looked at each other, nor addressed each other, though I could see that every look and movement of one was visible to the other. Nelly kept me up-stairs until it was time for me to go home. She came running out with me, with her red cloak round her, when the Admiral marched to the gate to see me home, as he made a rule of doing. She stood at the gate, in the foggy, wintry darkness, to wait for him until he came back from my door. And I waited on my own threshold, and saw them going back—Nelly, poor child, clinging fast to her father's arm. My heart ached; and yet not so much even for her as for the other. What was he doing indoors, left alone with the girl he was engaged to, and did not love?

Next morning, to the astonishment and dismay of everybody but myself, Captain Llewellyn was summoned back to his ship by telegraph. Martha was more excited about it than I should have supposed possible. It was so hard upon poor dear Ellis, she said, before they had been able to arrange anything, or even to talk of anything. She had not the slightest doubt of him. His wretched looks, and his hesitation and coldness, had taught nothing to Martha. If she was perhaps disappointed at first by his want of ardour, the disappointment had soon passed. It was his way; he was not the sort of man to make a fuss. By this means she quite accounted for it to herself. For my own part, I cannot say that I was satisfied with his conduct. If he had put a stop to it boldly—if he had said at once it was all a mistake—then, whatever had come of it, I could have supported and sympathized with him; but it made an end of Captain Llewellyn, as a man, in my estimation, when he thus ran away. I was vexed, and I was sorry; and yet I cannot say I was surprised.

He wrote afterwards to say it was important business, and that he had no hope of being able to come back. And then he wrote that he had been transferred to another ship just put into commission, and had to sail at once. He could not even come to wish his betrothed good-bye. He assured her it could not be for long, as their orders were only for the Mediterranean; but it was a curious reversal of all their former ideas. 'He must retire,' Martha said, when she had told me this news with tears. 'The idea of a man with a good property of his own being ordered about like that! Papa says things have changed since his days; he never heard of anything so arbitrary. After all he said about our marriage taking place first, to think that he should have to go away now, without a moment to say good-bye!'

And she cried and dried her eyes, while I sat by and felt myself a conspirator, and was very uncomfortable. Nelly was present too. She sat working in the window, with her head turned away from us, and took no part in the conversation. Perhaps it was a relief; perhaps—and this was what she herself thought—it would have been better to have got it over at once. Anyhow, at this present juncture, she sat apart, and took no apparent notice of what we said.

'And Nelly never says a word,' sobbed Martha. 'She has no sympathy. I think she hates poor dear Ellis. She scarcely looked at him when he was here. And she won't say she is sorry now.'

'When everybody is sorry what does it matter if I say it or not?' said Nelly, casting one rapid glance from her work. She never was so fond of her work before. Now she had become all at once a model girl: she never was idle for a moment; one kind of occupation or another was constantly in her hands. She sat at her knitting, while Martha, disappointed and vexed, cried and folded up her letter. I don't know whether an inkling of the truth had come to Nelly's mind. Sometimes I thought so. When the time approached which Llewellyn had indicated as the probable period of his return, she herself proposed that she should go on a visit to her godmother in Devonshire. It was spring then, and she had a cough; and there were very good reasons why she should go. The only one that opposed it was Martha. 'It will look so unkind to dear Ellis,' she said; 'as if you would rather not meet him. At Christmas you were out all the time. And if she dislikes him, Mrs. Mulgrave, she ought to try to get over it. Don't you think so? It is unkind to go away.'

'She does not dislike him,' said I. 'But she wants a change, my dear.' And so we all said. The Admiral, good man, did not understand it at all. He saw that something was wrong. 'There is something on the little one's mind,' he said to me. 'I hoped she would have taken you into her confidence. I can't tell what is wrong with her, for my part.'

'She wants a change,' said I. 'She has never said anything to me.'

It was quite true; she had never said a word to me. I might have betrayed Llewellyn, but I could not betray Nelly. She had kept her own counsel. While the Admiral was talking to me, I cannot describe how strong the temptation was upon me to tell him all the story. But I dared not. It was a thing from which the boldest might have shrunk. And though everybody on the Green had begun to wonder vaguely, and the Admiral himself was a little uneasy, Martha never suspected anything amiss. She cried a little when 'poor Ellis' wrote to say his return was again postponed; but it was for his disappointment she cried. Half an hour after she was quite serene and cheerful again, looking forward to the time when he should arrive eventually. 'For he must come some time, you know; they can't keep him away for ever,' she said; until one did not know whether to be impatient with her serenity, or touched by it, and could not make up one's mind whether it was stupidity or faith.

CHAPTER III

Nelly paid her visit to her godmother, and came back; and spring wore into summer, and the trees were all in full foliage again in the Dingle, and the cricketers had returned to the Green; but still Captain Llewellyn was unaccountably detained. Nelly had come home looking much better than when she went away. His name still disturbed her composure I could see; though I don't suppose a stranger who knew nothing of the circumstances would have found it out. And when Martha threatened us with a visit from him, her sister shrank up into herself; but otherwise Nelly was much improved. She recovered her cheerful ways; she became the soul of all our friendly parties again. I said to myself that I had been a truer prophet than I had the least hope of; and that she was not the sort of girl to let herself be crushed in any such way. But she never spoke to me of her sister's marriage, nor of her sister's betrothed. I mentioned the matter one day when we were alone, cruelly and of set purpose to see what she would say. 'When your sister is married, and when you are married,' I said, 'it will be very dull both for the Admiral and me.'

'I shall never marry,' said Nelly, with a sudden closing up and veiling of all her brightness which was more expressive than words. 'I don't know about Sister; but you need not weave any such visions for me.'

'All girls say so till their time comes,' said I, with an attempt to be playful; 'but why do you say you don't know about Martha? she must be married before long, of course?'

'I suppose so,' said Nelly, and then she stopped short; she would not add another word; but afterwards, when we were all together, she broke out suddenly—Martha's conversation at this period was very much occupied with her marriage. I suppose it was quite natural. In my young days girls were shy of talking much on that subject, but things are changed now. Martha talked of it continually: of when dear Ellis would come; of his probable desire that the wedding should take place at once; of her determination to have two months at least to prepare her trousseau; of where they should go after the marriage. She discussed everything, without the smallest idea, poor girl, of what was passing in the minds of the listeners. At last, after hearing a great deal of this for a long time, Nelly suddenly burst forth—

'How strange it would be after all, if we were to turn out a couple of old maids,' she cried, 'and never to marry at all. The two old sisters! with chairs on each side of the fire, and great authorities in the village. How droll it would be!—and not so very unlikely after all.'

'Speak for yourself,' cried Martha indignantly. 'It is very unlikely so far as I am concerned. I am as good as married already. As for you, you can do what you please—'

'Yes, I can do what I please,' said Nelly, with a curious ring in her voice; and then she added, 'But I should not wonder if we were both old maids after all.'

'She is very queer,' Martha said to me when her sister had left the room, in an aggrieved tone. 'She does not mean it, of course; but I don't like it, Mrs. Mulgrave. It does not seem lucky. Why should she take it into her head about our being old maids? I am as good as married now.'

'Yes,' I said vaguely. I could not give any assent more cordial. And then she resumed her anticipations. But I saw in a moment what Nelly meant. This was how she thought it was to end. It was a romantic girl's notion, but happily she was too young to think how unlikely it was. No doubt she saw a vision of the two maiden sisters, and of one who would be their devoted friend, but who could never marry either. That was the explanation she had put in her heart upon his abrupt departure and his many delays. He had made a fatal mistake, and its consequences were to last all his life. They were all three, all their lives long, to continue in the same mind. He could never marry either of them; and neither of them, none of the three, were ever to be tempted to marry another. And thus, in a pathetic climax of faithfulness and delicate self-sacrifice, they were to grow old and die. Nelly was no longer miserable when she had framed this ideal in her mind. It seemed to her the most natural solution of the difficulty. The romance, instead of ending in a prosaic marriage, was to last all their lives. And the eldest of them, Llewellyn himself, was but seven-and-twenty! Poor Nelly thought it the most likely thing in the world.

If she had consulted me, I could have told her of something much more likely—something which very soon dawned upon the minds of most people at Dinglefield Green. It was that a certain regiment had come back to the barracks which were not very far from our neighbourhood. Before Captain Llewellyn made his appearance among us, there had been a Major Frost who had 'paid attention' to Martha; and he did not seem at all disinclined to pay attention to her now that he had come back. Though he was told of her engagement, the information seemed to have very little effect upon him. He came over perpetually, and was always at hand to ride, or walk, or drive, or flirt, as the young ladies felt disposed. Before he had been back a fortnight it seemed to me that Martha had begun to talk less about dear Ellis. By degrees she came the length of confessing that dear Ellis wrote very seldom. I had found out that fact for myself, but she had never made any reference to it before. I watched her with an interest which surpassed every other interest in my life at that moment. I forgot even Nelly, and took no notice of her in comparison. The elder sister absorbed me altogether. By degrees she gave up talking of her marriage, and of her wedding-dress, and where they were to live; and she began to talk of Major Frost. He seemed always to be telling her something which she had to repeat; and he told her very private details, with which she could have nothing to do. He told her that he was much better off than when he was last at the Green. Somebody had died and had left him a great deal of money. He was thinking of leaving the army, and buying a place in our county, if possible. He asked Martha's advice where he should go. 'It is odd that he should tell you all this,' I said to her one day, when she was re-confiding to me a great many of Major Frost's personal affairs; and though she was not usually very quick of apprehension, something called upon Martha's cheek the shadow of a blush.

'I think it is quite natural,' she said; 'we are such old friends; and then he knows I am engaged. I always thought he was very nice—didn't you? I don't think he will ever marry,' Martha added, with a certain pathos. 'He says he could never have married but one woman; and he can't have her now. He was poor when he was last here you know.'

'And who was the woman he could have married?' said I.

'Oh, of course I did not ask him,' said Martha with modest consciousness. 'Poor fellow! it would have been cruel to ask him. It is hard that he should have got his money just after I— I mean after she was engaged.'

'It is hard that money should always be at the bottom of everything,' said I. And though it was the wish nearest to my heart that Martha should forget and give up Llewellyn, still I was angry with her for what she said. But that made no difference. She was not bright enough to know that her faith was wavering. She went on walking and talking with Major Frost, and boring us all with him and his confidences, till I, for one, was sick of his very name. But she meant no treachery; she never even thought of deserting her betrothed. Had any accident happened to bring him uppermost, she would have gone back to dear Ellis all the same. She was not faithless nor fickle, nor anything that was wicked: she was chiefly stupid, or, rather, I stolid. And to think the two were sisters! The Admiral was not very quick-sighted, but evidently he had begun to notice how things were going. He came to me one afternoon to consult me when both the girls were out. I suppose they were at croquet somewhere. We elders found that afternoon hour, when they were busy with the balls and mallets, a very handy time for consulting about anything which they were not intended to know.

'I think I ought to write to Llewellyn,' he said. 'Things are in a very unsatisfactory state. I am not satisfied that he was obliged to go away as he said. I think he might have come to see her had he tried. I have been consulting the little one about it, and she thinks with me.'

'What does she think?' I asked with breathless interest, to the Admiral's surprise.

'She thinks with me that things are in an unsatisfactory state,' he said calmly; 'that it would be far better to have it settled and over, one way or another. She is a very sensible little woman. I was just about to write to Llewellyn, but I thought it best to ask you first what your opinion was.'

Should I speak and tell him all? Had I any right to tell him? The thought passed through my mind quick as lightning. I made a longer pause than I ought to have done; and then all I could find to say was:

'I think I should let things take their course if I were you.'

'What does that mean?' said the Admiral quickly. 'Take their course! I think it is my duty to write to him and let things be settled out of hand.'

It was with this intention he left me. But he did not write, for the very next morning there came a letter from Llewellyn, not to Martha, but to her father, telling him that he was coming home. The ship had been paid off quite unexpectedly I heard afterwards. And I suppose that unless he had been courageous enough to give the true explanation of his conduct he had no resource but to come back. It was a curious, abrupt sort of letter. The young man's conscience, I think, had pricked him for his cowardice in running away; and either he had wound himself up to the point of carrying out his engagement in desperation, or else he was coming to tell his story and ask for his release. I heard of it immediately from the Admiral himself, who was evidently not quite at ease in his mind on the subject. And a short time afterwards Martha came in, dragging her sister with her, full of the news.

'I could scarcely get her to come,' Martha said. 'I can't think what she always wants running after those village people. And when we have just got the news that Ellis is coming home!'

'Yes, I heard,' said I. 'I suppose I ought to congratulate you. Do you expect him soon? Does he say anything about—?'

'Oh, his letter was to papa,' said Martha, interrupting my very hesitating and embarrassed speech; for my eyes were on Nelly, and I saw in a moment that her whole expression had changed. 'He could not be expected to say anything particular to papa, but I suppose it must be very soon. I don't think he will want to wait now he is free.'

'I shall be very glad when it is all over,' said Nelly, to my great surprise. It was the first time I had heard her make any comment on the subject. 'It will make so much fuss and worry. It is very entertaining to them, I suppose, but it is rather tiresome to us. Mrs. Mulgrave, I am going to see Molly Jackson; I can hear all about the trousseau at home, you know.'

'Nelly!' said I, as I kissed her; and I could not restrain a warning look. She flushed up, poor child, to her hair, but turned away with a sick impatience that went to my heart.

'If you had the worry of it night and day as I shall have!' she said under her breath, with an impatient sigh. And then she went away.

I knew all that was in her heart as well as if she had told me. She had lost her temper and patience as well as her peace of mind. It is hard to keep serene under a repeated pressure. She did it the first time, but she was not equal to it the second. She had no excuse to go away now. She had to look forward to everything, and hear it all discussed, and go through it in anticipation. She had to receive him as his future sister; to be the witness of everything, always on the spot; a part of the bridal pageant, the first and closest spectator. And it was very hard to bear. As for Martha, she sat serene in a chair which she had herself worked for me, turning her fair countenance to the light. She saw nothing strange in Nelly's temper, nor in anything that happened to her. She sat waiting till I had taken my seat again, quite ready to go into the question of the trousseau. The sight of her placidity made me desperate. Suddenly there came before me the haggard looks of poor Llewellyn, and the pale exasperation and heart-sickness of my bright little Nelly's face. And then I looked at Martha, who was sitting, serene and cheerful, just in the same spot and the same attitude in which, a few days before, she had told me of Major Frost. She had left off Major Frost now and come back to her trousseau. What did it matter to her which of them it was? As for giving her pain or humiliating her, how much or how long would she feel it? I became desperate. I fastened the door when I closed it after Nelly that nobody might interrupt us, and then I came and sat down opposite to my victim. Martha was utterly unconscious still. It never occurred to her to notice how people were looking, nor to guess what was in anybody's mind.

'You are quite pleased,' said I, making my first assault very gently, 'that Captain Llewellyn is coming home?'

'Pleased!' said Martha. 'Of course I am pleased. What odd people you all are! Anybody might see that it is pleasanter to be settled and know what one is doing. I wish you would come up to town with me some day, Mrs. Mulgrave, and help me with my things.'

'My dear,' said I, 'in the first place, there is something more important than your things; there is Major Frost. What do you mean to do with him?'

'I—with him?' said Martha, opening her eyes. 'He always knew I was engaged. Of course I am very sorry for him; but if he did not choose to come forward in time, he could not expect that one was to wait.'

'And is that how you mean to leave him,' said I severely, 'after all the encouragement you have given him? Every day, for a month past, I have expected to hear you say that you had made a mistake about Captain Llewellyn, and that it was the Major you liked best.'

'Oh, fancy me doing such a thing!' cried Martha, really roused, 'after being engaged to Ellis a whole year. If he had come forward at the proper time perhaps— But to make a change when everything was settled! You never could have believed it of me!'

'If you like the other better, it is never too late to make a change,' said I, carried away by my motive, which was good, and justified a little stretch of ethics. 'You will be doing a dreadful injury to poor Captain Llewellyn if you marry him and like another man best.'

Martha looked at me with a little simper of self-satisfaction. 'I think I know my duty,' she said. 'I am engaged. I don't see that anything else is of any consequence. Of course the gentleman I am engaged to is the one I shall like best.'

'Do you mean that you are engaged to him because you like him best?' said I. 'Martha, take care. You may be preparing great bitterness for yourself. I have no motive but your good.' This was not true, but still it is a thing that everybody says; and I was so much excited that I had to stop to take breath. 'You may never have it in your power to make a choice again,' I said with solemnity. 'You ought to pause and think seriously which of the two you love. You cannot love them both. It is the most serious question you will ever have to settle in your life.'

Martha looked at me with a calm surprise which drove me wild. 'Dear Mrs. Mulgrave,' she said, 'I don't know what you mean. I am engaged to Ellis—and Major Frost has never proposed even. He may have been only flirting, for anything I can tell; and how foolish it would be to give up the one without any real hold on the other! but of course it is nonsense altogether. Why, Ellis is coming back on purpose; and as Major Frost did not come forward in time, I don't see how he can complain.'

All this she said with the most perfect placidity, sitting opposite the window, lifting her serene countenance to the light. It was a practical concern to Martha. It did not so much matter which it was; but to interfere with a thing fully arranged and settled, because of any mere question of liking! I was not by a very long way so cool as she was. Everything seemed to me to depend upon this last throw, and I felt myself suddenly bold to put it to the touch. It was not my business, to be sure; but to think of those two young creatures torn asunder and made miserable! It was not even Nelly I was thinking of. Nelly would be free; she was young; she would not have her heartbreak always kept before her, and time would heal her wounds. But poor Llewellyn was bound and fettered. He could not escape nor forget. It was for him I made my last attempt.

'Martha, I have something still more serious to say to you,' I said. 'Do you remember, when you told me of Captain Llewellyn's proposal first, I asked you if it was not a mistake?'

'Yes, I remember very well,' said Martha. 'It was just like you. I never knew any one who asked such odd questions. I should have been angry had it been any one but you.'

'Perhaps you will be angry now,' I said. 'I know you will be vexed, but I can't help it. Oh, my dear, you must listen to me! It is not only your happiness that is concerned, but that of others. Martha, I have every reason to think that it was a mistake. Don't smile; I am in earnest. It was a mistake. Can't you see yourself how little heart he puts into it? Martha, my dear, it is no slight to you. You told me you had never thought of him before he wrote to you. And it was not you he meant to write to. What can I say to convince you? It is true; it is not merely my idea. It was all a mistake.'

'Mrs. Mulgrave,' said Martha, a little moved out of her composure, 'I am not angry. I might be; but I am sure you don't mean it. It is one of the fancies you take into your head. How could it be a mistake? It was me he wrote to, not anybody else. Of course I was not fond of him before; but when a man asks you to marry him, how is it possible there can be any mistake?'

'Oh, Martha,' I said, wringing my hands, 'let me tell you all; only hear me, and don't be vexed. Did you never notice all that summer how he followed Nelly about? Try and remember. He was always by her side; wherever we went those two were together. Ask anybody; ask Lady Denzil; ask your father. Oh, my dear child, I don't want to hurt your feelings! I want to save you from something you will be very sorry for. I want you to be happy. Can't you see what I mean without any more explanations from me?'

Martha had, notwithstanding her composure, grown pale. Her placid looks had changed a little. 'I see it is something about Sister,' she said. 'Because you like her best, you think everybody else must like her best too. I wonder why it is that you are so unkind to me!'

As she spoke she cried a little, and turned her shoulder towards me, instead of her face.

'Not unkind,' I said, 'oh, not unkind; I am speaking only because I love you all.'

'You have never loved me,' said Martha, weeping freely; 'never, though I have been so fond of you. And now you want to make me ridiculous and miserable. How can I tell what you mean? What has Sister to do with it? Ellis was civil to her for—for my sake. It was me he proposed to. How can I tell what you are all plotting in your hearts? When people write letters to me, and ask me to marry them, am I not to believe what they say?'

'When he wrote, he thought Nelly was the eldest,' I said. 'You know what I have always told you about your names. He wrote to her, and it came to you. Martha, believe me, it is not one of my fancies; it is true.'

'How do you know it is true?' she cried, with a natural outburst of anger and indignation. 'How do you dare to come and say all this now? Insulting Ellis, and Sister, and me! Oh, I wish I had never known you! I wish I had never, never come into this house! I wish—'

Her voice died away in a storm of sobs and tears. She cried like a child—as a baby cries, violently, with temper, and not with grief. She was not capable of Nelly's suppressed passion and misery; neither did the blow strike deep enough for that; and she had no pride to restrain her. She cried noisily, turning her shoulder to me, making her eyes red and her cheeks blurred. When I got up and went to her, she repulsed me; I had nothing to do but sit down again, and wait till the passion had worn itself out. And there she sat sobbing, crushing her pretty hat, and disfiguring her pretty face, with the bright light falling upon her, and revealing every heave of her shoulders. By degrees the paroxysm subsided; she dried her eyes, poor child, and put up her hair, which had got into disorder, with hasty and agitated hands. Then she turned her flushed, tear-stained face upon me. It was almost prettier than usual in this childish passion.

'I don't believe you!' she cried. 'I don't believe it one bit! You only want to vex me. Oh, I wish I had never known you. I wish I might never see you again—you, and—all the rest! I wish I were dead! But I shall tell papa, Mrs. Mulgrave, and I know what he will think of you.'

'Martha, I am very sorry—' I began, but Martha had rushed to the door.

'I don't want to hear any more!' she said. 'I know everything you can say. You are fond of Sister, and want her to have everything. And you always hated me!'

With these words she rushed out, shutting not only the door of the room behind her in her wrath, but the door of the house, which stood always open. She left me, I avow, in a state of very great agitation. I had not expected her to take it in this way. And it had been a great strain upon my nerves to speak at all. I trembled all over, and as soon as she was gone I cried too, from mere nervousness and agitation, not to speak of the terrible thought that weighed on my mind—had I done harm or good? What would the others say if they knew? Would they bless or curse me? Had I interfered out of season? Had I been officious? Heaven knows! The result only could show.

Most people know what a strange feeling it is when one has thus estranged, or parted in anger from, a daily and intimate companion; how one sits in a vague fever of excitement, thinking it over—wondering what else one could have said; wondering if the offended friend will come or send, or give any sign of reconciliation; wondering what one ought to do. I was so shaken by it altogether that I was good for nothing but lying down on the sofa. When my maid came to look for me, she was utterly dismayed by my appearance. 'Them young ladies are too much for you, ma'am,' she said indignantly. 'It's as bad as daughters of your own.' I think that little speech was the last touch that wanted to make me break down. As bad as daughters of my own! but not as good; very different. When I thought how those girls would cling round their father, it was more than I could bear. Not that I envied him. But I was ready to do more for them than he was; to risk their very love in order to serve them; and how different was their affection for me!

All day long I stayed indoors, recovering slowly, but feeling very miserable. Nobody came near me. The girls, who were generally flitting out and in twenty times in a day, never appeared again. The very door which Martha shut in her passion remained closed all day. When it came to be evening, I could bear it no longer; I could not let the sun go down upon such a quarrel; I was so lonely I could not afford to be proud. I drew my shawl round me, though I was still trembling, and went softly in at the Admiral's gate. It was dusk, and everything was very sweet. It had been a lovely autumn day, very warm for the season, and the twilight lingered as if it were loth to make an end. I thought the girls would probably be in the drawing-room by themselves, and that I might invent some excuse for sending Nelly away, and try to make my peace with her sister. I did not love Martha as I loved Nelly, but I was fond of her all the same, as one is fond of a girl one has seen grow up, and watched over from day to day; and I could not bear that she should be estranged from me. When I went in however Nelly was all alone. She was sitting in a low chair by the fire, for they always had a fire earlier than other people. She was sitting over it with her face resting in her hands, almost crouching towards the friendly blaze. And yet it was a warm evening, very warm for the time of the year. She started when she heard my step, and turned round and for the moment I saw that I was not welcome to Nelly either. Her thoughts had been better company: or was it possible that Martha could have told her? I did not think however that this could be the case, when she drew forward my favourite chair for me, and we began to talk. Nelly had not passed through any crisis such as that which Martha and I had made for ourselves. She told me her sister had a headache, and had been lying down before dinner, but that now she had gone out for a little air.

'Only in the garden,' Nelly said. And then she added, 'Major Frost is here. He is with her—and I don't think he ought to come so often—now—'

'Major Frost!' I said, and my heart began to beat; I don't know what I feared or hoped, for at this moment the Admiral came in from the dining-room, and joined us, and we got into ordinary conversation. What a strange thing ordinary conversation is! We sat in the dark, with only the firelight making rosy gleams about the room, and wavering in the great mirror over the mantelpiece, where we were all dimly reflected—and talked about every sort of indifferent subject. But I wonder if Nelly was thinking of what she was saying? or if her heart was away, like mine, hovering over the heads of these two in the garden, or with poor Llewellyn, who was creeping home an unwilling bridegroom? Even the Admiral, I believe, had something on his mind different from all our chit-chat. For my own part I sat well back in my corner, with my heart thumping so against my breast that it affected my breathing. I had to speak in gasps, making up the shortest sentences I could think of. And we talked about public affairs, and what was likely to be the result of the new measures; and the Admiral, who was a man of the old school, shook his head, and declared I was a great deal too much of an optimist, and thought more hopefully than reasonably of the national affairs. Heaven help me! I was thinking of nothing at that moment but of Martha and Major Frost.

Then there was a little stir outside in the hall. The firelight, and the darkness, and the suspense, and my own feelings generally, recalled to my mind so strongly the evening on which Llewellyn arrived, that I should not have been surprised had he walked in, when the door opened. But it was only Martha who came in. The firelight caught her as she entered, and showed me for one brief moment a different creature from the Martha I had parted with that morning in sobs and storms. I don't know what she wore; but I know that she was more elaborately dressed than usual, and had sparkling ornaments about her, which caught the light. I almost think, though I never could be sure, that it was her poor mother's diamond brooch which she had put on, though they were alone. She came in lightly, with something of the triumphant air I had noticed in her a year ago, before Captain Llewellyn's Christmas visit. It was evident at all events that my remonstrance had not broken her spirit. I could see her give a little glance to my corner, and I know that she saw I was there.

'Are you here, papa?' she said. 'You always sit, like crows, in the dark, and nobody can see you.' Then she drew a chair into the circle. She took no notice of me or any one, but placed herself directly in the light of the fire.

'Yes, my dear,' said her father. 'I am glad you have come in. It begins to get cold.'

'We did not feel it cold,' said Martha, and then she laughed—a short little disconnected laugh, which indicated some disturbance of her calm; then she went on, with a tendency to short and broken sentences, like myself—'Papa,' she said, 'I may as well tell you at once. When the Major was here last he was poor, and could not speak—now he's well off. And he wants me to marry him. I like him better than—Ellis Llewellyn. I always—liked him better—and he loves me!'

Upon which Martha burst into tears.

If I were to try to describe the consternation produced by this unlooked-for speech, I should only prolong my story without making it more clear. The want of light heightened it, and confused us all doubly. If a bomb had burst in the peaceful place I don't think it could have produced a greater commotion. It was only the Admiral however who could say a word, and of course he was the proper person. Martha very soon came out of her tears to reply to him. He was angry, he was bewildered, he was wild for the moment. What was he to say to Llewellyn? What did she mean? How did Major Frost dare—? I confess that I was crying in my corner—I could not help it. When the Admiral began to storm, I put my hand on his arm, and made him come to me, and whispered a word in his ear. Then the good man subsided into a bewildered silence. And after a while he went to the library, where Major Frost was waiting to know his fate.

It is unnecessary to follow out the story further. Llewellyn, poor fellow, had to wait a long time after all before Nelly would look at him. I never knew such a proud little creature. And she never would own to me that any spark of human feeling had been in her during that painful year. They were a proud family altogether. Martha met me ever after with her old affectionateness and composure—never asked pardon, nor said I was right, but at the same time never resented nor betrayed my interference. I believe she forgot it even, with the happy facility that belonged to her nature, and has not an idea now that it was anything but the influence of love and preference which made her cast off Llewellyn and choose Major Frost.

Sometimes however in the gray of the summer evenings, or the long, long winter nights, I think I might just as well have let things alone. There are two bright households the more in the world, no doubt. But the Admiral and I are both dull enough sometimes, now the girls are gone. He comes, and sits with me, which is always company, and it is not his fault I have not changed my residence and my lonely condition. But I say to him, why should we change, and give the world occasion to laugh, and make a talk of us at our age? Things are very well as they are. I believe we are better company to each other living next door, than if we were more closely allied; and our neighbours know us too well to make any talk about our friendship. But still it often happens, even when we are together,—in the still evenings, and in the firelight, and when all the world is abroad of summer nights—that we both of us lament a little in the silence, and feel that it is very dull without the girls.

LADY DENZIL

CHAPTER I

The Denzils were the chief people at Dinglefield Green. Their house was by much the most considerable-looking house, and the grounds were beautiful. I say the most considerable-looking, for my own impression is that Dinglewood, which was afterwards bought by the stockbroker whose coming convulsed the whole Green, was in reality larger than the Lodge; but the Lodge, when Sir Thomas Denzil was in it, was all the same the centre of everything. It was like Windsor Castle to us neighbours, or perhaps in reality it was more what her Majesty's actual royal habitation is to the dwellers within her castle gates. We were the poor knights, the canons, the musical and ecclesiastical people who cluster about that mingled stronghold of the State and Church—but to the Lodge was it given to bestow distinction upon us. Those of us who visited Lady Denzil entered into all the privileges of rank; those who did not receive that honour fell into the cold shade—and a very uncomfortable shade it must have been. I speak, you will say, at my ease; for my people had known the Denzils ages before, and Sir

Thomas most kindly sent his wife to call, almost before I had settled down into my cottage; but I remember how very sore Mrs. Wood felt about it, though it surprised me at the time. 'I have been here five years, and have met them everywhere, but she has never found the way to my door. Not that I care in the least,' she said, with a flush on her cheek. She was a clergyman's widow, and very sensitive about her 'position,' poor thing—and almost found fault with me, as if I was to blame for having known the Denzils in my youth.

Lady Denzil, who had so much weight among us, was a very small personage. She would have been tiny and insignificant had she not been so stately and imposing. I don't know how she did it. She was some way over sixty at the time I speak of. Whatever the fashion was, she always wore long flowing dresses which swept the ground for a yard behind her, and cloaks ample and graceful: always large, always full, and always made of black silk. Even in winter, though her carriage would be piled with heaps of furs, she wore upon her little majestic person nothing but silk. Such silk!—you should have touched it to know what it was. The very sound of it, as it rustled softly after her over the summer lawn or the winter carpet, was totally different from the frôlement of ordinary robes. Some people said she had it made for herself expressly at Lyons. I don't know how that might be, but I know I never saw anything like it. I believe she had every variety in her wardrobe that heart of woman could desire: Indian shawls worth a fortune I know were among her possessions; but she never wore anything but that matchless silk—long dresses of it, and long, large, ample cloaks to correspond. Her hair was quite white, like silver. She had the brightest dark eyes, shining out from under brows which were curved and lined as finely as when she was eighteen. Her colour was as fresh as a rose. I think there never was a more lovely old lady. Eighteen, indeed! It has its charms, that pleasant age. It is sweet to the eye, especially of man. Perhaps a woman, who has oftenest to lecture the creature, instead of falling down to worship, may not see so well the witchery which lies in the period; but find me any face of eighteen that could match Lady Denzil's. It had wrinkles, yes; but these were crossed by lines of thought, and lighted up by that soft breath of experience and forbearance which comes only with the years. Lady Denzil's eyes saw things that other eyes could not see. She knew by instinct when things were amiss. You could tell it by the charitable absence of all questioning, by a calm taking for granted the most unlikely explanations. Some people supposed they deceived her, but they never deceived her. And some people spoke of her extraordinary insight, and eyes that could see through a millstone. I believe her eyes were clear; but it was experience, only experience—long knowledge of the world, acquaintance with herself and human nature, and all the chances that befall us on our way through this life. That it was, and not any mere intuition or sharpness that put insight into Lady Denzil's eyes.

The curious thing however was that she had never had any troubles of her own. She had lived with Sir Thomas in the Lodge since a period dating far beyond my knowledge. It was a thing which was never mentioned among us, chiefly, I have no doubt, because of her beautiful manners and stately look, though it came to be spoken of afterwards, as such things will; but the truth is, that nobody knew very clearly who Lady Denzil was. Sir Thomas's first wife was from Lancashire, of one of the best old families in the county, and it was not an unusual thing for new comers to get confused about this, and identify the present Lady Denzil with her predecessor; but I am not aware that any one really knew the rights of it or could tell who she was. I have heard the mistake made, and I remember distinctly the gracious and unsatisfactory way with which she put it aside. 'The first Lady Denzil was a Lancashire woman,' she said; 'she was one of the Tunstalls of Abbotts Tunstall, and a very beautiful and charming person.' This was all; she did not add, as anybody else would have done, Loamshire or Blankshire is my county. It was very unsatisfactory, but it was fine all the same—and closed everybody's mouth. There were always some connections on the Denzil side staying at the Lodge at the end of the year. No one could be kinder than she was to all Sir Thomas's young connections. But nobody belonging to Lady Denzil was ever seen among us. I don't think it was remarked at the time, but it came to be noted afterwards, and it certainly was very strange.

I never saw more perfect devotion than that which old Sir Thomas showed to his wife. He was about ten years older than she—a hale, handsome old man, nearly seventy. Had he been twenty-five and she eighteen he could not have been more tender, more careful of her. Often have I looked at her and wondered, with the peaceful life she led, with the love and reverence and tender care which surrounded her, how she had ever come to know the darker side of life, and understand other people's feelings. No trouble seemed ever to have come near her. She put down her dainty little foot only to walk over soft carpets or through bright gardens; she never went anywhere where those long silken robes might not sweep, safe even from the summer dust, which all the rest of us have to brave by times. Lady Denzil never braved it. I have seen her sometimes—very seldom—with her dress gathered up in her arms in great billows, on the sheltered sunny lime-walk which was at one side of the Lodge, taking a little gentle exercise; but this was quite an unusual circumstance, and meant that the roads were too heavy or too slippery for her horses. On these rare occasions Sir Thomas would be at her side, like a courtly old gallant as he was. He was as deferential to his wife as if she had been a princess and he dependent on her favour: and at the same time there was a grace of old love in his reverence which was like a poem. It was a curious little paradise that one looked into over the ha-ha across the verdant lawns that encircled the Lodge. The two were old and childless, and sometimes solitary; but I don't think, though they opened their house liberally to kith, kin, and connections, that they ever felt less lonely than when they were alone. Two, where the two are one, is enough. To be sure the two in Eden were young. Yet it does but confer a certain tender pathos upon that companionship when they are old. I thought of the purest romance I knew, of the softest creations of poetry, when I used to see old Sir Thomas in the lime-walk with his old wife.

But I was sorry she had not called on poor Mrs. Wood. It would have been of real consequence to that good woman if Lady Denzil had called. She was only a clergyman's widow, and a clergyman's widow may be anything, as everybody knows: she may be such a person as will be an acquisition anywhere, or she may be quite the reverse. It was because Mrs. Wood belonged to this indefinite class that Lady Denzil's visit would have been of such use. Her position was doubtful, poor soul! She was very respectable and very good in her way, and her daughters were nice girls; but there was nothing in themselves individually to raise them out of mediocrity. I took the liberty to say so one day when I was at the Lodge: but Lady Denzil did not see it somehow; and what could I do? And on the other hand it was gall and wormwood to poor Mrs. Wood every time she saw the carriage with the two bays stop at my door.

'I saw Lady Denzil here to-day,' she would say. 'You ought to feel yourself honoured. I must say I don't see why people should give in to her so. In my poor husband's time the duchess never came into the parish without calling. It need not be any object to me to be noticed by a bit of a baronet's wife.'

'No, indeed!' said I, being a coward and afraid to stand to my guns; 'I am sure you need not mind. And she is old, poor lady—and I am an old friend—and indeed I don't know that Lady Denzil professes to visit,' I went on faltering, with a sense of getting deeper and deeper into the mud.

'Oh, pray don't say so to spare my feelings,' said Mrs. Wood with asperity. 'It is nothing to me whether she calls or not, but you must know, Mrs. Mulgrave, that Lady Denzil does make a point of calling on every one she thinks worth her while. I am sure she is quite at liberty to do as she pleases so far as I am concerned.' Here she stopped and relieved herself, drawing a long breath and fanning with her handkerchief her cheeks, which were crimson. 'But if I were to say I was connected with the peerage, or to talk about the titled people I do know,' she added with a look of spite, 'she would very soon find out where I lived: oh, trust her for that!'

'I think you must have taken up a mistaken idea,' I said, meekly. I had not courage enough to stand up in my friend's defence. Not that I am exactly a coward by nature, but Mrs. Wood was rather a difficult person to deal with; and I was sorry in the present instance, and felt that the grievance was a real one. 'I don't think Lady Denzil cares very much about the peerage. She is an old woman and has her fancies, I suppose.'

'Oh, you are a favourite!' said Mrs. Wood, tossing her head, as if it were my fault. 'You have the entrées, and we are spiteful who are left out, you know,' she added with pretended playfulness. It was a very affected little laugh however to which she gave utterance, and her cheeks flamed crimson. I was very sorry—I did not know what to say to make things smooth again. If I had been Lady Denzil's keeper, I should have taken her to call at Rose Cottage next day. But I was not Lady Denzil's keeper. It was great kindness of her to visit me: how could I force her against her will to visit other people? A woman of Mrs. Wood's age, who surely could not have got so far through the world without a little understanding of how things are managed, ought to have known that it could do her very little good to quarrel with me.

And then the girls would come to me when there was anything going on at the Lodge. 'We met the Miss Llewellyns the other day,' Adelaide said on one occasion. 'We thought them very nice. They are staying with Lady Denzil, you know. I wish you would make Lady Denzil call on mamma, Mrs. Mulgrave. It is so hard to come and settle in a place and be shut out from all the best parties. Until you have been at the Lodge you are considered nobody on the Green.'

'The Lodge can't make us different from what we are,' said Nora, the other sister, who was of a different temper. 'I should be ashamed to think it mattered whether Lady Denzil called or not.'

'But it does matter a great deal when they are going to give a ball,' said Adelaide very solemnly. 'The best balls going, some of the officers told me; and everybody will be there—except Nora and me,' said the poor girl. 'Oh, Mrs. Mulgrave, I wish you would make Lady Denzil call!'

'But, my dear, I can't make Lady Denzil do anything,' I said; 'I have no power over her. She comes to see me sometimes, but we are not intimate, and I have no influence. She comes because my people knew the Denzils long ago. She has her own ways. I could not make her do one thing or another. It is wrong to speak so to me.'

'But you could if you would try,' said Adelaide; as she spoke, we could hear the sound of the croquet balls from the Lodge, and voices and laughter. We were all three walking along the road, under shelter of the trees. She gave such a wistful look when she heard them, that it went to my heart. It was not a very serious trouble, it is true. But still to feel one's self shut out from anything, is hard when one is twenty. I had to hurry past the gate, to restrain the inclination I had to brave everything, and take them in with me, as my friends, to join the croquet party. I know very well what would have happened had I done so. Lady Denzil would have been perfectly sweet and gracious, and sent them away delighted with her; but she would never have crossed my threshold again. And what good would that have done them? The fact was, they had nothing particular to recommend them; no special qualities of their own to make up for their want of birth and connection; and this being the case what could any one say?

It gave one a very different impression of Lady Denzil, to see how she behaved when poor Mrs. Stoke was in such trouble about her youngest boy. I had been with her calling, and Mrs. Stoke had told us a whole long story about him; how good-hearted he was, and how generous, spending his money upon everybody. It was a very hard matter for me to keep my countenance, for of course I knew Everard Stoke, and what kind of boy he was. But Lady Denzil took it all with the greatest attention and sympathy. I could not but speak of it when we came out. 'Poor Mrs. Stoke!' said I, 'it is strange how she can deceive herself so—and she must have known we knew better. You who have seen poor Everard grow up, Lady Denzil—'

'Yes, my dear,' she said, 'you are right; and yet, do you know, I think you are wrong too? She is not deceived. She knows a great deal better than we do. But then she is on the other side of the scene, and she sees into the boy's heart a little. I hope she sees into his heart.'

'I fear it is a very bad heart; I should not think it was any pleasure to look into it,' said I in my haste. Lady Denzil gave me a soft, half-reproachful look. 'Well,' she said, and gave a sigh, 'it has always been one of my great fancies, that God was more merciful than man, because He saw fully what was in all our hearts—what we meant, poor creatures that we are, not what we did. We so seldom have any confidence in Him for that. We think He will forgive and save, but we don't think He understands, and sees everything, and knows that nothing is so bad as it seems. Perhaps it is dangerous doctrine; at least the vicar would think so, I fear.'

'In the case of Everard Stoke,' said I stupidly, coming back to the starting point.

'My dear,' said Lady Denzil with a little impatience, 'the older one grows, the less one feels inclined to judge any one. Indeed when one grows quite old,' she went on after a pause, smiling a little, as if it were at the thought that she, whom no doubt she could remember so thoughtless and young, was quite old, 'one comes to judge not at all. Poor Everard, he never was a good boy—but I dare say his mother knows him best, and he is better than is thought.'

'At least it was a comfort to her to see you look as if you believed her,' said I, not quite entering into the argument. Lady Denzil took no notice of this speech. It was a beautiful bright day, and it was but a step from Mrs. Stoke's cottage to the Lodge gates, which we were just about entering. But at that moment there was a little party of soldiers marching along the high-road, at right angles from where we stood. It is not far from the Green to the barracks, and their red coats were not uncommon features in the landscape. These men however were marching in a business-like way, not lingering on the road: and among them was a man in a shooting-coat, handcuffed, poor fellow! It was a deserter they were taking back to the punishment that awaited him. I made some meaningless exclamation or other, and stood still, looking after them for a moment. Then I suppose my interest failed as they went on, at their rapid, steady pace, turning their backs upon us. I came back to Lady Denzil, my passing distraction over; but when I looked at her, there was something in her face that struck me with the deepest wonder. She had not come back to me. She was standing absorbed, watching them; the colour all gone out of her soft old cheeks, and the saddest, wistful, longing gaze in her eyes. It was not pity—it was something mightier, more intense. She did not breathe or move, but stood gazing, gazing after them. When they had disappeared, she came to herself; her hands, which had been clasped tightly, fell loose at her sides; she gave a long deep sigh, and then she became conscious of my eyes upon her, and the colour came back with a rush to her face.

'I am always interested about soldiers,' she said faintly, turning as she spoke to open the gate. That was all the notice she took of it. But the incident struck me more than my account of it may seem to justify. If such a thing had been possible as that the deserter might have been her husband or her brother, one could have understood it. Had I seen such a look on Mrs. Stoke's face, I should have known it was Everard. But here was Lady Denzil, a contented childless woman, without anybody to disturb her peace. Sympathy must indeed have become perfect, before such a wistfulness could come into any woman's eyes.

Often since I have recalled that scene to my mind, and wondered over it; the quick march of the soldiers on the road; the man in the midst with death environing him all round, and most likely despair in his heart; and that one face looking on, wistful as love, sad as death—and yet with no cause either for her sadness or her love. It did not last long, it is true; but it was one of the strangest scenes I ever witnessed in my life.

It even appeared to me next day as if Lady Denzil had been a little shaken, either by her visit to Mrs. Stoke, or by this strange little episode which nobody knew of. She had taken to me, which I confess I felt as a great compliment; and Sir Thomas came in to ask me to go to her next afternoon. 'My lady has a headache,' he said in a quaint way he had of speaking of her: I think he would have liked to call her my queen or my princess. When he said 'my lady' there was something chivalric, something romantic in his very tone. When I went into the drawing-room at the Lodge the great green blind was drawn over the window on the west side, and the trees gave the same green effect to the daylight, at the other end. The east windows looked out upon the lime-walk, and the light came in softly, green and shadowy, through the silken leaves. She was lying on the sofa, which was not usual with her. As soon as I entered the room she called me to come and sit by her—and of course she did not say a word about yesterday. We went on talking for an hour and more, about the trees, and the sunset; about what news there was; girls going to be married, and babies coming, and other such domestic incidents. And sometimes the conversation would languish for a moment, and I did think once there was something strange in her eyes, when she looked at me, as if she had something to tell and was looking into my face to see whether she might or might not do it. But it never went any further; we began to speak of Molly Jackson, and that was an interminable subject. Molly was a widow in the village, and she gave us all a great deal of trouble. She had a quantity of little children, to whom the people on the Green were very kind, and she was a good-natured soft soul, always falling into some scrape or other. This time was the worst of all; it was when the talk got up about Thomas Short. People said that Molly was going to marry him. It would have been very foolish for them both, of course. He was poor and he was getting old, and would rather have hindered than helped her with her children. We gentlefolks may, or may not, be sentimental about our own concerns; but we see things in their true light when they take place among our poor neighbours. As for the two being a comfort to each other we never entered into that question; there were more important matters concerned.

'I don't know what would become of the poor children,' said I. 'The man would never put up with them, and indeed it could not be expected; and they have no friends to go to. But I don't think Molly would be so wicked; she may be a fool but she has a mother's heart.'

Lady Denzil gave a faint smile and turned on her sofa as if something hurt her; she did not answer me all at once—and as I sat for a minute silent in that soft obscurity, Molly Jackson, I acknowledge, went out of my head. Then all at once when I had gone on to something else, she spoke; and her return to the subject startled me, I could not have told how.

'There are different ways of touching a mother's heart,' she said; 'she might think it would be for their good; I don't think it could be, for my part; I don't think it ever is; a woman is deceived, or she deceives herself; and then when it is too late—'

'What is too late?' said Sir Thomas behind us. He had come in at the great window, and we had not noticed. I thought Lady Denzil gave a little start, but there was no sign of it in her face.

'We were talking of Molly Jackson,' she said. 'Nothing is ever too late here, thanks to your precise habits, you old soldier. Molly must be talked to, Mrs. Mulgrave,' she said, turning to me.

'Oh, yes, she will be talked to,' said I; 'I know the rector and his wife have both called; and last time I saw her, Mrs. Wood—'

'You are not one of the universal advisers,' said Lady Denzil, patting my arm with her white hand. It was no virtue on my part, but she spoke as if she meant it for a compliment. And then we had to tell the whole story over again to Sir Thomas, who was very fond of a little gossip like all the gentlemen, but had to have everything explained to him, and never knew what was coming next. He chuckled and laughed as men do over it. 'Old fool!' he said. 'A woman with half-a-dozen children.' It was not Molly but Thomas Short that he thought would be a fool; and on our side, it is true that we had not been thinking of him.

Molly Jackson has not much to do with this story, but yet it may be as well to say that she listened to reason, and did not do anything so absurd. It was a relief to all our minds when Thomas went to live in Langham parish the spring after, and married somebody there. I believe it was a girl out of the workhouse, who might have been his daughter, and led him a very sad life. But still in respect to Molly it was a relief to our minds. I hope she was of the same way of thinking. I know for one thing that she lost her temper, the only time I ever saw her do it—and was very indignant about the young wife. 'Old fool!' she said, and again it was Thomas that was meant. We had a way of talking a good deal about the village folks, and we all did a great deal for them—perhaps, on the whole, we did too much. When anything happened to be wanting among them, instead of making an effort to get it for themselves, it was always the ladies on the Green they came to. And, of course, we interfered in our turn.

CHAPTER II

It was in the spring of the following year that little Mary first came to the Lodge. Sir Thomas had been absent for some time, on business, Lady Denzil said, and it was he who brought the child home. It is all impressed on my mind by the fact that I was there when they arrived. He was not expected until the evening, and I had gone to spend an hour with Lady Denzil in the afternoon. It was a bright spring day, as warm as summer; one of those sweet surprises that come upon us in England in intervals between the gray east wind and the rain. The sunshine had called out a perfect crowd of golden crocuses along the borders. They had all blown out quite suddenly, as if it had been an actual voice that called them, and God's innocent creatures had rushed forth to answer to their names. And there were heaps of violets about the Lodge which made the air sweet. And there is something in that first exquisite touch of spring which moves all hearts. Lady Denzil had come out with me to the lawn. I thought she was quieter than usual, with the air of a woman listening for something. Everything was very still, and yet in the sunshine one felt as if one could hear the buds unfolding, the young grass and leaflets thrilling with their new life. But it did not seem to me that Lady Denzil was listening to these. I said, 'Do you expect Sir

Thomas now?' with a kind of vague curiosity; and she looked in my face with a sudden quick glance of something like suspicion which I could not understand.

'Do I look as if I expected something?' she said. 'Yes—I expect some news that probably I shall not like. But it does not matter, my dear. It is nothing that affects me.'

She said these words with a smile that was rather dreary to see. It was not like Lady Denzil. It was like saying, 'So long as it does not affect me you know I don't care,'—which was so very, very far from my opinion of her. I did not know what to answer. Her tone somehow disturbed the spring feeling, and the harmony of the flowers.

'I wish Sir Thomas had been here on such a lovely day,' she said, after a while; 'he enjoys it so. Peace is very pleasant, my dear, when you are old. You don't quite appreciate it yet, as we do.' And then she paused again and seemed to listen, and permitted herself the faintest little sigh.

'I think I am older than you are, Lady Denzil,' I said.

Then she laughed in her natural soft way. 'I dare say you are,' she said. 'That is the difference between your restless middle age and our oldness. You feel old because you feel young. That's how it is; whereas, being really old, we can afford to be young again—sometimes,' she added softly. The last word was said under her breath. I don't suppose she thought I heard it; but I did, being very quick of hearing, and very fond of her, and feeling there was something underneath which I did not know.

Just then there came the sound of wheels upon the road, and Lady Denzil started slightly. 'You have put it into my head that Sir Thomas might come by the three o'clock train,' she said. 'It would be about time for it now.' She had scarcely stopped speaking and we had just turned towards the gate, when a carriage entered. I saw at once it was one of the common flys that are to be had at the station, and that it was Sir Thomas who put his head out at the window. A moment after it stopped. He had seen Lady Denzil on the lawn. He got out with that slight hesitation which betrays an old man; and then he turned and lifted something out of the carriage. For the first moment one could not tell what it was—he made a long stride on to the soft greensward, with his eyes fixed upon Lady Denzil, and then he put down the child on the lawn. 'Go to that lady,' he said. For my part I stood and stared, knowing nothing of the feelings that might lie underneath. The child stood still with her little serious face and looked at us both for a moment, and then she walked steadily up to Lady Denzil, who had not moved. I was quite unprepared for what followed. Lady Denzil fell down on her knees on the grass—she took the child to her, into her arms, close to her breast. All at once she fell into a passion of tears. And yet that does not express what I saw. It was silent; there were no cries nor sobs, such as a young woman might have uttered. The tears fell as if they had been pent up all her life, as if all her life she had been waiting for this moment: while Sir Thomas stood looking on, half sad, half satisfied. It seemed a revelation to him as it was to me. All this time when she had looked so serene and had been so sweet, had she been carrying those tears in her heart! I think that must have been what was passing through Sir Thomas's mind. I had stood and stared, as one does when one is unexpectedly made the spectator of a crisis in another life. When I came to myself I was ashamed of spying as it were upon Lady Denzil's feelings. I hastened away, shaking hands with Sir Thomas as I passed him. And so entirely was his mind absorbed in the scene before him, that I scarcely think he knew who I was.

After this it may be supposed I took a very great interest in little Mary. At first I was embarrassed and did not quite know what to do—whether I should go back next day and ask for the child, and give Lady

Denzil an opportunity of getting over any confusion she might feel at the recollection that I had been present—or whether I should stay away; but it turned out that Lady Denzil was not half so sensitive as I was on the subject. I stayed away for one whole day thinking about little else—and the next day I went, lest they should think it strange. It seemed quite curious to me to be received as if nothing had happened. There was no appearance of anything out of the ordinary course. When I went in Lady Denzil held out her hand to me as usual without rising from her chair. 'What has become of you?' she said, and made me sit down by her, as she always did. After we had talked a while she rang the bell. 'I have something to show you,' she said smiling. And then little Mary came in, in her little brown holland overall, as if it was the most natural thing in the world. She was the most lovely child I ever saw. I know when I say this that everybody will immediately think of a golden-haired, blue-eyed darling. But she was not of that description. Her hair was brown—not dark, but of the shade which grows dark with years; and it was very fine silky hair, not frizzy and rough as is the fashion now-a-days. Her eyes were brown too, of that tender wistful kind which are out of fashion like the hair. Every look the child gave was an appeal. There are some children's eyes that look at you with perfect trust, believing in everybody; and these are sweet eyes. But little Mary's were sweeter still, for they told you she believed in you. 'Take care of me: be good to me—I trust you,' was what they said; 'not everybody, but you.' This was the expression in them; and I never knew anybody who could resist that look. Then she had the true child's beauty of a lovely complexion, pure red and white. She came up to me and looked at me with those tender serious eyes, and then slid her soft little hand into mine. Even when I had ceased talking to her and petting her, she never took her eyes away from my face. It was the creature's way of judging of the new people among whom she had been brought—for she was only about six, too young to draw much insight from words. I was glad to bend my head over her, to kiss her sweet little face and smooth her pretty hair by way of hiding a certain embarrassment I felt. But I was the only one of the three that was embarrassed. Lady Denzil sat and looked at the child with eyes that seemed to run over with content. 'She is going to stay with me, and take care of me,' she said, with a smile of absolute happiness; 'are not you, little Mary?'

'Yes, my lady,' said the little thing, turning, serious as a judge, to the old lady. I could not help giving a little start as I looked from one to the other, and saw the two pair of eyes meet. Lady Denzil was sixty, and little Mary was but six; but it was the same face; I felt quite confused after I had made this discovery, and sat silent and heard them talk to each other. Even in the little voice there was a certain trill which was like Lady Denzil's. Then the whole scene rushed before me. Lady Denzil on her knees, her tears pouring forth and the child clasped in her arms. What did it mean? My lady was childless—and even had it been otherwise, that baby never could have been her child—who was she? I was so bewildered and surprised that it took from me the very power of speech.

After this strange introduction the child settled down as an inmate of the Lodge, and was seen and admired by everybody. And every one discovered the resemblance. The neighbours on the Green all found it out, and as there was no reason we knew of why she should not be Lady Denzil's relation, we all stated our opinion plainly—except perhaps myself. I had seen more than the rest, though that was almost nothing. I had a feeling that there was an unknown story beneath, and somehow I had not the courage to say to Lady Denzil as I sat there alone with her, and had her perhaps at a disadvantage. 'How like the child is to you!' But other people were not so cowardly. Not long after, two or three of us met at the Lodge, at the hour of afternoon tea, which was an invention of the time which Lady Denzil had taken to very kindly. Among the rest was young Mrs. Plymley, who was not precisely one of us. She was one of the Herons of Marshfield, and she and her husband had taken Willowbrook for the summer. She was a pleasant little woman, but she was fond of talking—nobody could deny that. And she had children of her own, and made a great fuss over little Mary the moment she saw her. The child was too much a little lady to be disagreeable, but I could see she did not like to be lifted up on a stranger's knee, and admired and chattered over. 'I wish my Ada was half as pretty,' Mrs. Plymley said; 'but Ada is so like her poor dear papa,' and here she pretended to sigh. 'I am so fond of pretty children. It is hard upon me to have mine so plain. Oh, you little darling! Mary what? you have only told me half your name. Lady Denzil, one can see in a moment she belongs to you.'

Lady Denzil at the moment was pouring out tea. All at once the silver teapot in her hand seemed to give a jerk, as if it were a living creature, and some great big boiling drops fell on her black dress. It was only for a single second, and she had presence of mind to set it down, and smile and say she was awkward, and it was nothing. 'My arm is always shaky when I hold anything heavy,' she said; 'ever since I had the rheumatism in it. Then she turned to Mrs. Plymley, whose injudicious suggestion we had all forgotten in our fright. Perhaps Lady Denzil had lost her self-possession a little. Perhaps it was only that she thought it best to reply at once, so that everybody might hear. 'Belongs to me?' she said with her clear voice. And somehow we all felt immediately that something silly and uncalled for had been said.

'I mean your side of the house,' said poor Mrs. Plymley abashed. She was young and nervous, and felt, like all the rest of us, that she was for the moment the culprit at the bar.

'She belongs to neither side of the house,' said Lady Denzil, with even unnecessary distinctness. 'Sir Thomas knows her people, and in his kindness he thought a change would be good for her. She is no— connection; nothing at all to us.'

'Oh, I am sure I beg your pardon,' said Mrs. Plymley; and she let little Mary slide down from her lap, and looked very uncomfortable. None of us indeed were at our ease, for we had all been saying it in private. Only little Mary, standing in the middle, looked wistfully round upon us, questioning, yet undisturbed. And Lady Denzil, too, stood and looked. At that moment the likeness was stronger than ever.

'It is very droll,' said Mrs. Damerel, the rector's wife, whose eye was caught by it, like mine. 'She is very like you, Lady Denzil; I never saw an incidental likeness so strong.'

'Poor little Mary! do you think she is like me?' said Lady Denzil with a curious quiver in her voice; and she bent over the child all at once and kissed her. Sir Thomas had been at the other end of the room, quite out of hearing. I don't know by what magnetism he could have known that something agitating was going on—I did not even see him approach or look; but all at once, just as his wife betrayed that strange thrill of feeling, Sir Thomas was at her elbow. He touched her arm quite lightly as he stood by her side.

'I should like some tea,' he said.

She stood up and looked at him for a moment as if she did not understand. And then she turned to the tea-table with something like a blush of shame on her face. Then he drew forward a chair and sat down by Mrs. Plymley and began to talk. He was a very good talker when he pleased, and in two seconds we had all wandered away to our several subjects, and were in full conversation again. But it was some time before Lady Denzil took any part in it. She was a long while pouring out those cups of tea. Little Mary, as if moved by some unconscious touch of sympathy, stole away with her doll into a corner. It was as if the two had been made out of the same material and thrilled to the same touch—they both turned their backs upon us for the moment. I don't suppose anybody but myself noticed this; and to be sure it was simply because I had seen the meeting between them, and knew there was something in it more than the ordinary visit to the parents' friends of a little delicate child.

Besides, the child never looked like a little visitor; she had brought no maid with her, and she spoke very rarely of her home. I don't know how she might be dressed under those brown holland overalls, but these were the only outside garb she ever wore. I don't mean to say they were ugly or wanting in neatness; they were such things as the children at the Rectory wore in summer when they lived in the garden and the fields. But they did not look suitable for the atmosphere of the Lodge. By and by however these outer garments disappeared. The little creature blossomed out as it were out of her brown husk, and put forth new flowers. After the first few weeks she wore nothing but dainty white frocks, rich with needlework. I recognized Lady Denzil's taste in everything she put on. It was clear that her little wardrobe was being silently renewed, and every pretty thing which a child of her age could fitly wear was being added to it. This could never have been done to a little visitor who had come for change of air. Then a maid was got for her, whom Lady Denzil was very particular about; and no one ever spoke of the time when little Mary should be going away. By degrees she grew to belong to the place, to be associated with everything in it. When you approached the house, which had always been so silent, perhaps it was a burst of sweet childish laughter that met your ears; perhaps a little song, or the pleasant sound of her little feet on the gravel in the sunny lime-walk. The servants were all utterly under her sway. They spoke of little Miss Mary as they might have spoken of a little princess whose word was law. As for Sir Thomas, I think he was the first subject in her realm. She took to patronizing and ordering him about before she had been a month at the Lodge. 'Sir Thomas,' she would say in her clear little voice, 'come and walk;' and the old gentleman would get up and go out with her, and hold wonderful conversations, as we could see, looking after them from the window. Lady Denzil did not seem either to pet her, or to devote herself to her, as all the rest of the house did. But there was something in her face when she looked at the child which passes description. It was a sort of ineffable content and satisfaction, as if she had all that heart could desire and asked no more. Little Mary watched her eye whenever they were together with a curious sympathy more extraordinary still. She seemed to know by intuition when my lady wanted her. ''Es, my lady,' the child would say, watching with her sweet eyes. It was the only little divergence she made from correctness of speech, and somehow it pleased my ear. I suppose she said 'My Lady' because Sir Thomas did, and that I liked too. To an old lady like Lady Denzil it is such a pretty title; I fell into it myself without being aware.

CHAPTER III

Thus the world went softly on, till the roses of June had come instead of the spring crocuses. Everything went on softly at the Green. True, there was a tragedy now and then, even among us, like that sad affair of Everard Stoke; and sometimes a very troublesome complication, going near to break some hearts, like that of Nelly Fortis—but for the most part we were quiet enough. And that was a very quiet time. Little Mary had grown the pet of the Green before June. The little Damerels, who were nice children enough, were not to be compared with her; and then there were so many of them, whereas Mary was all alone like a little star. We all petted her—but she was one of the children whom it is impossible to spoil. She was never pert or disagreeable, like little Agatha Damerel. She had her little childish fits of temper by times, but was always sorry and always sweet, with her soft appealing eyes—a little woman, but never knowing or forward, like so many children now-a-days. She was still but a baby, poor darling, not more than seven years old, when that dreadful scene broke in upon our quietness which I have now to tell.

It was June, and there was a large party on the lawn before the Lodge. As long as the season lasted, while there were quantities of people in town, Lady Denzil often had these parties. We were all there of course; everybody on the Green whom she visited—(and I used to be very sorry for Mrs. Wood and her daughters when one of them was going to take place). We were in the habit of meeting continually in the same way, to see the young people play croquet and amuse themselves; and there was perhaps a little monotony in it. But Lady Denzil always took care to have some variety. There would be a fine lady or two from town, bringing with her a whiff of all the grandeurs and gaieties we had no particular share in, and setting an example to the girls in their dress and accessories. I never was extravagant in my dress, nor encouraged such a thing—I think no true lady ever does—but a real fashionable perfect toilette is generally so complete, and charming, and harmonious, that it is good for one to see it now and then, especially for girls, though of course ignorant persons and men don't understand why. And then there were a few gentlemen—with all the gossip of the clubs, and town talk, which made a very pleasant change to us. It was an unusually brilliant party that day. There was the young Countess of Berkhampstead, who was a great beauty and had married so strangely; people said the Earl was not very right in his head, and told the oddest stories about him. Poor thing, I fear she could not help herself— but she was the loveliest creature imaginable, and very nice then, though she went wrong afterwards. She sat by Lady Denzil's side on the sofa, which was placed just before the great bank of roses. It was pretty to see them together: the lovely young lady, with her fits of gaiety and pretty languid stillnesses, letting us all admire her as if she felt what a pleasure it was to us; and the lovely old lady, so serene, so fair, so kind. I don't know, for my part, which was the more beautiful. There were other fine ladies besides Lady Berkhampstead, and, as I have just said, it was a very brilliant party. There never was a more glorious day; the sky was a delight to look at, and the rich full foliage of the trees clustered out against the blue, as if they leant caressingly upon the soft air around them. The breath of the roses went everywhere, and behind Lady Denzil's sofa they threw themselves up into space—great globes of burning crimson, and delicate blush, and creamy white. They were very rich in roses at the Lodge—I remember one wall quite covered with the Gloire de Dijon—but that is a digression. It was a broad lawn, and left room for several sets of croquet players, besides all the other people. The house was on a higher level at one side, the grounds and woods behind, and in front over the ha-ha we had a pretty glimpse of the Green, where cricket was being played, and the distant houses on the other side. It was like fairy-land, with just a peep of the outer world, by which we kept hold upon the fact that we were human, and must trudge away presently to our little houses. On the grass before Lady Denzil little Mary was sitting, a little white figure, with a brilliant picture-book which somebody had brought her. She was seated sideways, half facing to Lady Denzil, half to the house, and giving everybody from time to time a look from her tender eyes. Her white frock which blazed in the sunshine was the highest light in the picture, as a painter would have said, and gave it a kind of centre. I was not playing croquet, and there came a moment when I was doing nothing particular, and therefore had time to remark upon the scene around me. As I raised my eyes, my attention was all at once attracted by a strange figure, quite alien to the group below, which stood on the approach to the house. The house, as I have said, was on a higher level, and consequently the road which approached it was higher too, on the summit of the bank which sloped down towards the lawn. A woman stood above gazing at us. At first it seemed to me that she was one of the servants: she had a cotton gown on, and a straw bonnet, and a little black silk cloak. I could not say that she was shabby or wretched-looking, but her appearance was a strange contrast to the pretty crowd on the lawn. She seemed to have been arrested on her way to the door by the sound of voices, and stood there looking down upon us—a strange, tall, threatening figure, which awoke, I could not tell how, a certain terror in my mind. By degrees it seemed to me that her gaze fixed upon little Mary—and I felt more frightened still; though what harm could any one do to the child with so many anxious protectors looking on? However people were intent upon their games, or their talks, or their companions, and nobody saw her but myself. At last I got so much alarmed that I left my seat to tell Sir

Thomas of her. I had just made one step towards him, when all at once, with a strange cry, the woman darted down the bank. It was at little Mary she flew: she rushed down upon her like a tempest, and seized the child, crushing up her pretty white frock and her dear little figure violently in her arms. I cried out too in my fright—for I thought she was mad—and various people sprang from their chairs, one of the last to be roused being Lady Denzil, who was talking very earnestly to Lady Berkhampstead. The woman gave a great loud passionate outcry as she seized upon little Mary. And the child cried out too, one single word which in a moment transfixed me where I stood, and caught Lady Denzil's ear like the sound of a trumpet. It was a cry almost like a moan, full of terror and dismay and repugnance; and yet it was one of the sweetest words that ever falls on human ears. The sound stopped everything, even the croquet, and called Sir Thomas forward from the other end of the lawn. The one word that Mary uttered, that filled us all with such horror and consternation, was 'Mamma!'

'Yes, my darling,' cried the woman, holding her close, crumpling, even crushing her up in her arms. 'They took you from me when I wasn't myself! Did I know where they were going to bring you? Here! Oh, yes, I see it all now. Don't touch my child! don't interfere with my child!—she sha'n't stay here another day. Her father would curse her if he knew she was here.'

'Oh, please set me down,' said little Mary. 'Oh, mamma, please don't hurt me. Oh, my lady!' cried the poor child, appealing to her protectress. Lady Denzil got up tottering as she heard this cry. She came forward with every particle of colour gone from her face. She was so agitated her lips could scarcely form the words; but she had the courage to lay her hand upon the woman's arm,—

'Set her down,' she said. 'If you have any claim—set her down—it shall be seen into. Sir Thomas—'

The stranger turned upon her. She was a woman about five-and-thirty, strong and bold and vigorous. I don't deny she was a handsome woman. She had big blazing black eyes, and a complexion perhaps a little heightened by her walk in the heat. She turned upon Lady Denzil, shaking off her hand, crushing little Mary still closer in one arm, and raising the other with a wild theatrical gesture.

'You!' she cried; 'if I were to tell her father she was with you, he would curse her. How dare you look me in the face—a woman that's come after her child! you that gave up your own flesh and blood. Ay! You may stare at her, all you fine folks. There's the woman that sold her son to marry her master. She's got her grandeur, and all she bid for; and she left her boy to be brought up in the streets, and go for a common soldier. And she's never set eyes on him, never since he was two years old; and now she's come and stole my little Mary from me!'

Before this speech was half spoken every soul in the place had crowded round to hear. No one thought how rude it was. Utter consternation was in everybody's look. As for Lady Denzil, she stood like a statue, as white as marble, in the same spot, hearing it all. She did not move. She was like an image set down there, capable of no individual action. She stood and gazed, and heard it all, and saw us all listening. I cannot tell what dreadful pangs were rending her heart; but she stood like a dead woman in the sunshine, neither contradicting her accuser nor making even one gesture in her own defence.

Then Sir Thomas, on whom there had surely been some spell, came forward, dividing the crowd, and took the stranger by the arm. 'Set down the child,' he said in a shaking voice. 'Set her down. How dare you speak of a mother's rights? Did you ever do anything for her? Set down the child, woman! You have no business here.'

'I never forsook my own flesh and blood,' cried the enraged creature, letting poor little Mary almost fall down out of her arms, but keeping fast hold of her. 'I've a better right here than any of these strangers. I'm her son's wife. She's little Mary's grandmother, though she'll deny it. She's that kind of woman that would deny to her last breath. I know she would. She's the child's grandmother. She's my mother-in-law. She's never seen her son since he was two years old. If he hears the very name of mother he curses and swears. Let me alone, I have come for my child! And I've come to give that woman her due!'

'Go!' cried Sir Thomas. His voice was awful. He would not touch her, for he was a gentleman; but the sound of his voice made my very knees bend and tremble. 'Go!' he said—'not a word more.' He was so overcome at last that he put his hand on her shoulder and pushed her away, and wildly beckoned to the servants, who were standing listening too. The woman grasped little Mary by her dress. She crushed up the child's pretty white cape in her hot hand and dragged her along with her. But she obeyed. She dared not resist his voice; and she had done all the harm it was possible to do.

'I'll go,' she said. 'None of you had better touch me. I'm twice as strong as you, though you're a man. But I'll go. She knows what I think of her now; and you all know what she is!' she cried, raising her voice. 'To marry that old man, she deserted her child at two years old, and never set eyes on him more. That's Lady Denzil. Now you all know, ladies and gentlemen; and I'll go.'

All this time Lady Denzil never stirred; but when the woman moved away, dragging little Mary with her, all at once my lady stretched out her hands and gave a wild cry. 'The child!' she cried; 'the child!' And then the little thing turned to her with that strange sympathy we had all noticed. I don't know how she twitched herself out of her mother's excited, passionate grasp, but she rushed back and threw herself at Lady Denzil's feet, and clutched hold of her dress. My lady, who had not moved nor spoken except those two words—who was old and capable of no such exertion, stooped over her and lifted her up. I never saw such a sight. She was as pale as if she had been dead. She had received such a shock as might well have killed her. Notwithstanding, this is what she did. She lifted up the child in her arms, broke away from us who were surrounding her, mounted the steep bank like a girl, with her treasure clasped close to her bosom, and before any one knew, before there was time to speak, or even almost think, had disappeared with her into the house. The woman would have rushed at her, sprung upon her, if she had not been held fast. It may easily be imagined what a scene it was when the mistress of the feast disappeared, and a family secret so extraordinary was thus tossed to public discussion. The house door rang after Lady Denzil, as she rushed in, with a sound like a cannon shot. The stranger stood struggling in the midst of a group of men, visitors and servants, some of whom were trying to persuade, some to force her away. Sir Thomas stood by himself, with his old pale hands piteously clasped together, and his head bent. He was overwhelmed by shame and trouble, and the shock of this frightful scene. He did not seem able for the first moment to face any one, to lift his eyes to the disturbed and fluttering crowd, who were so strangely in the way. And we all stood about thunderstruck, staring in each other's faces, not knowing what to do or to say. Lady Berkhampstead, with the instinct of a great lady, was the first to recover herself. She turned to me, I scarcely know why, nor could she have told why. 'I know my carriage is waiting,' she said, 'and I could not think of disturbing dear Lady Denzil to say good-bye. Will you tell her how sorry I am to go away without seeing her?' They all came crowding round me with almost the same words, as soon as she had set the example. And presently Sir Thomas roused up as it were from his stupor. And for the next few minutes there was nothing but shaking of hands, and the rolling up of carriages, and an attempt on the part of everybody to smile and look as if nothing had happened. 'So long as it does not make dear Lady Denzil ill,' one of the ladies said. 'This is one of the dangers of living so close upon the road. It might have happened to any of us,' said another. 'Of course the creature is mad; she should be shut up somewhere.' They said such words with the natural impulse of saying anything to break the terrible impression of the scene; but they were all almost as much shocked and shaken as the principals in it. I never saw such a collection of pale faces as those that went from the Lodge that afternoon. I was left last of all. Somehow the woman who had made so dreadful a disturbance had disappeared without anybody knowing where. Sir Thomas and I were left alone on the lawn, which ten minutes ago—I don't think it was longer—had been so gay and so crowded. So far as I was myself concerned, that was the most trying moment of all. Everybody had spoken to me as if I belonged to the house, but in reality I did not belong to the house; and I felt like a spy as I stood with Sir Thomas all alone. And what was worse, he felt it too, and looked at me with the forced painful smile he had put on for the others, as if he felt I was just like them, and it was also needful for me.

'I beg your pardon for staying,' I said, 'don't you think I could be of any use? Lady Denzil perhaps—'

Sir Thomas took my hand and shook it in an imperative way. 'No, no,' he said with his set smile. He even turned me towards the gate and touched my shoulder with his agitated hand—half no doubt, because he knew I meant kindly—but half to send me away.

'She might like me to do something,' I said piteously. But all that Sir Thomas did was to wring my hand and pat my shoulder, and say, 'No, no.' I was obliged to follow the rest with an aching heart. As I went out one of the servants came after me. It was a man who had been long in the family, and knew a great deal about the Denzils. He came to tell me he was very much frightened about the woman, who had disappeared nobody could tell how. 'I'm afraid she's hiding about somewhere,' he said, 'to come again.' And then he glanced round to see that nobody was by, and looked into my face. 'All that about my lady is true,' he said—'true as gospel. I've knowed it this forty years.'

'They've been very kind to you, Wellman,' I said indignantly—'for shame! to think you should turn upon your good mistress now.'

'Turn upon her!' said Wellman; 'not if I was to be torn in little bits; but being such a friend of the family, I thought it might be a satisfaction to you, ma'am, to know as it was true.'

If anything could have made my heart more heavy I think it would have been that. He thought it would be a satisfaction to me to know! And after the first moment of pity was past, were there not some people to whom it would be a satisfaction to know? who would tell it all over and gloat upon it, and say to each other that pride went before a fall? My heart was almost bursting as I crossed the Green in the blazing afternoon sunshine, and saw the cricketers still playing as if nothing had happened. Ah me! was this what brought such sad indulgent experience to Lady Denzil's eyes?—was this what made her know by instinct when anything was wrong in a house? I could not think at first what a terrible accusation it was that had been brought against her. I thought only of her look, of her desperate snatch at the child, of her rush up the steep bank with little Mary in her arms. She could scarcely have lifted the child under ordinary circumstances—what wild despair, what longing must have stimulated her to such an effort! I put down my veil to cover my tears. Dear Lady Denzil! how sweet she was, how tender, how considerate of everybody. Blame never crossed her lips. I cannot describe the poignant aching sense of her suffering that grew upon me till I reached my own house. When I was there, out of sight of everybody, I sat down and cried bitterly. And then gradually, by degrees it broke upon me what it was that had happened—what the misery was, and the shame.

She must have done it forty years ago, as Wellman said, when she was quite young, and no doubt ignorant of the awful thing she was doing. She had done it, and she had held by it ever since—had given her child up at two years old, and had never seen him again. Good Lord! could any woman do that and live? Her child, two years old. My mind seemed to grow bewildered going over and over that fact: for evidently it was a fact. Her child—her own son.

And for forty years! To keep it all up and stand by it, and never to flinch or falter. If it is difficult to keep to a good purpose for so long, what can it be to keep by an evil one? How could she do it? Then a hundred little words she had said came rushing into my mind. And that look—the look she cast after the deserter on the road! I understood it all now. Her heart had been longing for him all the time. She had loved her child more than other mothers love, every day of all that time.

Poor Lady Denzil! dear Lady Denzil! this was the end of all my reasonings on the matter. I went over it again and again, but I never came to any ending but this:—The thing was dreadful; but she was not dreadful. There was no change in her. I did not realize any guilt on her part. My heart only bled for the long anguish she had suffered, and for the shock she was suffering from now.

But before evening on this very same day my house was filled with people discussing the whole story. No one had heard any more than I had heard: but by this time a thousand versions of the story were afloat. Some people said she had gone astray when she was young, and had been cast off by her family, and that Sir Thomas had rescued her; and there were whispers that such stories were not so rare, if we knew all: a vile echo that always breathes after a real tragedy. And some said she was of no family, but had been the former Lady Denzil's maid; some thought it was Sir Thomas's own son that had been thus cast away; some said he had been left on the streets and no provision made for him. My neighbours went into a hundred details. Old Mr. Clifford thought it was a bad story indeed; and the rector shook his head, and said that for a person in Lady Denzil's position such a scandal was dreadful; it was such an example to the lower classes. Mrs. Damerel was still more depressed. She said she would not be surprised at anything Molly Jackson could do after this. As for Mrs. Wood, who came late in the evening, all agape to inquire into the news, there was something like a malicious satisfaction in her face, I lost all patience when she appeared. I had compelled myself to bear what the others said, but I would not put up with her.

'Lady Denzil is my dear friend,' I broke out, not without tears; 'a great trouble has come upon her. A madwoman has been brought against her with an incredible story; and when a story is incredible people always believe it. If you want to hear any more, go to other people who were present. I can't tell you anything, and if I must say so, I won't.'

'Good gracious, Mrs. Mulgrave, don't go out of your senses!' said my visitor. 'If Lady Denzil has done something dreadful, that does not affect you!'

'But it does affect me,' I said, 'infinitely; it clouds over heaven and earth; it changes—Never mind, I cannot tell you anything about it. If you are anxious to hear, you must go to some one else than me.'

'Well, I am very glad I was not there,' said Mrs. Wood, 'with my innocent girls. I am very glad now I never made any attempt to make friends with her, though you know how often you urged me to do it. I am quite happy to think I did not yield to you now.'

I had no spirit to contradict this monstrous piece of pretence. I was glad to get rid of her anyhow; for though I might feel myself for an instant supported by my indignation, the blow had gone to my heart, and I had no strength to struggle against it. The thought of all that Lady Denzil might be suffering confused me with a dull sense of pain. And yet things were not then at their worst with my lady. Next morning it was found that little Mary had been stolen away.

CHAPTER IV

That was a dreadful morning on the Green. After the lovely weather we had been having, all the winds and all the fiends seemed to have been unchained. It blew a hurricane during the night, and next day the Green was covered with great branches of trees which had been torn off and scattered about like wreck on a seashore. After this came rain; it poured as if the windows of heaven were opened, when Sir Thomas himself stepped in upon me like a ghost, as I sat at my solitary breakfast. These twenty-four hours had passed over him like so many years. He was haggard and ashy pale, and feeble. His very mind seemed to be confused. 'We have lost the child,' he said to me, with a voice from which all modulation and softness had gone. 'Will you come and see my wife?'

'Lost! little Mary?' I cried.

And then all his courage gave way; he sat down speechless, with his lips quivering, and bitter tears in his worn old eyes. Then he got up restless and shaking. 'Come to my wife,' he said. There was not another word exchanged between us. I put on my cloak with the hood over my head, and went with him on the moment. As we crossed the Green a sort of procession arrived, two or three great vans packed with people, with music and flags, which proceeded to discharge their contents at the 'Barley-Mow' under the soaking rain. They had come for a day's pleasure, poor creatures, and this was the sort of day they got. The sight of them is so associated in my mind with that miserable moment, that I don't think I could forget it were I to live a hundred years. It seemed to join on somehow to the tragical breaking-up of the party on the day before. There was nothing wrong now but in the elements; yet it chimed in with its little sermon on the vanity of all things. My lady was in her own room when I entered the Lodge. The shock had struck her down, but she was not calm enough, or weak enough to go to bed. She lay on a sofa in her dressing-gown; she was utterly pale, not a touch of her sweet colour left, and her hands shook as she held them out to me. She held them out, and looked up in my face with appealing eyes, which put me in mind of little Mary's. And then, when I stooped down over her in the impulse of the moment to kiss her, she pressed my hands so in hers, that frail and thin as her fingers were, I almost cried out with pain. Mrs. Florentine, her old maid, stood close by the head of her mistress's sofa. She stood looking on very grave and steady, without any surprise, as if she knew it all.

For a few minutes Lady Denzil could not speak. And when she did, her words came out with a burst, all at once. 'Did he tell you?' she said. 'I thought you would help me. You have nobody to keep you back; neither husband nor— I said I was sure of you.'

'Dear Lady Denzil,' I said, 'if I can do anything—to the utmost of my strength—'

She held my hand fast, and looked at me as if she would look me through and through. 'That was what I said—that was what I said!' she cried; 'you can do what your heart says; you can bring her back to me; my child, my little child! I never had but a little child—never that I knew!'

'I will do whatever you tell me,' I said, trying to soothe her; 'but oh! don't wear yourself out. You will be ill if you give way.'

I said this, I suppose, because everybody says it when any one is in trouble. I don't know any better reason. 'That's what I'm always telling my lady, ma'am,' said Mrs. Florentine; 'but she pays no heed to me.'

Lady Denzil gave us both a faint little smile. She knew too much not to know how entirely a matter of conventional routine it was that we should say this to her. She made a pause, and then she took my hand once more.

'I ought to tell you,' she said—'it is all true—every word. Florentine knows everything, from the first to the last. I was a poor soldier's widow, and I was destitute. I was too young to know what I was doing, and I was pretty, they said, and there were men that would have taken advantage of my simplicity. But Sir Thomas was never like that. I married him to buy a livelihood for my child; and he was very good to me. When he married me, I was a forlorn young creature, with nothing to give my helpless baby. I gave up my child, Florentine knows; and yet every day, every year of his life, I've followed him in my heart. If he had been living in my sight, I could not have known more of him. What I say is every word true, Florentine will tell you. I want you,' grasping my hand tightly, 'to tell everything to him.'

'To him!' said I, with a gasp of astonishment, not knowing what she meant.

'Yes,' said Lady Denzil, holding my hand fast, 'to my boy—I want you to see my boy. Tell him there has never been a day I have not followed him in my heart. All his wilfulness I have felt was my fault. I have prayed God on my knees to lay the blame on me. That day when I saw the deserter—I want you to tell him everything. I want you to ask him to give me back the child.'

I gave a cry of astonishment; an exclamation which I could not restrain. 'Can you expect it?' I said.

'Ah, yes, I expect it,' said Lady Denzil; 'not that I have any right—I expect it from his heart. Florentine will tell you everything. It is she who has watched over him. We never talked of anything else, she and I; never a day all these forty years but I have figured to myself what my darling was doing; I say my darling,' she cried as with a sharp pang, with a sudden gush of tears, 'and he is a man and a soldier, and in prison. Think of that, and think of all I have had to bear!'

I could not make any answer. I could only press her hand with a dumb sympathy. As for Mrs. Florentine, she stood with her eyes cast down, and smoothed the chintz cover with her hand, taking no part by look or word. The story was no surprise to her. She knew everything about it; she was a chief actor in it; she had no need to show any sympathy. The union between her mistress and herself was deeper than that.

'When he married this woman, I was ready to believe it would be for his good,' said my lady, when she had recovered herself. 'I thought it was somehow giving him back what I had taken from him. I sent her presents secretly. He has been very, very wilful; and Sir Thomas was so good to him! He took his mother from him; but he gave him money, education, everything a young man wants. There are many young men,' said Lady Denzil pathetically, 'who think but little of their mothers—' and then she made a pause. 'There was young Clifford, for example,' she added, 'and the rector's brother who ran away—their mothers broke their hearts, but the boys did not care much. I have suffered in everything he suffered by; but yet if he had been here, perhaps he would not have cared for me.'

'That is not possible,' I said, not seeing what she meant.

'Oh, it is possible, very possible,' she said. 'I have seen it times without number. I have tried to take a little comfort from it. If it had been a girl, I would never, never have given her up; but a boy— That was what I thought. I don't defend myself. Let him be the judge—I want him to be the judge. That woman is a wicked woman; she has disgraced him and left him; she will bring my child up to ruin. Ask him to give me back my poor little child.'

'I will do what I can,' I said, faltering. I was pledged; yet how was I to do it? My courage failed me as I sat by her dismayed and received my commission. When she heard the tremulous sound of my voice, she turned round to me and held my hand close in hers once more.

'You can do everything,' she said. Her voice had suddenly grown hoarse. She was at such a supreme height of emotion, that the sight of her frightened me. I kissed her; I soothed her; I promised to do whatever she would. And then she became impatient that I should set out. She was not aware of the rain or the storm. She was too much absorbed in her trouble even to hear the furious wail of the wind and the blast of rain against the windows: but had I been in her case she would have done as much for me. Before Florentine followed me with my cloak, I had made up my mind not to lose any more time. It was from her I got all the details: the poor fellow's name, and where he was, and all about him. He had been very wild, Florentine said. Sir Thomas had done everything for him; but he had not been grateful, and had behaved very badly. His wife was an abandoned woman, wicked and shameless; and he too had taken to evil courses. He had strained Sir Thomas's patience to the utmost time after time. And then he had enlisted. His regiment was in the Tower, and he was under confinement there for insubordination. Such was the brief story. 'Many a time I've thought, ma'am,' said Mrs. Florentine, 'if my lady did but know him as she was a-breaking of her heart for! If he'd been at home he'd have killed her. But all she knows is that he's her child—to love, and nothing more.'

'The Tower is a long way from our railway,' I said; 'but it does not much matter in a cab.'

'Law, ma'am, you're never going to-day?' said Florentine. But I had no intention of arguing the question with her. I went into the library to Sir Thomas to bid him good-bye. And he too was amazed when I told him. He took my hand as his wife had done, and shook it, and looked pitifully into my face. 'It is I who ought to go,' he said. But he knew as well as I did that it was impossible for him to go. He ordered the carriage to come round for me, and brought me wine—some wonderful old wine he had in his cellar, which I knew no difference in from the commonest sherry. But it pleased him, I suppose, to think he had given me his best. And before I went away, he gave me much more information about the unfortunate man I was going to see. 'He is not bad at heart,' said Sir Thomas; 'I don't think he is bad at heart; but his wife is a wicked woman.' And when I was going away, he stooped his gray aged countenance over me, and kissed me solemnly on the forehead. When I found myself driving along the wet roads, with the rain sweeping so in the horses' faces that it was all the half-blinded coachman could do to keep them going against the wind, I was so bewildered by my own position that I felt stupid for the moment. I was going to the Tower to see Sergeant Gray, in confinement for disrespect to his superior officer—going to persuade him to exert himself to take his child from his wife's custody, and give her to his mother, whom he did not know! I had not even heard how it was that little Mary had been stolen away. I had taken that for granted, in face of the immediate call upon me. I had indeed been swept up as it were by the strong wind of emotion, and carried away and thrust forward into a position I could not understand. Then I recognized the truth of Lady Denzil's words. I had nobody to restrain me: no husband at home to find fault with anything I might do; nobody to wonder, or fret, or be annoyed by the burden I had taken upon me. The recollection made my heart swell a little, not with pleasure. And yet it was very true. Poor

Mr. Mulgrave, had he been living, was a man who would have been sure to find fault. It is dreary to think of one's self as of so little importance to any one; but perhaps one ought to think more than one does, that if the position is a dreary one, it has its benefits too. One is free to do what one pleases. I could answer to myself; I had no one else to answer to. At such a moment there was an advantage in that.

At the station I met the rector, who was going to town by the same train. 'Bless my soul, Mrs. Mulgrave,' he said, 'what a dreadful day you have chosen for travelling. I thought there was no one afloat on the world but me.'

'There was no choice, Mr. Damerel,' I said. 'I am going about business which cannot be put off.'

He was very kind: he got my ticket for me, and put me into a carriage, and did not insist that I should talk to him on the way up. He talked enough himself it is true, but he was satisfied when I said yes and no. Just before we got to town however he returned to my errand. 'If your business is anything I can do for you,' he said, 'if there is anything that a man could look after better than a lady—you know how glad I should be to be of any use.'

'Thank you,' I said. My feelings were not mirthful, but yet I could have burst out laughing. I wonder if there is really any business that a man can do better than a lady, when it happens to be her business and not his? I have never got much help in that way from the men that have belonged to me. And to think of putting my delicate, desperate business into Mr. Damerel's soft, clerical hands, that had no bone in them! He got me a cab, which was something—though to be sure a porter would have done it quite as well—and opened his eyes to their utmost width when he heard me tell the coachman to go to the Tower.

What a drive it was! our thirty miles of railway was nothing to it: through all those damp, dreary, glistening London streets—streets narrow and drearily vicious; streets still more drearily respectable; desert lines of warehouses and offices; crowded thoroughfares with dreary vehicles in a lock, and dreary people crowding about surmounted with umbrellas—miles upon miles, streets upon streets, from Paddington to the Tower. I think it was the first drive of the kind I ever took, and if you can suppose me wrapped up in my waterproof cloak, a little excited about the unknown man I was going to see; trying to form my sentences, what I was to say; pondering how I should bring in my arguments best; wondering where I should have to go to find the mother and the child. Poor little Mary! after the little gleam of love and of luxury that had opened upon her, to be snatched off into the dreary world of poverty, with a violent mother whom it was evident she feared! And poor mother too! She might be violent and yet might love her child; she might be wicked and yet might love her child. To go and snatch the little creature back, at all hazards, was an act which to the popular mind would always look like a much higher strain of virtue than dear Lady Denzil's abandonment. I could not defend Lady Denzil, even to myself; and what could I say for her to her son, who knew her not?

At least an hour was lost before I got admittance to Sergeant Gray. As it happened, by a fortunate chance, Robert Seymour was colonel of the regiment, and came to my assistance. But for that I might have failed altogether. Robert was greatly amazed by the request I made him, but of course he did what I wanted. He told me Sergeant Gray was not in prison, but simply confined to his quarters, and that he was a very strange sort of man. 'I should like to know what you can want with him,' he said. 'Yes, of course, I am dreadfully curious—men are—you know it is our weakness. You may as well tell me what you want with Gray.'

'It is nothing to laugh about,' said I; 'it is more tragic than comical. I have a message to him from his mother. And there is not a moment to lose.'

'I understand,' said Robert, 'I am to take myself off. Here is the door; but you must tell me anything you know about him when you have seen him. He is the strangest fellow in the regiment. I never can make him out.'

And in two minutes more I was face to face with Sergeant Gray.

He must have been like his father. There was not a feature in his face which recalled Lady Denzil's. He was an immensely tall, powerful man, with strong chestnut brown hair, and vigour and life in every line of his great frame. I expected to find a prisoner partially sentimental; and I found a big man in undress marching freely about his room, with a long pipe by the fire, and his beer and glasses on the table. I had expected a refined man, bearing traces of gentleman written on him, and the fine tastes that became Lady Denzil's son. There was something about him, when one came to look at him a second time—but what was it? Traces of dissipation, a look of bravado, an instant standing to his arms in self-defence, whatever I might have come to accuse him of; and the insufferable coxcomb air which comes naturally to the meanest member of the household troops. Such was the rapid impression I formed as I went in. He took off his cap with an air of amazement yet assurance, but put it on again immediately. I stood trembling before this big, irreverent, unknown man. If the door had been open I think I should have run away. But as it was I had no resource.

'Mr. Gray,' I said all at once, half from cowardice, half to get it over, 'I have come to you—from your mother.'

The man actually staggered as he stood before me—he fell back and gazed at me as if I had been a ghost. 'From my—mother?' he said, and his lips seemed to refuse articulation. His surprise vanquished him; which was more than with my individual forces I could have hoped to do.

'From your mother,' I repeated. 'I have come direct from her, where she is lying ill and much shaken. She has told me all her story—and I love her dearly—that is why she sent me to you.'

All the time I was speaking he stood still and stared at me; but when I stopped, he appeared gradually to come to himself. He brought forward, from where it stood against the wall, very deliberately, another chair, and sitting down looked at me intently. 'If she has told you all her story,' he said, 'you will know how little inducement I have to listen to anything she may say.'

'Yes,' said I, feeling not a fictitious but a real passion swelling up into my throat, 'she has told me everything, more than you can know. She has told me how for forty years—is it forty years?—she has watched over you in secret, spent her days in thinking of you, and her nights in praying for you. Ah, don't smile! if you had seen her pale and broken in all her pride, lying trembling and telling me this, it would have touched your heart.'

And I could see that it did touch his heart, being so new and unusual to him. He was not a cynical, over-educated man, accustomed to such appeals, and to believe them nonsense. And it touched him, being so unexpected. Then he made a little effort to recover himself, and the natural bravado of his character and profession. 'In all her pride!' he said bitterly. 'Yes, that's very well said; she liked her pride better than me.'

'She liked your life better than you,' said I—and heaven forgive me if I spoke like a sophist—'and your comfort. To secure bread to you and education she made that vow. When she had once made it, she had to keep it. But I tell you what she told me not three hours ago. "There has never been a day I have not followed him in my heart." That is what she said. She and her old maid who used to see you and watch over you talked of nothing else. Fancy! you a young man growing up, taking your own way, going against the wishes of your best friends; and your mother, who dared not go to you, watching you from far off, weeping over you, praying on her knees, thinking of nothing else, talking of nothing else when she was alone and dared do it. At other times she had to go into the world to please her husband, to act as if you had no existence. And all the time she was thinking of nothing but you in her heart.'

He had got up before I came so far. He was unquestionably moved; his step got quicker and quicker. He made impatient gestures with his hands as if to put my voice away. But all the same he listened to me greedily. When I had done—and I got so excited that I was compelled to be done, for tears came into my throat and choked me—he turned to me with his face strongly swept by winds of feeling. 'Who told you?' he cried abruptly. 'Why do you come to disturb me? I was thinking nothing about my circumstances. I was thinking how I could best be jolly in such a position. What do I know about anybody who may choose to call herself my mother? Probably I never had a mother. I can do nothing for her, and she can do nothing for me.'

'You can do something for her,' I cried. 'She sent me to you to beg it of you. Sir Thomas saw how your wife was living. He saw she should not have a little girl to ruin. He brought away the child. I was there when he came home. Your mother knew in a moment who it was, though he never said a word. She rushed to her, and fell on her knees, and cried as if her heart would break. She thought God had sent the child. Little Mary is so like her, so like her! You cannot think how beautiful it was to see them together. Look! if you don't know what your mother is, look at that face.'

He had stood as if stupefied, staring at me. When I mentioned his wife he had made an angry gesture; but his heart melted altogether when I came to little Mary. I had brought Lady Denzil's photograph with me, thinking it might touch his heart, and now I thrust it into his hand before he knew what I meant. He gave one glance at it, and then he fell back into his chair, and gazed and gazed, as if he had lost himself. He was not prepared. He had been wilful—perhaps wicked—but his heart had not got hardened like that of a man of the world. It had been outside evils he had done, outside influences that had moved him. When anything struck deep at his heart he had no armour to resist the blow. He went back upon his chair with a stride, hiding from me, or trying to hide, that he was obliged to do it to keep himself steady; he knitted his brows over the little picture as if it was hard to see it. But he might have spared himself the trouble. I saw how it was. One does not live in the world and learn men's ways for nought: I knew his eyes were filling with tears; I knew that sob was climbing up into his throat; and I did not say a word more. It was a lovely little photograph. The sun is often so kind to old women. It was my lady with all the softness of her white hair, with her gracious looks, her indulgent, benign eyes. And those eyes were little Mary's eyes. They went straight into the poor fellow's heart. After he had struggled as long as he could, the sob actually broke out. Then he straightened himself up all at once, and looked at me fiercely; but I knew better than to pretend to hear him.

'This is nothing to the purpose,' he said; and then he stopped, and nature burst forth. 'Why did she cast me upon the world? Why did she give me up? You are a good woman, and you are her friend. Why did she cast me away?'

I shook my head, it was all I could do. I was crying, and I could not articulate. 'God knows!' I gasped through my tears. And he got up and went to the window, and turning his back on me, held up the little picture to the light. I watched no longer what he was doing. Nature was working her own way in his heart.

When he turned round at last, he came up to me and held out his hand. 'Thank you,' he said, in a way that, for the first time, reminded me of Lady Denzil. 'You have made me think less harshly about my mother. What is it she wants me to do?'

He did not put down the photograph, or give it back to me, but held it closely in his hand, which gave me courage. And then I entered upon my story. When I told him how his wife had insulted his mother, his face grew purple. I gave him every detail: how little Mary clung to my lady; how frightened she was of the passionate claimant who seized her. When I repeated her little cry, 'My lady!' a curious gleam passed over his face. He interrupted me at that point. 'Who is my lady?' he said, with a strange consciousness. The only answer I made was to point at the photograph. It made the most curious impression on him. Evidently he had not even known his mother's name. Almost, I think, the title threw a new light for him upon all the circumstances. There are people who will say that this was from a mean feeling; but it was from no mean feeling. He saw by this fact what a gulf she had put between herself and him. He saw a certain reason in the separation which, if she had been a woman of different position, could not have existed. And there is no man living who is not susceptible to the world's opinion of the people he is interested in. He changed almost imperceptibly—unawares. He heard all the rest of my story in grave silence. I told him what my lady had said—that he was to be the judge; and henceforward it was with the seriousness of a judge that he sat and listened. He heard me out every word, and then he sat and seemed to turn it over in his mind. So far as I was concerned, that was the hardest moment of all. His face was stern in its composure. He was reflecting, putting this and that together. His mother was standing at the bar before him. And what should I do, did he decide against her? Thus I sat waiting and trembling. When he opened his lips my heart jumped to my mouth. How foolish it was! That was not what he had been thinking of. Instead of his mother at the bar, it was his own life he had been turning over in his mind. It all came forth with a burst when he began to speak: the chances he had lost; the misery that had come upon him; the shame of the woman who bore his name; and his poor little desolate child. Then the man forgot himself, and swore a great oath. 'As soon as I am free I will go and get her, and send her to— my lady!' he said, with abrupt, half-hysterical vehemence. And then he rose suddenly and went to the window, and turned his back on me again.

I was overcome. I did not expect it so soon, or so fully. I could have thrown myself upon his neck, poor fellow, and wept. Was he the one to bear the penalties of all? sinned against by his mother in his childhood, and more dreadfully by his wife in his maturity. What had he done that the closest of earthly ties should thus be made a torment to him? When I had come to myself I rose and went after him, trembling. 'Mr. Gray,' I said, 'is there nothing that can be done for you?'

'I don't want anything to be done for me,' he cried abruptly. The question piqued his pride. 'Tell her she shall see yet that I understand the sacrifice she has made,' he said. If he spoke ironically or in honesty I cannot tell; when his mouth had once been opened the stream came so fast. 'I want to go away, that is all,' he said, with a certain heat, almost anger; 'anywhere—I don't care where—to the Mauritius, if they like, where that fever is. No fear that I should die. I have been brought up like a gentleman—it is quite true. And yet I am here. What was the use? My father was a common soldier. She— but it's no good talking; I am no credit to anybody now. If I could get drafted into another regiment, and go—to India or anywhere—you should see a difference. I swear you should see a difference!' his voice rose high in these last words, then he paused. 'But she is old,' he said, sinking his voice; 'ten years—I couldn't do in less than ten years. She'll never be living then, to see what a man can do.'

'She is a woman that would make shift to live, somehow, to see her son come back,' I cried. 'Give her little Mary, and try.'

'She shall have little Mary, by God!' cried the excited man; and then he broke down, and wept. I cannot describe this scene any more. I grasped his hand when I left him, feeling as if he were my brother; he had his mother's picture held fast and hidden in his other hand. If that dear touch of natural love had come to him before! But God knows! perhaps he was only ready and open to it then.

But he could not tell me where to find the child. I had to be content with his promise that when he was free he would restore her to us. I went out from him as much shaken as if I had gone through an illness, and stole out, not to see Robert Seymour, whom I was not equal to meeting just at that moment. But the end of my mission was nearer than I thought. When I got outside there was a group of excited people about the gateway, close to which my cab was waiting me. They were discussing something which had just happened, and which evidently had left a great commotion behind. Among the crowd was a group of soldiers' wives, who shook their heads, and talked it over to each other with lowered voices. 'It's well for her she was took bad here, and never got nigh to him,' one of them said. 'He'd have killed her, I know he would! It's well for her she never got in to tempt that man to her death.'

'It was brazen of her to come nigh him at all,' said another, 'and him so proud. She always was a shameless one. What my heart bleeds for is that poor little child.'

'Where is the child?' asked a third. 'It would be well for her, poor innocent, if the Lord was to take her too.'

I was standing stupefied, listening to them, when I heard a little cry, and the grasp of something at my dress. The cry was so feeble, and the grasp so light, that I might never have noticed it but for those women. I turned round, and the whole world swam round me for a moment. I did what Lady Denzil did—I staggered forward and fell on my knees, though this was not the soft green grass, but a stony London pavement, and clasped little Mary tight with a vehemence that would have frightened any other child; but she was not frightened. The little creature was drenched with the pitiless rain. She had been tied up in an old shawl, to hide the miserable, pretty white frock, now clogged with mud and soaked with water. Her little hat was glued to her head with the floods to which she had been exposed. I lifted my treasure wildly in my arms, as soon as I had any strength to do it, and rushed with her to my carriage. I felt like a thief triumphant; and yet it was no theft. But my eagerness aroused the suspicions of the soldiers' wives who had been standing by. They explained to me that the child was Sergeant Gray's child; that her mother had been took very bad in a fit, and had been carried off to the hospital; and that I, a stranger, had no right to interfere. I don't know what hurried explanation I made to them; but I know that at last I satisfied their fears, and with little Mary in my arms actually drove away.

It was true, though I never could believe it. I got her as easily as if it had been the most natural thing in the world. I could not believe it, even when I held her fast and drew from her her little story. She had been taken away early, very early in the morning, when she had run to the door as soon as she was up to satisfy herself that it rained. No doubt the wretched mother had hung about the grounds all night in the storm and rain to get at the child. She had snatched up little Mary in her arms, and rushed out with her before any one was aware. The child had been dragged along the dreary roads in the rain. If the woman had really loved her, if it had been the passion of a tender mother, and not of a revengeful creature, she never would have subjected the child to this. She was wet to the skin, with pools in her little boots, and the water streaming from her dress. I took her to a friend's house and got dry clothes to put upon her. The unhappy mother had, no doubt, been out all night exposed to the storm. She was mad with rage and misery and fatigue, and probably did not feel her danger at the moment; but just as she reached the Tower to claim, building upon a common opposition to one object, her husband's support, had fallen down senseless on his very threshold as it were. Nothing indeed but madness could have led her to the man whom she had disgraced. When the surrounding bystanders saw that nothing was to be done for her, and that she would not come out of her faint, they had her carried in alarm to the hospital. Such was the abrupt conclusion of the tale. Had I known I need not have given myself the trouble of seeing Sergeant Gray—but that, at least, was a thing which I could not find in my heart to regret.

When I took her back Lady Denzil held me in her arms, held me fast, and looked into my face, even before she listened to little Mary's call. She wanted me to tell her of her child—her own child—and I was so weak that I could not speak to her. I fell crying on her tender old bosom, like a fool, and had to be comforted, as if it could be anything to me—in comparison. I don't know afterwards what I said to her, but she understood all I meant. As for Sir Thomas he was too happy to ask any questions. The child had wound herself into his very heart. He sat with little Mary in his arms all that evening. He would scarcely allow her to be taken to bed. He went up with his heavy old step to see her sleeping safe once more under his roof, and made Wellman, with a pistol, sleep in a little room below. But little Mary was safe enough now. Her father was confined in his barrack room, with my lady's photograph in his hands, and a host of unknown softenings and compunctions in his heart. Her mother was raving wildly in the hospital on the bed from which she was never to rise. I don't know that any one concerned, except myself, thought of this strange cluster of divers fortunes, of tragic mystery and suffering, all hanging about the little angel-vision of that child. Sin, shame, misery, every kind of horror and distress, and little Mary the centre of all; how strange it was!—how terrible and smiling and wretched is life!

It is not to be supposed that such a frightful convulsion and earthquake could pass over and leave no sign. Little Mary was very ill after her exposure, and the shadow of death fell on the Lodge. Perhaps that circumstance softened a little the storm of animadversion that rose up in the neighbourhood. For six months after, Lady Denzil, who had been our centre of society, was never seen out of her own gates. Then they went away, and were absent a whole year. It was the most curious change to everybody on the Green. For three months no one talked on any other subject, and the wildest stories were told: stories with just so much truth in them as to make them doubly wild. It was found out somehow that that wretched woman had died, and then there were accounts current that she had died in the grounds at the Lodge—on the road—in the workhouse—everywhere but the real place, which was in the hospital, where every indulgence and every comfort that she was capable of receiving had been given to her, Sir Thomas himself going to town on purpose to see that it was so. And then it was said that it was she who was Lady Denzil's child. It was a terrible moment, and one which left its mark upon everybody concerned. Sergeant Gray lost his rank, but got his wish and was drafted into another regiment going to India. I saw him again, I and poor old Mrs. Florentine.

But he did not see his mother. They were neither of them able for such a trial. 'I will come back in ten years,' he said to me. I do not know if he will. I don't know if Lady Denzil will live so long. But I believe if she does that then for the first time she will see her son.

They returned to the Lodge two years ago, and the neighbourhood now, instead of gossiping, is very curious to know whether Lady Denzil ever means to go into society again. Everybody calls, and admires little Mary—how she has grown, and what a charming little princess she is; and they all remind my lady, with tender reproach, of those parties they enjoyed so much. 'Are we never to have any more, dear Lady Denzil?' Lucy Stoke asked the other day, kneeling at my lady's side, and caressing her soft old ivory-white hand. My lady—to whom her tender old beauty, her understanding of everybody's trouble, even the rose-tint in her cheek, have come back again—made no answer, but only kissed pretty Lucy. I don't know if she will give any more parties; but she means to live the ten years.

As for Sir Thomas he was never so happy in his life before. He follows little Mary about like an old gray tender knight worshipping the fairy creature. Sometimes I look on and cannot believe my eyes. The wretched guilty mother is dead long ago, and nobody remembers her very existence. The poor soldier has worked himself up to a commission, and may be high in rank before he comes back. If Lady Denzil had been the most tender and devoted of mothers, could things have turned out better? Is this world all a phantasmagoria and chaos of dreams and chances? One's brain reels when Providence thus contradicts all the laws of life. Is it because God sees deeper and 'understands,' as my lady is so fond of saying? It might well be that He had a different way of judging from ours, seeing well and seeing always what we mean in our hearts.

THE STOCKBROKER AT DINGLEWOOD

CHAPTER I

Those who saw Dinglewood only after the improvements had been made could scarcely be able to form to themselves any idea of what it was before the Greshams came. I call them improvements because everybody used the word; but I cannot say I thought the house improved. It was an old-fashioned red-brick house, nothing to speak of architecturally—in the style of Kensington Palace and Kew, and the rest of those old homely royal houses. The drawing-room opened its tall narrow windows upon a little terrace, which was very green and grassy, and pleasant. I should be sorry to undertake to say why it was called Dinglewood. Mr. Coventry made very merry over the name when he had it. He used to say it was because there were no trees; but that was not strictly the case. It was quite open and bare, it is true, towards the river, which we could not see from the Green; but there was a little grove of trees which interposed between us and the house, as if to shut out Dinglewood from the vulgarity of neighbours. It was a popular house in a quiet way when the Coventrys were there. They did not give parties, or pretend to take much trouble in the way of society, for Lady Sarah was always delicate; but when we were tired with our view on the Green, and our lawns and trees, we were always welcome on the Dinglewood terrace, where the old people were constantly to be found sitting out in the summer afternoons, Lady Sarah on her sofa, and Mr. Coventry with the newspapers and his great dog. The lawn went sloping down towards the river, which lay still and white under the sunshine, with a little green island, and a little gray house making a centre to the picture. As long as the sloping bank was lawn it was closely cut and kept like velvet; but when it became field these niceties stopped, and Lady Sarah's pet Alderney stood up to her knees in the cool clover. There was an old mulberry-tree close to the wall of the house, which shaded the sofa; and a gloomy yew on the other side did the same thing for Mr. Coventry, though he was an old Indian and a salamander, and could bear any amount of sunshine. Lady Sarah's perpetual occupation was knitting. She knitted all sorts of bright-coloured things in brilliant German wool with big ivory pins, and her husband used to read the news to her. They read all the debates together, stopping every now and then to exchange their sentiments. Lady Sarah would say with her brisk little voice, 'He might have made a better point there. I don't see that he proves his case. I don't agree with that;' and Mr. Coventry would stop and lay down the paper on his knees, and discuss it leisurely. There was no reason why they should not do it at their leisure. The best part of the summer days were spent thus by the old couple; and the sunshine lay warm and still round them, and the leaves rustled softly, and the cool grass kept growing under their peaceful old feet. These feet tread mortal soil no longer, and all this has nothing in the world to do with my story. But it was a pretty sight in its way. They were not rich, and the furniture and carpets were very faded, and everything very different from what it came to be afterwards; yet we were all very fond of Mr. Coventry and his old wife, and the old-fashioned house was appropriate to them. I like to think of them even now.

We were all anxious, of course, after Mr. Coventry's death, to know who would buy the house (Lady Sarah could not bear it after he was gone, and indeed lived only a year after him); and when it was known that young Mr. Gresham was the purchaser, it made quite a sensation on the Green. He was the son of old Gresham, who had bought Bishop's Hope, a noble place at Cookesley, about a dozen miles off, but had made all his fortune as a stockbroker, and, they say, not even the best kind of that. His son had succeeded him in business, and had lately married somebody in his own class. He was a nice-looking young fellow enough, and had been brought up at Eton, to be sure, like so many of those people's sons; but still one felt that it was bringing in a new element to the Green. If his wife had been, as so often happens, a gentlewoman, it would have made things comparatively easy. But she was only the daughter of a mercantile man like himself, and there was great discussion among us as to what we should do when they came. Some families made up their minds at once not to call; and some, on the other hand, declared that such rich people were sure to fête the whole county, and that everybody would go to them. 'If they had only been a little rich, it would never have answered; but they are frightfully rich, and, of course, we must all go down on our knees,' Lottie Stoke said. She was the most eager of all to know them; for her youth was passing away, and she was not likely to marry, and the Stokes were poor. I confess I was curious myself to see how things would turn out.

Their first step however was one which took us all by surprise. Young Gresham dashed over in his Yankee waggon from Cookesley to go over the house, and the same day a charming barouche made the tour of the Green, with a very pretty young woman in it, and a lovely little girl, and a matchless tiny Skye terrier—all going to inspect Dinglewood. The arms on the carriage were quartered to the last possibility of quartering, as if they had come through generations of heiresses and gentlemen of coat-armour, and the footman was powdered and dazzling to behold. Altogether it was by far the finest equipage that had been seen in these parts for a long time. Not to speak of Lady Denzil's, or the other great people about, her Majesty's own carriage, that she drives about the neighbourhood in, was not to be compared to it. Its emblazoned panels brushed against the privet hedges in poor old Lady Sarah's drive, which was only wide enough for her little pony-carriage, and I have no doubt were scratched and spoiled; but the next thing we heard about Dinglewood was that a flood of workmen had come down upon it, and that everything was to be changed. Young Mrs. Gresham liked the situation, but the house was far too small for her. My maid told me a new dining-room and drawing-room, with bed-rooms over, were to be added, and already the people had set to work. We all looked on thunderstruck while these 'improvements' were going on: he had a right to do it, no doubt, as he had bought it, but still it did seem a great piece of presumption. The pretty terrace was all cut up, and the poor old mulberry-tree perished in the changes, though it is true that they had the sense not to spoil the view. They added two wings to the old house, with one sumptuous room in each. Poor Lady Sarah's drawing-room, which was good enough for her, these millionaires made into a billiard-room, and put them all en suite, making a passage thus between their two new wings. I don't deny, as I have already said, that they had a perfect right to do it; but all the same it was very odd to us.

And then heaps of new furniture came down from town; the waggons that brought it made quite a procession along the road. All this grandeur and display had a bad effect upon the neighbourhood. It really looked as if these new people were already crowing over us, whose carpets and hangings were a little faded and out of fashion. There was a general movement of indignation on the Green. All this expense might be well enough, for those who could afford it, in a town-house, people said, but in the country it was vulgar and stupid. Everything was gilded and ornamented and expensive in the new Dinglewood; Turkey carpets all over the house, and rich silk curtains and immense mirrors. Then after a while 'the family' arrived. They came with such a flutter of fine carriages as had never been seen before among us. The drive had been widened, down which Lady Sarah's old gray pony used to jog so comfortably, and there was nothing to be seen all day long but smooth, shining panels and high-stepping horses whisking in and out. In the first place there was Mr. Gresham's Yankee waggon, with a wicked-looking beast in it, which went like the wind. Then there would be a cosy brougham carrying Mrs. Gresham to Shoreton shopping, or taking out the nurse and baby for an airing; and after lunch came the pretty open carriage with the armorial bearings and the men in powder. We were too indignant to look round at first when these vehicles passed; but custom does a great deal, and one's feelings soften in spite of one's self. Of all the people on the Green, Lottie Stoke was the one who did most for the new people. 'I mean to make mamma call,' she said: and she even made a round of visits for the purpose of saying it. 'Why shouldn't we all call on them? I think it is mean to object to them for being rich. It looks as if we were ashamed of being poor; and they are sure to have quantities of people from town, and to enjoy themselves—people as good as we are, Mrs. Mulgrave: they are not so particular in London.'

'My dear Lottie,' said I, 'I have no doubt the Greshams themselves are quite as good as we are. That is not the question. There are social differences, you know.'

'Oh, yes! I know,' cried Lottie; 'I have heard of them all my life, but I don't see what the better we are, for all our nicety; and I mean to make mamma call.'

She was not so good as her word however, for Mrs. Stoke was a timid woman, and waited to see what the people would do. And in the meantime the Greshams themselves, independent of their fine house and their showy carriages, presented themselves as it were before us for approval. They walked to church on Sunday without any show, which made quite a revulsion in their favour; and she was very pretty and sweet-looking, and he was so like a gentleman that you could never have told the difference. And the end of it all was, that one fine morning Lady Denzil, without saying a word to any one, called; and after that, everybody on the Green.

I do not pretend to say that there was not a little air of newness about these young people. They were like their house, a little too bright, too costly, too luxurious. Mrs. Gresham gave herself now and then pretty little airs of wealth, which, to do her justice, were more in the way of kindness to others than display for herself. There was a kind of munificence about her which made one smile, and yet made one grow red and hot and just a little angry. It might not have mattered if she had been a princess, but it did not answer with a stockbroker's wife. She was so anxious to supply you with anything or everything you wanted. 'Let me send it,' she would say in a lavish way, whenever there was any shortcoming, and opened her pretty mouth and stared with all her pretty eyes when her offers were declined. She wanted that delicate sense of other people's pride, which a true great lady always has. She did not understand why one would rather have one's own homely maid to wait, than borrow her powdered slave; and would rather walk than be taken up in her fine carriage. This bewildered her, poor little woman. She thought it was unkind of me in particular. 'You can't really prefer to drive along in the dust in your little low carriage,' she said, with a curious want of perception that my pony carriage was my own. This was the only defect I found in her, and it was a failing which leant to virtue's side. Her husband was more a man of the world, but he too had money written all over him. They were dreadfully rich, and even in their freest moment they could not get rid of it—and they were young and open-hearted, and anxious to make everybody happy. They had people down from town as Lottie prophesied—fashionable people sometimes, and clever people, and rich people. We met all kinds of radicals, and artists, and authors, and great travellers at Dinglewood. The Greshams were rather proud of their literary acquaintances indeed, which was surprising to us. I have seen old Sir Thomas look very queer when he was told he was going to meet So-and-So, who had written some famous book. 'Who is the fellow?' he said privately to me with a comical look, for he was not very literary in his tastes;—neither were the Greshams for that matter: but then, having no real rank, they appreciated a little distinction, howsoever it came; whereas the second cousin of any poor lord or good old decayed family was more to the most of us than Shakespeare himself or Raphael; though of course it would have been our duty to ourselves to be very civil to either of those gentlemen had we met them at dinner anywhere on the Green.

But there was no doubt that this new lively household, all astir with new interests, new faces, talk and movement, and pleasant extravagance, woke us all up. They were so rich that they took the lead in many things, in spite of all that could be done to the contrary. None of us could afford so many parties. The Greshams had always something on hand. Instead of our old routine of dinners and croquet-parties, and perhaps two or three dances a year for the young people, there was an endless variety now at Dinglewood; and even if we elders could have resisted Mrs. Gresham's pretty winning ways on her own account, it would have been wicked to neglect the advantage for our children. Of course this did not apply to me, who have no children; but I was never disposed to stand very much on my dignity, and I liked the young couple. They were so fond of each other, and so good-looking, and so happy, and so ready—too ready—to share their advantages with everybody. Mrs. Gresham sent her man over with I don't know how much champagne the morning of the day when they were all coming to play croquet on my little lawn, and he wanted to know, with his mistress's love, whether he should come to help, or if there was anything else I wanted. I had entertained my friends in my quiet way before she was born, and I did not like it. Lottie Stoke happened to be with me when the message arrived, and took the reasonable view, as she had got into the way of doing where the Greshams were concerned.

'Why should not they send you champagne?' she said. 'They are as rich as Crœsus, though I am sure I don't know much about him; and you are a lady living by yourself, and can't be expected to think of all these things.'

'My dear Lottie,' said I—and I confess I was angry—'if you are not content with what I can give you, you need not come to me. The Greshams can stay away if they like. Champagne in the afternoon when you are playing croquet! It is just like those nouveaux riches. They would think it still finer, I have no doubt, if they could drink pearls, like Cleopatra. Champagne!'

'They must have meant it for Cup, you know,' said Lottie, a little abashed.

'I don't care what they meant it for,' said I. 'You shall have cups of tea; and I am very angry and affronted. I wonder how they think we got on before they came!'

And then I sat down and wrote a little note, which I fear was terribly polite, and sent it and the baskets back with John Thomas, while Lottie went and looked at all the pictures as if she had never seen them before, and hummed little airs under her breath. She had taken up these Greshams in the most curious way. Not that she was an unreasonable partisan; she could see their faults like the rest of us, but she was always ready to make excuses for them. 'They don't know any better,' she would say softly when she was driven to the very extremity of her special pleading. And she said this when I had finished my note and was just sending it away.

'But why don't they know better?' said I; 'they have had the same education as other people. He was at Eton where a boy should learn how to behave himself, even if he does not learn anything else. And she went to one of the fashionable schools—as good a school as any of you ever went to.'

'We were never at any school at all,' said Lottie with a little bitterness. 'We were always much too poor. We have never learned anything, we poor girls; whereas Ada Gresham has learned everything,' she added with a little laugh.

It was quite true. Poor little Mrs. Gresham was overflowing with accomplishments. There never was such an education as she had received. She had gone to lectures, and studied thorough bass, and knew all about chemistry, and could sympathize with her husband, as the newspapers say, and enter into all his pursuits. How fine it sounds in the newspapers! Though I was angry, I could not but laugh too—a young woman wanted an elaborate education indeed to be fit to be young Gresham's wife.

'Well,' I said, 'after all, I don't suppose she means to be impertinent, Lottie, and I like her. I don't think her education has done her much harm. Nobody could teach her to understand other people's feelings; and to be rich like that must be a temptation.'

'I should like to have such a temptation,' said Lottie, with a sudden sparkle in her eyes. 'Fancy there are four Greshams, and they are all as rich. The girl is married, you know, to a railway man; and, by the by,' she went on suddenly after a pause, 'they tell me one of the brothers is coming here to-day.'

She said this in an accidental sort of way, but I could see there was nothing accidental about it. She drew her breath hard, poor girl, and a little feverish colour got up in her cheeks. It is common to talk of girls looking out for husbands, and even hunting that important quarry. But when now and then in desperate cases such a thing does actually come before one's eyes, it is anything but an amusing sight. The Stokes were as poor as the Greshams were rich. Everard had ruined himself, and half-killed everybody belonging to him only the year before; and now poor Lottie saw a terrible chance before her, and rose to it with a kind of tragic valour. I read her whole meaning and resolution in her face, as she said, with an attempt at a smile, these simple-sounding words; and an absolute pang of pity went through me. Poor Lottie!—it was a chance, for her family and for herself—even for poor Everard, whom they all clung to, though he had gone so far astray. What a change it would make in their situation and prospects, and everything about them! You may say it was an ignoble foundation to build family comfort upon. I do not defend it in any way; but when I saw what Lottie meant, my heart ached for her. It did not seem to me ridiculous or base, but tragic and terrible; though to be sure in all likelihood there is nobody who will think so but me.

Before Lottie left me, Mrs. Gresham came rushing over in her pretty summer dress, with her curls and ribbons fluttering in the breeze. She came to ask me why I had been so unkind, and to plead and remonstrate. 'We have so much, we don't know what to do with it,' she said; 'Harry is always finding out some new vintage or other, and the cellars are overflowing. Why would not you use some of it? We have so much of everything we don't know what to do.'

'I would rather not, thanks,' I said, feeling myself flush; 'what a lovely day it is. Where are you going for your drive? The woods will be delicious to-day.'

'Oh, I have so much of the woods,' cried Mrs. Gresham. 'I thought of going towards Estcott to make some calls. But, dear Mrs. Mulgrave, about the Champagne?'

'It is a little too early for the heath,' said Lottie, steadily looking our visitor in the face. 'It is always cold there. What they call bracing, you know; but I don't care about being braced, the wind goes through and through one, even on a sunny day.'

'It is because you are so thin,' said Mrs. Gresham; 'I never feel the cold for my part; but I shall not drive at all to-day—I forgot—I shall go and fetch Harry from the station, and come to you, Mrs. Mulgrave: and you will not be cross, but let me send back John Thomas with—'

'My dear, I am going to give you some tea,' said I, 'and my maids can manage beautifully; the sight of a gorgeous creature like John Thomas distracts them; they can do nothing but stare at his plush and his powder. We shall be very glad to have Mr. Gresham and you.'

'But—' she began eagerly. Then she caught Lottie's look, who had made some sign to her, and stopped short, staring at me with her blue eyes. She could not make it out, and no hint short of positive demonstration could have shown her that she had gone too far. She stopped in obedience to Lottie's sign, but stared at me all the same. Her prosperity, her wealth, her habit of overcoming everything that looked in the least like a difficulty, had taken even a woman's instinct from her. She gazed at me, and by degrees her cheeks grew red: she saw she had made a mistake somehow, but even up to that moment could not tell what it was.

'Harry's brother is coming with him,' she said, a little subdued; 'may I bring him? He is the eldest, but he is not married yet. He is such a man of the world. Of course he might have married when he liked, as early as we did, there was nothing to prevent him: but he got into a fashionable set first, and then he got among the artists. He is quite what they call a Bohemian you know. He paints beautifully—Harry always consults Gerald before buying any pictures; I don't know what he does with all his money, for he keeps up no establishment, and no horses nor anything. I tell him sometimes he is an old miser, but I am sure I have no reason to say so, for he gives me beautiful presents. I should so like to bring him here.'

'Yes, bring him by all means,' said I; but I could not help giving a little sigh as I looked at Lottie, who was listening eagerly. When she saw me look at her, her face flamed scarlet, and she went in great haste to the window to hide it from Mrs. Gresham. She saw I had found her out, and did not know what compassion was in my heart. She gave a wistful glance up into my face as she went away. 'Don't despise me!' it said. Poor Lottie! as if it ever could be lawful to do evil that good might come! They went away together, the poor girl and the rich, happy young wife. Lottie was a little the older of the two, and yet she was not old, and they were both pretty young women. They laid their heads together and talked earnestly as girls do, as they went out of my gate, and nobody could have dreamed that their light feet were entangled in any web of tragedy. The sight of the two who were so unlike, and the thought of the future which might bring them into close connection made me melancholy, I could not have told why.

CHAPTER II

We did not miss the Champagne-cup that afternoon; indeed I do not approve of such beverages for young people, and never sanction anything but tea before dinner. The Dinglewood people were doing their best to introduce these foolish extravagances among us, but I for one would not give in. Young Gresham, though he took some tea, drew his wife aside the moment after, and I heard him question her.

'It was not my fault, Harry,' she cried, not knowing I was so near. 'She sent it all back, and Lottie said I had hurt her feelings. I did not know what to do. She would not even have John Thomas to wait.'

'Nonsense!' said Harry Gresham; 'you should have insisted. We ought not to let her go to any expense. I don't suppose she has a shilling more than she wants for her own affairs.'

'But I could not help it,' said his wife.

I don't know what Lottie had said to her, but she was evidently a little frightened. As for Harry, I think he would have liked to leave a bank-note for me on one of the tables. People have told me since that it was a very bad sign, and that it is only when people are getting reckless about money that they think of throwing it away in presents; but I cannot say I have had much experience of that weakness. The new brother who had come with them was a very different kind of man. I cannot say I took to him at first. He was not a wealthy, simple-minded, lavish creature like his brother. He was more like other people. Harry Gresham was red and white, like a girl, inclining to be stout, though he was not above thirty, and with the manners which are, or were, supposed to be specially English—downright and straightforward. Gerald was a few years older, a little taller, bronzed with the sun, and bearing the indescribable look of a man who has mixed much with the world. I looked at Lottie Stoke when I made my first observations upon the stranger, and saw that she too was looking at him with a strange expression, half of repugnance, half of wistfulness in her eyes. Lottie had not done her duty in the way of marrying, as she ought to have done, in her early youth. She had refused very good offers, as her mother was too apt to tell with a little bitterness. Now at last, when things were going so badly with the family, she had made up her mind to try; but when she did so she expected a second Harry Gresham, and not this man of the world. She looked at him as a martyr might look standing on the edge of a precipice, gathering up her strength for the plunge, shrinking yet daring. My party was quite dull for the first hour because of this pause which Lottie made on the brink, for she was always the soul of everything. When I saw her all at once rise up from the chair where she had been sitting obstinately beside old Mrs. Beresford, and go up to Mrs. Gresham, who was standing aside with her brother-in-law looking on, I knew she had made up her mind at last, and taken the plunge. An experienced rich young man of the nineteenth century! I thought to myself she might spare her pains.

Just at that moment I saw the gorgeous figure of John Thomas appear at the end of my lawn, and a sudden flush of anger came over me. I got up to see what he wanted, thinking they had sent him back again notwithstanding my refusal. But just before I reached him I perceived that his errand was to his master, to whom he gave a telegram. Mr. Gresham tore it open at my side. He ran his eye over the message, and muttered something between his teeth, and grew red all over in indignation or trouble. Then, seeing me, he turned round, with an effort, with one of his broad smiles.

'Business even in the midst of pleasure,' he said. 'Is it not too bad?'

'If it is only business—' said I. Whenever I see one of those telegraph papers, it makes my heart beat. I always think somebody is ill or dead.

'Only business, by Jove!' said Harry. His voice was quite subdued, but he laughed—a laugh which sounded strange and not very natural. Then he gave himself a sort of shake, and thrust the thing into his pocket, and offered me his arm, to lead me back to my place. 'By the by,' he said, 'I am going to quarrel with you, Mrs. Mulgrave. When we are so near why don't you let us be of some use to you? It would give the greatest pleasure both to Ada and me.'

'Oh, thanks; but indeed I don't want any help,' I cried, abruptly coming to a sudden stop before Lady Denzil's chair.

'You are so proud,' he said with a smile, and so left me to plunge into the midst of the game, where they were clamouring for him. He played all the rest of the afternoon, entering into everything with the greatest spirit; and yet I felt a little disturbed. Whether it was for Lottie, or whether it was for Harry Gresham I could not well explain to myself; a feeling came over me like the feeling with which one sometimes wakes in the morning without any reason for it—an uneasy restless sense that something somehow was going wrong.

The Greshams were the last of my party to go away, and I went to the gate with them, as I had a way of doing, and lingered there for a few minutes in the slanting evening light. It was nearly seven o'clock, but they did not dine till eight, and were in no hurry. She wore a very pretty dress—one of those soft pale grays which soil if you look hard at them—and had gathered the long train over her arm like a figure in a picture; for though she was not very refined, Ada Gresham was not a vulgar woman to trail her dress over a dusty road. She had taken her husband's arm as they went along the sandy brown pathway, and Gerald on the other side carried her parasol and leant towards her to talk. As I looked at them I could not but think of the strange differences of life: how some people have to get through the world by themselves as best they may, and some have care and love and protection on every side of them. These two would have kept the very wind from blowing upon Ada; they were ready to shield her from every pain, to carry her in their arms over any thorns that might come in her way. The sunshine slanted sideways upon them as they went along, throwing fantastic broken shadows of the three figures on the hedgerow, and shining right into my eyes. I think I can see her now leaning on her husband's arm, looking up to his brother, with the pretty sweep of the gray silk over her arm, the white embroidered skirts beneath, and the soft rose-ribbons that caught the light. Poor Ada! I have other pictures of her, beside this one, in my memory now.

Next day we had a little discussion upon the new brother, in the afternoon when my visitors looked in upon me. We did not confine ourselves to that one subject. We diverged, for instance, to Mrs. Gresham's toilette, which was so pretty. Lottie Stoke had got a new bonnet for the occasion; but she had made it herself, and though she was very clever, she was not equal to Elise.

'Fancy having all one's things made by Elise!' cried Lucy the little sister, with a rapture of anticipation. 'If ever I am married, nobody else shall dress me.'

'Then you had better think no more of curates,' said some malicious critic, and Lucy blushed. It was not her fault if the curates amused her. They were mice clearly intended by Providence for fun and torture. She was but sixteen and meant no harm, and what else could the kitten do?

Then a great controversy arose among the girls as to the claims of the new brother to be called handsome. The question was hotly discussed on both sides, Lottie alone taking no part in the debate. She sat by very quietly, with none of her usual animation. Nor did she interpose when the Gresham lineage and connection—the little cockney papa who was like a shabby little miser, the mother who was large and affable and splendid, a kind of grand duchess in a mercantile way—were taken in hand. Lottie could give little sketches of them all when she so pleased; but she did not please that day.

'This new one does not look like a nobody,' said one of my visitors. 'He might be the Honourable Gerald for his looks. He is fifty times better than Mr. Gresham, though Mr. Gresham is very nice too.'

'And he has such a lovely name!' cried Lucy. 'Gerald Gresham! Any girl I ever heard of would marry him just for his name.'

'They have all nice names,' said the first speaker, who was young too, and attached a certain weight to this particular. 'They don't sound like mere rich people. They might be of a good old family to judge by their names.'

'Yes; she is Ada,' said Lucy, reflectively, 'and he is Harry, and the little boy's name is Percy. But Gerald is the darling! Gerald is the one for me!'

The window was open at the time, and the child was talking incautiously loud, so that I was not much surprised, for my part, when a peal of laughter from outside followed this speech, and Ada, with her brother-in-law in attendance, appeared under the veranda. Of course Lucy was covered with confusion; but her blushes became the little creature, and gave her a certain shy grace which was very pretty to behold. As for Lottie, I think the contrast made her paler. Looking at her beautiful refined head against the light, nobody could help admiring it; but she was not round and dimpled and rosy like her little sister. After a while Gerald Gresham managed to get into the corner where Lottie was, to talk to her; but his eyes sought the younger creature all the same. A man has it all his own way when there is but one in the room. He was gracious to all the girls, like a civilized English sultan; but they were used to that, poor things, and took it very good-naturedly.

'It is not his fault if he is the only man in the place,' said Lucy; and she was not displeased, though her cheeks burned more hotly than ever when he took advantage of her incautious speech.

'I must not let you forget that it is Gerald who is the darling,' he said laughing. Of course it was quite natural, and meant nothing, and perhaps no one there but Lottie and myself thought anything of this talk; but it touched her, poor girl, with a certain mortification, and had a curious effect upon me. I could not keep myself from thinking, Would it be Lucy after all? After her sister had made up her mind in desperation; after she had screwed her courage to the last fatal point; after she had consciously committed herself and compromised her maiden up-rightness, would it be Lucy who would win the prize without an effort? I cannot describe the effect it had upon me. It made me burn with indignation to think that Lottie Stoke was putting forth all her powers to attract this stranger—this man who was rich, and could buy her if he pleased; and, at the same time, his looks at Lucy filled me with the strangest sense of disappointment. I ought to have been glad that such humiliating efforts failed of success, and yet I was not. I hated them, and yet I could not bear to think they would be in vain.

'And Harry has gone to town again to-day,' said Ada, with a pout of her pretty mouth, 'though he promised to stay and take me up the river. They make his life wretched with those telegrams and things. I ask him, What is the good of going on like this, when we have plenty of money? And then he tells me I am a little fool and don't understand.'

'I always feel sure something dreadful has happened whenever I see a telegram,' said Mrs. Stoke.

'Oh, we are quite used to them: they are only about business,' said Ada, taking off her hat and smoothing back, along with a twist of her pretty hair, the slightest half visible pucker of care from her smooth young brow.

'Only business!' said Gerald. They were the same words Harry had said the day before, and they struck me somehow. When he caught my eye he laughed, and added something about the strange ideas ladies had. 'As if any accident, or death, or burial could be half so important as business,' he said, with the half sneer which we all use as a disguise to our thoughts. And some of the little party exclaimed, and some laughed with him. To be sure, a man in business, like Harry Gresham, or a man of the world, like his brother, must be less startled by such communications than such quiet country people as we were. That was easy enough to see.

That same night, when I came across from the Lodge, where I had been spending the evening, Dinglewood stood blazing out against the sky with all its windows lighted up. Sir Thomas, who was walking across the Green with me, as it was so fine a night, saw me turn my head that way and looked too. The whole house had the air of being lighted up for an illumination. It always had; it revealed itself, its different floors, and even the use of its different rooms to all the world by its lights. The Greshams were the kind of people who have every new improvement that money can procure. They made gas for themselves, and lighted up the entire house, in that curious mercantile, millionaire way which you never see in a real great house. Sir Thomas's look followed mine, and he shook his gray head a little.

'I hope no harm will come of it,' he said; 'they are going very fast over there, Mrs. Mulgrave. I hope they are able to keep it up.'

'Able!' said I, 'they are frightfully rich;' and I felt half aggrieved by the very supposition.

'Yes,' said Sir Thomas, 'they would need to be rich. For a little while that may do; but I don't think any man in business can be rich enough to stand that sort of thing for a long time together.'

'Oh, they can bear it, no doubt,' I said, impatient of Sir Thomas's old-fashioned ways. 'Of course it was very different in the Coventrys' time.'

'Ah, in the Coventrys' time,' said Sir Thomas regretfully; 'one does not often get such neighbours as the Coventrys. Take care of that stone. And now, here we are at your door.'

'Good-night!' said I, 'and many thanks;' but I stood outside a little in the balmy evening air, as Sir Thomas went home across the Green. I could not see Dinglewood from my door, and the Lodge, which was opposite, glimmered in a very different way, with faint candles in Lady Denzil's chamber, and some of the servants' sleeping rooms, and the soft white lamp-light in the windows below; domestic and necessary lights, not like the blaze in the new house. Sir Thomas plodded quietly home, with his gray head bent and his hands behind him under his coat, in the musing tranquillity of old age; and a certain superstitious feeling came over me. It was my gaze at the illuminated house which made him say those uncomfortable words. I felt as if I had attracted to the Greshams, poor children, in their gaiety and heedlessness, the eye of some sleeping Fate.

CHAPTER III

I have often been impatient in reading books, to find the story go on from one party to another, from one ball to another, as if life had nothing more important in it. But sometimes no doubt it does happen so. The life of the Greshams was made up of balls and parties; they were never alone; Dinglewood blazed out to the skies every evening, and the carriages flashed out and in, and one kind of merry-making or another went on all day. Lottie Stoke was there continually, and there grew up a curious friendship, half strife, half accord, between Gerald and herself. He had nothing to do with the business as it turned out, and consequently was not half so rich as his brother. But still he was very well off. I don't know what it is about people in business which gives them a kind of primitive character: they are less sophisticated than the rest of us, though possibly not more simple. The Greshams took a simple pleasure in pleasure for itself, without making it a mere medium for other things, as most of us do. They were fond of company, fond of dancing, delighted with picnics, and even with croquet, without any ulterior motive, like children. They were fond even of their wealth, which gave them so many pretty and so many pleasant things. They enjoyed it with all their hearts, and took an innocent, foolish delight in it, which spiteful people set down to purse-pride; but which in reality was more like the open satisfaction of children in their dear possessions. Gerald was a very different being: I never saw him without feeling that his visit was not a mere visit, but had some motive in it. Before Lottie roused him to talk and battle with her, he would look on at their great parties with a curious, anxious, dissatisfied air, as if he suspected or feared something. I think poor Lottie went further than she meant to go: she grew interested herself, when she had meant only to interest him, and was more excited by his presence than he was by hers. They carried on a kind of perpetual duel, very amusing to the spectators: and there was no doubt that he liked it. But he liked Lucy's funny little shy speeches too; and he had some interest more absorbing, more serious than either, which made his face very grave when the two girls were not there. Harry Gresham had sometimes the air of getting impatient of his brother's presence. Now and then they passed my house walking together, and not enjoying their walk, according to appearances. Once as I stood at my gate I heard Harry say sharply, 'In any case Ada has her settlement,' with a defiant air. And Gerald's face was full of remonstrance and expostulation. I could not help taking a great interest in these young people, and feeling a little anxious at the general aspect of affairs.

Things were in this state when the ball was given on Mrs. Gresham's birthday. I had nobody to take charge of for a wonder, and nothing to do but look on. The entire suite of rooms was thrown open, ablaze with light and sweet with flowers. There were great banks of geraniums in every corner where they could be piled, and the whole neighbourhood had been ravaged for roses. The room in which I took refuge was the smallest of all, which had been old Lady Sarah's boudoir in old times, and was a little removed from the dancing, and cooler than the rest. It had one little projecting window, not large enough to be called a bay, which looked out upon the terrace just above the spot where the old couple used to sit in the summer days. It was open, and the moon streamed in, making a curious contrast with the floods of artificial light. Looking out from it, you could see the Thames, like a silver ribbon, at the bottom or the slope, and the little island and the little house gleaming out white, with intense black shadows. Lottie Stoke came up to me while I stood at the window, and looked out over my shoulder. 'It looks like the ghost of the river and the ghost of the island,' she said, putting her pretty arm round my waist with an agitated grasp. 'I almost think we are all ghosts too.'

'A curious moment to think so,' said Gerald Gresham. My back was turned to them, so that I did not see him, but there sounded something like a thrill of excitement in the half laugh of his voice.

'Not curious at all,' said Lottie: 'how many of us are really here do you think? I know where Mrs. Mulgrave is. She is outside on the terrace with old Lady Sarah, listening to the old people's talk, though I am holding her fast all the same. We are in all sorts of places the real halves of us, but our doubles do the dancing and the laughing, and eat the ices quite as well. It is chilly to be a ghost,' said Lottie with a laugh; 'come in from the window, I am sure there is a draught there.'

'There is no draught,' said Gerald; 'you are afraid of being obliged to go into particulars, that is all.'

'I am not in the least afraid,' said Lottie. 'There is Mrs. Damerel. She is in the nursery at the rectory, though you think you have her here. She is counting Agatha's curl-papers to see if there is the right number, for children are never properly attended to when the mother's eye is wanting. I don't know where you are, Mr. Gerald Gresham; that would be too delicate an inquiry. But look, your brother has gone upon 'Change, though he is in the middle of his guests. He looks as like business as if he had all the Reduced Consols on his mind; he looks as if— good heavens!'

Lottie stopped, and her tone was so full of alarm and astonishment, that I turned suddenly round to look too, in a fright. Harry Gresham was standing at the door; he had a yellow envelope in his hand, another of those terrible telegrams which are always bringing misery. He had turned round unawares facing us, and facing the stream of people who were always coming and going. I never saw in all my life so ghastly a face. It showed the more that he was so ruddy and cheerful by nature. In a moment every tinge of colour had disappeared from it. His mouth was drawn down, his blue eyes looked awful, shrinking back as it were among the haggard lines of the eyelids. The sight of him struck Lottie dumb, and came upon me like a touch of horror. But Gerald, it was evident, was not taken by surprise. Some crisis which he had been looking for had come at last.

'He has had some bad news,' he said; 'excuse me, my mother is ill—it must be that;' and he went through the stream of guests, fording the current as it were with noiseless rapidity. As for Lottie, she drew me back into the recess of the window and clung to me and cried—but not for Harry Gresham. Her nerves were at the highest strain, and broke down under this last touch; that was all.

'I knew something was going to happen,' she said. 'I felt it in the air; but I never thought it was coming upon them.'

'It must be his mother,' I said, though I did not think so. 'Hush, Lottie! Don't frighten her, poor child.'

Lottie was used to restraining herself, and the tears relieved her. She dried her eyes and gave me a nervous hug as she loosed her arm from my waist.

'I cannot stand this any longer,' she said; 'I must go and dance, or something. I know there is trouble coming, and if I sit quiet I shall make a fool of myself. But you will help them if you can,' she cried in my ear. Alas! what could I do?

By the time she left me the brothers had disappeared, and after half an hour's waiting, as nothing seemed to come of it, and as the heat increased I went to the window again. The moon had gone off the house, but still shone white and full on the lawn like a great sheet of silvery gauze, bound and outlined by the blackest shadow. My mind had gone away from that temporary interruption. I was not thinking about the Greshams at all, when all at once I heard a rustle under the window. When I looked down two figures were standing there in the shadow. I thought at first they were robbers, perhaps murderers, waiting to waylay some one. All my self-command could not restrain a faint exclamation. There seemed a little struggle going on between the two. 'You don't know her,' said the one; 'why should you trust her?' 'She is safer than the servants,' said the other, 'and she is fond of poor Ada.' If my senses had not been quickened by excitement and alarm I should never have heard what they said. Then something white was held up to me in a hand that trembled.

'Give it to Ada—when you can,' said Harry Gresham in a quick, breathless, imperative voice.

I took the bit of paper and clutched it in my hand, not knowing what I did, and then stood stupefied, and saw them glide down in the dark shadow of the house towards the river. Where were they going? What had happened? This could be no sudden summons to a mother's death-bed. They went cautiously in the darkness the two brothers, keeping among the trees; leaning out of the window as far as I could, I saw Gerald's slighter figure and poor Harry's portly one emerge into the moonlight close to the river, just upon the public road. Then I felt some one pull me on the other side. It was Lottie who had come back, excited, to ask if I had found out anything.

'I thought you were going to stretch out of the window altogether,' she said, with a half-suspicious glance; and I held my bit of paper tight, with my fan in my other hand.

'I was looking at the moon,' I said. 'It is a lovely night. I am sorry it has gone off the house. And then the rooms are so hot inside.'

'I should like to walk on the terrace,' said Lottie, 'but my cavalier has left me. I was engaged to him for this dance, and he has never come to claim it. Where has he gone?'

'I suppose he must have left the room,' I said. 'I suppose it is their mother who is ill; perhaps they have slipped out quietly not to disturb the guests. If that is the case, you should go and stand by Mrs. Gresham, Lottie. She will want your help.'

'But they never would be so unkind as to steal away like this and leave everything to Ada!' cried Lottie. 'Never! Harry Gresham would not do it for twenty mothers. As for Gerald, I dare say any excuse—'

And here she stopped short, poor girl, with an air of exasperation, and looked ready to cry again.

'Never mind,' I said; 'go to Mrs. Gresham. Don't say anything, Lottie, but stand by her. She may want it, for anything we know.'

'As you stood by us,' said Lottie affectionately; and then she added with a sigh and a faint little smile, 'But it never could be so bad as that with them.'

I did not make her any reply. I was faint and giddy with fear and excitement; and just then, of course, Admiral Fortis's brother, a hazy old gentleman, who was there on a visit, and havered for hours together, whenever he could get a listener, hobbled up to me. He had got me into a corner as it were, and built entrenchments round me before I knew, and then he began his longest story of how his brother had been appointed to the Bellerophon, and how it was his interest that did it. The thing had happened half a century before, and the Admiral had not been at sea at all for half that time, and here was a present tragedy going on beside us, and the message of fate crushed up with my fan in my hand. Lottie Stoke made her appearance in the doorway several times, casting appealing looks at me. Once she beckoned, and pointed energetically to the drawing-room in which poor little Mrs. Gresham was. But when I got time to think, as I did while the old man was talking, I thought it was best, on the whole, to defer giving my letter, whatever it was. It could not be anything trifling or temporary which made the master of the house steal away in the darkness. I have had a good many things put into my hands to manage, but I don't think I ever had anything so difficult as this. For I did not know, and could not divine, what the sudden misfortune was which I had to conceal from the world. All this time Mr. Fortis went on complacently with his talk about the old salt-water lords who were dead and gone. He stood over me, and was very animated; and I had to look up to him, and nod and smile, and pretend to listen. What ghosts we were, as Lottie said! My head began to swim at last as Mr. Fortis's words buzzed in my ear. '"My lord," I said, "my brother's services—not to speak of my own family influence—"' This formed a kind of chorus to it, and came in again and again. He was only in the middle of his narrative when Lottie came up, making her way through all obstacles. She was trembling, too, with excitement which had less foundation than mine.

'I can't find Mr. Gresham anywhere,' she whispered. 'He is not in any of the rooms; none of the servants have seen him, and it is time for supper. What are we to do?'

'Is Ada alarmed?' said I.

'No; she is such a child,' said Lottie. 'But she is beginning to wonder. Come and say something to her. Come and do something. Don't sit for ever listening to that tiresome old man. I shall go crazy if you do not come; and she dancing as if nothing had happened!'

Mr. Fortis had waited patiently while this whispering went on. When I turned to him again he went on the same as ever. 'This was all to the senior sea-lord, you understand, Mrs. Mulgrave. As for the other—'

'I hope you will tell me the rest another time,' I said, like a hypocrite. 'I must go to Mrs. Gresham. Lottie has come to fetch me. I am so sorry—'

'Don't say anything about it,' said Mr. Fortis. 'I shall find an opportunity,' and he offered me his arm. I had to walk with him looking quite at my ease through all those pretty groups, one and another calling to me as I passed. 'Oh, please tell me if my wreath is all right,' Nelly Fortis whispered, drawing me from her uncle. 'Mrs. Mulgrave, will you look if I am torn?' cried another. Then pair after pair of dancers came whirling along, making progress dangerous. Such a sight at any time, when one is past the age at which one takes a personal interest in it, is apt to suggest a variety of thoughts; but at this moment! Lottie hovered about me, a kind of avant-coureur, clearing the way for me. There was something amazing to me in her excitement, especially as, just at the moment when she was labouring to open a way for me,

Ada Gresham went flying past, her blue eyes shining, her cheeks more like roses than ever. She gave me a smiling little nod as her white dress swept over my dark one, and was gone to the opposite end of the room before I could say a word. Lottie drew her breath hard at the sight. Her sigh sounded shrill as it breathed past me. 'Baby!' she whispered. 'Doll!' And then the tears came to her eyes. I was startled beyond description by her looks. Had she come to care for Gerald in the midst of that worldly dreadful scheme of hers? or what did her agitation mean?

It was time for supper however, and the elders of the party began to look for it; and there were a good many people wondering and inquiring where was Mr. Gresham? where were the brothers? Young ladies stood with injured faces, who had been engaged to dance with Harry or Gerald; and Ada herself, when her waltz was over, began to look about anxiously. By this time I had got rid of Mr. Fortis, and made up my mind what to do. I went up to her and stopped her just as she was asking one of the gentlemen had he seen her husband?—where was Harry? I kept Harry's bit of paper fast in my hand. I felt by instinct that to give her that would only make matters worse. I made up the best little story I could about old Mrs. Gresham's illness.

'They both went off quite quietly, not to disturb the party,' I said. 'I was to put off telling you as long as I could, my dear, not to spoil your pleasure. They could not help themselves. They were very much put out at the thought of leaving you. But Sir Thomas will take Mr. Gresham's place; and you know they were obliged to go.'

Tears sprang to poor Ada's eyes. 'Oh, how unkind of Harry,' she cried, 'to go without telling me. As if I should have kept on dancing had I known. I don't understand it at all—to tell you, and go without a word to me!'

'My dear, he would not spoil your pleasure,' I said; 'and it would have been so awkward to send all these people away. And you know she may get better after all.'

'That is true,' said easy-minded Ada. 'It would have been awkward breaking up the party. But it is odd about mamma. She was quite well yesterday. She was to have been here to-night.'

'Oh, it must have been something sudden,' I cried, at the end of my invention. 'Shall I call Sir Thomas? What can I do to be a help to you? You must be Mr. and Mrs. Gresham both in one for to-night.'

Ada put her laced handkerchief up to her eyes and smiled a little faint smile. 'Will you tell Sir Thomas?' she said. 'I feel so bewildered I don't know what to do.'

Then I commenced another progress in search of Sir Thomas, Lottie Stoke still hovering about me as pale as a spirit. She took my arm as we went on. 'Was that all a story?' she whispered in my ear, clasping my arm tightly with her hands. I made her no answer; I dared not venture even to let her see my face. I went and told the same story very circumstantially over again to Sir Thomas. I hope it was not a great sin; indeed it might be quite true for anything I could tell. It was the only natural way of accounting for their mysterious absence; and everybody was extremely sorry, of course, and behaved as well as possible. Old Mrs. Gresham was scarcely known at Dinglewood, and Ada, it was evident, was not very profoundly affected after the first minute by the news, so that, on the whole, the supper-table was lively enough, and the very young people even strayed into the dancing-room after it. But of course we knew better than that when trouble had come to the house. It was not much above one o'clock in the morning when they were all gone. I pretended to go too, shaking off Lottie Stoke as best I could, and keeping out of sight in a corner while they all streamed away. On the whole, I think public opinion was in favour of Harry Gresham's quiet departure without making any disturbance. 'He was a very good son,' people said: and then some of them speculated if the poor lady died, how Harry and his wife would manage to live in the quietness which family affliction demanded. 'They will bore each other to death,' said a lively young man. 'Oh, they are devoted to each other!' cried a young lady. Not a suspicion entered any one's mind. The explanation was quite satisfactory to everybody but Lottie Stoke; but then she had seen Harry Gresham's face.

When I had made quite sure that every one was gone, I stole back quietly into the blazing deserted rooms. Had I ever been disposed to moralize over the scene of a concluded feast, it certainly would not have been at that moment. Yet there was something pathetic in the look of the place—brilliant as day, with masses of flowers everywhere, and that air of lavish wealth, prodigality, luxury—and to feel that one carried in one's hand something that might turn it into the scene of a tragedy, and wind up its bright story with the darkest conclusion. My heart beat loud as I went in. My poor little victim was still in the dancing-room—the largest and brightest of all. She had thrown herself down on a sofa, with her arms flung over her head like a tired child. Tears were stealing down her pretty cheeks. Her mouth was pouting and melancholy. When she saw me she rose with a sudden start, half annoyed, half pleased, to have some one to pour out her troubles upon. 'I can't help crying,' she said. 'I don't mean to blame Harry; but it was unkind of him to go away without saying a word to me. We never, never parted in that way before;' and from tears the poor little woman fell into sobs—grievous, innocent sobs, all about nothing, that broke one's heart.

'I have come to tell you something,' I said, 'though I don't know myself what it is. I am afraid it is something worse than you think. I said that because your brother-in-law said it; but I don't believe it is anything about Mrs. Gresham. Your husband put this into my hand through the window as he went away. Take courage, dear. You want all your courage—you must keep up for the sake of the children, Ada!'

I babbled on, not knowing what words I used, and she stared at me with bewildered eyes. 'Into your hand through the window!' she said. She could not understand. She looked at the paper as if it were a charm. Then she opened it slowly, half afraid, half stupefied. Its meaning did not seem to penetrate her mind at first. After a while she gave a loud sudden shriek, and turned her despairing eyes on me. Her cry was so piercing and sudden that it rang through the house and startled every one. She was on the verge of hysterics, and incapable of understanding what was said to her, but the sight of the servants rushing to the door to ask what was the matter brought her to herself. She made a brave effort and recovered something like composure, while I sent them away; and then she held out to me the letter which she had clutched in her hand. It was written in pencil, and some words were illegible. This was what Harry said:—

'Something unexpected has happened to me, my darling. I am obliged to leave you without time even to say good-bye. You will know all about it only too soon. It is ruin, Ada—and it is my own fault—but I never meant to defraud any man. God knows I never meant it. Try and keep up your heart, dear; I believe it will blow over, and you will be able to join me. I will write to you as soon as I am safe. You have your settlement. Don't let anybody persuade you to tamper with your settlement. My father will take care of that. Why should you and the children share my ruin? Forgive me, dearest, for the trouble I have brought on you. I dare not pause to think of it. Gerald is with me. If they come after me, say I have gone to Bishop's Hope.'

'What does it mean?' cried poor Ada close to my ear. 'Oh, tell me, you are our friend! What does it mean?'

'God knows,' I said. My own mind could not take it in, still less could I express the vague horrors that floated across me. We sat together with the lights blazing round us, the grand piano open, the musicians' stands still in their places. Ada was dressed like a queen of fairies, or of flowers: her gown was white, covered with showers of rosebuds; and she had a crown of natural roses in her bright hair. I don't know how it was that her dress and appearance suddenly impressed themselves on me at that moment. It was the horror of the contrast, I suppose. She looked me piteously in the face, giving up all attempt at thought for her own part, seeking the explanation from me. 'What is it?' she asked. 'Why has he gone away? Who is coming after him? Oh, my Harry! my Harry!' the poor young creature moaned. What could I say? I took her in my arms and kissed her. I could do no more.

At this moment there came a loud knocking at the door. The house had fallen into deadly stillness, and at that hour of the night, and in the state we were, the sound was horrible. It rang through the place as if it had been uninhabited, waking echoes everywhere. Ada's very lips grew white—she clasped her small hands over mine holding me fast. 'It is some one who has forgotten something,' I said, but my agitation was so great that I felt a difficulty in speaking. We sat and listened in frightful suspense while the door was opened and the sound of voices reached us. It was not Harry who had come back; it was not any one belonging to the place. Suddenly Ada rushed to the door with a flash of momentary petulance which simulated strength. 'If it is any one for Mr. Gresham, bring him in here,' she cried imperiously. I hurried after her and took her hand. It was like touching an electric machine. She was so strung to the highest pitch that only to touch her made me thrill and vibrate all over. And then the two men—two homely black figures—startled even in spite of their acquaintance with strange sights, came hesitatingly forward into the blazing light to confront the flower-crowned, jewelled, dazzling creature, made up of rose and lily, and diamond and pearl. They stood thunderstruck before her, notwithstanding the assurance of their trade. Probably they had never in their lives seen such an apparition before. The foremost of the two took off his hat with a look of deprecation. I do not think Ada had the least idea who they were. They were her husband's enemies, endowed with a certain dignity by that fact. But I knew in a moment, by instinct, that they must be London detectives in search of him, and that the very worst possibility of my fears had come true.

I cannot tell what we said to these men or they to us; they were not harsh nor unfeeling; they were even startled and awe-struck in their rough way, and stepped across the room cautiously, as if afraid of hurting something. We had to take them over all the house, through the rooms in which not a single light had been extinguished. To see us in our ball dresses, amid all that silent useless blaze of light, leading these men about, must have been a dreadful sight. For my part, though my share in it was nothing, I felt my limbs shake under me when we had gone over all the rooms below. But Ada took them all over the house. They asked her questions and she answered them in her simplicity. Crime might have fled out of that honest, joyous home, but it was innocence, candid and open, with nothing to conceal, which dwelt there. I had to interfere at last and tell them we would answer no more questions; and then they comforted and encouraged us in their way. 'With this fine house and all these pretty things you'll have a good bit of money yet,' said the superior of the two; 'and if Mr. Gresham was to pay up, they might come to terms.'

'Then is it debt?' cried I, with a sudden bound of hope.

The man gave a short laugh. 'It's debt to the law,' he said. 'It's felony, and that's bad; but if you could give us a bit of a clue to where he is, and this young lady would see 'em and try, why it mightn't be so bad after all. Folks often lets a gentleman go when they won't let a common man.'

'Would money do it?' cried poor Ada; 'and I have my settlement. Oh, I will give you anything, everything I have, if you'll let my poor Harry go.'

'We haven't got him yet, ma'am,' said the man. 'If you can find us any clue—'

And it was then I interfered; I could not permit them to go on with their cunning questions to poor Ada. When they went away she sank down on a sofa near that open window in the boudoir from which I had seen Harry disappear. The window had grown by this time 'a glimmering square,' full of the blue light of early dawn. The birds began to chirp and stir in the trees; the air which had been so soft and refreshing grew chill, and made us shiver in our light dresses; the roses in Ada's hair began to fade and shed their petals silently over her white shoulders. As long as the men were present she had been perfectly self-possessed; now suddenly she burst into a wild torrent of tears. 'Oh, Harry, my Harry, where is he? Why did not he take me with him?' she cried. I cannot say any more, though I think every particular of that dreadful night is burned in on my memory. Such a night had never occurred in my recollection before.

Then I got Ada to go to bed, and kept off from her the sleepy, insolent man in powder who came to know if he was to sit up for master. 'Your master has gone to Bishop's Hope,' I said, 'and will not return to-night.' The fellow received what I said with a sneer. He knew as well, or perhaps better than we did, what had happened. Everybody would know it next day. The happy house had toppled down like a house of cards. Nothing was left but the helpless young wife, the unconscious babies, to fight their battle with the world. There are moments when the sense of a new day begun is positive pain. When poor Ada fell into a troubled sleep, I wrapped myself up and opened the window and let in the fresh morning air. Looking out over the country, I felt as if I could see everything. There was no charitable shadow now to hide a flying figure: every eye would be upon him, every creature spying his flight. Where was Harry? When I looked at the girl asleep—she was but a girl, notwithstanding her babies— and thought of the horror she would wake to, it made my heart sick. And her mother was dead. There seemed no one to stand by her in her trouble but a stranger like me.

CHAPTER IV

When Ada woke however, instead of being, as I was, more hopeless, she was almost sanguine. 'There is my money, you know,' she said. 'After all, so long as it is only money—I will go and see them, as the men said, and they will come to terms. So long as we are together, what do I mind whether we have a large house or a little one? And Harry himself speaks of my settlement. Don't cry. I was frightened last night; but now I see what to do. Will you come up to town with me by the twelve o'clock train? And you shall see all will come right.'

I had not the heart to say a word. I went home, and changed that wretched evening dress which I had worn all through the night. It was a comfort to throw it off and cast it away from me; and I never wore it again; the very sight of it made me ill ever after. I found Ada almost in high spirits with the strength of her determination and certainty that she was going to redeem her husband and make all right, when I went back. Just before noon however, when she was putting on her bonnet to start, a carriage swept up to the door. I was at the window of the dining-room when it came in sight, waiting for the brougham to convey us to the station. And the rector and his wife were coming up the avenue with 'kind inquiries,' in full belief that old Mrs. Gresham was dying, and that the house was 'in affliction.' No wonder they started and stared at the sight. It was old Mrs. Gresham herself, in her pink ribbons, fresh and full and splendid, in robust health, and all the colours of the rainbow, who came dashing up with her stately bays, to the door.

I had only time to realize that all our little attempts to keep up appearances were destroyed for ever when the old people came in; for Harry's father had come too, though no one ever noticed him in presence of his wife. Mrs. Gresham came in smiling and gracious, in her usual affable and rather overwhelming way. She would have dismissed me majestically before she went to her daughter-in-law, but I was in reality too obtuse, by reason of fatigue and excitement, to understand what she meant. When she went to Ada the old man remained with me. He was not an attractive old man, and I had scarcely spoken to him before. He walked about the room looking at everything, while I sat by the window. If he had been an auctioneer valuing the furniture, he could not have been more particular in his investigations. He examined the handsome oak furniture, which was the envy of the Green, the immense mirrors, the great china vases, the pictures on the walls, as if making a mental calculation. Then he came and stood by me, and began to talk. 'In my time young people were not so extravagant,' he said. 'There are thousands of pounds, I believe, sunk in this house.'

'Mr. Gresham had a great deal of taste,' I said faltering.

'Taste! Nonsense. You mean waste,' said the old man, sitting down astride on a carved chair, and looking at me across the back of it. 'But I admit the things have their value—they'll sell. Of course you know Harry has got into a mess?' he went on. 'Women think they can hush up these things; but that's impossible. He has behaved like an idiot, and he must take the consequences. Fortunately the family is provided for. Her friends need not be concerned in that respect.'

'I am very glad,' said I, as it was necessary to say something.

'So am I,' said old Mr. Gresham. 'I suppose they would have come upon me if that had not been the case. It's a bad business; but it is not so bad as it might have been. I can't make out how a son of mine should have been such an ass. But they all go so fast in these days. I suppose you had a very grand ball last night? A ball!' he repeated, with a sort of snort. I don't know if there was any fatherly feeling at all in the man, but if there was he hid it under this mask of harshness and contempt.

'Will not Mr. Gresham return?' I asked foolishly; but my mind was too much worn out to have full control of what I said.

The old man gave a shrug, and glanced at me with a mixture of scorn and suspicion. 'I can't say what may happen in the future,' he said dryly. 'I should advise him not. But Ada can live where she likes—and she will not be badly off.'

Old Mrs. Gresham stayed a long time up-stairs with her daughter-in-law; so long that my patience almost deserted me. Mr. Gresham went off, after sitting silent opposite to me for some time, to look over the house, which was a relief; and no doubt I might have gone too, for we were far too late for the train. But I was too anxious to go away. When the two came down the old lady was just as cheerful and overwhelming as usual, though poor Ada was deadly pale. Mrs. Gresham came in with her rich, bustling, prosperous look, and shook hands with me over again. 'I am sure I beg your pardon,' she said; 'I had so much to say to Ada. We have not met for a whole month; and poor child, they gave her such a fright last night. My dear, don't you mean to give us some luncheon? Grandpapa never takes lunch; you need not wait for him, but I am quite hungry after my long drive.'

Then poor Ada rose and rang the bell; she was trembling so that she tottered as she moved. I saw that her lips were dry, and she could scarcely speak. She gave her orders so indistinctly that the man could not hear her. 'Luncheon!' cried the old lady in her imperious way. 'Can't you hear what Mrs. Gresham says? Lunch directly—and tell my people to be at the door in an hour. Ada, a man who stared in my face like that, and pretended not to understand, should not stay another day in my house; you are a great deal too easy. So your ball was interrupted last night, Mrs. Mulgrave,' she went on with a laugh, 'and the blame laid on me. Oh, those boys! I hope the good people hereabouts will not take offence. I will never forgive them, though, for giving Ada such a fright, poor child. She thought I was dying, I suppose; and it was only one of Gerald's sporting scrapes. Some horse was being tampered with, and he would have lost thousands if they had not rushed off; so they made out I was dying, the wretched boys. Ha, ha! I don't look much like dying to-day.'

'No, indeed,' was all I could say. As for Ada she never opened her white lips, except to breathe in little gasps like a woman in a fever. The old lady had all the weight of the conversation to bear; and indeed she was talking not for our benefit, but for that of the servants, who were bringing the luncheon. She looked so rich and assured of herself that I think they were staggered in their certainty of misfortune and believed her for the moment. The young footman, who had just been asking me privately to speak a word for him to secure him another place, gave me a stealthy imploring look, begging me as it were not to betray him. The old gentleman was out, going over the house and grounds, but Mrs. Gresham ate a very good luncheon and continued her large and ample talk. 'They sent me a message this morning,' she said, as she ate, 'and ordered me to come over and make their excuses and set things right. Just like boys! Give me some sherry, John Thomas. I shall scold them well, I promise you, when they come back— upsetting poor Ada's nerves, and turning the house upside down like this. I don't know what Ada would have done without you, Mrs. Mulgrave; and I hear you had their stable-men, trainers, or whatever they call them, to puzzle you too.'

'Yes,' I said, struck dumb with wonder. Was this all an invention, or was she herself deceived? Poor Ada sat with her eyes cast down, and never spoke except in monosyllables; she could scarcely raise to her lips the wine which her mother-in-law made her swallow. I could not but admire the energy and determination of the woman. But at the same time she bewildered me, as she sat eating and drinking, with her elbow on the table and her rich lace mantle sweeping over the white tablecloth, conversing in this confident way. To meet her eyes, which had not a shade of timidity or doubt about them, and see her evident comfort and enjoyment, and believe she was telling a downright lie, was almost more than was possible. 'I did not know Mr. Gerald was a racing man,' I faltered, not knowing what to say.

'Oh, yes, he is on the turf,' said Mrs. Gresham, shrugging her shoulders; 'he is on everything that don't pay. That boy has been a nuisance all his life. Not that there is anything bad about him; but he's fashionable, you know, and we are known to be rich, and everybody gives him his own way; and Harry's such a good brother—' said the rash woman all at once, to show how much at her ease she was. But this was taking a step too much. Ada could bear it no longer. There was a sudden sound of choking sobs, and then she sprang from the table. The strain had gone too far.

'I hear baby crying; I must go to baby,' she sobbed; and rushed from the room without any regard to appearances. Even Mrs. Gresham, self-possessed as she was, had gone too far for her own strength. Her lip quivered in spite of herself. She looked steadily down, and crumbled the bread before her in her strong agitated fingers. Then she gave a little laugh, which was not much less significant than tears.

'Poor little Ada,' she said, 'she can't bear to be crossed. She has had such a happy life, when anything goes contrary it puts her out.' Perhaps it was the quivering of her own lip that brought back her vernacular. And then we began to discuss the ball as if nothing had happened. Her husband came in while we were talking, and shrugged his shoulders and muttered disapprobation, but she took no notice. She must have been aware that I knew all; and yet she thought she could bewilder me still.

I went home shortly after, grieved and disgusted and sick at heart, remembering all the wicked stories people tell of mercantile dishonesty, of false bankruptcies, and downright robberies, and the culprits who escape and live in wealth and comfort abroad. This was how it was to be in the case of Harry Gresham. His wife had her settlement, and would go to him, and they would be rich, and well off, though he had as good as stolen his neighbour's property and squandered it away. Of course I did not know all the particulars then; and I had got to be fond of these young people. I knew very well that Harry was not wicked, and that his little wife was both innocent and good. When one reads such stories in the papers, one says, 'Wretches!' and thinks no more of it. But these two were not wretches, and I was fond of them, and it made me sick at heart. I went up-stairs and shut myself into my own room, not being able to see visitors or to hear all the comment that, without doubt, was going on. But it did not mend matters when I saw from my window Mrs. Gresham driving past, lying back in her carriage, sweeping along swift as two superb horses could carry her, with her little old husband in the corner by her side, and a smile on her face, ready to wave her hand in gracious recognition of any one she knew. She was like a queen coming among us, rather than the mother of a man who had fled in darkness and shame. I never despised poor Mrs. Stoke or thought less of her for Everard's downfall, but I felt scorn and disgust rise in my heart when these people passed my door; though Mrs. Gresham, too, was her son's champion in her own worldly way.

Some hours later Ada sent me a few anxious pleading words, begging me to go to her. I found her in the avenue, concealing herself among the trees; though it was a warm summer day she was cold and shivering. I do not know any word that can express her pallor. It was not the whiteness of death, but of agonized and miserable life, palpitating in every nerve and straining every faculty.

'Hush!' she said. 'Don't go to the house—I can't bear it—I am watching for him—here!'

'Is he coming back?' I cried in terror.

'I do not know; I can't tell where he is, or where he is going!' cried poor Ada, grasping my arm; 'but if he should come back he would be taken. The house is watched. Did you not see that old man sitting under the hedge? There are people everywhere about watching for my Harry; and they tell me I am to stay quiet and take no notice. I think I will die—I wish I could die!'

'No, my darling!' I said, crying over her. 'Tell me what it is? Did they bring you no comfort? He will not come back to be taken. There is no fear. Did they not tell you what it means?'

'They told me,' cried Ada, with a violent colour flushing over her face, 'that I was to keep my money to myself, and not to pay back that—that—what he has taken! It is true; he has taken some money that was not his, and lost it; but he meant to pay it back again, Mrs. Mulgrave. We were so rich; he knew he could pay it all back. And now he has lost everything and can't pay it. And they will put him in prison. Oh, I wish he had died! I wish we had all died!' cried Ada, 'rather than this—rather than to feel what I do to-day!'

'My dear,' I cried, 'don't say so; we cannot die when we please. It is a terrible misfortune; but when he did not mean it—'

Great tears rushed to Ada's eyes. 'He did not mean that,' she said; 'but I think he meant me to keep my money and live on it. Oh, what shall I do! They say I will be wicked if I give it up. I will work for him with all my heart. But I cannot go on living like this, and keep what is not mine. If your husband had done it, Mrs. Mulgrave—don't be angry with me—would not you have sold the cottage and given up everything? And what am I to do?'

'You must come in and rest,' I said. 'Never mind what they said to you. You must do what is right, Ada, and Gerald will stand by you. He will know how to do it. Come in now and rest.'

'Ah, Gerald!' cried the poor child, and then she leant on my shoulder and cried. The moment she heard even the name of one man whom she could trust her strength broke down. 'Gerald will know how to do it,' she said faintly, as I led her in, and tried to smile at me. It was a gleam of comfort in the darkness.

I cannot describe the period of terrible suspense that followed. I stayed with her, making no pretence of going back to my own house; though when the story came to be in the newspapers all my friends wrote letters to me and disapproved of my conduct. I did not care; one knows one's own duties better than one's friends do. The day after the ball hosts of cards, and civil messages, and 'kind inquiries' had poured upon Ada; but after that they totally stopped. Not a carriage nor a visitor came near the house for the three last days. The world fell away from us and left the poor young creature to bear her burden alone. In the midst or all this real suffering there was one little incident which affected my temper more than all the rest. Old Thomas Lee, an old man from the village, who used to carry little wares about in a basket, and made his living by it, had taken his place under the hedge close to the gates of Dinglewood, and sat there watching all day long. Of course he was paid to do it, and he was very poor. But I don't think the money he has earned so has done him much good. I have never given a penny or a penny's worth to old Lee since that time. Many a sixpence poor Harry had tossed at him as he passed in his Yankee waggon every morning to the station. I had no patience with the wretched old spy. He had the assurance to take off his hat to me when I went into the house he was watching, and I confess that it was with a struggle, no later back than last winter, when the season was at its coldest, that I consented to give him a little help for his children's sake.

It was nearly a week before we got any letters, and all these long days we watched and waited, glad when every night fell, trembling when every morning rose; watching at the windows, at the gates, everywhere that a peep could be had of the white, blinding, vacant road. Every time the postman went round the Green our hearts grew faint with anxiety: once or twice when the telegraph boy appeared, even I, though I was but a spectator, felt the life die out of my heart. But at last this period of dreadful uncertainty came to a close. It was in the morning by the first post that the letters came. They were under cover to me, and I took them to Ada's room while she was still sleeping the restless sleep of exhaustion. She sprang up in a moment and caught at her husband's letter as if it had been a revelation from heaven. The happiest news in the world could not have been more eagerly received. He was safe. He had put the Channel between him and his pursuers. There was no need for further watching. The relief in itself was a positive happiness. Ten days ago it would have been heart-rending to think of Harry Gresham as an escaped criminal, as an exile, for whom return was impossible; disgraced, nameless, and without hope. To-day the news was joyful news; he was safe, if nothing more.

Then for the first time Ada indulged in the luxury of tears—tears that came in floods, like those thunder-showers which ease the hearts of the young. She threw herself on my neck and kissed me again and again. 'I should have died but for you: I had no mamma of my own to go to,' she sobbed like a baby. Perhaps the thing that made these childish words go so to my heart was that I had no child.

Of course I expected, and everybody will expect, that after this excitement she should have fallen ill. But she did not. On the contrary, she came down-stairs with me and ate (almost for the first time) and smiled, and played with her children, while I stood by with the feeling that I ought to have a brain fever myself if Ada would not see what was expected of her. But as the day ran on she became grave, and ever graver. She said little, and it was mostly about Gerald; how he must come home and manage everything; how she was determined to take no rest, to listen to no argument, till the money was paid. I went home to my own house that evening, and she made no opposition. I said good-night to her in the nursery, where she was sitting close by her little girl's bed. She was crying, poor child, but I did not wonder at that; and nurse was a kind woman, and very attentive to her little mistress. I went round to the terrace and out by the garden, without having any particular reason for it. But before I reached the gate some one came tripping after me, and looking round I saw it was Ada, wrapped in a great waterproof cloak. She was going to walk home with me, she said. I resisted her coming, but it was in vain. It was a warm, balmy night, and I could not understand why she should have put on her great cloak. But as soon as she was safe in my little drawing-room, her secret came out. Then she opened her mantle with a smile. On one of her arms hung a bundle; on the other rested her sleeping baby. She laughed at my amaze, and then she cried. 'I am going to Harry,' she said; and held her child closer, and dried her eyes and sat immovable, ready to listen to anything I chose to say. Heaven knows I said everything I could think of—of the folly of it, of her foolhardiness; that she was totally unable for the task she was putting on herself; that Harry had Gerald, and could do without her. All which she listened to with a smile, impenetrable, and not to be moved. When I had come to an end of my arguments, she stretched out to me the arm on which the bundle hung, and drew me close to her and kissed me again. 'You are going to give me some biscuits and a little flask of wine,' she said, 'to put in my pocket. I have one of the housekeeper's old-fashioned pockets, which is of some use. And then you must say "God bless you," and let me go.'

'God bless you, my poor child,' I said, overcome; 'but you must not go; little Ada too—'

Then her eyes filled with tears. 'My pretty darling!' she said; 'but grandmamma will take her to Bishop's Hope. It is only baby that cannot live without his mother. Baby and Harry. What is Gerald? I know he wants me.'

'But he can wait,' I cried; 'and you so young, so delicate, so unused to any trouble!'

'I can carry my child perfectly,' said Ada. 'I never was delicate. There is a train at eleven down to Southampton, I found it out in the book: and after that I know my way. I am a very good traveller,' she said with a smile, 'and Gerald must come to settle everything. Give me the biscuits, dear Mrs. Mulgrave, and kiss me and let me go.'

And it had to be so, though I pleaded with her till I was hoarse. When the moment came, I put on my cloak too and walked with her, late as it was, a mile off to the new station, which both she and I had thought too far for walking in the cheerful daylight. I carried the bundle, while she carried the baby, and we looked like two homely country women trudging home. She drew her hood over her head while she got her ticket, and I waited outside. Then in the dark I kissed her for the last time. I could not speak, nor did she. She took the bundle from me, grasping my hand with her soft fingers almost as a man might have done; and we kissed each other with anguish, like people who part for ever. And I have never seen her again.

As I came back, frightened and miserable, all by myself along the moonlit road, I had to pass the Stokes' cottage. Lottie was leaning out of the window, though it was now nearly midnight, with her face, all pallid in the moon, turned towards Dinglewood. I could scarcely keep myself from calling to her. She did not know what we had been doing, yet her heart had been with us that night.

CHAPTER V

I will not describe the tumult that arose when it was discovered. The servants rushed over to me in a body, and I suggested that they should send for Mrs. Gresham, and that great lady came, in all her splendour, and took little Ada away, and gave everybody 'notice.' Then great bills of the auction covered the pillars at the gate, and strangers came in heaps to see the place. In a month everything had melted away like a tale that is told. The Greshams, and their wealth, and their liberality, and their good-nature fell out of the very recollection of the people on the Green, along with the damask and the gilding and the flowers, the fine carriages and the powdered footmen. Everything connected with them disappeared. The new tenant altered the house a second time, and everything that could recall the handsome young couple and their lavish ways was cleared away. Of course there was nothing else talked of for a long time after. Everybody had his or her account of the whole business. Some said poor Harry met his pursuers in the field close to the river, and that Gerald and he fought with them, and left them all but dead in the grass; some said that Ada and I defended the house, and would not let them in; and there were countless romances about the escape and Ada's secret following after. The imagination of my neighbours made many a fancy sketch of that last scene; but never hit upon anything so touching as my last glimpse of her, with her baby under her cloak, going into the train. I held my peace, and let them talk. She had been as my own child for about a week, just a week of our lives; before that she was a common acquaintance, after it a stranger; but I could not let any vulgar tongues meddle with our relationship or her story in that sacred time.

And after a while the tale fell into oblivion, as every story does if we can but wait long enough. People forgot about the Greshams; sometimes a stranger would observe the name of Mr. Gresham, of Bishop's Hope, in some list of county charities, and would ask if he was a Gresham of Greshambury, or if he was any connection of the man who ran away. Of course, at the time, it was in all the newspapers. He had taken money that somebody had trusted him with and used it in his speculations. Of course he meant to pay it back; but then a great crash came. The men say there was no excuse for him, and I can see that there is no excuse; but he never meant it, poor Harry! And then the papers were full of further incidents, which were more unusual than Harry's sin or his flight. The Times devoted a leading article to it which everybody read, holding Mrs. Gresham up to the applause of the world. Ada gave up her settlement and all her own fortune, and 'one of his brothers,' the papers said, came forward, too, and most of the money was paid back. But Harry, poor fellow, disappeared. He was as if he had gone down at sea. His name and every sign of his life went out of knowledge—waves of forgetfulness, desertion, exile closed over them. And at Dinglewood they were never either seen or heard of again.

As long as it continued to be in the papers, Lottie Stoke kept in a very excited state. She came to me for ever, finding out every word that was printed about it, dwelling on everything. That evening when the article appeared about Mrs. Gresham's heroic abandonment of her fortune, and about 'one of his brothers,' Lottie came with her eyes lighted up like windows in an illumination, and her whole frame trembling with excitement. She read it all to me, and listened to my comments, and clasped my hand in hers when I cried out, 'That must be Gerald!' She sat on the footstool, holding the paper, and gazed up into my face with her eyes like lamps. 'Then I do not mind!' she cried, and buried her face in her hands and sobbed aloud. And I did not ask her what she meant—I had not the heart.

It was quite years after before I heard anything more of the Greshams, and then it was by way of Lottie Stoke that the news came. She had grown thinner and more worn year by year. She had not had the spirits to go out, and they were so poor that they could have no society at home. And by degrees Lottie came to be considered a little old, which is a dreadful business for an unmarried girl when her people are so poor. Mrs. Stoke did not upbraid her; but still, it may be guessed what her feelings were. But, fortunately, as Lottie sank into the background, Lucy came to the front. She was pretty, and fresh, and gay, and more popular than her sister had ever been. And, by and by, she did fulfil the grand object of existence, and married well. When Lucy told me of her engagement she was very angry with her sister.

'She says, how can I do it? She asks me if I have forgotten Gerald Gresham?' cried Lucy. 'As if I ever cared for Gerald Gresham; or as if anybody would marry him after— I shall think she cared for him herself if she keeps going on.'

'Lucy!' said Lottie, flushing crimson under her hollow eyes. Lucy, for her part, was as bright as happiness, indignation, high health, and undiminished spirits could make her. But, for my part, I liked her sister best.

'Well!' she said, 'and I do think it. You would lecture me about him when we were only having a little fun. As if I ever cared for him. And I don't believe,' cried Lucy courageously, 'that he ever cared for me.'

Her sister kissed her, though she had been so angry. 'Don't let us quarrel now when we are going to part,' she said, with a strange quiver in her voice. Perhaps the child was right; perhaps he had never cared for her, though Lottie and I both thought he did. He cared for neither of them, probably; and there was no chance that he would ever come back to Dinglewood, or show himself where his family had been so disgraced. But yet Lottie brightened up a little after that day, I can scarcely tell why.

Some time after she went on a visit to London in the season; and it was very hard work for her, I know, to get some dresses to go in, for she never would have any of Lucy's presents. She was six weeks away, and she came back looking a different creature. The very first morning after her return she came over to me, glowing with something to tell. 'Who do you think I met?' she said with a soft flush trembling over her face. Her look brought one name irresistibly to my mind. But I would not re-open that old business; I shook my head, and said I did not know.

'Why, Gerald Gresham!' she cried. 'It is true, Mrs. Mulgrave; he is painting pictures now—painting, you understand, not for his pleasure, but like a trade. And he told me about Ada and poor Harry. They have gone to America. It has changed him very much, even his looks; and instead of being rich, he is poor.'

'Ah,' I said, '"one of his brothers." You always said it was Gerald;' but I was not prepared for what was to come next.

'Did not I?' cried Lottie, triumphant; 'I knew it all the time.' And then she paused a little, and sat silent, in a happy brooding over something that was to come. 'And I think she was right,' said Lottie softly. 'He had not been thinking of Lucy; it was not Lucy for whom he cared.'

I took her hands into my own, perceiving what she meant; and then all at once Lottie fell a crying, but not for sorrow.

'That was how I always deceived myself,' she said. 'It was so base of me at first; I wanted to marry him because he was rich. And then I thought it was Lucy he liked; she was so young and so pretty—' Then she made a long pause, and put my hands upon her hot cheeks and covered herself with them. 'Your hands are so cool,' she said, 'and so soft and kind. I am going to marry him now, Mrs. Mulgrave, and he is poor.'

This is a kind of postscript to the story, but still it is so connected with it that it is impossible to tell the one without the other. We were much agitated about this marriage on the Green. If Gerald Gresham had been rich, it would have been a different matter. But a stockbroker's son, with disgrace in the family, and poor. I don't know any one who was not sorry for Mrs. Stoke under this unexpected blow. But I was not sorry for Lottie. Gerald, naturally, is not fond of coming to the Green, but I see them sometimes in London, and I think they suit each other. He tells me of poor Ada every time I see him. And I believe old Mr. Gresham is very indignant at Harry's want of spirit in not beginning again, and at Ada for giving up her settlement, and at Gerald for expending his money to help them—'A pack of fools,' says the old man. But of course they will all, even the shipwrecked family in America, get something from him when he dies. As for the mother, I met her once at Lottie's door, getting into her fine carriage with the bays, and she was very affable to me. In her opinion it was all Ada's fault. 'What can a man do with an extravagant wife who spends all his money before it is made?' she said as she got into her carriage; and I found it a little hard to keep my temper. But the Greshams and their story, and all the brief splendours of Dinglewood are almost forgotten by this time by everybody on the Green.

THE SCIENTIFIC GENTLEMAN

PART I

CHAPTER I

There were a great variety of houses on the Green; some of them handsome and wealthy, some very old-fashioned, some even which might be called tumbledown. The two worst and smallest of these were at the lower end of the Green, not far from the 'Barleymow.' It must not be supposed however that they were unpleasantly affected by the neighbourhood of the 'Barleymow.' They were withdrawn from contact with it quite as much as we were, who lived at the other end; and though they were small and out of repair, and might even look mouldy and damp to a careless passer-by, they were still houses for gentlefolk, where nobody need have been ashamed to live. They were built partly of wood and partly of whitewashed brick, and each stood in the midst of a very luxuriant garden. At the time Mr. Reinhardt, of whom I am going to speak, came to East Cottage, as it was called, the place had been very much neglected; the trees and bushes grew wildly all over the garden; the flower-beds had gone to ruin; the kitchen-garden was a desert, with only a dreary cabbage or great long straggling onion-plant run to seed showing among the gooseberries and currants, which looked like the copsewood in a forest. It is miserable to see a place go to destruction like this, and I could not but reflect often how many poor people there were without a roof to shelter them, while this house was going to ruin for want of an inhabitant. 'My dear lady, that is communism, rank communism,' the Admiral said to me when I ventured to express my sentiments aloud; but I confess I never could see it.

The house belonged to Mr. Falkland, who was a distant relation of Lord Goodwin's, and lived chiefly in London. He was a young man, and a barrister, living, I suppose, in chambers, as most of them do; but I wondered he did not furnish the place and keep it in order, if it had been only for the pleasure of coming down with his friends from Saturday to Monday, to spend Sunday in the country. When I suggested this, young Robert Lloyd, Mrs. Damerel's brother, took it upon him to laugh.

'There is nothing to do here,' he said. 'If it were near the river, for boating, it would be a different matter, or even if there was a stream to fish in; but a fellow has nothing to do here, and why should Falkland come to bore himself to death?' Thus the young man ended with a sigh for himself, though he had begun with a laugh at me.

'If he is so afraid to be bored himself,' said I—for I was rather angry to hear our pretty village so lightly spoken of—'I am sure he must know quantities of people who would not be bored. Young barristers marry sometimes, I suppose, imprudently, like other young people—'

'Curates, for instance,' said Robert, who was a saucy boy.

'Curates, and young officers, and all sorts of foolish people,' said I; 'and think what a comfort that little house would be to a poor young couple with babies! Oh no, I do not like to see such a waste; a house going to rack and ruin for want of some one to live in it, and so many people famishing for want of fresh air, and the country. Don't say any more, for it hurts me to see it. I wish it were mine to do what I liked with it only for a year.'

'Communism, rank communism,' said the Admiral. But if that is communism, then I am a communist, and I don't deny it. I would not waste a Christian dwelling-place any more than I would throw away good honest wholesome bread.

However this state of things came to an end one spring, a good many years ago. Workmen came and began to put East Cottage in order. We all took the greatest interest in the work. It was quite a place to go to for our afternoon walks, and sometimes as many as three and four parties would meet there among the shavings and the pails of plaster and whitewash. It was being very thoroughly done up. We consulted each other and gave our opinions about all the papers, as if it mattered whether we liked them or not. The Green thought well of the new tenant's taste on the whole, though some of us had doubts about the decoration of the drawing-room, which was rather a dark little room by nature. The paper for it was terribly artistic. It was one of those new designs which I always think are too mediæval for a private house—groups of five or six daisies tied together, with long stalks detached and distinct, and all the hair on their heads standing on end, so to speak; but we who objected had a conviction that it was only our ignorance, and merely whispered to each other in corners, that we were not quite sure—

that perhaps it was just a little—but the people who knew better thought it showed very fine taste indeed.

It was some time before we found out who the new tenant was. He did not come down until after everything had been arranged and ready for some weeks. Then we found out that he was a Mr. Reinhardt, a gentleman who was well-known, people said, in scientific circles. He was of German extraction, we supposed, by his name, and as for his connections, or where he came from, nobody knew anything about them. An old housekeeper was the first person who made her appearance, and then came an old man-servant; both of them looked the very models of respectability, but I do not think, for my own part, that the sight of them gave me a very pleasant feeling about their master. They chilled you only to look at them. The woman had a suspicious, watchful look, her eyes seemed to be always on the nearest corner looking for some one, and she had an air of resolution which I should not have liked to struggle against. The man was not quite so alarming, for he was older and rather feeble on his legs. One felt that there must be some weakness in his character to justify the little deviousness that would now and then appear in his steps. These two people attracted our notice in the interval of waiting for their master. The man's name was White—an innocent, feeble sort of name, but highly respectable—and he called the woman something which sounded like Missis Sarah; but whether it was her Christian name or her surname we never could make out.

It was on a Monday evening, and I had gone to dine at the Lodge with Sir Thomas and Lady Denzil, when the first certain news of the new tenant of East Cottage reached us. The gentlemen, of course, had been the first to hear it. Somehow, though it is taken for granted that women are the great traffickers in gossip, it is the men who always start the subject. When they came into the drawing-room after dinner they gave us the information, which they had already been discussing among themselves over their wine.

'Mr. Reinhardt has arrived,' Sir Thomas said to Lady Denzil; and we all asked, 'When?'

'He came yesterday, I believe,' said Sir Thomas.

'Yesterday! Why, yesterday was Sunday,' cried some one; and though we are, as a community, tolerably free from prejudice, we were all somewhat shocked; and there was a pause.

'I believe Sunday is considered the most lucky day for everything abroad,' said Lady Denzil, after that interval; 'for beginning a journey, and no doubt for entering a house. And as he is of German extraction—'

'He does not look like a German,' said Robert Lloyd; 'he is quite an old fellow—about fifty, I should say—and dark, not fair.'

At this speech the most of us laughed; for an old fellow of fifty seemed absurd to us, who were that age, or more; but Robert, at twenty, had no doubt on the subject.

'Well,' he said, half offended, 'I could not have said a young fellow, could I? He stoops, he is awfully thin, like an old magician, and shabbily dressed, and—'

'You must have examined him from head to foot, Robert.'

'A fellow can't help seeing,' said Robert, 'when he looks; and I thought you all wanted to know.'

Then we had a discussion as to what notice should be taken of the new comer. We did not know whether he was married or not, and, consequently, could not go fully into the question; but the aspect of the house and the looks of the servants were much against it. For my own part, I felt convinced he was not married; and, so far as we ladies were concerned, the question was thus made sufficiently easy. But the gentlemen felt the weight proportionably heavy on their shoulders.

'I never knew any one of the name of Reinhardt,' Sir Thomas said with a musing air.

'Probably he will have brought letters from somebody,' the Admiral suggested: and that was a wonderful comfort to all the men.

Of course he must have letters from somebody; he must know some one who knew Sir Thomas, or Mr. Damerel, or the Admiral, or General Perronet, or the Lloyds. Surely the world was not so large as to make it possible that the new comer did not know some one who knew one of the people on the Green. As for being a scientific notability, or even a literary character, I am afraid that would not have done much for him in Dinglefield. If he had been cousin to poor Lord Glyndon, who was next to an idiot, it would have been of a great deal more service to him. I do not say that we were right; I think there are other things which ought to be taken into consideration; but, without arguing about it, there is no doubt that so it was.

The Green generally kept a watchful eye for some time on the East Cottage. There were no other servants except those two whom we had already seen. Sometimes the gardener, who kept all the little gardens about in order—'doing for' ladies like myself, for instance, who could not afford to keep a gardener—was called in to assist at East Cottage; and I believe (of course I could not question him on the subject; I heard this through one of the maids) that he was very jocular about the man-servant, who was a real man-of-all-work, doing everything you could think of, from helping to cook, down to digging in the garden. Our gardener opened his mouth and uttered a great laugh when he spoke of him. He held the opinion common to a great many of his class, that to undertake too much was a positive injury to others. A servant who kept to his own work, and thought it was 'not his place' to interfere with anything beyond it, or lend a helping hand in matters beyond his own immediate calling, was Matthew's model of what a servant ought to be, and a man who pretended to be a butler, and was a Jack-of-all-trades, was a contemptible object to our gardener: 'taking the bread out o' other folks's mouths,' he said. He thought the man at the East Cottage was a foreigner, and altogether had a very poor opinion of him. But however what was a great deal worse was the fact that neither the man-servant, nor the woman, nor the master, appeared to care for our notice, or in any way took the place they ought to have done in our little community. They had their things down from London; they either did their washing 'within themselves' or sent it also away to a distance; they made no friends, and sought none. Mr. Reinhardt brought no letters of introduction. Sometimes—but rarely—he might be seen of an evening walking towards the Dell, with an umbrella over his head to shield him from the setting sun, but he never looked at anybody whom he met, or showed the least inclination to cultivate acquaintance, even with a child or a dog. And the worst of all was that he certainly never went to church. We were very regular church-goers on the Green. Some of us preferred sometimes to go to a little church in the woods, which was intended for the scattered population of our forest district, and was very pretty and sweet in the midst of the great trees, instead of to the parish. But to one or other everybody went once every Sunday at least. It was quite a pretty sight on Sunday morning to see everybody turning out—families all together, and lonely folk like myself, who scarcely could feel lonely when there was such a feeling of harmony and friendliness about. The young people set off walking generally a little while before us; but most of the elder people drove, for it was a good long way. And though some rigid persons thought it was wrong on the Sunday, yet the nice carriages and horses looked pleasant, and the servants always had time to come to church; and an old lady like Lady Denzil, for instance, must have stayed at home altogether if she had not been allowed to drive. I think a distinction should be made in such cases. But when all the houses thus opened their doors and poured forth their inhabitants, it may be supposed how strange it looked that one house should never open and no figure ever come from it to join the Sunday stream. Even the housekeeper, so far as we could ascertain, never had a Sunday out. They lived within those walls, within the trees that were now so tidy and trim. One morning when I had a cold, and was reading the service by myself in my own room, I had a glimpse of the master of the house. It was a summer day, very soft and blue, and full of sunshine. You know what I mean when I say blue—the sky seemed to stoop nearer to the earth, the earth hushed itself and looked up all still and gentle to the sky. There were no clouds above, and nobody moving below; nothing but a little thrill and flicker of leaves, a faint rustle of the grass, and the birds singing with a softer note, as if they too knew it was Sunday. My room is in the front of the house, and overlooks all the Green. The window was open, and the click of a latch sounding in the stillness made me lift my head without thinking from the lesson I was reading. It was Mr. Reinhardt, who had come out of his cottage. He came to the garden gate and stood for a moment looking out. I was not near enough to see his face, but in every line of his spare, stooping figure there was suspicion and doubt. He looked to the right and to the left with a curious prying eagerness, as if he expected to see some one coming. And then he came out altogether, and began to walk up and down, up and down. The stillness was so great that, though he walked very softly, the sound of his steps on the gravel of the road reached me from time to time. I stopped in my reading to watch him, in spite of myself. Every time he turned he looked about him in the same suspicious, curious way. Was he waiting for some one? Was he looking out for a visitor? or was he (the thought sprang into my mind all at once) insane perhaps, and had escaped from his keepers in the cottage? This thought made my heart jump, but a little reflection calmed me, for he had not the least appearance of insanity. The little jar now and then of his foot when he turned kept me in excitement; I felt it impossible to keep from watching him. When I found how abstracted my mind was getting, I changed my place that I might not be tempted to look out any more, feeling that it was wrong to yield to this curiosity; and when I had finished my reading the first carriage—the Denzils' carriage—was coming gleaming along the distant road in the sunshine, coming back from church, and the lonely figure was gone. I did not know whether he had gone in again or had extended his walk. But I felt somehow all that day, though you will say with very little reason, that I knew something more about our strange neighbour than most people did on the Green.

CHAPTER II

This seclusion and isolation of East Cottage did not however last very long. Before the summer was over Sir Thomas, who, though he stood on his dignity sometimes, was very kind at bottom, began to feel compunctious about his solitary neighbour: now and then he would say something which betrayed this. 'It worries me to think there is some one there who has been taken no notice of by anybody,' he would say. 'Of course it is his own fault—entirely his own fault.' The next time one met him he would return to the subject. 'What a lovely day! Everybody seems to be out-of-doors—except at East Cottage, where they have the blinds drawn down.' This would be said with a pucker of vexation and annoyance about his mouth. He was angry with the stranger, and sorry, and did not know what to do. And I for one knew what would follow. But we were all very curious when we heard that Sir Thomas had actually called. The Stokes came running in to tell me one afternoon. 'Oh, fancy, Mrs. Mulgrave, Sir Thomas has called!'

cried Lucy. 'And he has been admitted, which is still greater fun,' said Robert Lloyd, who was with them. I may say in passing that this was before Robert had passed his examination, when he was an idle young man at home, trying hard to persuade Lucy Stoke that he and she were in love with each other. Their parents, of course, would never have permitted such a thing for a moment, and fortunately there turned out to be nothing in it; but at present this was the chief occupation of Robert's life.

'I am very glad,' said I. 'I knew Sir Thomas never would be happy till he had done it.'

'And oh, you don't know what funny stories there are about,' said Lucy. 'They say he killed his wife, and that he is always thinking he sees her ghost. I wonder if it is true? They say he can never be left alone or in the dark; he is so frightened. I met him yesterday, and it made me jump. I never saw a man who killed his wife before.'

'But who says he killed his wife?'

'Oh, everybody; we heard it from Matthew the gardener, and I think he heard it at the "Barleymow," and it is all over the place. Fancy Sir Thomas calling on such a person! for I suppose,' said Lucy, 'though you are so very superior, you men, and may beat us, and all that, it is not made law yet that you may kill your wives.'

'It might just as well be the law: for I am sure there are many other things quite as bad,' said Lottie, while Robert, who had been appealed to, whispered some answer which made Lucy laugh. 'Poor man, I wonder if she was a very bad woman, and if she haunts him. How disappointed he must have been to find he could not get rid of her even that way!'

'Lottie, my dear, here is Sir Thomas coming; don't talk so much nonsense,' said I hurriedly.

I am afraid however that Sir Thomas rather liked the nonsense. He had not the feeling of responsibility in encouraging girls to run on, that most women have. He thought it was amusing, as men generally do, and never paused to think how bad it was for the girls. But to-day he was too full of his own story to care much for theirs. He came in with dusty boots, which was quite against his principles, and stretched his long spare limbs out on the beautiful rug which the Stokes had worked for me in a way that went to my heart. That showed how very much pre-occupied he was; for Sir Thomas was never inconsiderate about such matters.

'Well,' he said, pushing his thin white hair off his forehead, and stretching out his legs as if he were quite worn out, 'there is one piece of work well over. I have had a good many tough jobs in my life, but I don't know that I ever had a worse.'

'Oh, tell us what happened. Is he mad? Has he shut himself in? Has he hurt you?' cried the Stokes.

Sir Thomas smiled upon this nonsense as if it had been perfectly reasonable, and the best sense in the world.

'Hurt me! well, not quite: he was not likely to try that. He is a little mite of a man, who could not hurt a fly. And besides,' added Sir Thomas, correcting himself, 'he is a gentleman. I have no reason to doubt he is a perfect gentleman. He conducts himself quite as—as all the rest of us do. No, it was the difficulty of getting in that bewildered me.'

'Was there a difficulty in getting in?'

'You shall hear. The servant looked as if he would faint when he saw me. "Mr. Reinhardt at home?" Oh! he could not quite say; if I would wait he would go and ask. So I waited in the hall,' said Sir Thomas with a smile. 'Well, yes, it was odd, of course; but such an experience now and then is not bad for one. It shows you, you know, of how little importance you are the moment you get beyond the circle of people who know you. I think really it is salutary, you know, if you come to that—and amusing,' he added, this time with a little laugh.

'Oh, but what a shame: how shocking! how horrid! You, Sir Thomas, whom everybody knows!'

'That is just what makes it so instructive,' he said. 'I must have stood in the hall a quarter of an hour: allowing for the tediousness of waiting, I should say certainly a quarter of an hour; and then the man came back and asked me, what do you think? if I had come of my own accord, or if some one had sent me! It was ludicrous,' said Sir Thomas with a half laugh; 'but if you will think of it, it was rather irritating. I am afraid I lost my temper a little. I said, "I am Sir Thomas Denzil. I live at the Lodge, and I have come to call upon your master," in a tone which made the old fool of a man shake, and then some one else appeared at the top of the stairs. It was Mr. Reinhardt, who had heard my voice.'

'What did he say for himself?' I asked.

'It was not his fault,' said Sir Thomas; 'he knew nothing of it. He is a very well-informed man, Mrs. Mulgrave. He is quite able to enter into conversation on any subject. He was very glad to see me. He is a sort of recluse, it is easy to perceive, but quite a proper person; very well-informed, one whom it was a pleasure to converse with, I assure you. He made a thousand apologies. He said something about unfortunate circumstances, and a disagreeable visitor, as an excuse for his man; but whether the disagreeable visitor was some one who had been there or who was expected—'

'Oh, I know,' cried Lucy Stoke, with excitement. 'It was his wife's ghost.'

Sir Thomas stopped short aghast, and looked at me to ask if the child had gone mad.

'How could they think Sir Thomas was the wife's ghost?' cried Lottie, 'you little goose! and besides, most likely it is not true.'

'What is not true?' asked Sir Thomas in dismay.

'Oh, they say he killed her,' said Lucy, 'and that she haunts him. They say his man sleeps in his room, and the housekeeper just outside. He cannot be left by himself for a moment: and I do not wonder he should be frightened if he has killed his wife.'

'Nonsense, nonsense,' said Sir Thomas, raising his voice. 'Nonsense!' he was quite angry. He had taken up the man and felt responsible for him, 'My dear child, I think you are going out of your little wits,' he cried. 'Killed his wife! why, the man is a thorough gentleman. A most well-informed man, and knows my friend Sir Septimus Dash, who is the head of the British Association. Why, why, Lucy! you take away my breath.'

'It was not I who said it,' cried Lucy. 'It is all over the Green—everybody knows. They say she disappeared all at once, and never was heard of more; and then there used to be sounds like somebody crying and moaning; and then he got so frightened, he never would go anywhere, nor look any one in the face. Oh! only suppose; how strange it would be to have a haunted house on the Green. If I had anybody to go with me I should like to walk down to East Cottage at midnight.'

'Let me go with you,' whispered Robert; but fortunately I heard him, and gave Lucy a look. She was a silly little girl certainly, but not so bad as that.

'This is really very great nonsense,' said Sir Thomas. 'A haunted house at this time of day! Mrs. Mulgrave, I hope you will use all your influence to put down this story if it exists. I give you my word, Mr. Reinhardt is quite an addition to our society, and knows Sir Septimus Dash. A really well-bred, well-informed man. I am quite shocked, I assure you. Lucy, I hope you will not spread this ridiculous story. I shall ask your mother what she thinks. Poor man! no wonder he looked uncomfortable, if there is already such a rumour abroad.'

'Then he did look uncomfortable?' said Lottie.

'No, I can't say he did. No; I don't mean uncomfortable,' said Sir Thomas, seeing he had committed himself. 'I mean— it is absurd altogether. A charming man; one whom you will all like immensely. I think Lady Denzil must have returned from her drive. We are to see you all to-morrow, I believe, in the afternoon? Now, Lucy, no more gossip; leave that to the old women, my dear.'

'Sir Thomas does not know what to make of it,' said Lottie, as we watched him cross the Green. 'He has gone to my lady to have his mind made up whether he ought to pay any attention to it or not.'

'And my lady will say not,' said I; 'fortunately we are all sure of that. Lady Denzil will not let anybody be condemned without a hearing. And, Lucy, I think Sir Thomas gave you very good advice; when you are old it will be time enough to amuse yourself with spreading stories, especially such dreadful stories as this.'

Lucy took offence at what I said, and went away pouting—comforted by Robert Lloyd, and very indignant with me. Lottie stayed for a moment behind her to tell me that it was really quite true, and that the report had gone all over the Green, and everybody was talking of it. No one knew quite where it had come from, but it was already known to all the world at Dinglewood, and a very unpleasant report it was.

However time went on, and no more was heard of this. In a little place like Dinglewood, as soon as everybody has heard a story, a pause ensues. We cannot go on indefinitely propagating it, and renewing our own faith in it. When we all know it, and nothing new can be said on the subject, we are stopped short; and unless there are new facts to comment upon, or some new light thrown upon the affair, it is almost sure to die away, as a matter of course. This was the case in respect to the report about Mr. Reinhardt. We got no more information, and we could not go on talking about the old story for ever. We exhausted it, and grew tired of it, and let it drop; and thus, by degrees, we got used to him, and became acquainted with him, more or less.

The other gentlemen called, one by one, after Sir Thomas. Mr. Reinhardt was asked, timidly, to one or two dinner-parties, and declined, which we thought at first showed, on the whole, good taste on his part. But he became quite friendly when we met him on the road, and would stop to talk, and showed no moroseness, nor fear of any one. He had what was generally pronounced to be a refined face—the features high and clear, with a kind of ivory paleness, and keen eyes, which were very sharp to note everything. He was, as Sir Thomas said, very well-informed. There seemed to be nothing that you could talk about that he did not know; and in science, the gentlemen said he was a perfect mine of knowledge. I am not sure however that they were very good judges, for I don't think either Sir Thomas or the Admiral knew much about science. One thing however which made some of us still doubtful about him was the fact that he never talked of people. When a name was mentioned in conversation he never said, 'Oh, I know him very well—I knew his father—a cousin of his was a great friend of mine,' as most people do. All the expression went out of his face as soon as we came to this kind of talk; and it may be supposed how very much at a loss most people were in consequence for subjects to talk about. But this, though it was strange, was not any sort of proof that he had done anything wicked. It might be—and the most of us thought it was—an evidence that he had not lived in society. 'He knows my friend, Sir Septimus Dash,' Sir Thomas always said in his favour; but then, of course, Sir Septimus was a public personage, and Mr. Reinhardt might have made his acquaintance at some public place. But still, a man may be of no family, and out of society, and yet not have murdered his wife. After a while we began to think, indeed, that whether he had killed her or not, it was just as well there was no wife in the question—'Just as well,' Mrs. Perronet said, who was great in matters of society. 'A man whom nobody knows does not matter; but what should we have done with a woman?'

'He must have killed her on purpose to save us the trouble,' said Lottie. But the General's wife was quite in earnest, and did not see the joke.

CHAPTER III

It is a good thing, on the whole, to have a house with a mystery about it in one's immediate neighbourhood. Gradually we ceased to believe that Mr. Reinhardt had anything criminal about him. But it was quite certain that there was a mystery—that we knew nothing about him, neither where he came from, nor what his family was. For one thing, he had certainly no occupation: therefore, of course, he must be sufficiently well off to do without that: and he had no relations—no one who ever came to see him, nor of whom he talked; and though the men who called upon him had been admitted, they were never asked to go back, nor had one of us ladies ever crossed his threshold. It would seem indeed that he had made a rule against admitting ladies, for when Mrs. Damerel herself called to speak of the soup-kitchen, old White came and spoke to her at the gate, and trembled very much, and begged her a hundred pardons, but nevertheless would not let her in—a thing which made her very indignant. Thus the house became to us all a mysterious house, and, on the whole, I think we rather liked it. The mystery did no harm, and it certainly amused us, and kept our interest alive.

Thus the summer passed, and Dinglefield had got used to the Scientific Gentleman. That was the name he generally went by. When strangers came to the Green, and had it all described to them—Sir Thomas here, the Admiral there, the General at the other side, and so on, we always gave a little special description of Mr. Reinhardt.

'He is a Fellow of the Royal Society,' one would say, not knowing much what that meant. 'He belongs to the British Association,' said another. 'He is a great scientific light.' We began even to feel a little proud of him. Even I myself, on the nights when I did not sleep well, used to feel quite pleased, when I looked out, to see the Scientific Gentleman's light still burning. He was sitting up there, no doubt, pondering things that were much beyond our comprehension—and it made us proud to think that, on the Green, there was some one who was going over the abstrusest questions in the dead of the night.

It was about six months after his arrival when, one evening, for some special reason, I forget what, I went to Mrs. Stoke's to tea. She lives a little way down the lane, on the other side of the 'Barleymow.' It is not often that she asks any one even to tea. As a rule, people generally ask her and her daughters, for we are all very well aware of her circumstances; but on this particular night, I was there for some reason or other. It was October, and the nights had begun to be cold; but there was a full moon, and at ten o'clock it was as light as day. This was why I would not let them send any one home with me. I must say I have never understood how middle-aged women like myself can have a pretty young maid-servant sent for them, knowing very well that the girl must walk one way alone, and that, if there is any danger at all, a young woman of twenty is more in the way of it, than one who might be her mother. I remember going to the door to look out, and protesting that I was not the least nervous—nor was I. I knew all the roads as well as I knew my own garden, and everybody round about knew me. The way was not at all lonely. To be sure, there were not many people walking about; but then there were houses all along— and lastly, it was light as day. The moon was shining in that lavish sort of way which she only has when she is at the full. The houses amid their trees stood whitened over, held fast by the light as the wedding-guest was held by the eye of the Ancient Mariner. The shadows were as black as the light was white. There was a certain solemnity about it, so full of light, and yet so colourless. After I had left the house, and had come out—I and my shadow—into the full whiteness, it made an impression upon me which I could scarcely resist. My first idea when I glanced back was that my own shadow was some one stealing after me. That gave me a shake for a moment, though I laughed at myself. The lights of the 'Barleymow' neutralized this solemn feeling, and I went on, thinking to myself what a good story it would be for my neighbours—my own shadow! I did not cross the Green, as I generally did, partly from a vague feeling that, though it was so light and so safe, there was a certain company in being close to the houses—not that I was the least afraid, or that indeed there was any occasion to fear, but just for company's sake. By this time, I think it must have been very nearly eleven o'clock, which is a late hour for Dinglefield. All the houses seemed shut up for the night. Looking up the Green, the effect of the sleeping place, with the moon shining on the pale gables and ends of houses, and all the trees in black, and the white stretch of space in the centre, looking as if it had been clean swept by the moonlight of every obstacle, had the strangest effect. I was not in the least afraid. What should I be afraid of, so close to my own door? But still I felt a little shiver run over me—a something involuntary, which I could not help, like that little thrill of the nerves, which makes people say that some one is walking over your grave.

And all at once in the great stillness and quiet I heard a sound quite near. It was very soft at first, not much louder than a sigh. I hurried on for a few steps frightened, I could not tell why, and then, disgusted with myself, I stopped to listen. Yes, now it came again, louder this time; and then I turned round to look where it came from. It was the sound of some one moaning either in sorrow or in pain; a soft, interrupted moan, now and then stopping short with a kind of sob. My heart began to beat, but I said to myself, it is some one in trouble, and I can't run away. The sound came from the side of East Cottage, just where the little railing in front ended; and, after a long look, I began to see that there was some one there. What I made out was the outline of a figure seated on the ground with knees drawn up, and looking so thin that they almost came to a point. It was straight up against the railing, and so overshadowed by the lilac-bushes that the outline of the knees, black, but whitened over as it were with a sprinkling of snow or silver, was all that could be made out. It was like something dimly seen in a picture, not like flesh and blood. It gave me the strangest sensation to see this something, this shrouded semblance of a human figure, at Mr. Reinhardt's door. All the stories that had been told of him came back to my mind. His wife! I would have kept the recollection out of my mind if I could, but it came without any will of mine. I turned and went on as fast as ever I could. I should have run like a frightened child had I followed my own instinctive feeling. My heart beat, my feet rang upon the gravel; and then I stopped short, hating myself. How silly and weak I was! It might be some poor creature, some tramp or wandering wretch, who had sunk down there in sickness or weariness, while I in my cowardice passed by on the other side frightened lest it should be a ghost. I do not know to this day how it was that I forced myself to turn and go back, but I did. Oh! what a moaning, wailing sound it was; not loud, but the very cry of desolation. I felt as I went, though my heart beat so, that such a moaning could only come from a living creature, one who had a body full of weariness and pain, as well as a suffering soul.

I turned back and went up to the thing with those sharp-pointed knees; then I saw the hands clasped round the knees, and the hopeless head bowed down upon them, all black and silvered over like something cut out of ebony. I even saw, or thought I saw, amid the flickering of the heavens above and the shadows below, a faint rocking in the miserable figure;—that mechanical, unconscious rocking which is one of the primitive ways of showing pain. I went up, all trembling as I was, and asked 'What is the matter?' with a voice as tremulous. There was no answer; only the moaning went on, and the movement became more perceptible. Fortunately, my terror died away when I saw this. The human sound and action, that were like what everybody does, brought me back at once out of all supernatural dread. It was a woman, and she was unhappy. I dismissed the other thought—or rather, it left me unawares.

This gave me a great deal of courage. I repeated my question; and then, as there was no answer, went up and touched her softly. The figure rose with a spring in a moment, before I could think what she was going to do. She put out one of her hands, and pushed me off.

'Ah! have I brought you out at last?' she cried wildly; and then stopped short and stared at me; while I stared, too, feeling, whoever it might be she had expected, that I was not the person. Her movement was so sudden, that I shrank back in terror, fearing once more I could not tell what. She was a very tall, slight woman, with a cloak tightly wrapped about her. In the confusion of the moment I could remark nothing more.

'Are you ill?' I said, faltering. 'My good woman, I—I don't want to harm you; I heard you moaning, and I—thought you were ill—'

She seized me by the arm, making my very teeth chatter. The grasp was bony and hard like the hand of a skeleton.

'Are you from that house? Are you from him?' she cried, pointing behind her with her other hand. 'Bid him come out to me himself; bid him come out and go down on his knees before I'll give in to enter his door. Oh! I've not come here for nought—I've not come here for nought! I've come with all my wrongs that he's done me. Tell him to come out himself; it is his part.'

Her voice grew hoarse with the passion that was in it, and yet it was a voice that had been sweet.

I put up my hand, pleading with her, trying to get a hearing, but she held me fast by the arm.

'I have not come from that house,' I said. 'You frighten me. I—I live close by. I was passing and heard you moan. Is there anything the matter? Can I be—of any use?'

I said this very doubtfully, for I was afraid of the strange figure, and the passionate speech.

Then she let go her hold all at once. She looked at me and then all round. There was not another creature visible except, behind me, I suppose, the open door and lights of the 'Barleymow.' She might have done almost what she would to me had she been disposed;—at least, at the moment that was how I felt.

'You live close by?' she said, putting her hand upon her heart, which was panting and heaving with her passion.

'Yes. Are you—staying in the neighbourhood? Have you—lost your way?'

I said this in my bewilderment, not knowing what the words were which came from my lips. Then the poor creature leaned back upon the wall and gasped and sobbed. I could not make out at first whether it was emotion or want of breath.

'Yes, I've lost my way,' she said; 'not here, but in life; I've lost my way in life, and I'll never find it again. Oh! I'm ill—I'm very ill. If you are a good Christian, as you seem, take me in somewhere and let me lie down till the spasm's past; I feel it coming on now.'

'What is it?' I asked.

She put her hand upon her heart and panted and gasped for breath. Poor wretch! At that moment I heard behind me the locking of the door at the 'Barleymow.' I know I ought to have called out to them to wait, but I had not my wits about me as one ought to have.

'Have you no home?' I asked; 'nowhere to go to? You must live somewhere. I will go with you and take you home.'

'Home!' she cried. 'It is here or in the churchyard, nowhere else—here or in the churchyard. Take me to one or the other, good woman, for Christ's sake: I don't care which—to my husband's house or to the churchyard—for Christ's sake.'

For Christ's sake! You may blame me, but what could I do? Could any of you refuse if you were asked in that name? You may say any one can use such words—any vagabond, any wretch—and, of course, it is true; but could you resist the plea—you who are neither a wretch nor a vagabond?—I know you could not, any more than me.

'Lean upon me,' I said; 'take my arm; try if you can walk. Oh! I don't know who you are or what you are, but when you ask for Christ's sake, you know, He sees into your heart. If you have any place that I can take you to, tell me; you must know it is difficult to take a stranger into one's house like this. Tell me if you have not some room—some place where you can be taken care of; I will give you what you want all the same.'

We were going on all this time, walking slowly towards my house; she was gasping, holding one hand to her heart and with the other leaning heavily on me. When I made this appeal to her she stopped and turned half round, waving her hand towards the house we were leaving behind us.

'If that is Mr. Reinhardt's house,' she said, 'take me there if you will. I am—his wife. He'll leave me to die—on the doorstep—most likely; and be glad. I haven't strength—to—say any more.'

'His wife!' I cried in my dismay.

'Lord have mercy upon us!' cried the panting creature. 'Ay! that's the truth.'

What could I do? She was scarcely able to totter along, panting and breathless. It was her heart. Poor soul! how could any one tell what she might have had to suffer? I took her, though with trembling—what could I do else?—to my own house.

CHAPTER IV

I cannot attempt to describe what my feelings were when I went into my own house with that strange woman. Though it was a very short way, we took a long time to get there. She had disease of the heart evidently, and one of the paroxysms had come on.

'I shall be better by and by,' she said to me, gasping as she leaned on my arm.

My mind was in such a confusion that I did not know what I was doing. She might be only a tramp, a thief, a vagabond. As for what she had said of being Mr. Reinhardt's wife—my head swam, I could neither understand nor explain to myself how this had come about. But, whether she was good or bad, I could not help myself; I was committed to it. Every house on the Green was closed and silent. The shutters were all put up at the 'Barleymow,' and silence reigned. No, thank Heaven! in the Admiral's window there were still lights, so that if anything happened I could call him to my aid. He was my nearest neighbour, and the sight of his lighted window gave me confidence.

My maid gave a little shriek when she opened the door, and this too roused me. I said, 'Mary, this—lady is ill; she will lie down on the sofa in the drawing-room while we get ready the west room. You will not mind the trouble, I am sure, when you see how ill she is.'

This I said to smooth matters, for it is not to be supposed that Mary, who was already yawning at my late return, should be quite pleased at being sent off to make up a bed and prepare a room unexpectedly as it were in the middle of the night. And I was glad also to send her away, for I saw her give a wondering look at the poor creature's clothes, which were dusty and soiled. She had been sitting on the dusty earth by Mr. Reinhardt's cottage, and it was not wonderful if her clothes showed marks of it. I made her lie down on the sofa, and got her some wine. Poor forlorn creature! The rest seemed to be life however to her. She sank back upon the soft cushions, and her heavy breathing softened almost immediately. I left her there (though, I confess, not without a slight sensation of fear), and went to the west room to help Mary. It was a room we seldom used, at the end of a long passage, and therefore the one best fitted to put a stranger, about whom I knew nothing, in. Mary did not say anything, but I could feel that she disapproved of me in every pat she gave to the fresh sheets and pillows. And I was conciliatory, as one so often is to one's servants. I drew a little picture of how I had found the 'poor lady' panting for breath and unable to walk—of how weak and how thin she was—and what a terrible thing to have heart-disease, which came on with any exertion—and how anxious her friends must be.

All this Mary listened to in grim silence, patting now and then the bedclothes with her hand, as if making a protest against all I said. At length, when I had exhausted my eloquence, and began to grow a little angry, Mary cleared her throat and replied,

'Please, ma'am, I know it ain't my place to speak—'

'Oh! you can say what you please, Mary, so long as it is not unkind to your neighbours,' said I.

'I never set eyes on the—lady—before, so she can't be a neighbour of mine,' said Mary; 'but she's been seen about the Green days and days. I've seen her myself a-haunting East Cottage, where that poor gentleman lives.'

'You said this moment that you never set eyes on her before.'

'Not to know her, ma'am,' said Mary; 'it's different. I saw her to-day walking up and down like a ghost, and I wouldn't have given sixpence for all she had on her. It ain't my place to speak, but one as you don't know, and as may have a gang ready to murder us all in our beds— Mother was in service in London when she was young, and oh! to hear the tales she knows. Pretending to be ill is the commonest trick of all, mother says, and then they get took in, and then, when all's still—'

'It is very kind of you, I am sure, to instruct me by your mother's experiences,' said I, feeling very angry. 'Now you can go to bed if you please, and lock your door, and then you will be safe. I shall not want you any more to-night.'

'Oh! but please, ma'am. I don't want to leave you by yourself—please, I don't!' cried Mary, with the ready tears coming to her eyes.

However I sent her away. I was angry, and perhaps unreasonable, as people generally are when they are angry; though, when Mary went to bed, I confess it was not altogether with an easy mind that I found myself alone with the stranger in the silent house. It is always a comfort to know that there is some one within reach. I went back softly to the drawing-room: she was still lying on the sofa, quite motionless and quiet, no longer panting as she had done. When I looked at her closely I saw that she had dropped asleep. The light of the lamp was full on her face, and yet she had dropped asleep, being, as I suppose, completely worn out. I saw her face then for the first time, and it startled me. It was not a face which you could describe by any of the lighter words of admiration as pretty or handsome. It was simply the most beautiful face I ever saw in my life. It was pale and worn, and looked almost like death lying back in that attitude of utter weakness on the velvet cushions; and, though the eyes were closed, and the effect of them lost, it was impossible to believe that the loveliest eyes in the world could have made her more beautiful. She had dark hair, wavy and slightly curling upon the forehead; her eyelashes were very long and dark, and curled upwards; her features, I think, must have been perfect; and the look of pain had gone from her face; she was as serene as if she had been dead.

I was very much startled by this: so much so that for the moment I sank down upon a chair, overcome by confusion and surprise, and did not even shade the lamp, as I had intended to do. You may wonder that I should be so much surprised, but then you must remember that great beauty is not common anywhere, and that to pick it out of the ditch as it were, and find it thus in the person of one who might be a mere vagabond and vagrant for aught you could tell, was very strange and startling. It took away my breath; and then, the figure which belonged to this face formed so strange a contrast with it. I know, as everybody else does, that beauty is but skin-deep; that it is no sign of excellence, or of mental or moral superiority in any way; that it is accidental and independent of the character of its possessor as money is, or anything else you are born to: I know all this perfectly well; and yet I feel, as I suppose everybody else does, that great beauty is out of place in squalid surroundings. When I saw the worn and dusty dress, the cloak tightly drawn across her breast, the worn shoes that peeped out from below her skirt, I felt ashamed. It was absurd, but such was my feeling; I felt ashamed of my good gown and lace, and fresh ribbons. To think that I, and hundreds like me, should deck ourselves, and leave this creature in her dusty gown! My suspicions went out of my mind in a moment. Instead of the uneasy doubt whether perhaps she might have accomplices (it made me blush to think I had dreamt of such a thing) waiting outside, I began to feel indignant with everybody that she could be in such a plight. Reinhardt's wife! How did he dare, that mean, insignificant man, to marry such a creature, and to be cruel to her after he had married her! I started up and removed the lamp, shading her face, and I took my shawl, which was my best shawl, an Indian one, and really handsome, and covered her with it. I did it—I can't tell why—with a feeling that I was making her a little compensation. Then I opened one of the windows to let in the air, for the night was sultry; and then I put myself into my favourite chair, and leant back my head, and made myself as comfortable as I could to watch her till she woke. I should have thought this a great hardship a little while before, but I did not think it a hardship now. I had become her partisan, her protector, her servant, in a moment, and all for no reason except the form of her features, the look of that sleeping face. I acknowledge that it was absurd, but still I know you would have done the same had you been in my place. I suspected her no more, had no doubts in my mind, and was not the least annoyed that Mary had gone to bed. It seemed to me as if her beauty established an immediate relationship between us, somehow, and made it natural that I, or any one else who might happen to be in the way, should give up our own convenience for her. It was her beauty that did it, nothing else, not her great want and solitude, not even the name by which she had adjured me;—her beauty, nothing more. I do not defend myself for having fallen prostrate before this primitive power; I could not help it, but I don't attempt to excuse myself.

I must have dozed in my chair, for I woke suddenly, dreaming that some one was standing over me and staring at me—a kind of nightmare. I started with a little cry, and for the first moment I was bewildered, and could not think how I had got there. Then all at once I saw her, and the mystery was solved. She had woke too, and lay on her side on the sofa, looking intently at me with a gaze which renewed my first impression of terror. She had not moved, she lay in the same attitude of exhaustion and grateful repose, with her head thrown back upon the cushions. There was only this difference—that whereas she had then been unconscious in sleep, she was now awake, and so vividly, intensely conscious that her look seemed an active influence. I felt that she was doing something to me by gazing at me so. She had woke me no doubt by that look. She made me restless now, so that I could not keep still. I rose up, and made a step or two towards her.

'Are you better? I hope you are better,' I said.

Still she did not move, but said calmly, without any attempt at explanation: 'Are you watching me from kindness or because you were afraid I should do some harm?'

She was not grateful: the sight of me woke no kindly feeling in her: and I was wounded in spite of myself.

'Neither,' said I; 'you fell asleep, and I preferred staying here to waking you; but it is almost morning and the oil is nearly burnt out in the lamp. There is a room ready for you; will you come with me now?'

'I am very comfortable,' she said; 'I have not been so comfortable for a very long time. I have not been well off. I have had to lie on hard beds and eat poor fare, whilst all the time those who had a right to take care of me—'

'Don't think of that now,' I said. 'You will feel better if you are undressed. Come now and go to bed.'

She kept her position, without taking any notice of what I said.

'I have a long story to tell you—a long story,' she went on. 'When you hear it you will change your mind about some things. Oh, how pleasant it is to be in a nice handsome lady's room again! How pleasant a carpet is, and pictures on the walls! I have not been used to them for a long time. I suppose he has every kind of thing, everything that is pleasant; and, if he could, he would have liked to see me die at his door. That is what he wants. It would be a pleasure to him to look out some morning and see me lying like a piece of rubbish under the wall. He would have me thrown upon the dust-heap, I believe, or taken off by the scavengers as rubbish. Yes, that is what he would like, if he could.'

'Oh, don't think so,' I cried. 'He cannot be so cruel. He has not a cruel face.'

Upon this she sat up, with the passion rising in her eyes.

'How can you tell?—you were never married to him!' she said. 'He never cast you off, never abandoned you, never—' Her excitement grew so great that she now rose up on her feet, and clenched her hand and shook it as if at some one in the distance. 'Oh, no!' she cried; 'no one knows him but me!'

'Oh, if you would go to bed!' I said. 'Indeed I must insist: you will tell me your story in the morning. Come, you must not talk any more to-night.'

I did not get her disposed of so easily as this, but after a while she did allow herself to be persuaded. My mind had changed about her again, but I was too tired now to be frightened. I put her into the west room. And oh! how glad I was to lie down in my bed, though I had a stranger in the house whom I knew nothing of, and though it only wanted about an hour of day!

CHAPTER V

When I got up, about two hours after, I was in a very uncomfortable state of mind, not knowing in the least what I ought to do. Daylight is a great matter to be sure, and consoles one in one's perplexity; but yet daylight means the visits of one's friends, and inquiries into all that one has done and means to do. I could not have such an inmate in my house without people knowing it. I was thrusting myself as it were into a family quarrel which I knew nothing of—I, one of the most peaceable people—!

When I went down-stairs the drawing-room was still as I had left it, and the sofa and its cushions were all marked with dust where my poor visitor had lain down. I believe, though Mary is a good girl on the whole, that there was a little spite in all this to show me my own enormity. A decanter of wine was left on the table too, with the glass which had been used last night. It gave the most miserable, squalid look to the room, or at least I thought so. Then Mary appeared with her broom and dustpan, severely disapproving, and I was swept away, like the dust, and took refuge in the garden, which was hazy and dewy, and rather cold on this October morning. The trees were all changing colour, the mignonette stalks were long and straggling, there was nothing in the beds but asters and dahlias and some other autumn flowers. And the monthly rose on the porch looked pale, as if it felt the coming frost. I went to the gate and looked out upon the Green with a pang of discomfort. What would everybody think? There were not many people about except the tradespeople going for orders and the servants at their work. East Cottage looked more human than usual in the hazy autumn morning sun. The windows were all open, and White was sweeping the fallen leaves carefully away from the door. I even saw Mr. Reinhardt in his dressing-gown come out to speak to him. My heart beat wildly and I drew back at the sight. As if Mr. Reinhardt was anything to me! But I was restless and uncomfortable and could not compose myself. When I went in I could not sit down and breakfast by myself as I usually did. I wanted to see how my lodger was, and yet I did not want to disturb her. At last I went to the door of the west room and listened. When I heard signs of movement inside I knocked and went in. She was still in bed; she was lying half-smothered up in the fine linen and downy pillows. On the bed there was an eiderdown coverlet covered with crimson silk, and she had stretched out her arm over it and was grasping it with her hand. She greeted me with a smile which lighted up her beautiful face like sunshine.

'Oh, yes, I am better—I am quite well,' she said. 'I am so happy to be here.'

She did not put out her hand, or offer any thanks or salutations, and it seemed to me that this was good taste. I was pleased with her for not being too grateful or affectionate. I believe if she had been very grateful and affectionate I should have thought that was best. For again the charm came over me—a charm doubled by her smile. How beautiful she was! The warm nest she was lying in, and the pleasure and comfort she evidently felt in being there, had brought a little colour to her cheeks—just a very little—but that became her beauty best. She was younger than I thought. I had supposed her to be over thirty last night, now she looked five or six-and-twenty, in the very height and fulness of her bloom.

'Shall I send you some breakfast?' I said.

'Oh, please! I suppose you don't know how nice it is to lie in a soft bed like this, to feel the nice linen and the silk, and to be waited upon? You have always been just so, and never known the difference? Ah! what a difference it is.'

'I have been very poor in my time,' said I.

'Have you? I should not have thought it. But never so poor as me. Let me have my breakfast please—tea with cream in it. May I have some cream? and—anything—whatever you please; for I am hungry; but tea with cream.'

'Surely,' I said; 'it is being prepared for you now.'

And then I stood looking at her, wondering. I knew nothing of her, not even her name, and yet I stood in the most familiar relation to her, like a mother to a child. Her smile quite warmed and brightened me, as she lay there in such childish enjoyment. How strange it was. And it seemed to me that everything had gone out of her mind except the delightful novelty of her surroundings. She forgot that she was a stranger in a strange house, and all the suspicious, unpleasant circumstances. When Mary came in with the tray she positively laughed with pleasure, and jumped up in bed, raising herself as lightly as a child.

'You must have a shawl to put round your shoulders,' I said.

'Oh, let me have the beautiful one you put over me last night. What a beauty it was! Let me have that,' she cried.

Mary gave me a warning look. But I was indignant with Mary. I went and fetched it almost with tears in my eyes. Poor soul! poor child! like a baby admiring it because it was pretty. I put it round her, though it was my best; and with my cashmere about her shoulders, and her beautiful face all lighted up with pleasure, she was like a picture. I am sure the Sleeping Beauty could not have been more lovely when she started from her hundred years' sleep.

I went back to the dining-room and took my own breakfast quite exhilarated. My perplexities floated away. I too felt like a child with a new toy. If I had but had a daughter like that, I said to myself—what a sweet companion, what a delight in one's life! But then daughters will marry; and to think of such a one, bound to a cruel husband, who quarrelled with her, deserted her—Oh, what cruel stuff men are made of! What pretext could he have for conduct so monstrous? She was as sweet as a flower, and more beautiful than any woman I ever saw; and to leave her sitting in the dust at his closed door! I could scarcely keep still; my indignation was so great. The bloodless wretch! without ruth, or heart, or even common charity. One has heard such tales of men wrapped up in some cold intellectual pursuit; how they get to forget everything, and despise love and duty, and all that is worth living for, for their miserable science. They would rather be fellows of a learned society than heads of happy houses; rather make some foolish discovery to be written down in the papers, than live a good life and look after their own. I have even known cases—certainly nothing so bad as this—but cases in which a man for his art, or his learning, or something, has driven his wife into miserable solitude, or still more miserable society. Yes, I have known such cases: and the curious thing is, that it is always the weak men, whose researches can be of use to no mortal being, who neglect everything for science. The great men are great enough to be men and philosophers too. All this I said in my heart with a contempt for our scientific gentleman which I did not disguise to myself. I finished my breakfast quickly, longing to go back to my guest, when all at once Martha and Nelly, the Admiral's daughters, came running in, as they had a way of doing. They were great favourites of mine, or, at least, Nelly was—but I was annoyed more than I could tell to see them now.

'We came in to ask if you were quite well,' said Nelly. 'Papa frightened us all with the strangest story. He insists that you came home quite late, leaning on Mary's arm, and was sure you must have been ill. You can't think how positive he is, and what a story he made out. He saw you from his window coming along the road, so he says; and now I look at you, Mrs. Mulgrave, you are a little pale.'

'It was not I, you can tell the Admiral,' I said. 'I wonder his sharp eyes were deceived. It was a—friend—I have staying with me.'

'A friend you have staying with you? Fancy, Nelly! and we not to know.'

'She came quite late—yesterday,' said I. 'She is in—very poor health. She has come to be—quiet. Poor thing, I had to give her my arm.'

'But I thought you were at the Stokes' last night?' said Martha.

'So I was; but when I came back it was such a lovely night; you should have been out, Nelly, you who are so fond of moonlight. I never saw the Green look more beautiful. I could hardly make up my mind to come in.'

Dear, dear, dear! I wonder if all our fibs are really kept an account of? As I went on romancing I felt a little shiver run over me. But what could I do?

Nelly gave me a look. She was wiser than her sister, who took everything in a matter-of-fact way. She gave me a kiss, and said, 'We had better go and satisfy papa. He was quite anxious.'

Nelly knew me best, and she did not believe me. But what story could I make up to Lady Denzil, for instance, whose eyes went through and through me, and saw everything I thought?

Then I went back to my charge. She had finished her breakfast, but she would not part with the shawl. She was sitting up in bed, stroking and patting it with her hand.

'It is so lovely,' she said, 'I can't give it up just yet. I like myself so much better when I have it on. Oh! I should be so much more proud of myself than I am if I lived like this. I should feel as if I were so much better. And don't ask me, please! I can't—I can't get up to put myself in those dusty hideous clothes.'

'They are not dusty now,' I said, and a faint little sense of difficulty crossed my mind. She was taking everything for granted, as if she belonged to me, and had come on a visit. I think if I had offered to give her my Indian cashmere and all the best things I had she would not have been surprised.

She made no answer to this. She continued patting and caressing the shawl, laying down her beautiful cheek on her shoulder for the pleasure of feeling it. It was very senseless, very foolish, and yet it was such pretty play that I was more pleased than vexed. I sat down by her, watching her movements. They were so graceful always—nothing harsh, or rough, or unpleasant to the eye, and all so natural—like the movements of a child.

I don't know how long I sat and watched her—almost as pleased as she was. It was only when time went on, and when I knew I was liable to interruption, that I roused myself up. I tried to lead her into serious conversation. 'You look a great deal better,' I said, 'than I could have hoped to see you last night.'

'Better than last night? Indeed, I should think so. Please, don't speak of it. Last night was darkness, and this is light.'

'Yes, but— I fear I must speak of it. I should like to know how you got there, and if some one perhaps ought to be written to—some one who may be anxious about you.'

'Nobody is anxious about me.'

'Indeed I am sure you must be mistaken,' I said. 'I am sure you have friends, and then— I don't want to trouble you, but you must remember I don't know your name.'

She threw back the shawl off her shoulders all at once, and sat up erect.

'My name is Mrs. Reinhardt: I told you,' she said, 'and I hope you don't doubt my word.'

It was impossible to look in her face, and say to her, 'I don't know anything about you. How can I tell whether your word is to be trusted or not?' This was true, but I could not say it.

I faltered, 'You were ill last night, and we were both excited and confused. I wish very much you would tell me now once again. I think you said you would.'

'Oh, I suppose I did,' she said, throwing the shawl away, and nestling down once more among the pillows. A look of irritation came over her face. 'It is so tiresome,' she said, 'always having to explain. I felt so comfortable just now, as if I had got over that.'

There was an aggrieved tone in her voice, and she looked as if, out of her temporary pleasure and comfort, she had been brought back to painful reality in an unkind and uncalled-for way. I felt guilty before her. Her face said plainly, 'I was at ease, and all for your satisfaction, for no reason at all, you have driven me back again into trouble.' I cannot describe how uncomfortable I felt.

'If I am to be of any use to you,' I said apologetically, 'you must see that I ought to know. It is not that I wish to disturb you.'

'Everybody says that,' she murmured, with an angry pull at the bedclothes; and then, all at once, in a moment, she brightened up, and met my look with a smile. My relief was immense.

'I am a cross thing,' she said; 'don't you think so? But it was so nice to be comfortable. I felt as it I should like to forget it all, and be happy. I felt good— But never mind; you cannot help it. I must go back to all the mud, and dirt, and misery, and tell you everything. Don't look distressed, for it is not your fault.'

Every word she said seemed to convince me more and more that it was my fault. I could scarcely keep from begging her pardon. How cruel I had been! And yet, and yet— My head swam, what with the dim consciousness in my mind of the true state of affairs, and the sense of her view of the question, which had impressed itself so strongly upon me since I came into the room. Which was the right view I could not tell for the moment, and bewilderment filled my mind. I could only stare at her, and wait for what she pleased to say.

PART II

CHAPTER VI

After my visitor had got over her little fit of passion I took up my shawl—my good shawl, which she had flung from her—and put it away; and then I sat down by the bedside to hear her story. She had begun to think; her face had changed again. Her bewildered sort of feeling (which I could not understand, but yet which seemed so natural) that she had got over all that was disagreeable, passed away, and her life came back to her, as it were. She remembered herself, and her past, which I did not know. She did not speak for some time, while I sat there waiting. She kept twitching at the clothes, and moving about restlessly from side to side. The look of content and comfort which had filled up the thin outline of her beautiful face, and given it for the moment the roundness of youth, disappeared. At last she looked up at me almost angrily as I sat waiting.

'Oh, you are so calm,' she said. 'You take it all so quietly. You don't know what it is to have your heart broken, and your character destroyed, and yourself driven mad. To see you so calm makes me wild. If I am to tell you my story I must get up; I must be my own self again; I must put on my filthy clothes.'

'They are not filthy now. There are some clean things, if you like to use them,' I said softly; but I was very glad she should get up. I left her to do so with an easier mind, and had the fire made up in the dining-room that she might not be in the way of visitors. It was a long time before she came, and when she at last made her appearance I found she had again wrapped herself in my Indian shawl. To tell the truth, I did not like it. I gave a slight start when I saw her, but I could not take it from her shoulders. She had put on her old black gown, which had been carefully brushed and the clean cuffs and collar I had put out for her, and had dressed her hair in a fashionable way. She was dressed as poorly as a woman could be, and yet it appeared she had all the pads and cushions, which young women were then so foolish as to wear, for her hair. She was tall, and very slight, as I had remarked last night, but my shawl about her shoulders took away the angularity from her figure, and made it dignified and noble. To find fault with such a splendid creature for borrowing a shawl! I could as soon have remonstrated with the Queen herself.

'This is not the pretty room you brought me to last night,' she said.

'No; this is the dining-room. I thought it would be quieter and pleasanter for you, in case any one should call.'

'Ah! yes, that was very considerate for my feelings,' she said, 'but I am used to it, I am always thrust into a corner now. It did not use to be so before that man came and ruined me. Whereabouts is it that he lives?'

'You can see the house from the window,' said I.

Then she went to the window and looked out. She shook her clenched fist at the cottage; her face grew dark like a sky covered by a thunder-cloud. She came back and seated herself in front of me, wrapping herself close in my shawl.

'When I married him I was as beautiful as the day. That was what they all said,' she began. 'I was nineteen, and the artists used to go on their knees to me to sit to them. I might have married anybody. I don't know why it was that I took him, I must have been mad; twenty years older than me at the least, and nothing to recommend him. Of course he was rich. Ah! and I was so young, and thought money could buy everything, and that it would last for ever. We had a house in town and a house in the country, and he gave me a lovely phaeton for the park, and we had a carriage and pair. It was very nice at first. He was always a curious man, never satisfied, but we did very well at first. He was not a man to make a woman happy, but still I got on well enough till he sent me away.'

'He sent you away!'

'Yes. Oh! that was nothing; that got to be quite common. When he thought I was enjoying myself, all at once he would say, "Pack up your things; we shall go to the country to-morrow;" always when I was enjoying myself.'

'But if he went with you, that was not sending you away.'

'Then it was taking me away—which is much the same—from all I cared for; and he did not always go with me. The last two times I was sent by myself as if I had been a prisoner. And then, at last, after years and years of oppression, he turned me out of the house,' she said—'turned me out! He dared to do it. Oh! only think how I hated him. He said every insult to me a man could say, and he turned me out of his house, and bade me never come back. One day I was there the mistress of all, with everything heart could desire, and the next day I was turned out, without a penny, without a home, still so pretty as I was, and at my age!'

'Oh! that was terrible,' I cried, moved more by her rising passion than by her words—'that was dreadful. How could he do it? But you went to your friends—?'

'I had no friends. My people were all dead, and I did not know much about them when they were living. He separated me from everybody, and he told lies of me—lies right and left. He had made up his mind to destroy me,' she cried, bursting into sobs. 'Oh! what a devil he is! Everything I could desire one day, and the next turned out!'

Looking at her where she sat, something came into my throat which choked me and kept me from speaking: and yet I felt that I must make an effort.

'Without any—cause?' I faltered with a mixture of confusion and pain.

'Cause?'

'I mean, did not he allege something—say something? He must have given some—excuse—for himself.'

She looked at me very composedly, not angry, as I had feared.

'Cause? excuse?' she repeated. 'Of course he said it was my fault.'

She kept her eyes on me when she said this; no guilty colour was on her face, no flush even of shame at the thought of having been slandered. She was a great deal calmer than I was; indeed I was not calm at all, but disturbed beyond the power of expression, not knowing what to think.

'He is very clever,' she went on. 'I am clever myself, in a kind of a way, but not a match for him. Men have education, you see. They are trained what to do; but I was so handsome that nobody thought I required any training. If I had been as clever as he is, ah! he would not have found it so easy. He drove me into a trap, and then he shut me down fast. That is four years ago. Fancy, four years without anything, wandering about, none of the comforts I was used to! I wonder how I gave in at the time: it was because he had broken my spirit. But I am different now; I have made up my mind, until he behaves to me as he ought, I will give him no peace, no grace!'

'But you must not be revengeful,' I said, knowing less and less what to say. 'And if you were not happy together before, I am afraid you would not be so now.'

She did not make any answer; a vague sort of smile flitted over her face, then she gave a little shiver as of cold, and wrapped the shawl closer. 'A shawl suits me,' she said, 'especially since I am so thin. Do you think a woman loses as much as they say by being thin? It is my heart-disease. When it comes on it is very bad, though afterwards I feel just as well as usual. But it must tell on one's looks. Could you tell that I was thin by my face?'

'No,' I said, and I did not add, though it was on my lips, 'O woman, one could not tell by your face that you were not an angel or a queen. And what are you? What are you?' Alas! she was not an angel, I feared.

A little while longer she sat musing in silence. How little she had told me after all. How much more she must know in that world within herself to which she had now retired. At length she turned to me, her face lighted up with the most radiant smile. 'Shall I be a great trouble to you?' she asked. 'Am I taking up anybody's room?'

She spoke as a favourite friend might speak who had arrived suddenly, and did not quite know what your arrangements were, though she was confident nothing could make her coming a burden to you. She took away my breath.

'N—no,' I said; and then I took courage and added: 'But your friends will be expecting you—the people where you live: and you are better now—'

I could not, had my life depended on it, have said more.

'Oh, they will not mind much,' she said. 'I don't live anywhere in particular. When one thinks that one's own husband, the man who is bound to support one, has a home, and is close at hand, how do you think one can stay in a miserable lodging! But he does not care: he will sit there doing his horrible problems, and what is it to him if I were to die at his door! He would be glad. Yes, he would be glad. He would have me carted away as rubbish. He cares for nothing but his books and his experiments. I have sat at his door a whole night begging him to take me in, begging out of the cold and the snow, and his light has burnt steady, and he has gone on with his work, and then he has gone to bed and taken no notice. Oh, my God! I should have let him in had he been a cat or a dog.'

'Oh, surely, surely you must be mistaken,' I cried.

'I am not mistaken. I heard the window open; he looked down at me, and then he went away. I know he knew me: and so he did last night. He knew I was there; and he had a fire lighted in the room where he works. So he knew it was cold, too; and I his wife, his lawful wedded wife, sitting out in the chill. Some time or other he thinks it will be too much for me, and I shall die, and he will be free.'

'It is too dreadful to think of,' said I. 'I don't think he could have known that you were there.'

She smiled without making any further reply. She held out her thin hands to the fire with a little nervous shiver. They would have been beautiful hands had they not been so thin, almost transparent. She wore but one ring, her wedding-ring; and that was so wide that it was secured to her finger with a silk thread. I suppose she perceived that I looked at it. She held it up to me with a smile.

'See,' she said, 'how worn it is. But I have never put it off my finger; never gone by another name, or done anything to forfeit my rights. Whatever he may say against me, he cannot say that.'

At this moment she espied a chair in a corner which looked more comfortable than the one she was seated in, and rose and wheeled it to the fire. She said no 'By'r leave' to me, but did it as if she had been at home; there was something so natural and simple in this that I did not know how to object to it, but yet—I have had many a troublesome responsibility thrown upon me by strangers, but I was never so embarrassed or perplexed in my life. She drew the easy chair to the fire, she found a footstool and put her feet on it, basking in the warmth. She had my velvet slippers on her feet, my Indian shawl round her shoulders, and here she was settled and comfortable—for how long? I dared not even guess. A sick sort of consciousness came upon me that she had established herself and meant to stay.

After a while, during which I sat and watched, sitting bolt upright on my chair and gazing with a consternation and bewilderment which I cannot express upon her graceful attitude as she reclined back, wooing every kind of comfort, she suddenly drew her chair a little nearer to me and put her hand upon my knee.

'Look here,' she said hurriedly, 'you must see him for me. If any one could move him to do his duty it would be you. You must see him, and tell him I am—willing to go back. Perhaps he may not listen to you at first, but if you keep your temper and persevere—'

'I?' said I, dismayed.

'Yes, indeed, who else? only you could do it. And if you are patient with him and keep your temper—the great thing with him is to keep your temper—I never could do it, but you could. It would not be difficult to you. You have not got that sort of a nature, one can see it in your face.'

'But you mistake me, I—I could not take it upon myself,' I gasped.

'Not when I ask you? You might feel you were not equal to it, I allow. But when I ask you? Oh, yes, you can do it. It is not so very hard, only to keep your temper, and to take no denial—no denial! Make him say he will not be so unkind any more. Oh, how tired it makes me even to think of it!' she cried, suddenly putting up her hands to her face. 'Please don't ask me any more, but do it—do it! I know you can.'

And then she sat and rocked herself gently with her hands clasped over her face. This explanation had been too much for her, and somehow I felt that I was blamable, that it was my fault. I sat by her in a kind of dream, wondering what had happened to me. Was I under a spell? I did not seem able to move a step or raise a hand to throw off this burden from me. And the curious thing was that she never thanked me, never expressed, nor apparently felt, any sort of gratitude to me, but simply signified her will, and took my acquiescence as a right.

CHAPTER VII

I cannot tell how I got through that day: she got through it very comfortably, I think. In the evening she asked me to go into the pretty room she had been in last night.

'I am so fond of what is pretty,' she said; 'I like everything that is nice and pleasant. I never would sit in any but the best rooms in the house if I had a house like this.'

'But—someone might come in,' I said. 'To be sure the time for callers is over, but still my neighbours are very intimate with me, and some one might come in.'

'Well?' she said, looking up in my face. 'If they do, I don't mind. You may have objections perhaps, but I have none. I don't mind.'

'Oh! if you don't mind,' I said in my consternation; and I took up the cushion she had placed in her chair, and carried it humbly for her, while she made her way to the drawing-room.

I think I was scarcely in possession of my senses. I was dazed. The whole position was so extraordinary. I was ashamed to think of any one coming in and finding her there: not because I was ashamed of her, but for my own sake. What was I to say to anybody? How was I to explain myself? I had taken her in without knowing anything of her, and she had taken possession of my house. Fortunately, no one came that night. She placed herself on the sofa, where she had lain in her wretchedness the night before. She stretched herself out upon it, lying back with an air of absolute enjoyment. She had got a book—a novel—which she was reading, not taking very much notice of me; but now and then she would pause to say a word. I think had any one seen us seated together that evening, without knowing anything of the circumstances, he would have decided that she was the lady of the house and I her humble and rather stupid companion. But I was more than rather stupid—I felt like a fool; and that in nothing more than this—that I could not for my life tell what to do.

'Nobody is coming to-night, I suppose?' she said at last, putting down her book.

'No, I suppose not.'

'I thought from what you said you had always some one coming; and I like seeing people; I should like of all things to see some of the people here. Do you think if they saw me it would make any difference—? Oh, I can't tell you exactly what I mean. I mean—but it is so very unpleasant to be always obliged to explain;' and then she yawned: and then she said: 'I am so tired; I think I shall go to bed. Hush! was not that some one at the door?'

'It is my next neighbour going home,' I said.

'Does Reinhardt know the people about here?'

'He has not gone into society at all; but many of them know him to speak to,' said I.

'Ah! that is always the way; you hide me out of sight, and you send word to your people not to come; but everybody is quite ready to make friends with him. Oh! I am so tired—I am tired of everything; life is so dull, so monotonous, always the same thing over, no pleasure, no amusement.'

'I live a very dull, quiet life,' I said, as firmly as I could; 'I cannot expect it to suit you; and perhaps to-morrow you will be able to make arrangements to go to your own home.'

'Ah!' she said, giving a curious little cry. She looked at me, catching her breath; and then she cried, 'My own home!—my own home! That is at the cottage yonder; you will open the door for me, and take me back there—'

'But how can I? Be reasonable,' I said. 'I scarcely know—your husband; I don't know—you; how can I mediate between you? I don't know anything of the circumstances. There must have been some cause for all this. Indeed it will be a great deal better to go home and get some one to interfere who knows all.'

'Don't you believe in feelings?' she said suddenly. 'I do. The first time I saw Reinhardt I had the feeling I ought not to have anything to do with him, and I neglected it. When I saw you, it went through and through me like an arrow: 'This is the person to do it. And I always trust my feelings. I am sure that you can do it, and no one else.'

'Indeed—indeed you are mistaken.'

'Oh! I am so tired,' she cried again. 'Let me go to bed. I can't argue to-night; I am so dreadfully tired.'

This was her way of getting over a difficulty, and what could I do? I could not stop her from going to bed; I could not turn her out of my house. I went to the door of the west room with her, more embarrassed and uncomfortable than could be described. She turned round and waved her hand to me as she shut the door. The light of the candle which she held shone upon her pale, beautiful face. She had my shawl still round her. I, too, had a candle in my hand, and as I strayed back through the long passage I am sure I looked like a ghost. Bewilderment was in my soul. Had I taken a burden on my shoulders for life? Was I never to be free again? Never alone as I used to be? It had only lasted one day; but there seemed no reason why it should ever come to an end.

Then I went back and sat over the fire in the drawing-room, till it died away into white ashes, trying to decide what I should do. To consult somebody was of course my first thought; but whom could I consult? There was not one creature on the Green who would not blame me, who would not be shocked at my foolishness. I did not dare even to confess it to Lady Denzil. I must keep her concealed till I could persuade her to go away. And to think she should have been disappointed that nobody came! Good heavens! if anybody did come and see her, what should I do? Looming up before my imagination, in spite of all my resistance to it, came a picture of a possible interview with Mr. Reinhardt. It drove me half wild with fear to think of such a thing, and yet I felt as one sometimes does, that out of mere terror I should be driven to do it, if I could not persuade her to go away. That was my only hope, and I felt already what a forlorn hope it was.

And thus another day passed, and another night. She was quite well-behaved, and sometimes her beauty overwhelmed me so that I felt I could do anything for her; and sometimes her strange calmness and matter-of-course way of taking everything filled me with irritation. She never looked or spoke as if she were obliged to me, neither did she ever imply, by anything she said or did, that she meant to go away. She would stand for a long time by the window, gazing at the East Cottage; she even stepped out into the garden through the drawing-room window, and went and stood at the gate, looking out, though I called her back, and trembled lest she should be seen (and, of course, she was seen); but the answer she gave me when I objected put a stop to the controversy.

'You are afraid to let people see me,' she said; 'but I don't mind. There is nothing to be ashamed of in looking at Reinhardt's house. If any one calls, it is quite the same to me. Indeed I would rather be seen than otherwise. I think it is right that people should see me.'

To this I made no answer, for my heart was growing faint. And then she turned, and seized my arm—it was in the garden.

'Oh!' she said, 'listen to me. When are you going to see him? Are you going to-day?'

As she spoke the sound of footsteps quite close to us made me start. I had my back to the gate, and she was standing close to the verandah, so that she saw who was coming though I could not. She dropped my arm instantly; she subdued her voice; she put on a smile; and then she half-turned, and began to gather some rosebuds from the great monthly rose, with the air of one who is waiting to be called forward.

'Oh, Mrs. Mulgrave! we have found you at last,' said a voice in my ear, and, turning round, I saw the Stokes—Lottie and Lucy, and their brother Everard, a short way behind, following them on to the lawn.

'At last?' I said.

'Yes, and I think we have a very good right to complain. Why, you have shut yourself up for two whole days. The Green is in a commotion about it,' said Lottie, as she kissed me; and she threw a quick glance at the stranger, whom she did not know, and asked me, 'Who is that?' with her eyes.

'And somebody said you had visitors, but we would not believe it,' Lucy began, open-mouthed.

'And so she has—one visitor, at least,' said my guest, turning round, with her hand full of roses. Then she stopped short, and a look, which was half alarm, crept over her face. Everard Stoke was coming up behind.

'How do you do, Mrs. Mulgrave?' he said in his languid way. 'It is not my fault if I came in unceremoniously. It's the girls who are to blame.'

'There is no one to blame,' said I, turning round, and holding out my hand to him.

But even in the moment of my turning round a change had come over him. He gave a slight start, and he looked straight over my shoulder at my companion. I said to myself that perhaps they knew each other, and forgave him his rudeness. But the next moment he went on hastily, 'We must not stay now. Lottie, I have just remembered something I promised to do for my mother. I have just thought of it. Mrs. Mulgrave will excuse me. Come away quick, please.'

'Why, we have but just arrived!' said Lucy, full of a girl's resistance.

'Come!' her brother said; and before I could speak he had swept them away again, leaving me in greater consternation than ever. My companion had turned back, and was busy again among the roses, gathering them. I had not even her to respond to my look of wonder. What was the meaning of it? Could they have known each other, Everard and she?

'Your friends are gone very soon,' she said without turning to me; 'it is rather strange; but I suppose they are strange people. Oh! how sweet these roses are—I never thought such pale roses could be so sweet.'

I made her no answer, and, what was strangest of all, she did not seem to expect it, for immediately after she went back into the drawing-room, and the next minute I heard her voice singing as if on the way to her own room. The more I thought of it the more strange it seemed.

That night she began to question me about my neighbours on the Green, and somehow managed to bring the conversation to the people who had called.

'I thought I knew the man's face; I must have met him out,' she said, looking at me steadily.

Everard Stoke did not bear a good character on the Green. To have known him was no recommendation to any one; and this encounter did not increase my happiness. But after that first evening it did not disturb her. Next day went on like the previous one. I told the servants not to admit any visitors, and I felt as if I must be going mad. I could think only of one subject, my imagination could bring forward but one picture before me, and that was of a meeting with Mr. Reinhardt, which I kept going over in my mind. I said to myself, 'I could not do it—I could not do it,' with an angry vehemence, and yet I seemed to see just how he would look, and to hear what we were to say. It seemed to be the only outlet out of this impossible position in which I stood.

CHAPTER VIII

'Lady Denzil says she must see you, please, ma'am,' said Mary at my room door.

It had lasted for a week and I was downright ill. She would not go away; when I represented to her that I could not go on keeping her, that she must go to her own home, wherever that was, she either moaned that she had no home, or that I must open a way for her back to her husband. She was quite unmoved by my attempts to dislodge her. I told her I had people coming, and she assured me she did not mind, that there was plenty of room in the house, and that, if I wished it, she would change into a smaller chamber. This drove me almost out of my senses, I could not turn her out by force. I dared not face the criticisms of my neighbours: I shut myself up. I got a headache which never left me, and the result was, that I was quite ill. I had been lying down in my own room to try to get a little quiet and respite from the pain in my head; and I was impatient in my trouble, and felt disposed to turn my back on all the world.

'I cannot see her,' I said impatiently. 'I am not well enough to see any one.'

'Please, ma'am, is that what I am to say?' asked Mary.

Then I recollected myself. Lady Denzil was my close friend and counsellor. I had been admitted into the secret places of her life, and she knew me in every aspect of mine. I would not send such a reply to my old friend. I rose from my sofa and went stumbling to the door, feeling more miserable than I can say. 'Tell her I have a very bad headache, Mary. I will try to see her to-morrow. Give her my love, and say that I could not talk to-day, nor explain anything. If she will please leave it till to-morrow!—'

'Please, ma'am,' said Mary, earnestly, 'I think it would be a deal better if you could make up your mind to see my lady to-day.'

'I cannot do it—I cannot do it!' I said. 'If you but knew how my head aches! Give her my dear love, but I must keep quiet. If you tell her that, she will understand.'

'If you won't give no other answer, ma'am—' said Mary, disapprovingly; and I had lost my wits so completely that I actually locked the door when she went down-stairs, in case some one should force the way. I went back to my sofa and lay down again. I had closed the shutters, I don't know why—not that the light hurt me, but because I did not feel able to bear anything. I never lost my head in the same way before. I was irritable to such a degree that I could not bear any one to speak to me—this was, I suppose, because I felt that nobody would approve of me, and was ashamed of myself and my weakness. While I lay thus, she began to sing down-stairs; she had a pretty voice; there was a quaver in it, which was in reality a defect, but did not appear so when she sang. Her voice, I felt sure, could be heard half over the Green, and Lady Denzil would be sure to hear it, and what would they think of me? They would think she was a relation, somebody belonging to me, whom I had motive for hiding. No one would believe that she was a mere stranger whom I knew nothing of.

I kept as much away from her as I could during the day, and in the evening, when I came down-stairs, I managed to steal out by myself for a walk. I thought the fresh air would do me good, and, as all the people were at dinner, I was not likely to meet any one. When I felt myself outside and free, I stood still for a moment, and in my weakness three or four different impulses came upon me. In the first place I had a temptation to run away. It seems absurd to write it, but my feeling of nervous irritation was so great that I actually entertained for a moment the idea of abandoning my own house because this strange woman had taken possession of it. And then I thought of rushing to Lady Denzil, whom I had not long before sent away from my door, and entreating her to come and save me. When I had made but a few steps from my own gate a nervous terror made me pause again, and, turning round suddenly, I almost ran against some one coming in the opposite direction. I made a half-conscious clutch at him when I saw who it was, and then tried to hurry past in the fluctuations of my despair. But he stopped, struck, I suppose, by the strangeness of my looks.

'Can I do anything for you?' he asked.

'Oh, yes—everything!' I gasped forth, not knowing what I said.

'I! That is strange—that is very strange! but if it should be so!—Will you lean upon my arm, Mrs. Mulgrave? you are very much agitated.'

'Yes,' I said, 'I am very much agitated, but I will not lean upon you, for perhaps you will think I am your enemy—though I don't mean to be anybody's enemy, Heaven knows.'

'Ah!' he said. This little cry came from him unawares, and he fell back a step, and his face, which was like ivory, took a yellower pale tint. I do not mean that I observed this in my agitation at the moment, but I felt it. His countenance changed. He already divined what it was.

'I am very sure of that—that you mean only to be kind to all the world,' he said. He had a slight foreign accent, a roll of the r which is not in an English voice, and he spoke very deliberately, like one to whom English was an acquired language. I think this struck me now for the first time.

Then we paused and looked at each other—he on his guard; I, trembling in every limb trying to remember what I had said in my imaginary interviews with him, and feeling as if my very mind had gone. I made a despairing attempt to collect myself, to state her case in the best possible way, but I might as well have tried any impossible feat of athletics. I could not do it.

'There is a lady,' I faltered, 'in my house.'

A kind of smile crossed his face at the first words. He gave a nod as if to say, 'I know it;' but again a change came over him when I finished my sentence.

'In your house!'

'Yes, in my house,' I went on, finding myself at last wound up to speech. 'I found her on Friday last at your door—seated in the dust, almost dying.'

Here he stopped, making an incredulous movement—a shrug of the shoulders, an elevation of the eyebrows.

'It is true,' I said: 'she has heart-disease: she could scarcely walk the little distance to my house. Had you seen her, as I did, panting, gasping for very breath—'

'I should have thought it a fiction,' he said, bitterly, 'and I know her best.'

'It was no fiction. Oh, you may have had your wrongs. I say nothing to the contrary,' I cried: 'for anything I can tell, you may have been deeply wronged; but she is so beautiful, and so young, and loves pleasure and luxury so—'

I think he heard only the half of what I said, and that struck him like an unexpected arrow. He turned from me and walked a few steps away, and then came back again. 'So beautiful and so young,' he cried. 'Who should know that so well as I?—who should know that so well as I?'

'You know it, and still you let her sit at your door all through the lonely night? I would not let a tramp shiver at mine if I could help it. You let her perish within reach of you. You condemn her at her age, with her lovely face, unheard—'

He put out his hand to stop me. He was as much agitated as I was. 'Her lovely face,' he said to himself,—'oh, her lovely face!' That was the point at which I touched him. It woke recollections in him which were more eloquent than anything I could say.

'Yes,' I said, 'think of it.' I do not know by what inspiration I laid hold upon this feature of the story—her beauty; perhaps because it was the real explanation of the power she had acquired over me.

But in a minute more he had overcome his agitation; he came to a sudden pause in front of me and looked at me in the face, though there were signs of a conflict in his. 'It is vain to attempt to move me,' he said, hoarsely. 'I do not know why you should take it in hand, or why you should try to attain your object in this way. I did not expect it from such as you. Her lovely face—does that make her good or true or fit for a man's wife?'

'No doubt it was for that you married her,' said I, with an impulse I could not restrain.

He turned away from me again; he made a few hasty steps and then he came back. 'I do not choose to discuss my own history with a stranger,' he said; and then softening into politeness: 'You said I could do something for you. What can I do?'

This question suddenly brought me to a standstill, for even in my perplexity and confusion, and the state of semi-despair I had been thrown into by my visitor, a vestige of reason still remained in my mind. After all he must know her and his own concerns better than I could. His question seemed to stop my breath. 'She is in my house,' I said.

'You are too charitable, Mrs. Mulgrave,' he answered harshly. His voice sounded loud and sharp to me after the subdued tone in which we had been speaking, for we were the only two living creatures visible on the Green. Everything was quiet around us, and the night beginning to fall.

'I did not mean to be charitable,' I said, feeling that there was, without any consciousness of mine, a tone of apology in my voice. 'I did not expect—what has happened. I meant her to leave me—next day.'

'She will never leave you as long as you will keep her and give her all she wants,' he said, in the same sharp, harsh voice.

'Then Heaven help me!' I cried, in my confusion, 'what am I to do?'

He seized my arm, so that he hurt me, in what seemed a sudden access of passion. 'It will teach you not to thrust yourself into other people's concerns, or meddle with what does not concern you,' he said. He had come quite close to me, and his face was flushed with passion. I think it was the only time I was ever so spoken to in my life. The effect was bewildering, but I was more surprised than afraid. In short, the curious shock of this unexpected rage, the rude, sudden touch, the angry voice, brought me to myself.

'I think you forget yourself, Mr. Reinhardt,' I said.

Then he dropped my arm as if the touch burned him, and turned away, and shook, as I could see, with the effort to control himself. His passion calmed me, but it swept over him like a storm. He muttered something at length, hurriedly, in which there was the word 'pardon,' as if he were forced most unwillingly to say it, and then he turned round upon me again: 'I may have forgotten myself, as you say; but you force me to face a subject I would give the world to forget, and in the only way that makes it unavoidable. Good heavens! your amiability, and your Christianity, and all that, force me to take up again what I had put from me for ever. And you look for politeness, too!'

I did not make any answer: what was the use? At bottom, I did blame myself; I should not have interfered; I should have been firm enough and strong enough to take her to her home, wherever it was: I did not stand upon my defence. I let him say what he would; and I cannot tell how long this went on. I suppose the interval was not nearly so long as it seemed to me. He stood before me, and he smiled and frowned, and ground his teeth and discharged, as it were, bitter sentences at me. Englishmen can be brutal enough, but no Englishman, I think, would have done it in this way. He seemed to take a pleasure in saying everything that was most disagreeable. When he scowled at me I could bear it, but when he smiled and affected politeness I grew so angry that I could have struck him. Poor wretch! perhaps there was some justification for him after all.

'Because you are a woman!' he cried. 'A woman!—what it is to be a woman! It gives you a right to set every power of hell in motion, and always to be spared the consequences; to upset every arrangement of the world, and disturb the quiet, and put your fingers into every mess, and always to be held blameless. That is your right. Oh, I like those women's rights! I should have knocked down the man who had interfered as you have done; but, because you are a woman, I must come out of my quiet, I must derange my life, to save you from your folly. God in heaven! was that what those creatures, those slaves, those toys were made for? To interfere—for ever to interfere—and to be spared the consequences at any cost to us?'

I don't know how I bore it all. I got tired after a while of the mere physical effort of standing to listen to him. I did not try to answer at first, and after the torrent began I could not, he spoke so fast and so vehemently. But at length I turned from him, and walked slowly, as well as I was able, to my own door. He paused for a moment as if in surprise, and then turned and walked on with me, talking and gesticulating. 'Nothing else would have disturbed me,' he said; 'I had made my arrangements. How was I to tell that a fool, a woman,—would thrust herself into it, and put it on my honour as a gentleman to free her? What has honour to do with it? Why should I trouble more for a woman—an old woman— than for a man? Bah! Ah, I will be rude; yes, I am rude; it is a pleasure—it is a compensation. You are plain; you are old. You have lost what charms. Therefore, what right have you to be considered? Why should you not bear your own folly? Why should I interfere?'

'Pray make yourself quite easy about me,' I said, roused in my turn. 'I did not appeal to you on my account, and anything you can do for me would be dearly purchased by submitting to this violence. Go your own way, and leave me to manage my own concerns.'

He stopped, bewildered; and then he asked with confusion, 'What do you call your own concerns?'

'Nothing that can any way affect you,' I said, and in my passion I went in at my own gate and closed it upon him. I stood on one side defying him, and he stood on the other with confusion and amazement on his face.

'You do not wish my help any more?'

'No more. I shall act for myself, without thought of you,' I said. He stood and gazed at me for a moment, and then suddenly he turned round and left me. I looked after him as he walked rapidly away, and I confess that, notwithstanding my indignation and pride, my heart sank. He was the only creature who could help me, and I had driven him away. I had taken once more upon myself the task which it had made me half frantic to think of. My heart fell. I looked back upon my house, which had been such a haven of quietness and rest for so many years, and felt that the Eden was spoiled—that it was no longer my paradise. And yet I had rejected the only help! I was very forlorn, standing there with my hand upon my gate under the chilly October stars, having thrust all my friends from me, and refused even the only possible deliverance. 'I cannot allow myself to be insulted,' I said to myself, trying to get some comfort from my pride, but that was cold consolation. I turned round to go in, sighing and ready to sink with fatigue and trouble; and then I suddenly heard moans coming from the house, and Mary calling and beckoning from the open door.

CHAPTER IX

'Oh, ma'am, the poor lady's took bad—the poor dear lady's took very bad!' This was Mary's cry as she hurried me in. The windows were all wide open to give her air. She was lying on the sofa gasping for breath, her mouth and her eyes open, two hectic circles of red upon her cheeks, and that wildly anxious look upon her face which always accompanies a struggle for breath. I did not feel at all sure that she was not dying. I called out to my cook to run instantly for the doctor. Both the women had been in the room running about as she gave them wild orders, opening the windows one after another, fetching her fans, eau-de-cologne, water, wine—as one thing after another occurred to her. She stretched out her hands to me as I came in, and grasped and pulled me to her; she said something which I could not make out in her gasping, broken voice, and I nodded my head and pretended to understand, saying, 'Yes, yes,' to calm her—'Yes, yes.' It did not seem to matter what one said or promised at such a moment. For some time, every gasp looked to me as if it must be her last. I bathed her forehead with eau-de-cologne, I wetted her lips with wine; I had hard ado not to cry out, too, in sympathy with her distress. I shut down now one window, now another, fearing the cold for her, and then opening them again, in obedience to her gestures to give her air. I seem to see and to feel now, as I recall it, the room so unlike itself, with the cold night air blowing through and through it, and the great squares of blackness and night, with a bit of sky in one, which broke confusedly the familiar walls, and made it doubtful to my bewildered and excited mind whether I was out of doors or in—whether the chairs and sofa and the lamp on the table had been transported into the garden, or the garden had invaded the house. The wind made me shiver; the flame of the lamp wavered even within its protecting glass; darkness and mystery breathed in; and, in the centre absorbing all thoughts, was this struggle between, as I thought, death and life. I cannot tell how time passed, or how long we were in this suspense; but it seemed to me that half the night must have been over before the doctor came, in evening dress, with huge white wristbands, as if he were going to perform an operation. Notwithstanding the anxiety I was in, this fantastic idea flashed across my mind: for his cuffs were always too long and white. But it was a relief beyond description when he came: the responsibility, at least, seemed to be taken off my shoulders. I had scarcely permitted myself to hope before that the paroxysm was already beginning to subside; but now it became evident to me; and Dr. Houghton gave her something, which at once relieved her. I sat down beside the sofa, feeling half stupefied with the sensation of relief, and watched her breathing gradually grow calmer, and the struggle abate. I think my own brain had given way slightly under the tension. It seemed to me that the room behind me was full of people whispering and flitting about, and that all kinds of echoes and murmurs of voices were coming in at the open windows. I suppose it was only my own maids, and Susan from the Admiral's next door who had come to see what was the matter; but the strange sensation of being almost in the open air, and the worn-out state in which I was, produced this effect. I could not move however to put a stop to it. I could do nothing but sit still and watch. And thus the scene of the first evening, when I brought this strange inmate home to my house, reproduced itself, with another bewildering effect, before my eyes. She was no longer dusty and miserable; her poor black dress was neat and covered by my shawl; her hair had been elaborately dressed, and, though a little disordered, still showed how carefully it had been arranged; but otherwise, the attitude, the look, were exactly the same. Her head was thrown back in utter exhaustion upon the dark velvet pillow, which showed it in relief, like a white cameo on the dark background of the pietra dura. Her eyes were softly closed, and her lips. The doctor, who had gone away to write a prescription, was struck by her wonderful beauty, as I had been that night. He started in his surprise when he came back and saw how she had dropped asleep. He drew me aside in his amazement; the discovery flashed upon him all in a moment, as it had done on me. When a woman is very ill, when one's mind is full of anxiety for her, her beauty is the last thing one thinks of. So that the sudden sight of her confounded him. 'How beautiful she is!' he said in my ear with a certain agitation; and though I am only a woman, I had been agitated, too, when I found it out.

It was just when the doctor had said this that my eye was suddenly caught by a strange figure at one of the open windows. It stepped on to the sill, dark against the blackness without, and there paused a moment. Had this occurred at any other time I should, no doubt, have been very much frightened, I should have rushed to the window and demanded to know what he wanted, with terror and indignation; but to-night I took it as a matter of course. I did not even move, but kept still by the side of my patient's sofa and looked at him: and when he came in it seemed to me the most natural thing in the world. He entered with a sudden, impetuous movement as if something had pushed him forward. He advanced into the middle of the room—into the little circle round the sofa. It was Mr. Reinhardt. He had never been in my house before, or in any house on the Green, and Dr. Houghton looked at him and looked at me with positive consternation. For my part, I gave him no greeting. I did not say a word. It seemed natural that he should come, that was all.

There was a curious sort of smile upon his face; he was wound up to some course of action or other. What he thought of doing I cannot tell. His face looked as if he had come with the intention of taking her by the shoulders and turning her out. I don't know why I thought so, but there was a certain mixture of fierceness, and contempt, and impatience in his look which suggested the idea. 'I have come to put a stop to all this. I shall not put up with it for a moment longer.' Though he did not speak a word, this seemed to sound in my ears, somehow, as if he had said it in his mind. But when he came to the sofa and saw her laid out in that dead sleep, her face white as marble, the blue veins visible on her closed eyelids, the breath faintly coming and going, he came to a sudden pause. I think for the first moment he thought she was dead. He gave a short cry, and then turned to me wildly, as if I were responsible. 'You have killed her,' he said. He was in that state of suppressed passion in which anything might happen. He would have railed at her had he found her conscious, he would have railed at me if I would have let him: he was half mad.

'Tell him,' I said, turning to the doctor. Dr. Houghton was a man of the world, and tried very hard not to look surprised. He put his hand upon Mr. Reinhardt's shoulder to draw him away: but he would not be drawn away. He stood fast there, with his brows contracted and his eyes fixed on the sleeping face: he listened to the doctor's explanations without moving or looking up. He said not a word further to any one, but drew a chair in front of the sofa and sat down there with his eyes fixed upon her. Oh, what thoughts must have been going through his mind. The woman whom he had loved—I do not doubt passionately in his way—whom he had married, whom he had cast away from him! And there she lay before him unconscious, unaware of his presence, beautiful as when she had been his, like a creature seen in a dream.

'He had better be got to go away before she wakes,' Dr. Houghton said in my ear. 'Do you think you can make one more exertion, Mrs. Mulgrave, and send him away? Can you hear what I am saying? She will be in a very weak state, and any excitement might be dangerous. I don't know what connection there is between them, but can't you send him away? Who is this next?'

This time it was a very timid figure at the window, a halting, furtive old man peeping in. And somehow this, too, seemed quite natural to me. I felt that I knew everything that happened as if I had planned it all beforehand. 'It is his servant come to look for him,' said I. And the doctor went to the window with impatience and pulled poor old White in, and shut it down.

'The draught goes through and through one,' he said, with a shiver. It was quite true; I was trembling with cold where I sat by the sleeping woman's side; but it had not occurred to me to shut the window; everything seemed unchangeable, as if we had nothing to do with it except to accept whatever happened. When White came in he looked round him with great astonishment, and made me a very humble, frightened bow, while he whispered and explained to the doctor how it was he had taken the liberty. Then he gradually approached his master;—but when he saw the figure on the sofa consternation swallowed up all his other sentiments. He flung his arms above his head and uttered a stifled cry, and then he rushed at his master with a sudden vehemence which showed how deeply the sight had moved him. He put his hand upon Mr. Reinhardt's shoulder and shook him gently.

'Sir, sir!' he cried; then stooped to his ear and whispered, 'Master; Mr. Reinhardt; master!' Reinhardt took no notice of the old man, he sat absorbed with his eyes fixed on that marble, beautiful face. 'Oh, sir, come with me! Oh! come with me, my dear master!' said the old man. 'You know what I'm saying is for your good—you know it's for your good. It's getting late, sir, time for the house to be shut up. Oh, Mr. Reinhardt—sir, come away with me! come with me—do!'

Mr. Reinhardt pushed him impatiently away, but did not answer a word; he never removed his eyes from her for a moment. They seemed to me to grow like Charon's eyes, like circles of fire, while he gazed at her. Was it in wrath—was it in love?

'Mrs. Mulgrave, ma'am,' cried White, turning to me, but always in a voice which was scarcely above a whisper, 'Oh, speak to him! It ain't for his good to sit and stare at her like that. I know what comes of it. If he sits like that and looks to her it'll all begin over again. He ain't a man that can stand it, he ain't indeed. Oh, my lady, if you'll be a friend to him, speak and make him go.'

'Ah!' said a soft, sighing voice. 'Ah! old White!' We all started as if a shell had fallen among us: and yet it was not wonderful that she should wake with all this conversation going on by her bed—and besides she had slept a long time, more than an hour. She had not changed her position in the least, all she had done was to open her eyes. I don't know whether it was simply her supreme yet indolent self-estimation which kept her from paying us the compliment of making any movement on our account, or if it was from some consciousness that her beauty could not be shown to greater advantage. But certainly she did not move. She only opened her eyes, and said, 'Ah, old White!'

But oh, to see how the man started, who was nearer to her than White! It was as if a ball or a sword-stroke had gone through him. He sprang from his chair, and then he checked himself and drew it close and sat down again. He glanced round upon us all as if he would have cleared not only the chamber but the world of us, had it been possible, and then he leant over her and said sternly, 'There are others here besides White.'

'Ah!' Either she was afraid of him or pretended to be; she clutched at my sleeve with her hand, she shrank back a little, but still did not change her attitude nor raise herself so as to see his face.

'I am here,' he went on, his voice trembling with passion. 'I whom you have hunted, whose life you have poisoned. Oh, woman! you dare not look at me nor speak to me, but you wrong me behind my back. You whisper tales of me wherever I go. Here I had a moment's peace and you have ruined it. Tell these people the truth once in your life. Is it I that am in the wrong or you?'

A frightened look had stolen over her face, her eyebrows contracted as with fear. Her eyes became full of tears, and the corners of her beautiful mouth quivered. Heaven forgive me! I asked myself was it all feigning, or had she something kinder and better in her which I had never seen till now? But those eyes, which were like great cups of light filled with dew, once more turned to him. She remained immovable, looking up to his face, when he repeated hoarsely, 'You or I, which is in the wrong?'

She answered with a shiver which ran all over her, 'I.' Her voice was like a sigh. I did not know what his wrongs might be, but whatever they were, at that moment there could be no doubt about it. He, a hard, unsympathetic, inhuman soul, it must be he that was in the wrong, not she, though she confessed it so sweetly; and if this effect was produced upon me, what should it be upon him?

Mr. Reinhardt shook like a leaf in the wind. He had not expected this. It was a surprise to him. He had expected to be blamed. It startled him so, that for the moment he was silent, gazing at her. But old White was not silent. 'Oh! master, master, come away, come home,' he pleaded, wringing his hands; and then he came and touched my shoulder and cried like a child. 'Speak to him, send him away!' he cried. 'It is for his own good. If she speaks to him like that, if she keeps her temper, it is all over; it will have all to be begun again.'

Reinhardt made a long pause. He looked as if he were gathering up his strength to speak again, and when he did so, it was with the fictitious heat of a man whose heart is melting. 'How dare you say "I,"' he said, 'when you do not mean it?—when all your life you have said otherwise? You have reproached me, stirred up my friends against me, kept your own sins in the background and published mine. You have done this for years, and now is it a new art you are trying? Do not think you can deceive me,' he cried, getting up in his agitation; 'it is impossible. I am not such a credulous fool.'

She kept her eyes on the ceiling, not looking at him; the moisture in them seemed to swell, but did not overflow. 'I may not change then?' she said, very low. 'I may not see that I am wrong? I am not to be permitted to repent?'

He turned from her and began to pace up and down the room; he plucked at his waistcoat and cravat as though they choked him. More than once he returned to the sofa as if with something to say, but went away again. When White approached, he was pushed away with impatience, and once with such force that he span round as he was driven back. This last repulse seemed to convince him. 'Be a fool, then, if you will, sir,' he said sharply, and withdrew altogether into a corner, where he watched the scene. I do not think Reinhardt even saw this or anything else. He was walking up and down hastily like a man out of his mind, struggling, one could not but see, with a hundred demons, and tempting his fate.

He came back again however in his tumultuous uncertainty, and bent over her once more. 'Talk of repentance—talk of change,' he cried bitterly. 'How often have you pretended as much? Do you hear me, woman?' (bending down so close that his breath must have touched her)—'how often have you done it? how often have you pretended? Oh, false, false as death!'

She put her hand upon his shoulder, almost on his neck. He broke away from her with a hoarse cry; he made another wild march round the room. Then he came back.

'Julia,' he cried, 'Julia, Julia, Julia! Mine!'

She lay still as a tiger that is going to spring. He fell on his knees beside her, weeping, storming in his passion. Good Lord! was it my doing? was I responsible? White gave me a furious look, and rushed out of the room. The husband and wife were reconciled.

CHAPTER X

This is about the end of the story so far as I am concerned. He spent the night there by her sofa, kissing her dress and her hands, and watching her in a transport of passion and perhaps delight. For the last I would not answer. It must have been at best a troubled joy; and a man's infatuation for a beautiful face is not what I call love, though it is often a very tragic and terrible passion. He took her away in the morning, but not to his own house. They went straight from mine to London, that great receptacle of everybody's misery and happiness. I saw them both before they left, though only for a moment. She was still lying on the sofa as when I left her, and the half disorder of her hair, the exhaustion in her face, seemed rather to enhance her beauty. Any one else would have looked jaded and worn out, but a faint flush of triumph and satisfaction had stolen over her (partly perhaps produced by her weakness) and woke the marble into life. She stretched out her hand to me carelessly as I went in. She said with a smile, 'You see my feeling was right. I always trust my feelings. I knew you were the person to do it, and you have done it. I felt it whenever I saw your face.'

'I hope it will be lasting, and that you may be happy,' I said, faltering, not knowing what tone to take.

'Oh, yes, it is to be hoped so. He is going to take me to London,' she answered carelessly. 'I am quite sorry to leave your nice house, everything has been so comfortable. It is small and it is plain, but you know how to make yourself comfortable. I suppose when one has lived so long one naturally does.'

This was all her thanks to me. The husband took the matter in a different way. They had a fire lighted and coffee taken to them in the drawing-room (which was left in the saddest confusion after all the disturbance of the night); and it was when the carriage he had ordered was at the door, and she had gone to make herself ready, that he came to me. I was in the dining-room with my breakfast on the table, which I was too much worn out to take. His face was very strange; it was full of suppressed excitement, with a wild, strained look about the eyes, and a certain air of heat and haste, though his colour was like ivory as usual. 'I have to thank you,' he said to me, very stiffly, 'and if I said anything amiss in my surprise last night, I hope you will forgive it. I can only thank you now; nothing else is possible. But I must add, I hope we shall never meet again.'

'I assure you, if we do, it shall not be with my will,' said I, feeling very angry as I think I had a right to be.

He bowed, but made no reply; not because words failed him. I felt that he would have liked nothing better than to have fallen upon me and metaphorically torn me to pieces. He had been overcome by his own heart or passions, and had taken her back, but he hated me for having drawn him to do so. He saw the tragic folly of the step he was taking. There was a gloom in his excitement such as I cannot describe. He had no strength to resist her, but she was hateful to him even while he adored her. And doubly hateful, without any counter-balancing attraction, was I, who had as it were betrayed him to his fate.

'I trust your wife and you will be happy—now,' I said, trying to speak firmly. He interrupted me with a hoarse laugh.

'My wife!'

'Is she not your wife?' I said in alarm.

He laughed again, even more hoarsely, with a sharp tone in the sound. 'What do you call a woman who is taken back after—everything? Who is taken back because— What is she, do you suppose? What is he, the everlasting dupe and fool! Don't speak to me any more.' He hurried away from me, and then turned round again at the door. 'I spoke a little wildly perhaps,' he said, with a smile, which was more disagreeable than his rage, 'without due thought for Mrs. Reinhardt's reputation. Make yourself quite easy—she is my wife.'

That was the last I saw of them. I was too much offended to go to the door to see them leave the house, but it is impossible to describe the relief with which I listened to the wheels ringing along the road as they went away. Was it really true?—was this nightmare removed from me, and my house my own again? I did not know whether to laugh or to cry. I fell down on my knees and made some sort of confused thanksgiving. It seemed to me as if I had been in this horrible bondage half my life.

Mary came in about half-an-hour after to take away the breakfast things. I had swallowed a cup of tea, but I had not been able to eat. Mary was still disapproving, but quieter than at first; she shook her head over the untouched food. 'We'll be having you ill next, ma'am,' she said, with an evident feeling that cook and she would in that case have good reason to complain; and then, after a pause, she added severely, 'I don't know if you knew, ma'am, as the lady is gone off in your best shawl?'

'My shawl!' I had thought no more of it: but this sudden news took away my breath.

'She was always fond of it,' said Mary grimly. 'She liked the best of everything did that lady; and she couldn't make up her mind to take it off when she went away.'

Though I was so confounded and confused, I made an effort to keep up appearances still. 'She will send it back, of course, as soon as she gets—home,' I said; 'as soon as she gets—her own things.'

'I am sure I hope so, ma'am,' said Mary, carrying off her tray. Her tone was not one to inspire hope in the listener, and I confess that for the rest of the morning my shawl held a very large place in my thoughts. It was the most valuable piece of personal property I possessed. When I used to take it out and wrap it round me, it was always with a certain pride. It was the kind of wrap which dignifies any dress. 'With that handsome shawl, it does not matter what else you wear,' Mrs. Stoke was in the habit of saying to me; and though Mrs. Stoke was not a great authority in most matters, she knew what she was saying on this point. I said to myself, 'Of course she will send it back,' but I had a very chill sensation of doubt about my heart.

All the morning I sat still over the fire, with a longing to go and talk to some one. For more than a week now, I had not exchanged a word with my neighbours, and this was terrible to a person like me, living surrounded by so many whose lives had come to be a part of mine. But I had not the courage to take the initiative. I cannot tell how I longed for some one to come, for the ice to be broken. And it was only natural that people should be surprised and offended, and even have learned to distrust me. For who could they suppose I was hiding away like that—some mysterious sinner belonging to myself—some one I had a special interest in? And then she had been recognized by Everard Stoke!

At about twelve o'clock my quietness was disturbed by the sound of some one coming; my heart began to beat and my face to flush, but it was only old White with his fellow-servant, Mississarah, as he called her, pronouncing the two words as if they were one. Their visit put me in possession of the whole miserable story. It was like a tale of enchantment all through. The man had been a mature man of forty or more, buried in science and learning, when he first saw the beautiful creature who since seemed to have been the curse of his life. She was an innkeeper's daughter, untaught and unrefined. He had tried to educate her, married her, done everything that a man mad with love could do to make her a lady— nay, to make her a decorous woman—but he had failed and over again failed. They did not tell me, and I did not wish to hear, what special sins she had done against him. I suppose she had done everything that a wicked wife could do. She had been put into honourable retirement with the hope of recovery again and again. Then she had been sent away in anger. But every time the unfortunate husband had fallen under her personal influence—the influence of her beauty—she had been taken back.

'She hates him,' poor White said, almost crying, 'but he can't resist her. He's mad, ma'am, mad, that's what it is. He could kill hisself for giving in, but he can't help hisself. We've had to watch him night and day as he shouldn't hear her nor see her, for when her money's done she always comes back to him. He'll kill her some day or kill hisself. Mississarah knows as I'm speaking true.'

'As true as the Bible,' said Mississarah; but she was softer than he towards the wife. 'He was too wise and too good for her, ma'am,' she said, 'a fool and a wise man can't walk together—it's hard on the wise man, but maybe it's a bit hard too on the fool. Folks don't make themselves. She mightn't have been so bad—'

'Oh, go along; go along, Mississarah, do,' said White. 'We'll have to go off from here where all was quiet and nice, and start again without knowing no more than Adam. But he'll kill her, some day, you'll see, or he'll kill hisself.'

Mississarah was a north-country woman, and had a little feeling that her master was a foreigner, and therefore necessarily more or less guilty; but White was half a foreigner himself and totally devoted to his master. When they had poured forth their sorrows to me, they went away disconsolate, and their fears about leaving East Cottage were so soon justified that I never saw them more.

And then came my melancholy luncheon, which was set on the table for me, and which I loathed the sight of. To escape from it I went into the drawing-room, from which all traces of last night's confusion were gone. I was so miserable, and lonely, and weary that I think I dropped asleep over the fire. I had been up almost all night, and there seemed nothing so comfortable in all the world as forgetting one's very existence and being able to get to sleep.

I woke with the murmur of voices in my ears. Lady Denzil was sitting by me holding my hand. She gave me a kiss, and whispered to me in her soft voice,—'We know all about it—we know all about it, my dear,' patting me softly with her kind hand. I'm afraid I broke down and cried like a child. I am growing old myself, to be sure, but Lady Denzil, thank Heaven, might have been even my mother—and if you consider all the agitation, all the disturbance I had come through!

I think everybody on the Green called that day, and each visitor was more kind than the other. 'I shall always consider it a special providence, however, that none of us called or were introduced to her,' Mrs. General Perronet said solemnly. But she was the only one who made any allusion to the terrible guest I had been hiding in my house. They took me out to get the air—they made me walk to the Dell to see the autumn colour on the trees. They carried me off to dine at the Lodge, and brought me home with a body-guard. 'You are not fit to be trusted to walk home by yourself,' Lottie Stoke said, giving me her arm. In short, the Green received me back with acclamations, as if I had been a returned Prodigal, and I found that I could laugh over the new and most unexpected rôle, which I thus found myself filling, as soon as the next day.

Some time after, I received my shawl in a rough parcel, sent by railway. It was torn in two or three places by the pins it had been fastened with, and had several small stains upon it. It was sent without a word, without any apologies, with Mrs. Reinhardt's compliments written outside the brown paper cover, in a coarse hand. And that was the only direct communication I ever had with my strange guest. Before Christmas however there was a paragraph in some of the papers that L. Reinhardt, Esq., had volunteered to accompany an expedition going to Africa in order to make some scientific observations. There was a great crowded, enthusiastic meeting of the Geographical Society, in which his wonderful devotion was dwelt on and the sacrifice he was making to the interests of science. And he was even mentioned in the House of Commons, where some great personage took it upon him to say that in the arrangement of the expedition the greatest assistance had been received from Mr. Reinhardt, who, himself a man of wealth and leisure, had generously devoted his energies to it, and smoothed away a great many of the difficulties in the way—a good work for which science and his country would alike be grateful to him, said the orator. Oh, me! oh, me! I looked up in Lady Denzil's face as Sir Thomas read out these words to us. Sir Thomas took it quite calmly, and was rather pleased indeed that Mr. Reinhardt, by getting himself publicly thanked in the House of Commons, had justified the impulse which prompted himself, Sir Thomas Denzil, head as it were of society on the Green, to call upon him. But my lady laid her soft old hand on mine, and her eyes filled with tears. 'Do not let us blame him, my dear,—do not let us blame him,' she said to me when we were alone. She had known what temptation was.

LADY ISABELLA

CHAPTER I

There was one house in our neighbourhood which was perfect and above criticism. I do not mean to say that it was a great house; but the very sight of it was enough to make you feel almost bitter if you were poor, and much pleased and approving if you were well-off. Naturally it was the very next house to Mrs. Merridew's, who had heaps of children and a small income, and could not have things so very nice as might have been wished. Mrs. Spencer and Lady Isabella lived within sight of her, with but two holly-hedges between; the hedge on the side of the Merridews' house was bristly and untidy, but on the other side it was trimmed and clipped till it looked like a barrier-wall of dark green Utrecht velvet; and inside that inclosure everything was in perfection; the lawn was mown every other day; there was never an obtrusive daisy on it, and no fallen leaf presumed to lie for half an hour. The flower-beds which surrounded it were more brilliant than any I ever saw—not mere vulgar geraniums and calceolarias, but a continual variety, and always such masses of colour. Inside everything was just as perfect. They had such good servants, always the best trained of their class; such soft carpets, upon which no step ever sounded harsh; and Mrs. Spencer's ferns were the wonder of the neighbourhood; and the flowers in the two drawing-rooms were always just at the point of perfection, with never a yellow leaf or a faded blossom. We poorer people sometimes tried to console ourselves by telling each other that such luxury was monotonous. 'Nothing ever grows and nothing ever fades,' said Lottie Stoke, 'but always one eternal beautifulness; I should not like it if it were I. I should like to watch them budding, and pick off the first faded leaves.' This Lottie said with confidence, though she was notoriously indifferent to such cares, and declared, on other occasions, that she could not be troubled with flowers, they required so much looking after; but poor little Janet Merridew used to shake her head and groan with an innocent envy that would bring the tears to her eyes; not that she wished to take anything from her neighbours, but she loved beautiful things so much, and they were so far out of her reach.

Mrs. Spencer and Lady Isabella lived together in this beautiful house; they were two friends so intimately allied, that I was in the habit of saying they were more like man and wife than anything else. It was a wonder to us all at Dinglefield how they managed their money matters in respect to housekeeping. Many a little attempt I have seen to find this out, and heard many a speculation; whether the house was Mrs. Spencer's, whether Lady Isabella only paid for her board, which of them was at the expense of the carriage, or whether they kept a rigid account of all their expenditure and divided it at the end of the year, as some thought—nobody could make out. When they first came to Dinglefield it was universally prophesied that it would not last. 'Depend upon it, these arrangements never answer,' was the opinion of old Mr. Lloyd, who was Mrs. Damerel's father, and lived with them at the rectory. 'They will quarrel in three months,' the Admiral said, who was not very favourable to ladies. But when seven years had come and gone, Mrs. Spencer and Lady Isabella still lived together and had not quarrelled. By this time Lady Isabella, who was really quite young when they came, must have been nearly five-and-thirty, and people had made up their minds she would not marry now, so that the likelihood was, as it had lasted so long, it would last all their lives. They did not, at the first glance, look like people likely to suit each other. Mrs. Spencer was a woman overflowing with activity; she was thin, she could not have been anything else, so energetic was she, always in motion, setting everybody right. She was shortsighted, or said she was shortsighted, so far as the outer world was concerned, but in her own house, and in all that involved her own affairs, she had the eye of a lynx; nothing escaped her. It was she who kept everything in such beautiful order, and made the lawns and the flowers the wonder of the neighbourhood. Lady Isabella's part was the passive one; she enjoyed it. She did not worry her friend by pretending to take any trouble. She was full ten years younger than Mrs. Spencer, inclining to be stout, pretty, but undeniably inactive. I am afraid she was a little indolent, or, perhaps, in such close and constant contact with her friend's more active nature, Lady Isabella had found it expedient to seem more indolent than she was. She left all the burdens of life on Mrs. Spencer's shoulders. Except the one habitual walk in the day, which it was said Mrs. Spencer compelled her to take, lest she should grow fat, we at Dinglefield only saw Lady Isabella in her favourite easy-chair in the drawing-room, or her favourite garden-bench on the lawn. Indolent—but not so perfectly good-tempered as indolent people usually are, and fond of saying sharp things without perhaps always considering the feelings of others. Indeed she seemed to live on such a pinnacle of ease and wealth and comfort, that she must have found it difficult to enter into the feelings of such as were harassed, or careworn, or poor. She had a way of begging everybody not to make a fuss when anything happened; and I am afraid most of us thought that a selfish regard for her own comfort lay at the bottom of this love of tranquillity. I don't think now that we were quite right in our opinion of her. She had to go through a great deal of fuss whether she liked it or not; and I remember now that when she uttered her favourite sentiment she used to give a glance, half-comic, half-pathetic, to where Mrs. Spencer was. But she bore with Mrs. Spencer's 'ways' as a wife bears with her husband. Mrs. Spencer had all the worry and trouble, such as it was. Plenty of money is a great sweetener of such cares; but still, to be sure, it was easy for Lady Isabella to sit and laugh and adjure everybody not to make a fuss, when she herself had no trouble about anything, never had even to scold a servant, or turn an unsatisfactory retainer away.

We were never very intimate, they and I; but it happened, one autumn evening, that I went in to call rather out of the regular order of calls which we exchanged punctiliously. When I say we were not intimate, I only mean that there was no personal and individual attraction between us. Of course we knew each other very well, and met twice or thrice every week, as people do at Dinglefield. I had been calling upon Mrs. Merridew, and I cannot tell what fascination one found—coming out of that full house, which was as tidy as she could make it, but not, alas! as tidy as it might have been—in the next house, which was so wonderful a contrast, where the regions of mere tidiness were overpast, and good order had grown into beauty and grace. I suppose it was the contrast. I found myself going in at the other gate almost before I knew it; and there I found Lady Isabella alone, seated in the twilight, for it was growing dark, in her favourite corner, not very far from the fire. She was not doing anything; and as I went in, I fancied, to my great surprise, that something like the ghost of a sigh came to greet me just half a moment in advance of Lady Isabella's laugh. She had a way of laughing, which was not disagreeable when one came to know her, though at first people were apt to think that she was laughing at them.

'Mrs. Spen is out,' she said, 'and I am quite fatigued, for I have been standing at my window watching the Merridew babies in their garden. They look like nice little fat puppies among the grass; but it must be damp for them at this time of the year.'

'Poor little things! there are so many of them that they get hardy; they are not used to being looked after very much. Some people's children would be killed by it,' said I.

'How lucky for the little Merridews that they are not those people's children!' said Lady Isabella; 'and I think they must like it, for it is a great bore being looked after too much.' As she spoke she leant back in her chair with something that sounded like another sigh. 'I was rather fond of babies once,' she added, with a laugh which quickly followed the sigh. 'Absurd, was it not? but don't say a word, or Mrs. Spen will turn me out.'

'It would take more than that to part you two,' said I.

'Well, I suppose it would. I think sometimes it would take a great deal. Mrs. Mulgrave, do you know I have been turning it over in my mind whether I could ask you to do something for me or not? and I think I have decided that I will—that is not to say that you are to do it, you know, unless you please.'

'I think most likely I shall please—unless it is something very unlike you,' said I.

'Well, it is unlike me,' said Lady Isabella; and though I could not make out her face in the least, I felt sure, by the sound of her voice, and a certain movement she made, and an odd little laugh that accompanied her words, that she was blushing violently in the dark. 'At least, it is very unlike anything you know of me. You might not think it, perhaps,' she went on, with again that little constrained laugh, 'but do you know I was young once?'

'My dear, I think you are young still,' said I.

'Oh dear, no; that is quite out of the question. When a woman is over thirty, she ought to give up all such ideas,' said Lady Isabella, with an amount of explanatoriness which I did not understand; and she began to fold hems in her handkerchief in a nervous way. 'When a woman is thirty, she may just as well be fifty at once for any difference it makes.'

'I don't think even fifty is anything so very dreadful,' said I. 'One's ideas change as one gets older; but twenty years make a wonderful difference, whatever you may think.'

'Perhaps, for some things,' she said hastily. 'And you must know, Mrs. Mulgrave, in that fabulous time when I was young other marvels existed. They always do in the fabulous period in all histories; and there was once somebody who was—or at least he said he was—in love with me. There, the murder is out,' she said, pushing her chair a little further back into the dark corner; and, to my amazement, her voice was full of agitation, as if she had been telling me the secret of her life.

'My dear Lady Isabella,' I said, 'do you really expect me to be surprised at that?'

'Well, no, perhaps not,' she said, with another laugh. 'Not at the simple fact. They say every woman has such a thing happen to her some time in her life. Do you think that is true?'

'The people in the newspapers say it can't be true,' said I, 'now-a-days: though I don't think I ever knew a woman who had not—'

'Mrs. Spen will be back directly,' cried Lady Isabella, hastily, 'and I don't want her to know. I need not tell you that it all came to nothing, for you can see that; but, Mrs. Mulgrave, now comes the funny part of it. His regiment is coming to the barracks, and he will be within five miles of us. Is it not odd?'

'I don't think it is at all odd,' said I. 'I dare say it is just in the natural order. If it will be painful to you to meet him, Lady Isabella—'

'That is the funniest of all,' she said. 'It will not be in the least painful to me to meet him. On the contrary, I want to meet him. It is very droll, but I do. I should so like to see what he looks like now, and if his temper is improved, and a hundred things. Besides, his sister used to be a great friend of mine; and when we broke it off I lost Augusta too. I want so much to know about her. Indeed, that is my chief reason,' she went on faltering, 'for wishing to meet him.' The words were scarcely spoken when she burst into a little peal of laughter. 'What a stupid I am,' she cried, 'trying to take you in. No, Mrs. Mulgrave, let me be honest; it is not for Augusta I want to see him. I should so like just to make sure— you know—if I was a very great fool, or if he was worth thinking of after all. Now,' with a little sigh, 'when one is perfectly dispassionate—and cool—'

'To be sure,' said I, glad that it was dark, and she could not see me smile; 'and now that we have settled all that, tell me what I am to do.'

'You are so very kind,' she said; and then went off again in that agitated laugh. 'I am betraying myself frightfully; but I am sure you will understand me, Mrs. Mulgrave, and not think anything absurd. You are sure to get acquainted with him, you know; and if you would ask him to the cottage—and ask us to meet him— Good heavens! what a fool you must think me,' she cried: 'but I should like it, I confess.'

'But, my dear, I never give dinners,' I said; 'and to ask a man, a strange man, to tea—'

'He would be sure to come—to you,' she said very quickly, as if her breath had failed her.

'But, my dear, you are just as likely as I am—more likely—to meet him at other houses. It would be impossible otherwise. Not that I should mind asking him—though it is so odd to ask a man to tea.'

'Hush!' she said, suddenly leaning forward and grasping my arm. 'Mrs. Spen has told Lady Denzil—she meant it for kindness—so we shall not be asked to meet him. And I do wish it, just for once. Hush, here she is coming. I don't want her to know.'

'Then, my dear, I will do it,' said I, grasping her hand. It trembled and was hot, and she grasped mine again in an agitated, impetuous way. Could this be Lady Isabella, who was always so calm and self-possessed? I was rather afraid of her in general, for she had the name of being satirical; and this was entirely a new light on her character. But just then Mrs. Spencer came in, and scolded us for sitting in the dark, and rang for lights; and then no more could be said.

It was curious to look at the two when the lamp came. Mrs. Spencer seated herself on her side of the fire, like the husband coming in from his day's work. She was a clever woman, but she was matter-of-fact, and notwithstanding the long years they had lived together, was never quite sure what was the meaning of her friend's jibes and jests. It was this as much as anything that gave a sort of conjugal character to their relationship. Friends who were merely friends, and were so different, would, one was inclined to suppose, have got rid of each other years ago. But these two clung together in spite of all their differences, as if there were some bond between them which they had to make the best of. Mrs. Spencer began talking the moment she came in.

'I met Mrs. Damerel on the Green and she was asking for you, Isabella; in short, she was quite surprised to see me out alone. "I thought Lady Isabella always walked once a day at least," she said. "And so she pretends to do," said I. And I told her what I said to you before I went out about your health. Depend upon it your health will suffer. A young woman at your age getting into these chimney-corner ways! Mrs. Mulgrave, don't you agree with me that it is very wrong?'

'Don't scold me, please,' said Lady Isabella, out of her corner; 'if you both fall upon me, I am rather nervous to-night, and I know I shall cry.'

At this Mrs. Spencer laughed; just as a husband would have done, taking it for the merest nonsense; yet somehow propitiated, for there was an inference of superior wisdom, importance, goodness on his—I mean her—part, such as mollifies the marital mind. No one could have been more utterly bewildered than she, had she known that what her friend said was literally true. Lady Isabella had drawn a little screen between her and the fire, which sheltered her also from the modest light of the lamp; and I felt by the sound of her voice, that though, no doubt, she could restrain herself, it would have been a relief to her to have shed the tears which made her eyes hot and painful. She would have laughed, probably, while she was shedding them, but that makes no difference.

'You don't do enough, and Lady Denzil does too much,' said Mrs. Spencer. 'She surprises me, and I think I am as active as most people. I can't tell why she does it, I am sure. She is an old woman; it can't be any pleasure to her. There is a dinner-party there to-night, and another on Saturday; and on Monday the dance for those young Fieldings that are staying there—enough to kill a stronger woman. But these little, fragile beings get through so much. She keeps up through it all and never looks a pin the worse.'

'Are you going there to-night?' said I. I had scarcely said it when I saw a little flutter behind the screen, and felt it was a foolish question. But it was too late.

'No,' said Mrs. Spencer, pointedly; and she looked straight at Lady Isabella's screen with a distinctness of intimation that this abstinence was on her account, which would have puzzled me much but for the previous explanation I had had. Words would have been much less emphatic. She nodded her head a great many times, and she gave me a look which promised further information. She was fond of her companion, and I am sure would have sheltered her from pain at almost any cost to herself; but yet she enjoyed the mystery, and the story which lay below. 'All the officers from the barracks will be there,' she added, after a pause. 'There is a Captain Fielding, an empty-headed—but they are all empty-headed. I don't care much about soldiers in an ordinary way, and I dislike guardsmen. So does Isabella.'

And then there followed one of those embarrassing pauses which come against one's will when there is any secret undercurrent which everybody knows and nobody mentions. Lady Isabella sat perfectly silent, and I, who ought to have come to the rescue,—I, after running wildly in my mind over every topic of conversation possible,—at last rose to take my leave, not finding anything to say.

'Are you going, Mrs. Mulgrave?' said Lady Isabella. 'I will go to the door with you. I must show you the new flowers in the hall.'

'Good gracious, something must be going to happen,' said Mrs. Spencer, 'when Isabella volunteers to show you flowers. Don't catch cold in the draught; but it is too dark: you can't possibly see any colour in them now.'

'Never mind,' said Lady Isabella in an undertone; and she hurried out leading the way,—a thing I had never seen her do before. She made no pretence about the flowers when we got out to the hall. It was quite dark, and of course I could see nothing. She grasped my hand in a nervous, agitated way. She was trembling,—she, who was always so steady and calm. It was partly from cold, to be sure, but then the cold was caused by emotion. 'His name is Colonel Brentford,' she whispered in my ear; and then ran up-stairs suddenly, leaving me to open the door for myself. I have received a great many confidences in my life, but seldom any so strange as this. I did not know whether to laugh or to be sorry, as I walked home thinking over it. Lady Isabella was the last person in the world to be involved in any romance; and yet this was romantic enough. And it was so difficult to make out how I could perform my part in it. Ask a guardsman, a strange colonel, a man, to tea! I could not but reflect how foolish I was, always undertaking things that were so difficult to perform. But I was pledged to do it, and I could not go back.

CHAPTER II

I was to dine at Sir Thomas Denzil's that same evening, and so no doubt would Mrs. Spencer and Lady Isabella have done, but for that obstacle which the elder lady had set up and in which the younger seemed determined to foil her. I dressed to go out, with my heart beating a little quicker than usual. For myself, as may be supposed, the officers from the barracks were not very much to me; but the undertaking with which I suddenly found myself burdened was very serious, and made me nervous in spite of myself; and then the man's very name was strange to me. I thought over all my acquaintances, and everybody I had ever known; but I could not remember any one of the name of Brentford. There were the Brentwoods of Northam, and the Bentleys, and a great many names came up to my mind which sounded like it at the first glance; but I could not recollect a single Brentford among all my acquaintance. 'I wonder who his mother was?' I said to myself; for, to be sure, there might be a means of getting at him in that way; but it was impossible to find out at so short a notice. I almost felt as if I were a designing woman when I went into Lady Denzil's drawing-room—and so I was, though I did not want to marry any of those unconscious warriors either personally or by proxy. Little did Lady Denzil suspect, as I went up to her—trying to look as innocent as possible—and little did the men of war think, of my evil projects, as they looked blandly at me, and set me down as that harmless and uninteresting being—an old lady. The one who took me in to dinner was an elderly, sober-looking, quiet gentleman. He was a Major Somebody, and I don't think he was so fine as the others. I drew breath when I had seated myself under his wing. It was a comfort to me to have escaped the young ones, who never forgive you, when they have to take you in to dinner, for not being young and pretty. This was a man who had no pretensions above me—a man, probably, with a wife of his own and a large family, whom one could speak to freely and ask questions of. But before I would go so far, I made what private inspection I could. It was quite evident to me where the gap was which Mrs. Spencer and Lady Isabella ought to have filled. It had been hastily filled up by Lottie and Lucy Stoke, who were very much more to the taste of the guardsmen, I don't doubt, than if they had been their own grandmothers, ladies of county influence and majesty. Lucy, whose blue eyes were dancing in her head with mingled fright and delight to find herself in such a grand party, sat by a handsome dark man, to whom my eyes returned a great many times. He looked the kind of man whom a woman might be faithful to for years. Could it be him? He was amused with Lucy's excitement and her fright; perhaps he was flattered by it as men so often are. After a little while, I could see he took great pains to make himself agreeable; and I felt quite angry and jealous, though I am sure I could not have told why.

'Perhaps you recognize him?' my companion said to me, as he caught me watching this pair across the table. 'He is one of the Elliots. His father had a place once in this neighbourhood. I am sure you must recollect his face.'

'No, indeed,' said I, denying by instinct. 'That gentleman opposite—is his name Elliot? I was looking at the young lady by him. She is a little friend of mine, and I am petrified to find her here. I did not think she was out.'

'That is why she likes it so well, I suppose,' said the Major with a little sigh.

'I am afraid you don't enjoy it much,' said I. 'Pray forgive me for being so very stupid. I should like to know which of these gentlemen is Colonel Brentford. I have heard his name—I should like to know which is he.'

'He is sitting beside Lady Denzil,' said my companion shortly; and he said no more. His brevity startled me. I think Colonel Brentford from that moment began to lose in my opinion. I grew more and more frightened by the thought of what I had undertaken to do. I began to think it was a great pity Lady Isabella, a sensible woman, should waste a thought upon this soldier—and all for no reason in the world but that my Major announced curtly, 'He is sitting beside Lady Denzil,' without adding a word to say, 'I like him,' or 'He is a very nice fellow,' or anything agreeable. I concluded he must be a bear or a brute, or something utterly frivolous and uninteresting. It never occurred to me that it might be my Major and not the unknown Colonel who was to blame. And I had pledged myself to ask such a man as this to tea!

We had gone back to the drawing-room before I got what I could call a good look at him; and then I was even more disappointed to find that he was as far from looking a brute or a bear as he was from looking a hero. There was nothing remarkable about him; he was neither handsome nor ugly; he was neither young nor old. He stood and talked a long time to Lady Denzil, and his voice was pleasant, but the talk was about nothing—it was neither stupid nor clever. He was a man of negatives it seemed. I was dreadfully disappointed for Lady Isabella's sake. I could not help figuring to myself what her feelings would be. No doubt he had been young when they had known each other, and youth has often a deceiving glitter about it, which never comes to anything. Chance threw my Major in my way again at that advanced period of the evening. He said to me, 'We have a long drive and the night is chilly, and I wish I could get my young fellows into motion. These proceedings don't always agree with the taste of a man at my time of life; and my wife is always fidgety when I am out late—it is her way.'

'Mrs. Bellinger is not here to-night?' I said.

'No, we are quite new to the place, and Lady Denzil has not had time to call yet: my wife, I am sure, would be delighted if you would go and see her. She is rather delicate, and far from her friends. Colonel Brentford is the only one—' And here he stopped short with an abruptness that made me hate Colonel Brentford and repent my temerity more and more.

'I am so sorry you don't seem to have a favourable opinion of him,' I said; 'not that I know him, but I have heard some friends of mine— Oh, I am sure you did not mean to say a word against him—'

'Against him!' said the Major, stammering; 'why, he is my best friend! He is the kindest fellow I know! He goes and sits with my wife when nobody else thinks of her. I don't want to find fault with any one; but Brentford—he is the man I am most grateful to in all the world!'

'Oh, I beg your pardon!' I cried. Good heavens! what a very bad manner the man must have had to give one such a false idea. 'I shall do myself the pleasure of calling on Mrs. Bellinger early next week,' I said; after all, it did not seem so insane to ask a man who was in the habit of going to sit with an invalid lady. And then a kind of inspiration stole into my mind. Afternoon tea! that was the thing; not an evening party, with all its horrors—which every man hates.

I don't know what Lady Denzil could think of me that evening; but I stayed until everybody had gone, with a determination to hear something more about him. I think she was surprised; but then she is one of those women who understand you, even when they don't in the least know what you mean. That seems foolish, but it is quite true. She saw I had a motive, and she forgave me, though she was tired, and Sir Thomas looked surprised.

'The fly has never come back for me,' I said. 'I must ask you to let George walk across the Green with me. I have got my big shawl, and I don't mind the cold.'

'Wait a little now they have all gone, and let us have a talk,' said Lady Denzil. What a blessing it is to have to do with a woman who understands!

'Our new friends are very much like all the others, I think,' said I. 'Captain Fielding seems nice. Is he brother or cousin to those pretty girls?'

'Brother, or I should not have him here,' said Lady Denzil; 'I have no confidence in cousins. Colonel Brentford looks sensible. I should not have thought him likely to do anything so foolish as that business you know. I suppose Mrs. Spencer must have told you.'

'No,' I said, with a little thrill running through me; for, of course, it was something about Lady Isabella that was meant—and I was actually an agent employed in the matter, and knew, and yet did not know.

'Lady Isabella and he were once engaged to be married,' said Lady Denzil, speaking low. 'Don't mention this, unless Mrs. Spencer tells you; but she is sure to tell you. And they quarrelled about some silly trifle. Mrs. Spencer says he flew into a passion, and that Lady Isabella had to give him up on account of his temper. He does not look like it, does he? Mrs. Spencer is most anxious that they should not meet.'

'Do you think it is right to prevent people meeting, if they wish it?' said I; 'perhaps Lady Isabella might think differently.'

'It is best never to interfere,' said Lady Denzil; 'that is my principle—unless I am sure I can be of real use. Are you going now? You must wrap up well, for the night is rather cold.'

'So my Major thought,' I said to myself, as I went across the Green; and I could not but smile at the thought of the poor gentleman buttoning up his great-coat as he drove with all those wild young fellows on their drag. Very likely he felt they might upset him at any moment driving through the dark—and it was a very dark night. My sympathies were much attracted by this good man. He had to give in to them a great deal, and put up with their foolish ways. I could not help wondering whether he had ever had such a commission given to him as mine; and then I reflected that Lady Isabella was not even young to be humoured and have her fancies given in to. The Colonel looked a sensible, commonplace sort of man, with whom nobody had any right to quarrel. And perhaps Mrs. Spencer was right in doing her utmost to keep them apart. Perhaps Mrs. Spencer was right; but then, on the other hand, Lady Isabella was old enough to know her own mind and decide for herself. Such were the various thoughts that passed through my mind as I took that little walk through the dark with George behind me. It was a perplexing business altogether. But that I should be mixed up in it! I could not but take myself to task, and ask myself what call had I to be thus mixed up with every sort of foolish business—a woman of my age?

I saw Lady Isabella two days after. She came running in quite early, before luncheon, to my extreme surprise, and gave me a wistful look of inquiry which went to my very heart. She could not say anything however, for the Fielding girls were with me, talking of nothing but the dance which Lady Denzil was going to give for them. They assailed Lady Isabella directly, the moment she entered.

'Oh, why are not you coming on Monday? Oh, Lady Isabella, do change your mind and come. It will be such a pretty dance. And all the officers are coming, so that there will be no want of partners. Lady Denzil says she always asks more men than ladies. Oh, Lady Isabella, do come!'

'That is very wise of Lady Denzil,' said Lady Isabella; 'but I wonder how the extra men like it. No; I don't think I shall go. I shall see all the officers, perhaps, another time.' And with that she gave me another look which made me tremble, holding me to my word.

'Perhaps you don't dance,' said Emma Fielding. 'Oh, it is such a pity you won't come.'

'My husband won't let me,' said Lady Isabella; 'and, by the by, she will be waiting for me now. I had something to ask, but never mind, another time will do.'

She asked the question all the same with her eyes. She looked at me almost sternly, inquiring, as plainly as words, 'Have you done it? Is my commission fulfilled?' which I could only answer by a deprecating, humble look, begging her as it were to have patience with me. She shook her head slightly as she shook hands with me, and smiled, and then she sighed. That was the worst of all. I read a reproach in the sound of that sigh.

'What does she mean by her husband?' said Edith Fielding. 'Is she married, and does she call her husband "she"? Isn't she very queer? That sort of person always bewilders me.'

I could not help saying, 'I dare say she does,' with a certain irritation. As if it were within the bounds of possibility that creatures like these should understand Lady Isabella. And yet, alas! if she were entering into the lists with them, how could she ever stand against them? She, five-and-thirty, and a little stout; they, eighteen and nineteen. Is there a man in the world that would not turn to the young ones, and leave the mature woman? That was the question I asked myself. I don't think I am cynical; I have not a bad opinion of my fellow-creatures in general; but still there are some matters which one knows beforehand. The first thing to be done however was to make acquaintance with Colonel Brentford as soon as possible. I had promised to go to the dance, to take Lottie and Lucy Stoke; but then he would be dancing; he would not want to stand in a corner and talk to an old woman like me. Lady Isabella, at five-and-thirty, had given up dancing; but this man, though he was nearly five years older, of course did not think of giving it up. Most likely he felt himself on the level of the Fieldings and Stokes and the other girls, not on that of his old love. Men and women are so different. But, at all events, I would do nothing before Monday: and in the meantime, I had promised to go and call on Major Bellinger's invalid wife. There had been something about him that pleased me. Not that he was attractive; but he had the look of a man who was not always at his ease, who had cares and perplexities in his life, and perhaps could not always make both ends meet. I always recognize that look. I am not very rich now, and never will be; but I once was poor, quite poor, and I know the look of it, and it goes to my heart.

Accordingly, the first day I was at liberty I drove into Royalborough to see Mrs. Bellinger. They were in a little house—one of the houses which people take for the purpose of letting them to the officers. It was opposite to a tall church, a three-storied house, with two rooms on each floor all the way up. There was a little oblong strip of garden in front and another oblong strip behind; and everything about it gave evidence that it was let furnished. But the little garden was rather pretty, and there was a virginian creeper hanging in rich red wreaths upon the walls. The drawing-room was the front room on the ground-floor. When I was shown in, it seemed to me that I interrupted the prettiest domestic scene. A lady, who looked very fragile and weak, though not ill, lay on a sofa in the room. Of course, she was Mrs. Bellinger. She was about forty, perhaps,—not much older than Lady Isabella. She had a lovely invalid complexion, a soft, delicate flush which came and went with every movement; her hair was beginning to get gray, and was partially covered by a cap. She looked very weak, very worn, very sweet and smiling, and cheerful. Near her, on a low chair, sat a gentleman with a book in his hand. He had been reading aloud, and had just stopped when I came to the door; and in front of him, at a little distance, seated on a stool, just by her mother's feet, sat a girl of seventeen or so, with her head bent over her work. This was Edith, the Major's favourite child, the only one at home. And the gentleman who had been reading aloud was Colonel Brentford, the man about whom my mind had been busy night and day.

I took the chair that was given me, and I began to talk, but all the freedom and ease were taken out of me. I felt as if I had received a blow. Poor Lady Isabella! I had already perceived that to put herself in competition with the young girls would be a hopeless notion indeed; but it was no longer the girls in general, some of whom were empty-headed enough, but Edith Bellinger in particular. Poor Lady Isabella! If she saw him once like this, I said to myself, she would not wish to see him again!

'My husband told me you were going to be so good,' said the invalid. 'He told me how kind you had been, asking for me. I am really quite well for me, and I am sure I could do a great deal more if they would but let me. Hush, Edie! I am dreadfully petted and spoiled, Mrs. Mulgrave. They make a baby of me, and Colonel Brentford is so kind as to come and read—'

'It is very good of him, I am sure,' I said mechanically; and then, without knowing what I was doing, I looked at Edith. She was quite unconscious of any meaning in my look. She smiled at me in return with all the sweet composure yet shyness of a child. Would he be equally unconscious? I raised my eyes and looked steadily at him. He bore my scrutiny very well indeed. I knew there was an angry flush on my face which I could not quite conceal, and an eager look of inquiry. It puzzled him, there was no doubt. A vague sort of wonder came into his eyes, and he smiled too. What could the old woman mean? I am sure he was thinking. Edith was very pretty, but then a great many girls are pretty. What was particular about her was her sweet look, which moved me even though I was so hostile to her. One saw she was ready to run anywhere, to do anything, at the least little glance from her mother. She was mending stockings—the homeliest work—and she looked such a serviceable, useful creature—so different from those Fielding girls, who thought of nothing but the dance. To be sure, the stockings and the useful look were much more likely to please me than to attract a guardsman; but I did not think of that in my sudden jealousy of her. Poor, poor Lady Isabella!

And he did not go away, as he would have done had this been a chance visit. He kept his place, and joined in the conversation as if he belonged to the house. When I asked Mrs. Bellinger to come and see me, he seconded me quite eagerly. He was sure she was able, he said; while Edith put her pretty head on one side, and looked very wise and very doubtful.

'Oh, Colonel Brentford, please don't be so rash—please don't!' said Edith. 'It is very, very kind of Mrs. Mulgrave, but we must think it over first—we must indeed.'

'I will send my pony,' said I; 'he is the steadiest little fellow, and it is such a pretty drive. The weather is so mild that I am sure it would do you good.'

'Now, Edith, please let me go,' said the invalid. 'Do not be such a little hard-hearted inexorable—Colonel Brentford is the kindest of you all. He is ready to let me have a little indulgence, and so is the Major, Mrs. Mulgrave; but Edith is the most odious little tyrant—'

'Mamma dear, it is for your good,' said Edith with the deepest gravity; and the mother and the friend looked at each other and laughed. How pretty it was to see her shaking her young head, looking so serious, so judicious, so full of care! 'No wonder if he is fond of her,' I said to myself. I felt my own heart melting; but, all the same, I steeled it against her, feeling that I was on the other side.

'And I am sure,' I said with an effort—for it seemed almost like encouraging him—'I shall be very glad to see Colonel Brentford too; if you will take the trouble to come so far for a cup of tea?'

He said it would give him the greatest pleasure, with a cordiality that made me cross, and got up and took his leave, shaking hands with me in his friendliness. Why was he so friendly, I wonder? When he was gone, Mrs. Bellinger launched into his praises.

'You must not think it is only me he is good to,' she said; 'he is kind to everybody. People laugh at the guardsmen, and make fun of them; but if they only knew George Brentford! Because they see him everywhere in society, they think he is just as frivolous as the rest. But if they knew what kind of places he goes to when nobody sees him—as we do, Edith?'

'Yes, mamma,' said Edith, as calm as any cabbage. The mother was quite moved by her gratitude and enthusiasm, but the daughter took it all very quietly. 'He means to be very kind, but he is rash,' said the little wise woman; 'he gives the boys knives and things, though he knows they always cut themselves. He thinks so much more of pleasing people than of what is right. If Mrs. Mulgrave would leave it open, mamma dear, and then we could see how you are.'

This was how it was finally decided; indeed, before I left, even after that first visit, I could see that things were generally decided as Edith thought best. They were to come on Saturday—the Saturday before the ball—if Mrs. Bellinger was well enough; and Colonel Brentford was to come too. I asked myself all the way back what Lady Isabella would think of the arrangement. That was not how she expected to meet him. She had wanted to see her old love—a man whom (I could not but feel) she had never quite put out of her heart—perhaps only to prove herself, perhaps to try if any lingerings of the old tenderness remained in him. And now that it was arranged, and she was really to see him, it was in company of a young bright creature who, there could be little doubt, was all to him that Lady Isabella had ever been. What a shock and bitter dispelling of all dreams for her! but yet, perhaps, to do that at once and at a blow was kindest after all.

CHAPTER III

As I drove home, strangely enough, I met the ladies on their afternoon walk. Mrs. Spencer was in advance as usual, talking rapidly and with animation, while Lady Isabella lagged a step behind, pausing to look at the ripe brambles and the beautiful ruddy autumn leaves.

'Just look what a bit of colour,' she was saying when I came up; but Mrs. Spencer's mind, it was evident, was full of other things.

'I wonder how you can care for such nonsense,' she said; 'I never saw any one so unexcitable. After me fussing myself into a fever, to preserve you from this annoyance! and I knew it would be too much for you—'

'Hush!' said Lady Isabella, emphatically, and then Mrs. Spencer perceived the pony carriage for the first time, and restrained herself. She changed her tone in a moment, and came up to me with her alert step when I drew the pony up.

'What a nice afternoon for a drive,' she said; 'have you been at Royalborough?—is there anything going on? I have dragged Isabella out for a walk, as usual much against her will.'

'I have been to make a call,' I said, 'on a poor invalid, the wife of Major Bellinger.'

'Oh, yes! I know, I know,' said Mrs. Spencer; 'he is to be the barrack-master. He rose from the ranks, I think, or something—very poor, and a large family. I know quite what sort of person she would be. The kind of woman that has been pretty, and has quite broken down with children and trouble—I know. It was very good of you; quite like yourself.'

'If it was very good of me, I have met with a speedy reward,' said I, 'for I have quite fallen in love with her—and her daughter. They are coming to me on Saturday—if Mrs. Bellinger is able—for afternoon tea.'

'I know exactly the kind of person,' said Mrs. Spencer, nodding her head. 'Ah, my dear Mrs. Mulgrave, you are always so good, and so—'

'Easily taken in,' she was going to say, but I suppose I looked very grave, for she stopped.

'Is the daughter pretty, too?' said Lady Isabella: a flush had come upon her face, and she looked at me intently, waiting, I could see, for a sign. She understood that this had something to do with the commission she had given me. And I was so foolish as to think she had divined my thoughts, and had fixed upon Edith, by instinct, as an obstacle in her way.

'Never mind the daughter,' I said hastily, 'but do come on Saturday afternoon, and see if I am not justified in liking the mother. I dare say they are not very rich, but they are not unpleasantly poor, or, if they are, they don't make a show of it; and a little society, I am sure, would do her all the good in the world.'

This time Lady Isabella looked so intently at me, that I ventured to give the smallest little nod just to show her that I meant her to come. She took it up in a moment. Her face brightened all over. She made me a little gesture of thanks and satisfaction. And she put on instantly her old laughing, lively, satirical air.

'Of course we shall come,' she said, 'even if this lady were not sick and poor. These qualities are great temptations to us, you are aware; but even if she were just like other people we should come.'

'Well, Isabella!' said Mrs. Spencer, 'you who are so unwilling to go anywhere!' but of course she could not help adding a civil acceptance of my invitation; and so that matter was settled more easily than I could have hoped.

I saw them the next day—once more by accident. We were both calling at the same house, and Lady Isabella seized the opportunity to speak to me. She drew me apart into a corner, on pretence of showing me something. 'Look here,' she said, with a flush on her face, 'tell me, do you think me a fool—or worse? That is about my own opinion of myself.'

'No,' I said, 'indeed I don't. I think you are doing what is quite right. This is not a matter which concerns other people, that you should be guided by them, but yourself.'

'Oh, it does not concern any one very much,' she said, with a forced laugh. 'I am not so foolish as to think that. It is a mere piece of curiosity—folly. The fact is, one does not grow wise as one grows old, though of course one ought. And—he is—really to be there on Saturday? Despise me, laugh at me, make fun of me!—I deserve it, I know.'

'He is really to come—I hope.' I said it faltering, with a sense of fright at my own temerity: and Lady Isabella gave me a doubtful, half-suspicious look as she left me. Now that it had come so near I grew alarmed, and doubted much whether I should have meddled. It is very troublesome having to do with other people's affairs. It spoiled my rest that night, and my comfort all day. I almost prayed that Saturday might be wet, that Mrs. Bellinger might not be able to come. But, alas! Saturday morning was the brightest, loveliest autumn morning, all wrapped in a lovely golden haze, warm and soft as summer, yet subdued and chastened and sweet as summer in its heyday never is: and the first post brought me a note from Edith, saying that her mamma felt so well, and was so anxious to come. Accordingly, I had to make up my mind to it. I sent the pony carriage off by twelve o'clock, that the pony might have a rest before he came back, and I got out my best china, and had my little lawn carefully swept clean of faded leaves, and my flower-beds trimmed a little. They were rather untidy with the mignonette, which had begun to grow bushy, but then it was very sweet; and the asters and red geraniums looked quite gay and bright. My monthly rose, too, was covered with flowers. I am very fond of monthly roses; they are so sweet and so pathetic in autumn, remonstrating always, and wondering why summer should be past; or at least that is the impression they convey to me. I know some women who are just like them, women who have a great deal to bear, and cannot help feeling surprised that so much should be laid upon them; yet who keep on flowering and blossoming in spite of all, brightening the world and keeping the air sweet, not for any reason, but because they can't help it. My visitor who was coming was, I think, something of that kind.

The first of the party to arrive were Major Bellinger and Colonel Brentford; they had walked over, and the Major was very eloquent about my kindness to his wife. 'Nothing could possibly do her so much good,' he said. 'I don't know how to thank you, Mrs. Mulgrave. Brentford says he made up his mind she must go the very first minute, whether she could or not—he said he was so sure you would do her good.'

'I am very glad Colonel Brentford had such a favourable opinion of me,' I said.

Then I stopped short, feeling very much embarrassed. If Lady Isabella had only come in then, before the ladies arrived—but, of course, she did not. She came only after Mrs. Bellinger was established on the sofa, and Edith had taken off her hat. They looked quite a family party, I could not but feel. Colonel Brentford, probably, was very nearly as old as the Major himself, and quite as old as the Major's wife; but then he had the unmarried look which of itself seems a kind of guarantee of youth, and his face was quite free of that cloud of care which was more or less upon both their faces. He was standing outside the open window with Edith when Mrs. Spencer and Lady Isabella came in. He did not see them. He was getting some of the monthly roses for her, which were high up upon the verandah. It was so high that it was very seldom we were able to get the flowers; but he was a tall man, and he managed it. Lady Isabella perceived him at once, and I saw a little shiver run over her. She gave Mrs. Bellinger, poor soul, but a very stiff salutation, and sat down on a chair near the window. She did not notice the girl. She had not thought of Edith, and no sort of suspicion as yet had been roused in her. She sat down quietly, and waited until he should come in.

How strange it was!—all bright full sunshine, no shadow or mystery to favour the romance; the Bellingers and Mrs. Spencer talking in the most ordinary way; the Colonel outside, pulling down the branch of pale roses; and Edith smiling, shaking off some dewdrops that had fallen from them upon her pretty hair. All so ordinary, so calm, so peaceable—but Lady Isabella seated there, silent, waiting—and I looking on with a chill at my very heart. He was a long time before he came in—talking to Edith was pleasant out in that verandah, with all the brilliant sunshine about, and the russet trees so sweet in the afternoon haze.

'You shall have some,' he said; 'but we must give some to your mother first.'

And then he came in with the branch in his hand. I don't know whether some sense of suppressed excitement in the air struck him as he paused in the window, but he did stand still there, and looked round him with an inquiring look. He had not left so many people in the room as were in it now, and he was surprised. He looked at me, and then I suppose my agitated glance directed him, in spite of myself, to Lady Isabella. He gave a perceptible start when he saw her, and smothered an exclamation. He recognized her instantly. His face flushed, and the branch of roses in his hand trembled. All this took place quite unobserved by anybody but me, and, perhaps, Edith, outside the window, who was coming in after him, and now stood on tiptoe, trying to see what was going on and wondering. Lady Isabella looked up at him with a face so uncertain in its expression that my terror was great. Was she angry? Was she going to betray herself, and show the nervous irritability which possessed her? She was very pale—white to her lips; and he so flushed and startled. She looked up at him, and then her lips parted and she smiled.

'I think I should like one of the roses,' she said.

Colonel Brentford did not say a word. He made her a bow, and with a trembling hand (how it did tremble!—it made me shake with sympathy to see it) he detached a spray from the great branch, which was all pink with roses, and gave it to her; and then he went away into the furthest corner, throwing down his roses on a table as he passed, and stared out of the window. To him the meeting was quite unexpected, I suppose—something utterly startling and sudden. The talk went on all the same. Edith, surprised, came in, and stood with her back to the open window, looking after him in a state of bewilderment. He had gone in smiling, to give her mother the flowers; and now he was standing with his back to us, the flowers cast down anywhere. As for Lady Isabella, she had buried her face in her roses, and sat quite silent, taking no notice of any one. Such was this meeting, which I had brought about. And all the time I had to talk to Major Bellinger, and look as if I were attending to what he said.

'Does Edith sing?' I asked in desperation. 'I am so glad! Do sing us something, my dear—oh, anything— and the simpler the better. How nice it is of you not to want your music! My piano is not in very good order, I play so seldom now; but it will not matter much to your young fresh voice.'

I said this, not knowing what I was saying, and hurried her to the piano, thinking, if she sang ever so badly, it still would be a blessed relief amid all this agitation and excitement.

'I only sing to mamma,' said Edith. 'I will try if you wish it; but papa does not care for my singing—and Colonel Brentford hates it,' she added, raising her voice.

There was a little spite, a little pique, in what Edith said. She was confounded by his sudden withdrawal, and anxious to call him back and punish him. This however was not the effect her words produced. Colonel Brentford took no notice, and kept his back towards us; but on another member of our little company the effect was startling enough.

'Colonel Brentford!' said Mrs. Spencer with a little shriek; and her nice comfortable commonplace talk with Mrs. Bellinger came to an end at once. She got up and came to me, and drew me into another corner. 'For Heaven's sake,' she said, 'tell me, what did the girl mean? Colonel Brentford! He is the one man in all the world whom we must not meet. That is not him surely at the window? Oh, good heavens! what is to be done? I wanted to tell you, but I never had an opportunity. Mrs. Mulgrave, he was once engaged to Isabella. They had a quarrel, and it nearly cost her her life. I think I would almost have given mine to preserve her from this trial. Has she seen him?—Oh, my poor dear! my poor dear!'

Let anybody imagine what was the scene presented in my drawing-room now. Colonel Brentford at the other end, with his back to us all, gazing out at the window: Major Bellinger at one side of the room, and his wife at the other, suddenly deserted by the people they had been respectively talking to, looking across at each other with raised eyebrows and questioning looks. Edith, confused and half-offended, stood before the closed piano, where I had led her; and Mrs. Spencer holding me by the arm in the opposite corner to that occupied by Colonel Brentford, was discoursing close to my ear with excited looks and voluble utterance. And these people were strangers to me, not like familiar friends, who could wait for an explanation. I could only whisper in Mrs. Spencer's ear, 'For heaven's sake, do not let us make a scene now—let us keep everything as quiet as possible now!'

Just then Lady Isabella suddenly rose from her seat, and sat down beside Mrs. Bellinger, and began to talk to her. I could not quite hear how she began, but I made out by instinct, I suppose, what she was saying:

'I cannot ask Mrs. Mulgrave to introduce me, for I see she is occupied; but I know who you are, and you must let me introduce myself. I am Lady Isabella Morton, and I live here with a great friend of mine. Colonel Brentford and I used to know each other long ago—'

'Yes,' said Mrs. Bellinger, drawing her breath quickly; 'I think I have heard—'

'He was startled to see me,' said Lady Isabella. 'Of course, he did not expect—but we are always meeting people we don't expect. Your daughter is going to sing. Hush! please hush! I want to hear it,' she cried, raising her hand with a little sign to the Major, who looked as though he might be going to talk. Every word she said was audible through the room, her voice was so clear and full.

Colonel Brentford turned round slowly. He turned almost as if he were a man upon a pedestal, which some pivot had the power to move. Either it was her voice which attracted him, or he had heard what she said, or perhaps he was recovering from the shock of the first meeting.

It was at this moment that Edith began to sing. I do not know what her feelings were, or if she cared anything about it; but certainly all the rest of the party, with the exception of her father and mother, were excited to such a strange degree, that I felt as if some positive explosion must occur. How is it that fire and air, and all sorts of senseless things, cause explosions, and that human feeling does not? Edith's girlish, fresh voice, rising out of the midst of all this electrified one. It was a pretty voice singing one of the ordinary foolish songs, which are all alike—a voice without the least passion or even sentiment in it, sweet, fresh, guiltless of any feeling. Lady Isabella leaned back in her chair, and listened with a faint smile upon her face; Colonel Brentford stood undecided between her and the piano, sometimes making a half-movement towards the singer, but turning his eyes the other way; while Mrs. Spencer, on the other side of the room, sat with her hands clasped, and gazed at her friend. The two Bellingers listened as people listen to the singing of their child; a soft little complacent smile was on the mother's face. When Edith approached a false note, or when she was a little out in her time, Mrs. Bellinger gave a quick glance round to see if anybody noticed it, and blushed, as it were, under her breath. The Major kept time softly with his finger; and we—listened with our hearts thumping in our ears, bewildered by the pleasant little song in its inconceivable calm, and yet glad of the moment's breathing time.

'Thank you, my dear,' said I, when the song was done; and we all said 'Thanks' with more or less fervour, while the parents, innocent people, looked on well pleased.

And then I went to Edith at the piano, and asked all about her music, what masters she had had, and a thousand other trifles, not hearing what she answered me. But I did hear something else. I heard Colonel Brentford speak to Lady Isabella, and took in every word. There was nothing remarkable about it; but he spoke low, as if his words meant more than met the ear.

'I knew you were living here,' was all he said.

'Oh, I suppose so,' said Lady Isabella. She had been quite calm before, but I knew by her voice she was flurried now. And then there followed that little agitated laugh, which in the last few days I had learnt to know. 'Most people know where everybody lives,' she added, with an attempt at indifference. 'I too knew that your regiment was here.'

'But I did not expect to see you just then,' he went on. 'And that rose— Pardon me if I was rude. I was taken altogether by surprise.'

'That I should ask you for a rose?' she said, holding it up. 'It is but a poor little thing, as these late flowers always are. Not much scent, and less colour, but sweet, because it is over—almost a thing of the past.'

'I was taken altogether by surprise,' said Colonel Brentford.

He did not make any reply to her. He was not clever, as she was. He repeated his little phrase of confused no-meaning, and his voice trembled. And while he was saying all this, Edith was telling me that she had had a few—only a very few—lessons from Herrmannstadt, but her mamma hoped that if they stayed at Royalborough, she might be able to have some from Dr. Delvey or Miss de la Pluie.

'If, my dear?' said I. 'I thought it was quite settled that you were to stay!' And then her answer became unintelligible to me; for my ears were intent upon what was going on behind us, and instead of listening to Edith, I heard only Colonel Brentford's feet shuffling uneasily upon the carpet, and Mrs. Spencer asking Lady Isabella if she did not think it was time to go.

'But you have not had any tea,' said I, rushing to the front: though, indeed, I was not at all sure that I wished them to stay.

'We never take any tea,' said Mrs. Spencer, unblushingly; though she knew that I knew she was the greatest afternoon tea-drinker in all Dinglefield; 'and we have to call upon old Mrs. Lloyd, who is quite ill. Did you know she was ill? We must not neglect the sick and the old, you know, even for the pleasantest society. Isabella, my dear!'

Colonel Brentford went after us to the door. He looked at them wistfully, watching their movements, until he saw that Mrs. Spencer had a cloak over her arm. Then he came forward with a certain heavy alacrity.

'Let me carry it for you,' he said.

'Oh, thanks! We are not going far; don't take the trouble. I would not for the world take you from your friends,' cried Mrs. Spencer wildly.

'It is no trouble, if you will let me,' he said.

He had taken the cloak out of her astonished hand, and Lady Isabella, in the meantime, with a smile on her face, had walked on in advance. Even I, though I felt so much agitated that I could have cried, could not but laugh to see Mrs. Spencer's look of utter discomfiture as she turned from my door, attended by this man whom she so feared. I stood and watched them as they went away, with a mingled feeling of relief and anxiety and wonder. Thus it was over. Was it over? Could this be a beginning or an end?

When I went back to the Bellingers they were consulting together, and I fear were not quite well pleased. The Major and his daughter drew back as I entered, but I saw it on their faces.

'I hope you will pardon me,' I said, 'for leaving you alone. My friends are gone, and Colonel Brentford has kindly walked with them to carry something. Now I know you must want some tea.'

'Indeed, mamma is a great deal too tired,' said Edith, who naturally was most nettled, 'I am sure we ought to go home.'

'I think she is over-tired,' said the Major doubtfully.

He did not want to be dragged away so suddenly; but yet he was a little surprised. Mrs. Bellinger, for her part, did not say anything, but she looked pale, and my heart smote me. And then there appeared a line of anxiety, which I had not noticed before, between her eyes.

'It is only that she wants some tea,' said I; and the Stokes coming in at the moment, to my infinite satisfaction, made a diversion, and brought things back to the ordinary channel of talk. And then they challenged the Major and Edith to croquet, for which all the hoops and things were set out on the lawn. Mrs. Bellinger and I began to talk when they went away: and presently Colonel Brentford came back and sat silently by us for five minutes—then went out to the croquet-players. A little silence fell upon us, as the sound of the voices grew merrier outside. It may be thought a stupid game now-a-days, but it is pretty to look at, when one is safe and out of it; and we two ladies sat in the cool room and watched the players, no doubt with grave thoughts enough. Colonel Brentford took Edith in hand at once. He showed her how to play, advised her, followed her, was always by her side. What did it mean? Was he glad that his old love had passed away like a dream, and left him free to indulge in this new one—to throw himself into this younger, brighter existence? Neither of us spoke, and I wondered whether we were both busy with the same thought.

At length Mrs. Bellinger broke the silence.

'I feel so anxious about our Colonel,' she said; 'he is so good and so nice. And your friends came by chance, quite by chance, Mrs. Mulgrave? How strange it is? Do you know that there was once— But of course you know. Oh, I hope this meeting will be for good, and not for harm.'

'For harm!' I said, with words that did not quite express my thoughts. 'They are both staid, sober people, not likely to go back to any youthful nonsense. How could it do harm?'

Mrs. Bellinger shook her head. There was a cloud upon her face.

'We shall see in time,' she said, in a melancholy, prophetic way, and sighed again.

To whom could it be that she apprehended harm? Not to Lady Isabella, whom she did not know. Was it to the child then, or to him?

CHAPTER IV

Next day I had a number of visitors. Mrs. Spencer had made it so well known in Dinglefield that nobody was to invite Lady Isabella to meet the new officers, that my unexampled temerity startled the whole neighbourhood. 'Of course they have met, notwithstanding all our precautions—and fancy, at Mrs. Mulgrave's! She was almost the only person Mrs. Spencer had not told,' my neighbours said; for the place is so small, that of course everybody knows what everybody else is doing on the Green. The Stokes were the first to call, and they were full of it.

'Fancy not telling us that Lady Isabella had been here?' cried Lottie. 'You must have known there was something, or you would have told us. And what did you mean by it? Did you think they ought to have another chance; or did you think—? Oh, I do so wish you would tell me what you meant!'

'Another chance, indeed!' said Lucy. 'As if Colonel Brentford—a handsome man, and just a nice age—would look twice at that old thing!'

'He is a good deal older than the old thing,' said I; 'and it is a poor account of both men and women, Lucy, if everything is to give way to mere youth. You yourself will not be seventeen always. You should remember that.'

'Well, but then I shall be married,' said Lucy; 'and I sha'n't mind if nobody pays me any attention. I shall have my husband and my children of course; but an old maid—'

'Be quiet, Lucy,' said her sister angrily. 'If you girls only knew how to hold your tongues, then you might have a chance; but please tell me, Mrs. Mulgrave—you won't say you did not mean anything, for of course you knew—?'

'I don't intend to say anything about it, my dear; and here is Mrs. Spencer coming, if you would like to make any further inquiries,' I said. I was quite glad to see her, to get rid of their questionings. Mrs. Spencer was very much flurried and disturbed, out of breath both of mind and body.

'Oh, my dear Mrs. Mulgrave, what an unfortunate business!' she said, the moment the girls were gone. 'I have nobody but myself to blame, for I never told you. I thought as you did not give many parties—and then I know you don't care much for those dancing sort of men: and how was I to suppose he would be thrown upon your hands like this? It has upset me so,' she said, turning to me, with her eyes full of tears; 'I have not slept all night.'

Her distress was a great deal too genuine to be smiled at. 'I am so sorry,' I said; 'but, after all, I do not think it is serious. It did not seem to disturb her much.'

'Ah, that is because she does not show it,' said Mrs. Spencer. 'She is so unselfish. You might stab her to the heart and she would never say a word, if there was any one near who could be made unhappy by it. She would not let me see, for she knows it would make me wretched. And I am quite wretched about her. If this were to bring up old feelings! And you know she nearly died of it—at the time.'

The tears came dropping down on poor Mrs. Spencer's thin nose. It was too thin, almost sharp in outline, but such tears softened all its asperity away. I could not help thinking of those dreadful French proverbs, which are so remorseless and yet so true; about 'l'un qui aime, et l'autre qui se laisse aimer;' about 'l'un qui baise et l'autre qui tend la joue.' Is it always so in this world? I could have beaten myself for having interfered at all in the matter. Why should anybody ever interfere? Life is hard enough without any assistance to make it worse.

Lady Isabella herself came in late, when, fortunately, I was alone; and she was in a very different mood. She came in, and gave a curious, humorous glance round the room, and then sat down in the chair by the window, where she had sat the day before, and asked Colonel Brentford for that rose.

'Is it possible it has been and is over,' she said, in her mocking way; 'that great, wonderful event, to which I looked forward so much? It happened just here: and yet the place is exactly the same. How funny it is when one remembers that it has happened, and yet feels one's self exactly like what one was before—'

'You are not sorry, then?' I cried, not knowing what to say.

'Sorry? oh, no,' she said with momentary fervour: and then blushed scarlet. 'On the contrary, I am very glad. It proved to me— I got all I wanted. I am quite pleased with myself. I can't have been such a fool after all; for—he is not clever, you know—but he is a man a woman need not be ashamed to have been in love with: and that is saying a great deal.'

'And is it only a "have been?"' said I; for after all when one had taken so much trouble it was hard that nothing should come of it. I felt as if I had taken a great deal of trouble, and all in vain.

'Indeed, I should hope so!' cried Lady Isabella, getting up and drawing her shawl round her hastily. 'You surely did not think that I meant anything more. I am in a great hurry, I have only a few minutes to spare; and thanks to you, good friend, I have had my whim, and I am satisfied. I don't feel at all ashamed of having been fond of him—once.'

And with these words she ran away, silencing all questions. Was this indeed all? Was it a mere whim? To tell the truth, when I tried to put myself in her position, it seemed to me much wiser of Lady Isabella to let it end so. She was very well off and comfortable: she had come to an age when one likes to have one's own way, and does not care to adopt the habits of others; and what an immense bouleversement it would make if she should marry and break up that pleasant house, and throw herself upon the chances of married life, abandoning Mrs. Spencer, who was as good as married to her, and who, no doubt, calculated on her society all her life. I said to myself—if I were Lady Isabella! And then there was the great chance, the almost certainty that he would never attempt to carry it any farther. He was a young-looking man, and no doubt (though it is very odd to me how they can do it) he felt himself rather on the level of a girl of twenty than of a woman of thirty-five. He had been a good deal startled and touched by the meeting, which was not wonderful: but he had returned to Edith's side all the same; and, no doubt, that was where he would stay. Edith was very young, and her parents were poor, and the best thing for her would be to marry a man who was able to take care of her, and make her very comfortable, and to whom, in return, she would be entirely devoted. Edith could consent to be swallowed up in him altogether, and to have no life but that of her husband; and except by means of a husband who was well off the poor child never was likely to do anything for herself or her family, but would have to live a life of hard struggling with poverty and premature acquaintance with care. This was of course the point of view from which the matter should be regarded. To Lady Isabella Colonel Brentford's means or position were unnecessary. She was very well off, very fully established in the world without him. And she could not be swallowed up in him, and renounce everything that was her own to become his wife. She was an independent being, with a great many independent ways and habits. It was better for him, better for her, better for Edith that nothing should come of this meeting; and yet—how foolish one is about such matters: what vain fancies come into one's head!

Everything sank into its ordinary calm however from that day. I did not see Mrs. Spencer and Lady Isabella for a week after, and then they were exactly as they had always been. Lady Isabella made no remark to me of any kind on the subject, but Mrs. Spencer took me aside to give me her opinion. 'I am so glad to tell you,' she said, 'that your little inadvertence has done no harm. Oh, I forgot: it was not an inadvertence on your part, but my own fault for not telling you. It has done no harm, I am so glad to say. Isabella seems to have quite settled down again. I don't believe she has given him another thought. Of course it was a shock just at the moment. But you must not blame yourself, indeed you must not. Probably she would have met him somewhere sooner or later. I really feel quite glad that it is over; and it has done her no harm.'

This was all I gained by my exertions; and I made a resolution that I would certainly never be persuaded to do anything of the kind again. For, indeed, it had complicated my relations with various people. What could I do, for instance, about the Bellingers? In the meantime I simply dropped them, after having rushed into such an appearance of intimacy. If anybody else had done it, I should have been indignant; but how could I help myself? I could not have Edith in my house and see him wooing her, after having taken such an interest in the other side. I could not insult Lady Isabella by letting that go on under her very eyes. And though I wondered sometimes what the respectable Major would think, and whether poor dear Mrs. Bellinger would be wounded, I had not the fortitude to continue the acquaintance. I simply dropped them: it was the only thing I could do.

And then the winter came on all at once, which was a sort of excuse. There was a week or two of very bad weather and I caught cold, and was very glad of it, for, of course, nobody could expect me to drive to Royalborough in my little open carriage with a bad cold, through the rain and wind. A very dreary interval of dead quiet to me, and miserable weather, followed this little burst of excitement. I felt sore about it altogether, as a matter in which I had somehow been to blame, and which was a complete failure—to say the least. One day when I had been out for half an hour's walk in the middle of the day, Colonel Brentford called; but the card which I found on my table was the only enlightenment this brought me, and my cold kept me away from all the society on the Green for six weeks, during which time I had no information on the subject. Sometimes, as usual, I saw Lady Isabella, but there was no change in her. She had quite settled down again, was the same as ever, and Mrs. Spencer had ceased to keep any watch upon her. And so it was all over, as a tale that is told.

The first time I was out after my influenza was at Lady Denzil's, where, to my surprise, I found Edith Bellinger. She scarcely looked at me, and it was with some difficulty I got our slender thread of acquaintance renewed. Her mother, she thanked me, was better; her father was quite well; they had been sorry to hear of my cold; yes, of course it was a long way to drive. Such was the fashion of Edith's talk; and I acknowledged to myself that it was perfectly just.

'Your mamma must think it very strange that I have never gone to see her again,' I was beginning to say, feeling uncomfortable and guilty.

'I don't suppose she has thought about it,' Edith said hastily; and then she stopped short and blushed. 'I beg your pardon, I did not mean to be rude.'

'You are quite right,' I said—'not in being rude, but in feeling as you do. I seem to have been very capricious and unfriendly; but I have been ill; and you do not look quite so well yourself as when I saw you last.'

'Oh, I am well enough,' said the girl; and then those quick youthful tears of self-compassion which lie so near the surface came rushing to her eyes. 'It is nothing, I—I am not very strong; and Lady Denzil, who is always kind, has asked me here for change of air.'

'Poor child,' I said, 'tell me what is the matter?' But I was not to learn at this moment at least. Colonel Brentford, whom I had not seen till now, came forward and bent over her.

'They are going to sing something, and they want you to take a part. I have come for you,' he said.

He looked down upon her quite tenderly, and held out his hand to help her to rise. Yes, of course, that was how it must have ended. It was all settled, of that I could have no doubt. I looked at them with, I fear, a look that had some pain and some pity in it, as they left me; and when I withdrew my eyes from them, my look met Lady Isabella's, who was seated at the other side of the room. She had her usual half-mocking, half-kindly smile on her lips, but it looked to me set and immovable, as if she had been painted so and could not change; and she was pale—surely she was pale. It troubled me sadly, and all the more that I dared not say a word to any one, dared not even make any manifestation of sympathy to herself. She had chosen to renew her old acquaintance with him, had chosen to break down the barrier which sympathizing friends had raised round her, and to meet him with all freedom as if he were totally indifferent to her. This had been her own choice; and now, to be sure, she had to look on, and see all there might be to be seen.

But he was very civil to me when he chanced to be thrown near me. He said, in a much more friendly tone than poor Edith's, that Mrs. Bellinger had been sorry to hear of my cold; that he hoped I should soon be able to go and see her; and when I said that Edith did not look strong, he shook his head. 'She is rather wilful, and does not know her own mind,' he said, and I thought he sighed. Was it that she could not make up her mind to accept him? Was it— But speculation was quite useless, and there was no information to be got out of his face.

A little after this I went to see Mrs. Bellinger, but was coldly received. Edith was not quite well, she said; she had been doing too much, and had gone away for a thorough change. Colonel Brentford? Oh, he had gone to visit his brother Sir Charles Brentford, in Devonshire. Edith was in Devonshire, too—at Torquay.

'They are a little afraid of her lungs,' Mrs. Bellinger said. 'Oh, not I; I don't think there is very much the matter; but still they are afraid—and of course it is better to prevent than to cure.'

It seemed to me a heartless way for a mother to speak, and I was discouraged by my reception. When I came away I made up my mind not to take any further trouble about the matter. Perhaps I had been mistaken in them at first, or perhaps— but then, to be sure, I had another motive, and that existed no longer. It was my fault more than theirs.

I heard no more of the Bellingers nor much more of Colonel Brentford for a long time after this. He, to be sure, went and came, as the other officers did, to one house and another, and I met him from time to time, and exchanged three words with him, but no more. And Lady Isabella made no reference whatever to that agitating moment when I, too, had a share in her personal history. Even Mrs. Spencer seemed to have forgotten all about it. Their house was more exquisite than ever that winter. They had built a new conservatory, which opened from the ante-room, and was full of the most bright, beautiful flowers—forced, artificial things to be sure they were, blooming long before their season, but still very lovely to look at in those winter days. The large drawing-room and the ante-room, and the conservatory at the end of all, were as warm and fragrant and soft and delicious as if they had been fairy-land—the temperature so equable, everything so soft to tread on, to sit on, to look at. It was a little drawing-room paradise—an Eden, with Turkey carpets instead of turf, and the flowers all in pots instead of growing free. And here Lady Isabella would sit, with that touch of mockery in her laugh, with little gibes at most people and most things, not quite so friendly or gentle as they once were. Now and then, I have thought, she cast a wistful glance at the door; now and then her spirits were fitful, her face paler than usual—but she had never been more lively or more bright.

It was past Christmas, and already a pale glimmer of spring was in the air, when this little episode showed signs of coming to its conclusion. I remember the day quite distinctly—a pale day in the beginning of February, when everything was quite destitute of colour. The sky was gray and so was the grass, and the skeletons of the trees stood bleak against the dulness. It was the kind of afternoon when one is glad to hear any news, good or bad—anything that will quicken the blood a little, and restore to the nervous system something like its usual tone.

This stimulus was supplied by the entrance to the house of our two neighbours Lucy Stoke—very important, and bursting with the dignity of a secret. She kept it in painfully for the first two minutes, moved chiefly by her reverential admiration for the fine furniture, the beautiful room, the atmosphere of splendour about her. But I was there, unfortunately, of whom Lucy was not afraid. It was to me, accordingly, that the revelation burst forth.

'Oh, Mrs. Mulgrave,' she said, 'you know her! Who do you think I met going down to Lady Denzil's, in a white bonnet,—though it's such a dismal day—and a blue dress—quite light blue—the dress she went away in, I should think?'

'A bride, I suppose,' I said; 'but whom?—I don't remember any recent bride.'

'Oh, yes, I know you know her! Young Mrs. Brentford—Edith Bellinger that was.'

'Edith Bellinger!' I cried, with a sudden pang. It was nothing to me. I had no reason to suppose it was anything to anybody, but yet—

'It must have been the dress she went away in,' said Lucy: 'blue trimmed with bands of satin and fringe, and a white bonnet with blue flowers. It was very becoming. But fancy, only three weeks married, and coming to see Lady Denzil alone!'

'And so she is Mrs. Brentford,' said Mrs. Spencer, in a tone of genuine satisfaction. She would have suffered herself to be cut in little pieces for Lady Isabella, she would have done anything for her—but she was glad, unfeignedly thankful and relieved, to feel that this danger was past.

And Lucy, well pleased, ran on for ten minutes or more. It felt like ten hours. When she went away at last, Mrs. Spencer went with her to the door, to hear further particulars. All this time Lady Isabella had never said a word. She was in the shade, and her face was not very distinctly visible. When they left the room, she rose all at once, pulling herself up by the arms of her chair. Such a change had come upon her face that I was frightened. Every vestige of colour had left her cheek; her lip was parched, and tightly drawn across her teeth. She laughed as she got up from the chair.

'We were all wishing for something to stir us up,' she said; 'but I never hoped for anything so exciting as Mrs. Brentford's blue dress.'

'Where are you going?' I said, in sudden terror.

'Up-stairs—only up-stairs. Where should I go?' she said, with that short hard laugh. 'Tell Mrs. Spencer— something. I have gone to fetch—Mrs. Brentford's blue dress.'

Oh, how that laugh pained me! I would rather, a thousand times rather, have heard her cry. She went away like a ghost, without any noise; and Mrs. Spencer, full of thanksgiving, came back.

'Where is Isabella? Oh, Mrs. Mulgrave, I can't tell you what a relief this news is,' she said. 'I have always been so dreadfully afraid. Of course, anything that was for her happiness I would have put up with; but this would not have been for her happiness. She is no longer young, you know—her habits are all formed—and, even though she was fond of him once, how could she have taken up a man's ways, and adapted herself? It would never have done—it would never have done! I am so thankful he is married, and that danger past.'

For my part, I could not make any answer. Perhaps Mrs. Spencer was right—perhaps, in the long run, it would be better so; but, in the meantime, I could not forget Lady Isabella's face. I went home, feeling I cannot tell how sad. It was all so perfectly natural and to be expected. The hardest things in this world are the things that are to be expected. Of course, I had felt sure when I saw them together that it was the little girl who would be the victor in any such struggle. And Lady Isabella had not attempted any struggle. She had stood aside and looked on; though, perhaps, she had hoped that the old love would have counted for something in the man's heart. But I said to myself that I had always known better. What was old love, with all its associations, in comparison with the little peachy cheek and childish ways of a girl of seventeen? I despised the man for it, of course; but I thought it natural all the same.

CHAPTER V

I was sitting next day by myself, with my mind full of these thoughts, when I was suddenly roused by a shadow which flitted across the light, and then by the sound of some one knocking at the window which opened into my garden. I looked up hurriedly, and saw Lady Isabella. She was very pale, yet looked breathless, as if she had been running. She made me a hasty, imperative gesture to open, and when I had done so, came in without suffering me to shut the window. 'Mrs. Mulgrave,' she said, panting between the words, 'I have a very strange—request—to make. I want to speak with—some one—for ten minutes—alone. May we—come—here? I have nothing to conceal—from you. It is him;—he has something—to say to me—for the last time.'

'Lady Isabella—' I said.

'Don't—say anything. It is strange—I know—but it must be; for the last time.'

She did not seem able to stand for another moment. She sank down into the nearest chair, making a great effort to command herself. 'Dear Mrs. Mulgrave—please call him,' she cried faintly: 'he is there. It will only be for ten minutes—there is something to explain.'

I went out into the garden, and called him. He looked as much agitated as she did, and I went round the house, and through the kitchen-door with a sense of bewilderment which I could not put into words. Edith Bellinger's bridegroom! What could he have to explain? What right had he to seek her, to make any private communication? I felt indignant with him, and impatient with her. Then I went into the dining-room and waited. My dining-room windows command the road, and along this I could see Mrs. Spencer walking in her quick, alert way. She was coming towards my house, in search, probably, of her companion. There was something absurd in the whole business, and yet the faces of the two I had just left were too tragical to allow any flippancy on the part of the spectator. Mrs. Spencer came direct to my door as I supposed, and I had to step out and stop the maid, who was about to usher her into the drawing-room where those two were. Mrs. Spencer was a little excited too.

'Have you seen Isabella?' she said. 'She was only about half-a-dozen yards behind me, round the corner at the Lodge; and when I turned to look for her she was gone. She could not have dropped into the earth you know, and I know she would never have gone to the Lodge. Is she here? It has given me quite a turn, as the maids say. She cannot have vanished altogether, like a fairy. She was too substantial for that.'

'She will be here directly,' said I; 'she is speaking to some one in the other room.'

'Speaking—to some one! You look very strange, Mrs. Mulgrave, and Isabella has been looking very strange. Who is she speaking to? I am her nearest friend and I ought to know.'

'Yes,' I said, 'you ought to know, that is certain—but wait, only wait, ten minutes—that was the time she said.'

And then we two sat and looked at each other, not knowing what to think. I knew scarcely more than she did, but the little that I knew made me only the more anxious. If his wife should hear of it—if Lady Isabella were to betray herself, compromise herself! And then what was the good of it all? No explanation could annul a fact, and the less explanation the better between a married man and his former love. This feeling made me wretched as the time went on. Time seems so doubly long when one is waiting, and especially when one is waiting for the result of some private, secret, mysterious interview. The house was so quiet, the maids moving about the kitchen, the chirp of the sparrows outside, the drip—drip of a shower, which was just over, from the leaves. All these sounds made the silence deeper, especially as there was no sound from that mysterious room.

'The ten minutes are long past,' said Mrs. Spencer. 'I don't understand what all this mystery can mean. It is more like an hour, I think.'

'Oh, do you think so?' said I, though I fully agreed with her. 'When one is waiting time looks so long. She will be here directly. I hear her now—that was her voice.'

And so it certainly was. But everything became silent again the next instant. It was a sharp exclamation, sudden and high; and then we heard no more.

'I cannot wait any longer,' said Mrs. Spencer. 'I don't know what this can mean; I must have an explanation. Mrs. Mulgrave, if you will not come with me, I will go myself to Isabella. I don't understand what she can mean.'

'I will go,' said I; and we rose at the same moment and hurried to the door. But we had not time to open it when a sudden sound was audible, which arrested us both. The door of the other room was opened, voices came towards us—two voices, and then a laugh. Was it Lady Isabella's laugh? Mrs. Spencer drew near me and pinched my arm violently. 'Is it Isabella? What, oh, what can it mean?' she said with a look of terror. And then the door was thrown suddenly open, driving us back as we stood in our consternation within.

It was Lady Isabella who stood before us, and yet it was not the Lady Isabella I had ever known. When Mrs. Spencer saw her she gave a suppressed groan and sat down suddenly on the nearest chair. This Lady Isabella was leaning on Colonel Brentford's arm. Her face was flushed and rosy; her eyes shining like stars, yet full of tears; dimples I had never seen before were in her cheeks and about her mouth. She was radiant, she was young, she was running over with joy and happiness. In her joy and triumph she did not notice, I suppose, the sudden despair of her friend. 'I have come to tell you,' she said hastily, 'he never meant it. It is all over. Oh, do you understand? All this cloud that has lasted for ten years, that has come between us and the skies—it is all over, all over. He never meant it. Do you understand?'

Mrs. Spencer stood up tottering, looking like a ghost. 'Isabella! I thought you had forgotten him. I thought it was this that was all over. I thought you were content.'

Lady Isabella gave her a look of that supreme happiness which is not considerate of other people's feelings. 'I am content now,' she said, clasping her hands upon Colonel Brentford's arm, 'more than content.'

Mrs. Spencer answered with a bitter cry. 'Then I am nothing to her, nothing to her!' she said.

It was at this moment that I interfered. I could keep silence no longer. I put myself between the two who were so happy and the one who was so miserable. 'Before another word is said I must have this explained to me,' I said. 'He is Edith Bellinger's husband. And this is my house—'

He interrupted me hurriedly: 'I am no one's husband but hers,' he said. 'You have been mistaken. Edith Bellinger has married my brother. There is no woman to me in the world but Isabella—never has been—never could be, though I lived a hundred years.'

'And it is you who have brought us together,' cried Lady Isabella, suddenly throwing her arms round me. 'God bless you for it! I should never have known, it would never have been possible but for you.'

And he came to me and took both my hands. 'God bless you for it, I say too! We might have been two forlorn creatures all our lives but for you.'

I was overwhelmed with their thanks, with the surprise, and the shock. If I had done anything to bring this about I had done it in ignorance; but they surrounded me so with their joy and their gratitude, and the excitement of the revolution which had happened in them, that it was some minutes before I could think of anything else. And there was so much to be explained. But when I recovered myself so far as to look round and think of the other who did not share in their joy, I found she was gone. She had disappeared while they were thanking me, while I was expressing my wonder and my good wishes. None of us had either heard or seen her departure, but she was gone.

'Was Mrs. Spencer to blame?' I asked with some anxiety when the tumult had subsided a little, and they had seated themselves like ordinary mortals and begun to accustom themselves to their delight. 'Had she anything to do with the quarrel between you?'

'Nothing at all,' said Lady Isabella. 'She never saw George till she saw him in your house.'

'When you asked me for that rose—' said he. 'The rose you used to be so fond of; and I felt as if the skies had opened—'

'You turned your back upon me all the same,' she said with the laugh that had suddenly become so joyous. They had forgotten everything but themselves and the new story of their reconciliation: which I suppose the old story of their estrangement thus recalled and reconsidered made doubly sweet.

'But about Mrs. Spencer?' I said.

'Poor Mrs. Spen! She had got to be fond of me. She thought we were to spend all our lives together,' said Lady Isabella with momentary gravity; and then the smile crept once more about the corners of her mouth, and the dimples which had been hidden all these years disclosed themselves, and her face warmed into sunshine as she turned to him. This was my fate whenever I tried to bring back the conversation to Mrs. Spencer, who, poor soul, had disappeared like a shadow before that sunshine. I was glad for their sakes to see them so happy; but still I could not but feel that it was hard to have given your life and love for years and to be rewarded at the end by that 'poor Mrs. Spen.'

The news made a great commotion through all Dinglefield, and Mrs. Spencer did not make so much difficulty about it as I fancied she would. The marriage was from her house, and she took a great deal of trouble, and no mother could have been more careful and tender about a bride. But she made no fuss, poor soul—she had not the heart; and though I don't like fuss, I missed it in this case, and felt that it was a sign how deep the blow had gone. Even Lady Isabella, pre-occupied as she was, felt it. She had not realized it perhaps—few people do. We are all in the habit of laughing at the idea of friendships so close and exacting, especially when they exist between women. But to Mrs. Spencer it was as if life itself had gone from her. Her companion had gone from her, the creature she loved best. Next to a man's wife deserting him, or a woman's husband, I know nothing more hard. Her pretty house, her flowers, her perfect comfort and grace of life palled upon her. She had kept them up chiefly, I think, for the young woman who, she had thought, poor soul, was wedded to her for life. Perhaps it was a foolish thought, perhaps it might be a little selfish to try to keep Colonel Brentford away. I suppose to be married is the happiest; but still I was very, very sorry, grieved more than I can say, for the woman who was forsaken; though she was only forsaken by another woman and not by a man.

However that, I fear, is a sentiment in which I should find few sympathizers. The Brentfords took a place in the neighbourhood, and I believe Lady Isabella was a very happy wife. As for poor little Edith Bellinger, she had married the Colonel's elder brother, Sir Charles, and was Lady Brentford, to her great astonishment and that of everybody about. It had been her doubt and reluctance, poor child, to marry a man older than her father, which had made her ill. I think her mother missed her almost as much as Mrs. Spencer missed Lady Isabella. For every new tie that is made in this world some old ties must be broken. But what does that matter? Is it not the course of nature and the way of the world?

AN ELDERLY ROMANCE

CHAPTER I

There is a house in Dinglefield, standing withdrawn in a mass of shrubbery, and overshadowed by some fine trees, which has been called by the name of Brothers-and-Sisters for a longer time than any one in the village can recollect. It presents to the outside world who peep at it over the palings, between the openings which have been carefully cut to afford to its inmates pleasant glimpses of the lower part of the Green, on which the cricket matches are played, the aspect of a somewhat low white house, with no apparent entrance, and a great number of chimneys of different heights, chimneys which I suppose suggested to some wag the unequal stature of a family of children, and thus procured the house its popular name. In the map or the estate on which Dinglefield stands it is called Bonport House, and this is how the General's letters, I need not say, are addressed. But yet the common name sticks, all the more because of the character of the family which now inhabits that hospitable place. It is literally a house of brothers and sisters. General Stamford, the head of the family, is a hale and ruddy old warrior of sixty, who has seen a great deal of service, and who has been knocked about, battered, and beaten from the age of sixteen until now: sent to every unfavourable place where a soldier without money or influence has to go, and engaged in every fierce little war in which it has been the pleasure of England to indulge, without any consideration for the feelings of her fighting men. He has been at Bermuda; he has been on the Gold Coast; he has braved all the fevers and fought all the savages within our ken; and outliving all this, has settled down with his sisters and brother in our village, one of the most peaceable yet the most active of men. It is for this last reason that General George (as we have all got to call him, partly because there are other generals about, and to say General Stamford every time you mention a man in a neighbourhood like ours is fatiguing—and partly for kindness) has so many things on his hands. He is one of the directors of our railway; he is on several boards in town, where he goes almost every day punctual as clockwork, brushed to perfection, and driven to the station by Miss Stamford in the pony-carriage, which always takes him there, and always meets him when he comes back. Miss Stamford is the eldest sister of all. She is very like her brother, and there never was such a tender brotherly sisterly union as between these two old people. They have known each other so long, longer than any husband and wife. They have the recollections of the nursery quite fresh in their minds, as if it were yesterday—

when it was always Ursula who found George's books for him, and gave him good advice, and most of her pocket-money, and looked after his linen when he was at home, and his pets when he went away. Miss Stamford knows all the occurrences of her brother's chequered life better than he does himself, and recollects everything, and knows all his friends, even if she never saw them, and can recall to him the exact relationship between the young man who comes to him with an introduction, and old Burton who was killed by his side among the Maoris; or Percival who died of the yellow fever at Barbadoes. She is his remembrancer, his counsellor, half his heart, and a good part of his mind; and indeed there is nobody among us who ever thinks of the one without thinking of the other. What she was doing with herself all those years when George was fighting on the outskirts of civilization, or sweltering in the tropics, none of us know, but some of us wonder now and then. Did nothing ever happen to Miss Stamford on her own account? Has all her life been only a reflection of her brother's? But this is what nobody can tell.

The next member of the family in due succession is Mrs. St. Clair, who is the second sister, and who has been so long a widow that she has forgotten that this is not the normal condition of women. I don't think, for my part, that she remembers much about her husband, though he did exist, I have every reason to believe. Her married life was a little episode, but the family is all her idea of ordinary existence. That little sip of matrimony however has made her different from the rest. I cannot quite tell how. There is a tone that is more mellow; she is a little more—stout, if I may use such a word: her outlines are a little fuller, both of mind and body. Miss Stamford takes care of the house and the General, but Mrs. St. Clair takes care of the parish. She is the Rector's lay curate, and a most efficient one. It is she who watches over, not only the poor, but the district visitors, and even the curates, whose juvenile importance she makes very light of, keeping down all rampant sacerdotalism. When a young man comes into a parish full of very fine ideas of priestly state and dignity, and fortified besides by all the talk in the newspapers about adoring ladies and worked slippers, it is hard for him to find himself confronted by a lively middle-aged woman who has no particular respect for him, and knows all his kind, and all their little ways. Mrs. St. Clair was of the greatest use to us all in this particular. She kept us from innovations. Our excellent Rector has not a very strong will, and how far he might have been induced to go in respect to vestments, or candles, or even Gregorians, it would be hard to say, but for Mrs. St. Clair, who kept the young men down. Everybody who has ever been at Dinglefield has met her about the roads, with her gray hair neatly braided, and her soft brown eyes smiling, yet seeing everything, and a basket in her hand. She always had the basket; and the basket, if it had been examined, would have been found always to contain something which was to do somebody good.

Miss Sophy, the third sister, was much younger than the others, and she was one of those who are always young. Nothing had changed much with her since she was eighteen. She lived quite the same sort of life as she had done then, and wore the same kind of dresses; and felt, I believe, very much the same. Life had never progressed into a second chapter with her, and she felt no need of a second chapter. She did little commissions for everybody, and carried little messages, and played croquet, and went out to tea, and performed her little pieces on the piano with undiminished and undiminishing satisfaction. She was as kind, as sweet, and as innocent as any girl need be; and, in short, she was a girl—but of forty-five. The reader may think this is a sneer; but nobody ever thought of sneering at Miss Sophy; that malign amusement found no encouragement in her simplicity. You smiled at her, perhaps, then blushed for yourself, abashed at your own heartlessness in finding anything absurd in a creature so guileless and true. She had no particular rôle of her own in the family, except to be kind to everybody, and to do what everybody wished, as far as a merely mortal sister could. If there was one thing that she thought especially her duty and privilege, it was to look after the faith and morals of the other brother, who occasionally formed part of the household. He was a barrister, an old bachelor like the rest, who had chambers in town and came when he pleased to Brothers-and-Sisters. He spent the Sundays there, and Miss Sophy took him to church. She would have made him say the Collect if she could; and, indeed, always questioned him about his opinions, and argued with him on the Sunday afternoons upon the points on which he was astray. And when I add that Mr. Charles was a clever lawyer and a man of the world, and astray upon a great many points, it will be seen that Sophy had her hands full. She argued herself into palpitations and headaches, but I fear her arguments were less potent than her intention. This energetic effort to keep Charles right in theology was, so far as any one knew, the only duty exclusively hers.

These delightful people were only a small part of the family to which they belonged. Behind them was a bodyguard of married brothers and sisters, a sort of milky way of family plenitude, from which arose an army of nephews and nieces who were always looming about, sure to come down upon us in force when anything was going on. There were always men to be had for a dance, and actors for theatricals on application to the Stamfords. 'Tell me how many you want and give me two or three days' notice,' Mrs. St. Clair would say, and then Sophy would write the letters, and after a while the air of Dinglefield would be thick with nephews. There was room for an untold number of them in the old, many-chimneyed house. When it was the time for garden parties, or when there was a bazaar for some charity, it was the turn of the nieces, who came like the swallows, with a skimming of wings, and a chirping and chattering of pleasant voices. It was astonishing how soon we got to know them all, discriminating Sophy Humphreys from Sophy Thistlethwaite, and both from Sophy Stamford number one, called Soff, or Henry's Sophy, to distinguish her from Sophy Stamford number two, who was called Fia, or William's Sophy. Sophy was the pet name of the race; the mother's name from whom they all sprang.

And it would be difficult to give any stranger an idea of the addition they were to our limited society at Dinglefield. Go when you would the genial house was always open, a pleasant party always to be found on the lawn in summer, by the drawing-room fire in winter. They had their anxieties and sorrows like other people, no doubt; but not so many as other people: for the time was over with them for personal pangs and trouble; and when one nephew out of twenty goes a little wrong, or one niece (also out of twenty) makes a bad marriage, the pang is not so keen or so lasting as when it is a son or a daughter who has broken down. And this was the worst that could now befall the house. It was a house made for the comfort and succour of every aching heart or troubled mind within its range. There was nothing they would not do for their neighbours and friends; how much more for their relations. General George lent his kindly ear, a little, just a little, hard of hearing (but no, not hard of anything, the word is unworthy to be used in his connection), to every request. He would do his best to place your son, or invest your money; or order early salmon or turbot for you when you were going to have a dinner-party. I should not have liked to ask Mr. Charles Stamford to order my fish, but I have no doubt he too would have done it, had he been asked; and as for the sisters, they would, as the poor people said, put their hand to anything.

One day Sophy came into my cottage with an air of some excitement to tell me that George had sent a telegram, and was bringing down a large party of his fellow-directors to dinner. 'Will you come, dear Mrs. Mulgrave? Fancy! how shall we ever entertain these twelve business gentlemen?' said Sophy in a flutter. 'If only some of the girls had been here. Not that the girls would have cared for these old creatures. But the worst is that Ursula herself is away. She went up to town this morning to see her great friend, Mrs. Biddulph. And though she will be back for dinner, all the responsibility will be upon Frances and me. I must run away now this moment to James the gardener, to see how many strawberries he can give us. Don't you think it was tiresome of George to bring down so many upon us without warning? It is just like him: no, he is not tiresome—never! he is a darling! But sometimes he does a tiresome thing.'

And Sophy tripped away, light-footed, light-hearted, with no greater thought than the strawberries. She was still as slim as a girl, and there was about her all the eagerness and breathless mixture of fright and pleasure which are natural at eighteen. She was eighteen, spiritually speaking. I watched her tripping along in her light summer dress, and smiled; I could not help it. I saw her again three times that day, and, indeed, I saw Mrs. St. Clair too, who was equally full of business. 'Twelve men!' Mrs. St. Clair cried. 'Is it not a nuisance? I can't think how George could do it. They have a nice bit of villainy in hand; they are going to cut up all our pretty view, and take away the poor people's gardens; and then they expect us to give them dinner!'

'Did Sophy get the strawberries?' I asked.

'Oh, yes; more than they deserve. But you are coming, and you shall see.' She went on, waving her hand, too busy to talk. A dinner of twelve gentlemen, when you have made no arrangements, and provided nothing but what was needed for the family, is a serious matter in a country place, especially when the real housekeeper is out of the way.

CHAPTER II

All this time Miss Stamford knew nothing of what was going on. She had gone up to town early in the morning, and she had spent the day with her friend, who was ailing; and in the afternoon she had missed the usual dinner train by which General George always travelled, coming by the next one, which was about half an hour later. She came down in the same carriage with a gentleman who, she afterwards admitted, attracted her attention at once. He was a tall man—well, not young, certainly—oldish, elderly, 'about the same age as other people'—with a long face, like Don Quixote. She remarked him; and he remarked her, apparently, showing her several little politenesses: opening and shutting the window, &c. He was very like Don Quixote. This was the chief remark Miss Stamford made.

She was a little late for dinner, having been taken entirely by surprise by the great preparations she found on her return. She had left everything in the ordinary quiet, no company expected, and had ordered the usual dinner for the family before she went away; and the sight of Williams the greengrocer, and Jones the verger, both in grand official costume, on duty in her own hall when she got back, astonished her.

'Company, ma'am, as the General has brought home from town, unexpected,' Williams said, as he opened the door. Their own homely butler, Simms, had been promoted to the rank of major-domo for the moment, and was a very great personage with two men under him. Miss Stamford changed her dress as quickly as possible, but dinner had begun before she got down-stairs. Mrs. St. Clair had taken the head of the table, and Ursula slid quietly into the vacant place which had been left for her. She nodded to me across the table as she sat down. She had not even put on her best cap, and her gown was anything but new. And it did not seem to me that Ursula Stamford was by any means looking her best. She was a little prim in appearance, though so liberal and generous in heart; and she looked sixty, while to my knowledge she was only fifty-seven. You will say that was not a difference which mattered much; but I assure you we think a great deal of a year or two up here among the snows of life. She sat down so quietly that the gentleman on one side did not at first notice that the place was taken by his side, and she occupied herself with the other, whom she happened to know. There was a great deal of talk going on at the table. Mrs. St. Clair had picked up a few ladies in haste to make the balance a little more even. Mrs. Stokes had sent Lucy, who was going to be married, and Miss Woodroff had come from the Rectory, and Mrs. Sommerville, the young widow who was living with her brother, the curate. There were seven of us altogether to thirteen gentlemen, for, by way of making the table a little more crowded, Charles Stamford had thought proper to come, though it was not his day. And we all talked as if our lives were at stake. The younger ones were much amused to be on duty thus, to be called upon to take care of the old gentlemen, and the rest of us understood the obligation we were under to talk, and worked resolutely at the conversation. For my part, I did very well, I had quite a pleasant neighbour; and, indeed, I have found that a great many of the City gentlemen are very pleasant to talk to. He told me all about the new railway it was intended to make, and scarcely laughed at all when I declared myself an enemy to new railroads, in our neighbourhood, at least.

'Why should you cut up our pleasant, smiling country?' I said. 'We have all the railways we want, and more. I do not say anything against what is necessary; but why make gashes across the country when it is not wanted—'

'Gashes—I don't think they are gashes,' said my neighbour. 'When I saw the white steam flying along the valley just now, I thought it very picturesque. I allow I do not like it too near; but Dinglefield is as safe as if it were in Paradise. No railway will climb your peaceable heights. If there was question however of a railway into Paradise itself, there is the man who would do it,' he said, looking across the table. 'I am a mere innocent myself. I do what other people tell me: but there is the dangerous man. I hope, for your sake, that he will give his word against this, for he would survey the moon if he thought it likely to answer.'

I peeped between the little thickets of flowers with which Sophy had covered the table, and looked at the man thus pointed out to me. He was sitting by Ursula Stamford, but he was not talking to her—she, as I have said, was occupied by her other neighbour at her right hand. He was an old man, not far from seventy, according to appearance, with snow-white hair, but a beard still almost black, a combination which is always striking. His features were fine, his dark eyes deeply sunk under eyebrows still dark like his beard. There was a gentleman on the other side of him whom he did not seem to care to talk to, and he was sitting, scarcely speaking, his face in repose.

'Do you mean that handsome old man?' I said.

'Old,' said my companion, slightly startled; he was about the same age himself if I had thought of it. 'Well, I suppose he is old,' he added, with a little laugh. 'You should talk to him. I don't know a more interesting man; and, as I tell you, he is the man to whom, if there was a railway to be made to the moon, everybody would turn. If he took the Channel tunnel in hand he would carry it through.'

'But that must be impossible,' said I. 'I hate the crossing; but I would not trust myself in a tunnel under the sea, not for— But you are laughing—it is impossible—'

'Impossible!—not in the very least—ask him. I think myself he's too speculative. But there is one thing certain. If Oakley took it up, it would go through. He'd do it. He is a man who does not believe in difficulties. There might be a great catastrophe next day, but one way or other he'd drive it through.'

I am a very quiet person myself, therefore it stands to reason that I should like a man who drives things through. Besides, he was a handsome old man. I looked at him again behind the flowers, while my companion went on talking, and I saw something which interested me. Miss Stamford came to a pause in her conversation with the man at her right hand, and she seized the opportunity to turn to the man on her left. At the first sound of her voice his abstract countenance lighted up. He turned hastily round with a look of recognition. How could he know Ursula Stamford, I said to myself? His face lighted up with a gleam of intelligence and pleasure, and something which, not knowing any other word, I can only call sweetness. He turned quite round to her, and began to talk with an interest and warmth which roused my immediate sympathy. I seemed to be looking on at an interesting scene in the theatre, seen from so great a distance that it was only the dumb-show which made it intelligible. And my neighbour carried on his discourse all the time.

'He has sprung from nothing,' he said. 'I don't know if he ever had a father. He began in the humblest way. The first time I heard of him was about thirty years ago, when he was struggling into business. He was not what you would call a young man then. (You ladies are hard upon age—you don't like it talked about when it concerns yourselves, but you stamp us down as old men without a bit of fellow-feeling—)'

Here I interrupted my instructor. 'I thought it was a weakness of ours only to dislike to be called old. I thought men were superior to such a little vanity—as to so many others.'

'You are satirical now. You think we are not superior to any vanity, and I shouldn't wonder if you were right. I was saying old Oakley was not a young man to start with. He was a sort of an engineer, self-taught, all self-taught, and he was trying to get into business as a contractor. Mrs. Mulgrave,' said my companion solemnly, 'have you any idea what that man is worth now? I thought so, as you didn't seem impressed. He is worth more than a million, that is the fact—he is made of money; losses don't seem to touch him. I do not suppose,' my friend added, with awe in his voice, 'that he knows how much he has.'

This information did not excite me as he expected, but I looked again between the geraniums at Mr. Oakley. I am afraid his handsome head interested me more than his fortune. 'And there are so many people who have nothing at all!' I said; 'but to look at him he might be a philosopher without a penny.'

'That is just like you ladies—you would think more of him if he were a philosopher without a penny. What an extraordinary mistake!' cried my companion, 'as if money were not a power, quite as interesting and a great deal more tangible than philosophy.'

His countenance flushed and changed. He was an enthusiast for money. I have met many such among General George's City friends: not in the sordid way we think of, but really as a great power.

When Mrs. St. Clair gave the sign to go away, I was quite sorry to break off this conversation, which was so much more interesting than the ordinary kind of talk. It was a beautiful June evening, and, instead of going into the drawing-room, we all went out upon the lawn where Simms had laid down the great lion-skin, of which they are all so proud, and some rugs which the General brought from India; for it is unnecessary to say that we elder people were a little afraid of the dew on the grass. But nobody could have taken cold on such a night. The borders were all red and white with roses standing out against the deep green of the shrubberies behind, and the colours seemed to repeat themselves in the sky, which was all one flush of rose above the blue, deepening into crimson as it descended, and burning like fire between the trees on the horizon line. Dinglefield stands high, with the broad Thames valley lying at its feet, of which you could get glimpses through the cuttings on the western side, if your eyes were not dazzled with all that blaze of gold. Miss Stamford was tired with her day in town, and established herself at once in her favourite basket-chair on the lawn. She sat there tranquil and happy while the rest walked about; her presence, her smile, the rest that seemed to breathe about her, gave stability and meaning to the whole place. She was only an old maid according to the vulgar, but you could not look at her without feeling sure that where she was, there was a home. I don't know that it had ever occurred to me to think so much about Ursula Stamford before. There was something in the air which affected me, though I did not know how. We could see the lighted windows of the dining-room, and hear the sound of the voices and laughter, though at a distance; and we all laughed too in sympathy, though we did not know what the jokes were. It was very pleasant and friendly, and rather droll. None of us had any particular desire to be joined by the gentlemen. We had done our duty by them, talked our very best to them, and flattered ourselves that it had all gone off very well; but though we were glad they were enjoying themselves, now that our part of the entertainment was over, we were not very sorry to think that they must all go away shortly by the last train. And no heart among us, I am safe to say, beat one pulsation the quicker when they came out upon the lawn, some of them slightly flushed with the laughter and the good cheer, to take their coffee, and their leave. It had grown almost dark by that time, and the white waistcoats (for they were in their morning dress, and most of them wore white waistcoats) made a great show in the half light. The greater part of them thanked us all for the delightful evening, not being quite clear which were, and which were not, the ladies of the house, but determined to fulfil all the duties of politeness. We walked with them to the gate to see them go, and shook hands with them all, though we did not know their names. I recollect the whole scene as clearly as a picture, though I knew at the time no reason why I should remember it: the dining-room brightly lighted, the table with all its fruit and flowers, and the vacant chairs pushed away, standing in all manner of groups: the drawing-room much more dim, just showing a glimmer of newly-lighted candles: the table on the lawn with Miss Stamford's white cap and half visible figure close to it: and all the rest of us standing about telling each other how well it had gone off, and listening to the voices of the gentlemen getting fainter and fainter as they streamed off behind the shrubberies along the road to the station. If any one had told us what changes would come from that visit! But how could any one have guessed the changes that were to come?

It was not the next day, but the day after that I met General George in the afternoon coming from the station. It was at least two hours before his usual time, and he was walking. The sight of him gave me a little shock. Something, I thought, must have happened. I ran over in my mind, as one naturally does, as I went up to him, the things that were most possible. There were nephews scattered about over all the world. Could it be that there was bad news of George Thistlethwaite in Ceylon, or Bertie Stamford at the Cape? or was it pleasanter intelligence from young Mrs. Thurston (née Ursula Humphreys) or Lucy Thistlethwaite, or one of the Lincolnshire girls? but that (I said to myself) would not be enough to bring the General home so much sooner than usual. When he came nearer however my mind became easier. He did not look unhappy, he looked puzzled, and now and then a gleam like laughter came over his face. When he saw me he came forward with an air of pleasure.

'You are the very person I wanted to see—if you will let me, I will walk home with you; but let us go the back way,' said General George to my intense surprise, 'for I don't want to see my sisters till I have taken your advice.'

'My advice! before you see your sisters, before you tell Ursula!' I cried, and then the General laughed and frowned, and looked angry and amused all in one. 'That is just where my difficulty lies,' he said. A difficulty about Ursula! it took away my breath.

'You will not believe it,' he said, 'but it is quite true. Charles came to me this morning with the absurdest question. He came to ask me who it was that sat next Mr. Oakley at dinner at Bonport on Tuesday—eh? what, did you notice anything?' he asked abruptly, for I had not been able to restrain a little exclamation. I have never boasted of my penetration, but from that moment I seemed to know exactly what he was going to say.

'I know who sat next Mr. Oakley at dinner,' I said.

'Ursula, wasn't it? we laid our heads together, and from all we could make out—he went to Charles first to find out who it was, and Charles, of course, made up his mind that it must have been one of the young ladies that had made such an impression. He proposed first Miss Woodroff and then the young widow: but no, no. Oakley said it was not a young lady. It was a lady whose hair was turning gray, who wore a cap, and used a double eye-glass. At last the conviction forced itself upon me. By Jove! it was Ursula—Ursula the man was thinking of! We both burst out laughing in his face— But afterwards,' the General added gloomily with a flush of displeasure, 'afterwards—I feel furious, Mrs. Mulgrave, though I may not show it; and that is why I have come first to you.

'What did he want?' I said, though I allow there was some hypocrisy in my question.

'What did he want?—you may well ask. He is a man of sixty-five, older than I am. He wants—to marry my sister,' said the General, with a half suppressed outcry of rage—'a man who has risen from the ranks—a stranger—a—a confounded— I beg you ten thousand pardons, Mrs. Mulgrave; he wants to pay his addresses, if you please, to Ursula! God bless us all—did you ever hear such a thing? I feel much more like cursing than blessing, to tell the truth.'

'But, General, he is very rich—richer than any one ever was before.'

'Ah, you have got bitten too,' he said, with a tone almost of disgust. 'That is what Charles says; but what is his money to me? What is it to any of us, Mrs. Mulgrave? You would not upset all the order of your life and change your habits, and give up your own ways for a million of money, would you? After all, when you have enough to be comfortable, what does money matter? Even the most extravagant of women can't put more than a certain number of yards of stuff into her dress. When you have enough, what does it matter whether the over-plus is counted by hundreds or by thousands?' said the General, with magnanimous but new-born indifference. If he cared so little about it, why should he go to the City every day, I could not help saying to myself; and, indeed, it came to my lips before I knew.

'If we all thought that,' I said, 'it would save a great deal of trouble. Perhaps you would not then have had these twelve gentlemen down to dinner and made all the mischief, General.'

General George laughed. 'Perhaps I shouldn't,' he said, 'but that is different. It is not for the money, but the occupation, Mrs. Mulgrave; and of course when one has money invested one wants to make something by it. However my opinion is that it would be much better to say nothing about this folly to Ursula. To be sure,' he added with a look of half-defiant assurance which he belied by a suspicious glance of inquiry at me,' it might amuse her; but it could have no other effect. I don't see why I should take any notice to Ursula.'

'But Mr. Oakley—will he be satisfied?'

'Old Oakley? Upon my word, I don't see why I should consider him or what will satisfy him,' said the General, growing red; but he was uneasy. He paused, then turned to me again. 'If you were in my position, what should you do?'

'I should tell her, and let her judge; after all, it is she who must decide.'

'Decide—judge! you speak,' cried General George, 'as if it were possible—as if it might be within the bounds of— Bah! do you suppose that Ursula—Ursula! my sister—would, could hesitate one moment?'

'No.' I said 'no,' half because I really thought so, but half because he was so much excited, and it was necessary to calm him. 'I do not suppose she would; but still, a woman should be told when a man— It is the greatest compliment he can pay her, and it is always flattering even when it is impossible!'

'Flattering—a compliment! What can you be thinking of?' the General cried in high disdain; 'that an old fellow like that should propose to appropriate and take possession of—a lady! I don't say my sister, which of course is the sting of it,' he said with a laugh, calming down again, 'but any lady—'

'Dear General, forgive me,' I said; 'you always talk, you gentlemen, of marriage as the end of every woman's ambition, and you are always ready to jibe at those who have not attained that great end. Then how, when this elevation is in her power, do you venture to think of keeping her in ignorance of it?'

He turned round upon me almost with violence. 'Elevation!' he cried; then perceiving, I suppose, by something in my eyes what I meant, laughed more uneasily than ever. 'Come,' he said, 'we may say silly things, I allow we all say silly things; but when you come to that—to speak of elevation for my sister from any offer, or that she should think it a compliment!—God bless us all!—there are a great many foolish things that one says, but you know better than to take it all for gospel. Of course when one speaks of women one does not think of— By Jove, I am only getting deeper. Don't hit a man when he is down, but be serious, and give me your advice.'

'One does not think of one's own sisters,' said I, for I did not mean to spare him, 'only of other people's sisters, or of those who have nobody to stand up for them; but I will not be ungenerous, General I will give you my advice. Tell Ursula, and let her judge for herself.'

'Judge!—she can have but one opinion. But that is what Charlie says. I suppose the two of you must be right,' said the General grudgingly. He walked on by my side in silence, cutting down the weeds by the roadside ferociously with his stick; then repeated with a still more churlish assent, 'I suppose what you two people of the world say must be right.'

I smiled within myself to be called a woman of the world; but one must not take the words of an angry man to heart. When he came to the turn of the road which led to Brothers-and-Sisters he muttered something about getting it over, and took off his hat and left me without another word. Poor General George! Under all his pretences at anger he was in a great fright. Either he believed his own careless talk, and thought that a husband was too fine a thing for any woman to refuse, or else— But I need not discuss the vague feeling of insecurity which had begun to creep over him. For my part, I did not feel alarmed. I had more confidence in Ursula's faithfulness than he had. At the same time, the crisis was exciting, and I thought the time very long until the evening began to darken, and I felt myself at liberty—

dinner being over—to run over the corner of the Green which lay between us, as I often did in the evening, and see what Ursula said.

CHAPTER III

The family party was on the lawn as usual; Miss Stamford seated in her own chair with her knitting and her feet upon the lion-skin; while Mrs. St. Clair beside her, with a basket full of bright scraps, had been dressing dolls for a bazaar. Sophy was cutting off the withered roses with a large pair of garden scissors; all their occupations were quite as usual. But there was an aspect about the family which was not usual. In the distance the General's step was audible pacing about; and there was an odour of his cigar in the air; all as peaceful, as homelike as it always was; but yet a something in the atmosphere which had not been there yesterday. As I came up with my shawl over my head, the General tossed his cigar away and came nearer, and Sophia put down the basket with the dead roses, and Mrs. St. Clair got up to get me a chair. The only one that had not changed in the least was Ursula, who raised her head and her eyes and gave me a friendly nod as she always did. She went on with her knitting without any intermission. It is work which does not demand attention, nor so much light as doll-dressing. They were all very glad to see me—more glad even than on ordinary occasions: for it was clear that the situation was highly tendu, as the French say, and that a new-comer was a relief.

'What a beautiful evening!' we all said together, and then stopped abashed, as people do who have rushed into the same commonplace speech.

Then Ursula added, 'Of course, that is the first thing we must say to each other. I think there never was such a summer—so bright, so steady, one fine day after another. Here is a fortnight, or nearly so, that we have not had one drop of rain.'

'Quite wonderful,' said I. 'The hay, I hear, is a sight to see. A day or two more, and we shall all begin to pray for rain. We are never content whatever we have.'

'A little variety is always pleasant,' Mrs. St. Clair said. Meanwhile, while we talked about the weather, the General hung about over our little group like a storm-cloud. He did not say anything, but he looked tempestuous; he, who was always so calm. Presently he turned away, and went off to say something to Simms, who appeared just then with a note or a message.

'I suppose,' said Mrs. St. Clair, turning to me, 'you know all about it. George told us that he had met you, and told you—'

'Yes, he told me;' but I did not know what to say; they all wore a look of agitation, except Ursula, who was as calm as usual—more calm than usual, I should have said; but, no doubt, that was only in comparison with the agitation of the rest.

'And I suppose you think like the rest, that I will jump at a husband the moment one is offered to me,' said Miss Stamford with a smile.

'We don't think so, Ursula. We know it is not the first time. It is only George that is so frightened, poor fellow.'

'Why should he be so frightened?' Miss Stamford cried. 'No; it is not the first time. I may take that little credit to myself. I might have my head turned, perhaps, if it had been the first time. But, after all, it is not so much to brag of. I suppose he wants somebody to take care of him when he gets old and feeble; but he ought to have somebody younger than me.'

Sixty-five is not what you would call young; but it was odd how we all were of opinion that Mr. Oakley's time for being old and feeble was still a good way off, a thing to come. I acknowledged that I shared this weakness. We were all about the same age, and it did not occur to us that we were already old.

'He shows his sense,' said I, taking the part of the absent to whom nobody did any justice, 'as well as his good taste. Poor man, though he is so rich, I am very sorry for him. I wish Ursula had met him twenty years ago when there would have been no harm—'

'No harm! do you know that he is a nobody—a man self-made?' said Mrs. St. Clair; 'not a match for Ursula Stamford if he had been ever so young!'

'But you did not think of that in Fia's case,' said Sophy; 'he was rich and you never said a word. You thought it quite reasonable. 'What do his grandfathers matter to us?' you said. I am not sure myself whether it does or not; but you said so, you know; and George proposed the bride and bridegroom at the wedding, and everybody was pleased. Now this Mr. Oakley is a very nice man, whatever you say, for I had a good deal of talk with him myself; and if Ursula chose—'

'You should not interfere,' said Mrs. St. Clair; 'you are always sentimental. Of course, if there is so much as a thought of a marriage, Sophy is always in favour of it; but to think of Ursula at her time of life!'

'You all talk very much at your ease about Ursula,' said Miss Stamford. 'I suppose Ursula may have a word, a little share in it, for herself. The way my family consult over me'—she said, turning to me with a slight blush and laugh. 'I think George might have held his tongue; that would have been the more satisfactory way.'

'It was my fault,' I cried hurriedly: 'he told me that he thought it would be best not to tell you. You must forgive me, Ursula, if I gave him bad advice; I thought you ought to know.'

Before I had half said this, I saw I had made a mistake; but one must finish one's sentence, however foolish it may be. Ursula suspended her knitting for a moment and looked at me with calm amazement.

'Not tell me!' she said. 'Why should he have kept it from me?'

The emphasis was very slight, but it meant a great deal. It never occurred to her that a thing which concerned her so closely should have been kept from herself; the question was why should we know; and I confess I felt very much ashamed of having any say in it, when I met the calm, astonished look of her eyes.

'It is getting a little chilly,' she said, rising up. 'I think it is time to go indoors.'

We all followed her quite humbly, and the General came stalking after us, more like a thunder-cloud than ever. He had been talking to poor Simms in a voice which was not pleasant, and he appeared at the drawings-room window by which we all entered with the large lion-skin in his arms.

'I can't have this left out all night in those heavy dews,' he said. I do not think I ever saw those signs of suppressed irritation, which are too common in families, among the Stamfords before.

Next morning General George came in for a moment before I had breakfasted, to tell me for my satisfaction that all was right. His face was quite clear again. 'I was a little cross last night. I fear you may have supposed that I for a moment doubted my sister. Not a moment, Mrs. Mulgrave. I have got to give him his answer, poor old fellow. I can't help feeling a little sorry for him all the same. What bad luck for the poor old beggar! Of all the women there to hit upon the one who was simply hopeless! Some men always have that sort of fate.'

'He showed his taste,' said I; 'but I heard he was the luckiest man in the world, General; that he always succeeded in everything; that however wild the project was, he was the man to carry it through.'

I said this partly in malice, I am bound to admit, and I was very successful. The General's face clouded over again: he set his teeth. 'He shall not succeed this time;' and he said something more in his moustache, some stronger words which I was not intended to hear. It was all over then, this odd little episode. I stood and watched him from my door half relieved, half wondering. Was it all over? I did not feel so satisfied or so certain as General George.

A few days of perfect quiet ensued. When a week passed we all felt really satisfied. It was over then? Mr. Oakley had accepted his refusal. To be sure one did not see what else he could have done, though I confess that I had not expected it for my part. However, on the Sunday morning the moment I looked across to the Stamfords' pew after getting settled in my own, it seemed to me that I could see indications of a new event. Both Mrs. St. Clair and Sophy were looking at me when I raised my head; they could not restrain themselves. They gave me anxious, significant glances with little hardly perceptible signs of the head and hand. When the service was over, and we were going out, Sophy was at my side in a moment. We were not actually out of church when I felt her arm slide into mine and a whisper in my ear. 'She has got a letter!' Sophy said, all in a tremble of eagerness. Mrs. St. Clair came up on the other side as soon as we were clear of the stream of people. 'It is getting really serious,' she said; 'he will not take a refusal. It is quite absurd, and George is dreadfully angry. He is just as absurd on the other side.'

'And what does Ursula say?'

'Oh, Ursula does not say anything. Of course we could not help knowing about the letter. It was very long and very much in earnest—'

'Oh, quite impassioned!' cried Sophy. She had not encountered anything so exciting for years. She was pale with interest and emotion, shaking her head in intense seriousness. 'He says that he appeals to her sense of justice not to condemn him without a hearing. It is quite beautiful. I am sure he is a nice man.'

'And then, you know, there is the other side of the question,' said Mrs. St. Clair seriously. 'I did not quite understand when we spoke of it last. Charlie says he is immensely rich—not just ordinarily comfortable like so many people, but a true millionnaire. That changes the aspect of the matter a little, don't you think? Not that I am a mercenary person, still less Ursula; but when you come to think of it, wealth to that extent is something to be considered. Just fancy the good she might do,' cried the sensible sister, 'and the number of young people we have looking to us! I do think it is not exactly right to ignore that side of the question.'

'Charlie thinks it is quite wrong,' said Sophy, shaking her head.

The General had not even stopped to say 'Good morning' outside the church door as he usually did. It was his brother Charles who was with Ursula. The General walked straight home, without looking to the right hand or the left. I felt a great sympathy for him. It was he that would feel it most if anything happened; and he was the only one of the family who had that fantastic delicacy of sentiment which some of us feel for those we love, so that the merest touch of anything that could be called ridicule, seemed sacrilege and desecration to him.

I must not attempt to go in detail into all that followed. Miss Stamford wrote a very beautiful letter (they all told me) to her antiquated lover, telling him how sorry she was to be the cause of any annoyance to him, and hoping that the vexation would be but temporary, as indeed she felt sure it must be—but that his proposals were quite out of the question. This, of course, was what every woman would have said in the circumstances. But neither did Mr. Oakley take this for an answer. There was another letter by return of post in which they said he implored her to believe that nothing about the matter was temporary—that it was a question of life and death to him; that now was his only chance of happiness. Happiness! for a man of sixty-five! For my part I could not help laughing, but it was no laughing matter for the household at Brothers-and-Sisters. A few days after this I met Mr. Oakley himself on his way to the house. He recognized me at once, but naturally he did not know who I was. He took me for one of the family, and came up to me carrying his hat in his hand. He was a very handsome old man. His hair was snow-white, a mass of it rising up in waves from his forehead, with eyebrows still black and strongly marked, and the finest brilliant dark eyes. I said to myself mentally: 'If it had been I, I should have given in at once.' And his manners were beautiful—not the manners of society—the deferential respect of a man who knows women chiefly through books, and does not understand the free and easy modern way of treating us. He kept his hat in his hand as he stood and spoke. 'I do not know,' he said, 'if I have the honour of speaking to a sister of Miss Stamford's, but I know I met you there.'

'Not a sister, but a very affectionate friend,' I said. His face lighted up instantly; he almost loved me for saying so. 'Then if that is the case we ought to be friends too,' he said. I was so much interested that I turned and walked with him, regardless of prudence. What would the Stamfords say if they saw me thus identifying myself with the cause of their assailant? but the interest of this strange little romance carried me away.

'I must see her,' he said. 'Don't you think I have a right to see her? They need not surely grudge me one opportunity of pleading my own cause. No, indeed, I don't blame them. If I had such a treasure—nay,' he went on with a smile, 'when I have that treasure, I will guard it from every wind that blows. I don't wonder at their precautions. But Stamford does not treat me with generosity; he does not trust to my honour: that is why I adopt his own tactics. I must try to effect an entrance while he is away.'

'I don't think Ursula will have you, Mr. Oakley,' I said.

'Perhaps not; but that remains to be seen. She has never seen me—that is, she has never seen the real John Oakley, only a director of her brother's company, two different persons, Mrs. Mulgrave, if you will allow me to say so.'

'But she saw you before she knew you were a director. She travelled with you. You were the gentleman like Don Quixote—'

How foolish I was! Of course I ought not to have said it. I felt that before the words were out of my mouth. Such encouragement as this was enough to counterbalance any number of severities. 'Ah! I am like Don Quixote, am I?' he said; and once more, and more brightly than ever, his handsome old face blazed into the brightest expression. Poor Mr. Oakley! I threw myself heart and soul into his faction after this; for indeed, as I afterwards heard, he had not at all a pleasant 'time,' as the Americans say, that afternoon. When he sent in his name at Brothers-and-Sisters he was told that the ladies were out, and, though he waited, all that he managed to obtain was a hurried interview with Mrs. St. Clair, who conveyed to him Ursula's entreaty that he would accept her answer as final, and not ask to see her. Sophy told me after (she must have hidden herself somewhere, for nobody but Frances was supposed to be present) that his behaviour was beautiful. He bowed to the ground, she said, and declared that no one could be so much interested as he was in observing Miss Stamford's slightest wish; that he would not for the world intrude upon her, but wait her pleasure another time. Mrs. St. Clair's heart softened too, and she did not protest, as perhaps she ought to have done, against this 'other time.' He passed by my cottage as he went away, and I do not deny that I was in my little garden looking out, 'I have had no luck,' he said, shaking his head, but still with a smile, 'no luck to-day; but another time I shall succeed better.'

I ran to the gate, I felt so much interested. 'Do you really think, Mr. Oakley,' I said, 'that it is worth your while to persevere?'

'Worth my while?' he said; 'certainly it is worth my while: for I am in no hurry. I can bide my time.'

Bide his time at sixty-five! I stood and looked at him as long as he was in sight. There is nothing like courage for securing the sympathy of the bystanders.

After this the excitement ran very high both in the house of the Stamfords and in the community in general. We all took sides: and while General George made himself more and more disagreeable, and we all watched and spied her every action, Ursula was subjected all the time to a ceaseless assault from the other side. Letters poured upon her; beautiful baskets of flowers arrived suddenly, secretly, so that no one knew how they came. After a while, when the autumn commenced, there came hampers of game and of fruit, all in the same anonymous, magnificent way. And then the clever old man found out a still more effectual way of siege. The Stamfords had always nephews who wanted appointments or who required to be pushed. For instance, there was young Charley, of the Inner Temple, sadly in want of a brief: when lo! all at once, briefs began to tumble down from heaven upon the young man. In a week he had more business than he knew what to do with. And Willie Thistlethwaite had a living offered to him; and Cecil, whom they were so anxious to place with an engineer, though the premium was so serious a matter, suddenly found a place open to him with no premium at all. I believe in my heart that it was Mr. Charles Stamford who helped the old lover to recommend himself in this effectual, quiet way; for how should he have found out all the nephews without help? But as one of these mysterious benefits after another happened to the distant members of the family, the feeling rose stronger and stronger among all their friends. We set down everything, from the flowers to the living, unhesitatingly to Mr. Oakley;

and at last public sentiment on the Green got to such a pitch that whereas people had laughed at the whole matter at first as little more than a joke, everybody now grew indignant, and protested that Ursula Stamford ought to be cut and sent to Coventry if she did not marry Don Quixote. I don't know who had betrayed this description which she had herself given of him. But everybody now called him Don Quixote, and the whole community took his cause to heart. While this feeling rose outside, a wave of the same sentiment, but still more powerful, got up within. Mr. Charles spoke out and declared (as, indeed, he had done from the first) that to neglect such an opportunity of strengthening the family influence would be a mere flying in the face of Providence; and then something still more extraordinary happened. Frances herself—who looked upon all married ladies in the light of prospective widows, and regarded the one state only as a preparation for the other—Frances herself suddenly threw off her allegiance to the General and went over boldly to the other side. Sophy had been Mr. Oakley's champion all along. They began to turn upon Ursula, to accuse her of behaving badly to her unwearied suitor—they accused her of playing fast and loose, of amusing herself with his devotion. They raised a family outcry against her, and brought down all the married sisters and the distant brothers upon her, with a storm of disapproving letters. 'The man that has provided for my Cecil,' one indignant lady wrote, 'surely, surely, deserves better at my sister's hands;' and 'I really think, my dear Ursula, that any petty objections of your own should yield before the evident advantage to the family,' was what the eldest brother of all, the father of the young barrister, said. On the other side, with gloom on his face, and a sneer upon his lip (where it was so completely out of place), and a bitter jibe now and then about the falsity and weakness of women, General George stood all alone, and kept a jealous watch upon her. His love for his favourite sister seemed to have turned to gall. He would have none of her usual services; he no longer consulted her about anything—no longer told her what he was going to do. It is to be supposed that by this cruel method the General intended to prove to his sister how much kinder and better a master he was than any other she could aspire to; but if this was the case, he took a very curious way of showing his superiority. And Ursula stood between these two parties, her home and her life becoming more and more unbearable every day.

At last she took a sudden resolution. Sophy ran over to tell me of it late one September evening. There were tears in Sophy's eyes, and she was full of awe. 'Ursula has made up her mind, she said, almost below her breath. 'It is all over, Mrs. Mulgrave. She has written him a terrible letter—it is quite beautiful, but it is something terrible at the same time; and she is going off abroad to-morrow. She says she cannot bear it any longer; she says we are killing her. She says she must make an end of it, and that she will go away. Poor Mr. Oakley!' Sophy said, and cried. As for me, I also felt deeply impressed and a little awe-stricken, but I had a lingering faith in Don Quixote notwithstanding all.

CHAPTER IV

There had been very little time left for preparations, and hardly any one, Sophy told me, was aware they were going away. Except myself, no one of the neighbours knew. All the arrangements were hastily made. Ursula wanted to be gone if possible before Mr. Oakley could take any further step. I went over early next morning to see if I could be of any use. Ursula was in her room, doing her packing. To see her in her old black silk with her simple little cap covering her gray hair, and to think she was being driven from her home by the importunities of a too-ardent lover, struck me as more ridiculous than it had ever done before. She saw it herself, and laughed as she stood for a moment before the long glass, in which she had caught a glimpse of herself.

'I am a pretty sort of figure for all this nonsense,' she said, permitting herself for the first time an honest laugh on the subject; but then her face clouded once more. 'The truth is,' she said, 'it would all be mere nonsense, but for George. It is he that takes it so much to heart.'

'Indeed,' said I. 'I think it is not at all nice of the General; and I don't think it would be nonsense in any case. There is some one else I acknowledge, Ursula, that I think of more than the General.'

She did not say anything more. Her face paled, then grew red again, and she went on with her packing. It is needless to say that I was of no manner of use. I got rid of a little of my own excitement by going, that was all. I went again in the evening to see the last of them. It was a lovely September evening. There had been a wonderfully fine sunset, and the whole horizon was still flaming, the trees standing out almost black in their deep greenness, though touched with points of yellow, against the broad lines of crimson and wide openings of wistful green blueness in the sky. The days were already growing short. There is no time of the year at which one gets so much good of the sunset. As I went across the corner of the Green the gables and irregular chimneys of the old house stood up among the heavy foliage against the lower band of colour where the green and blue died into yellow the 'daffodil sky' of the poet. They too looked black against that light, and there was a wistful look, I thought, about the whole place, protesting dumbly against its abandonment. Why should people go away from such a pleasant and peaceful place to wander over the world? There was a solitary blackbird singing clear and loud, filling the whole air with his song. I wonder if that song is really much less beautiful than the nightingale's. I was thinking how blank and cold the house would be when they were all gone. The chimneys and gables already looked so cold, smokeless, fireless, appealing against the glare of the summer, which carried away the dwellers inside, and extinguished the cheerful fire of home. As I went in I saw the fly from the 'Barleymow' creeping along towards the house to carry the luggage to the station. The old white horse came along quite reluctantly, as if he did not like the errand. I suppose all that his slow pace meant was that he had gone through a long day's work, and was tired; but it is so natural to convey a little of one's own feelings to everything, even the chimneys of the old house. There was nobody down-stairs when I went in. Simms told me in a dolorous tone that Miss Stamford was putting on her bonnet.

'And I don't like it, ma'am—I don't like it—going away like this, just when the country's at its nicest. If it was the General for his bit of sport, his shooting, or that, I wouldn't mind,' said Simms; 'but what call have the ladies got away from home? They'll go a-catching fevers or something, see if they don't. It's tempting Providence.'

'I hope not, Simms,' said I; but Simms took no comfort from my hoping. He shook his head and he uttered a groan as he set a chair for me in the centre of the drawing-room. No more cosy corners, the man seemed to say—no more low seats and pleasant talk—an uncompromising chair in the middle of the room, and a business object. These were all of which the old drawing-room would be capable when the ladies were away. I set down Simms along with the house itself, protesting with all its chimneys, and the old white horse lumbering reluctantly along to fetch the luggage, and the blackbird remonstrating loudly among the trees. They were all opposed to Ursula's departure, and so was I.

The door opened, and Sophy came in more despondent than all of these sundry personages and things put together. 'They are rather late—the boxes are just being put on to the fly. Will you come out here and bid her good-bye?' said Sophy, who was limp with crying. I never could tell whether it was imagination or a real quickening of my senses, but at that moment, as I rose to follow Sophy, I heard as clearly as I ever heard it in my life the galloping of horses on the dry, dusty summer road. I heard it as distinctly as I hear now the soft dropping of the rain, a sound as different as possible from all the other sounds I had been hearing—horses galloping at their very best, a whip cracking, the sound of a frantic energy of haste. Then I went out into the hall, following Sophy. It must have been imagination, for with all these lawns and shrubberies round, one could not, you may well believe, hear passing carriages like that. Ursula was standing at the foot of the stairs in her travelling dress. It was a large, long hall, more oblong than square, into which all the rooms opened; the drawing-room was opposite the outer door, and the General's room (the library as it was called) was further back nearer the stairs. He was inside, but the door was open. Ursula stood outside talking to the cook, who was to be a kind of housekeeper while they were away. 'Don't trouble Miss Sophy except when you are perplexed yourself. On ordinary occasions you will do quite nicely, I am sure; you will do everything that is wanted,' she was saying in her kind, cheerful voice, for Ursula did not show any appearance of regret, though all of us who were staying behind were melancholy. The men were hoisting up the trunks with which the hall was encumbered on the top of the fly, which was visible with its old white horse standing tired and pensive at the open door. And Mrs. St. Clair appeared behind her sister, slowly coming down-stairs with a cloak over her arm and a bag in her hand. There was nothing left but to say good-bye and wish them a good journey and a speedy return.

But all at once in a moment there was a change. The horses I had been dreaming of, or had heard in a dream, drew up with a whirlwind of sound at the gate. Then something darted across the unencumbered light beyond the fly and came between the old white horse and the door. I think he—for to use any neutral expressions about him from the first moment at which he showed himself would be impossible—I think he lifted his hand to the men who were putting up the trunks to arrest them; at all events they stopped and scratched their heads and opened their mouths, and stood staring at him, as did Sophy and I, altogether confounded, yet with sudden elation in our hearts. He stepped past us all as lightly as any young paladin of twenty, taking off his hat. His white hair seemed all in a moment to light up everything, to quicken the place. Ursula was the last to see him. She was still talking quite calmly to the cook, though even Mrs. St. Clair on the stairs had seen the new incident, and had dropped her cloak in amazement. He went straight up to her, without a pause, without drawing breath. I am sure we all held ours in spellbound anxiety and attention. When Ursula saw him standing by her side she started as if she had been shot—she made a hasty step back and looked at him, catching her breath too with sudden alarm. But he had the air of perfect self-command.

'Miss Stamford,' he said, 'will you grant me half an hour's interview before you go?'

For the first time Ursula lost her self-possession; she fluttered and trembled like a girl, and could not speak for a moment. Then she stammered out, 'I hope you will excuse me. We shall be—late for the train.'

'Half an hour?' he said; 'I only ask half an hour—only hear me, Miss Stamford, hear what I have got to say. I will not detain you more than half an hour.'

Ursula looked round her helplessly. Whether she saw us standing gazing at her I cannot tell, or if she was conscious that the General behind her had come out to the door, and was standing there petrified, staring like the rest of us. She looked round vaguely, as if asking aid from the world in general. And whether her impetuous old lover took her hand and drew it within his arm, or if she accepted his arm, I cannot say. But the next thing of which we were aware was that they passed us, the two together, arm in arm, into the drawing-room. He had noted the open door with his quick eye, and there he led her trembling past us. Next moment it closed upon the momentous interview, and the chief actors in this strange scene disappeared. We were left all gazing at each other—Sophy and I at one side of the hall, Mrs. St. Clair on the stairs, where she stood as if turned to stone, her cloak fallen from her arm; and the General at the door of his room with a face like a thunder-cloud, black and terrible. We stared at each other speechless, the central object at which we had all been gazing withdrawn suddenly from us. There were some servants also of the party, Simms standing over Miss Stamford's box, the address of which he affected to be scanning, and the cabman scratching his head. We all looked at each other with ludicrous, blank faces. It was the General who was the first to speak. He took no notice of us. He stepped out from his door into the middle of the hall, and pointed imperiously to the box. 'Take all that folly away,' he said harshly, and with another long step strode out of the house and disappeared.

He did not come back till late that night, when all thoughts of the train had long departed from everybody's head. Before that time need I say it was all settled? I had always been doubtful myself about Ursula. She had been afraid of making a joke of herself by a late marriage. She had shrunk, perhaps, too, at her time of life, from all the novelty and the change; but even at fifty-seven a woman retains her imagination, and it had been captivated in spite of herself by the bit of strange romance thus oddly introduced into her life. Is any one ever old enough to be insensible to the pleasure of being singled out and pursued with something that looked like real passion? I do not suppose so; Ursula had been alarmed by the softening of her own feelings; she had been remorseful and conscience-stricken about her secret treachery to her brother. In short, I had felt all along that she must have had very little confidence in herself when she was driven to the expedient of running away.

They would not let me go, though I felt myself out of place at such a moment, so that I had my share in the excitement as I had in the suspense. And after all the struggle and the suspense it is inconceivable how easy and natural the settlement of the matter seemed, and what a relief it was that it should be decided.

As soon as the first commotion was over Mrs. Douglas came to me, took my hands in hers, and led me out by the open window. 'George!' she said to me with a little gasp. 'What shall we do about George? How will he take it? And if he comes in upon us all without any preparation, what will happen? I don't know what to do.'

'He must know what has happened,' said I; 'he saw there was only one thing that could happen. He must know what he has to expect.'

Mrs. St. Clair clasped her hands together. What with the excitement and the pleasure and the pain the tears stood in her eyes. 'Ursula was always his favourite sister,' she said; 'how will he take it? and where is he?—wandering about, making himself wretched this melancholy night.'

It was not in reality a melancholy night. It was dark, and the colour had gone out of the sky, which looked of a deep wintry blue between the black tree-tops which swayed in the wind. Mrs. St. Clair shivered a little, partly from the contrast with the bright room inside, partly from anxiety. 'Where can he be?—where can he be wandering?' she said. We had both the same idea—that he must have gone into the woods and be wandering about there in wild resentment and distress. 'And we must not stay out here or Mr. Oakley will think something is wrong, and Ursula will be unhappy,' she said with a sigh.

It was then I proposed that I should stay outside to break the news to the General when he appeared—a proposal which, after a while, Mrs. Douglas was compelled to accept, though she protested—for after all, my absence would not be remarked, and it was easy to say that I had gone home, as I meant to do.

But I cannot say that the post was a pleasant one. I walked about for some time in front of the house, and then I came and sat down in the porch 'for company.' There was nothing, as I have said, specially melancholy about the night, but the contrast of the scene within and this without struck the imagination. When a door opened the voices within came with a kind of triumph into the darkness where the disappointed and solitary brother was wandering: and so absorbed was I in thoughts of General George and his downfall that I almost missed the subject of them, who came suddenly round the corner of the house when I was not looking for him. It was he who perceived me, rather than I who was on the watch for him. 'You here, Mrs. Mulgrave!' he said in amazement. I believe he thought, as I started to my feet, that I had been asleep.

'General!' I cried then in my confusion. 'Stop here a moment, do not go in. I have something to say to you.'

He laughed—which was a sound so unexpected that it bewildered me. 'My kind friend,' he said, 'have you stayed here to break the news to me? But it is unnecessary—from the moment I saw Oakley arrive I knew how it must be. Ursula has been going—she has been going. I have seen it for three or four weeks past.'

'And, General! thank Heaven you are not angry, you are taking it in a Christian way.'

He laughed again—a sort of angry laugh. 'Am I taking it in a Christian way? I am glad you think so, Mrs. Mulgrave. When a thing cannot be cured it must be endured, you know. I am out of court— I have no ground to stand upon, and he is master of the field. I don't mean to make her unhappy whatever happens. Is he here still?'

'Yes,' I said trembling. He offered me his arm precisely as Mr. Oakley had offered his to Ursula. 'Then we'll go and join them,' he said.

This was how it all ended. There was not a speck on his boots or the least trace of disorder. Instead of roaming the woods in despair, as we thought, he had been quietly drinking Lady Denzil's delightful tea and playing chess with Sir Thomas. They had seen nothing unusual about him, we heard afterwards, and never knew that he ought to have been starting for the Continent when he walked in that evening, warmly welcomed to tea—which shows what sentimental estimates we women form about the feelings of men.

The marriage took place very soon after. Mr. Oakley bought Hillhead, the finest place in the neighbourhood, very soon after; he was so rich that he bought a house whenever he found one that pleased him, as I might buy an old blue china pot. The one was a much greater extravagance to me than the other was to him. And they lived very happy ever after, and nobody, so far as I know, has ever had occasion to regret this love at first sight at sixty—this elderly romance.

MRS. MERRIDEW'S FORTUNE

CHAPTER I

There are two houses in my neighbourhood which illustrate so curiously two phases of life, that everybody on the Green, as well as myself, has been led into the habit of classing them together. The first reason of this of course is, that they stand together; the second, that they are as unlike in every way as it is possible to conceive. They are about the same size, with the same aspect, the same green circle of garden surrounding them; and yet as dissimilar as if they had been brought out of two different worlds. They are not on the Green, though they are undeniably a part of Dinglefield, but stand on the Mercot Road, a broad country road with a verdant border of turf and fine trees shadowing over the hedgerows. The Merridews live in the one, and in the other are Mrs. Spencer and Lady Isabella. The house of the two ladies, which has been already described, is as perfect in all its arrangements as if it were a palace: a silent, soft, fragrant, dainty place, surrounded by lawns like velvet; full of flowers in perfect bloom, the finest kinds, succeeding each other as the seasons change. Even in autumn, when the winds are blowing, you never see a fallen leaf about, or the least symptom of untidiness. They have enough servants for everything that is wanted, and the servants are as perfect as the flowers—noiseless maids and soft-voiced men. Everything goes like machinery, with an infallible regularity; but like machinery oiled and deadened, which emits no creak nor groan. This is one of the things upon which Mrs. Spencer specially prides herself.

And just across two green luxuriant hedges, over a lawn which is not like velvet, you come to the Merridews'. It is possible if you passed it on a summer day that, notwithstanding the amazing superiority of the other, you would pause longer, and be more amused with a glance into the enclosure of the latter house. The lawn is not the least like velvet; probably it has not been mown for three weeks at least, and the daisies are irrepressible. But there, tumbled down in the midst of it, are a bunch of little children in pinafores—'all the little ones,' as Janet Merridew, the eldest daughter, expresses herself, with a certain soft exasperation. I would rather not undertake to number them or record their names, but there they are, a knot of rosy, round-limbed, bright-eyed, living things, some dark and some fair, with an amazing impartiality; but all chattering as best they can in nursery language, with rings of baby laughter, and baby quarrels, and musings of infinite solemnity. Once tumbled out here, where no harm can come to them, nobody takes any notice of the little ones. Nurse, sitting by serenely under a tree, works all the morning through, and there is so much going on indoors to occupy the rest.

Mr. and Mrs. Merridew, I need not add, had a large family—so large that their house overflowed, and when the big boys were at home from school, was scarcely habitable. Janet, indeed, did not hesitate to express her sentiments very plainly on the subject. She was just sixteen, and a good child, but full of the restless longing for something, she did not know what, and visionary discontent with her surroundings, which is not uncommon at her age. She had a way of paying me visits, especially during the holidays, and speaking more frankly on domestic subjects than was at all expedient. She would come in, in summer, with a tap on the glass which always startled me, through the open window, and sink down on a sofa and utter a long sigh of relief. 'Oh, Mrs. Mulgrave!' she would say, 'what a good thing you never had any children!' taking off, as she spoke, the large hat which it was one of her grievances to be compelled to wear.

'Is that because you have too many at home?' I said.

'Oh, yes, far too many; fancy, ten! Why should poor papa be burdened with ten of us? and so little money to keep us all on. And then a house gets so untidy with so many about. Mamma does all she can, and I do all I can; but how is it possible to keep it in order? When I look across the hedges to Mrs. Spencer and Lady Isabella's and see everything so nice and so neat I could die of envy. And you are always so shady, and so cool, and so pleasant here.'

'It is easy to be neat and nice when there is nobody to put things out of order,' said I; 'but when you are as old as I am, Janet, you will get to think that one may buy one's neatness too dear.'

'Oh, I delight in it!' cried the girl. 'I should like to have everything nice, like you; all the books and papers just where one wants them, and paper-knives on every table, and ink in the ink-bottles, and no dust anywhere. You are not so dreadfully particular as Mrs. Spencer and Lady Isabella. I think I should like to see some litter on the carpet or on the lawn now and then for a change. But oh, if you could only see our house! And then our things are so shabby: the drawing-room carpet is all faded with the sun, and mamma will never have the blinds properly pulled down. And Selina, the housemaid, has so much to do. When I scold her, mamma always stops me, and bids me recollect we can't be as nice as you other people, were we to try ever so much. There is so much to do in our house. And then those dreadful big boys!'

'My dear,' said I, 'ring the bell, and we will have some tea; and you can tell Jane to bring you some of that strawberry jam you are so fond of—and forget the boys.'

'As if one could!' said Janet, 'when they are all over the place—into one's very room, if one did not mind; their boots always either dusty or muddy, and oh, the noise they make! Mamma won't make them dress in the evenings, as I am sure she should. How are they ever to learn to behave like Christians, Mrs. Mulgrave, if they are not obliged to dress and come into the drawing-room at night?'

'I dare say they would run out again and spoil their evening clothes, my dear,' I said.

'That is just what mamma says,' cried Janet; 'but isn't it dreadful to have always to consider everything like that? Poor mamma, too—often I am quite angry, and then I think—perhaps she would like a house like Mrs. Spencer and Lady Isabella's as well as I should, if we had money enough. I suppose in a nice big house with heaps of maids and heaps of money, and everything kept tidy for you, one would not mind even the big boys.'

'I think under those circumstances most people would be glad to have them,' said I.

'I don't understand how anybody can like boys,' said Janet, with reflective yet contemptuous emphasis. 'A baby-boy is different. When they are just the age of little Harry, I adore them; but those great long-legged creatures, in their big boots! And yet, when they're nicely dressed in their evening things,' she went on, suddenly changing her tone, 'and with a flower in their coats—Jack has actually got an evening coat, Mrs. Mulgrave, he is so tall for his age—they look quite nice; they look such gentlemen,' Janet concluded, with a little sisterly enthusiasm. 'Oh, how dreadful it is to be so poor!'

'I am sure you are very fond of them all the same,' said I, 'and would break your heart if anything should happen to them.'

'Oh, well, of course, now they are there one would not wish anything to happen,' said Janet. 'What did you say I was to tell Jane, Mrs. Mulgrave, about the tea? There now! Selina has never the time to be as nice as that—and Richards, you know, our man— Don't you think, really, it would be better to have a nice clean parlour-maid than a man that looks like a cobbler? Mrs. Spencer and Lady Isabella are always going on about servants,—that you should send them away directly when they do anything wrong. But, you know, it makes a great difference having a separate servant for everything. Mamma always says,

"They are good to the children, Janet," or, "They are so useful and don't mind what they do." We put up with Selina because, though she's not a good housemaid, she is quite willing to help in the nursery; and we put up with nurse because she gets through so much sewing; and even the cook— Oh, dear, dear! it is so disagreeable. I wish I were—anybody but myself.'

Just at this moment my maid ushered in Mrs. Merridew, hastily attired in a hat she wore in the garden, and a light shawl wrapped round her. There was an anxious look in her face, which indeed was not very unusual there. She was a little flushed, either by walking in the sunshine or by something on her mind.

'You here, Janet,' she said, when she had shaken hands with me, 'when you promised me to practise an hour after luncheon? Go, my dear, and do it now.'

'It is so hot. I never can play in the middle of the day; and oh, mamma, please it is so pleasant here,' pleaded Janet, nestling herself close into the corner of the sofa.

'Let her stay till we have had some tea,' I said. 'I know she likes my strawberry jam.'

Mrs. Merridew consented, but with a sigh; and then it was that I saw clearly she must have something on her mind. She did not smile, as usual, with the indulgent mother's smile, half disapproving, yet unwilling to thwart the child. On the contrary, there was a little constraint in her air as she sat down, and Janet's enjoyment of the jam vexed her, and brought a little wrinkle to her brow. 'One would think you had not eaten anything all day,' she said with a vexed tone, and evidently was impatient of her daughter's presence, and wished her away.

'Nothing so nice as this,' said Janet, with the frank satisfaction of her age; and she went on eating her bread and jam quite composedly, until Mrs. Merridew's patience was exhausted.

'I cannot have you stay any longer,' she said at length. 'Go and practise now, while there is no one in the house.'

'Oh, mamma!' said Janet, beginning to expostulate; but was stopped short by a look in her mother's eye. Then she gathered herself up reluctantly, and left the paradise of my little tea-table with the jam. She went out pouting, trailing her great hat after her; and had to be stopped as she stepped into the blazing sunshine, and commanded to put it on. 'It is only a step,' said the provoking girl, pouting more and more. And poor Mrs. Merridew looked so worried, and heated, and uncomfortable as she went out and said a few energetic words to her naughty child. Poor soul! Ten different wills to manage and keep in subjection to her own, besides all the other cares she had upon her shoulders. And that big girl who should have been a help to her, standing pouting and disobedient between the piano she did not care for, and the jam she loved.— Sometimes such a little altercation gives one a glimpse into an entire life.

'She is such a child,' Mrs. Merridew said, coming in with an apologetic, anxious smile on her face. She had been fretted and vexed, and yet she would not show it to lessen my opinion of her girl. Then she sank down wearily into that corner of the sofa from which Janet had been so unwillingly expelled. 'The truth is, I wanted to speak to you,' she said, 'and could not while she was here. Poor Janet! I am afraid I was cross, but I could not help it. Something has occurred to-day which has put me out.'

'I hope it is something I can help you in,' I said.

'That is why I have come: you are always so kind; but it is a strange thing I am going to ask you this time,' she said, with a wistful glance at me. 'I want to go to town for a day on business of my own; and I want it to be supposed that it is business of yours.'

The fact was, it did startle me for the moment—and then I reflected like lightning, so quick was the process (I say this that nobody may think my first feeling hard), what kind of woman she was, and how impossible that she should want to do anything that one need be ashamed of. 'That is very simple,' I said.

Then she rose hastily, and came up to me and gave me a sudden kiss, though she was not a demonstrative woman. 'You are always so understanding,' she said, with the tears in her eyes; and thus I was committed to stand by her, whatever her difficulty might be.

'But you sha'n't do it in the dark,' she went on; 'I am going to tell you all about it. I don't want Mr. Merridew to know, and in our house it is quite impossible to keep anything secret. He is on circuit now; but he would hear of "the day mamma went to town" before he had been five minutes in the house. And so I want you to go with me, you dear soul, and to let me say I went with you.'

'That is quite simple,' I said again; but I did feel that I should like to know what the object of the expedition was.

'It is a long story,' she said, 'and I must go back and tell you ever so much about myself before you will understand. I have had the most dreadful temptation put before me to-day. Oh, such a temptation! resisting it is like tearing one's heart in two; and yet I know I ought to resist. Think of our large family, and poor Charles's many disappointments, and then, dear Mrs. Mulgrave, read that.'

It was a letter written on a large square sheet of thin paper which she thrust into my hand: one of those letters one knows a mile off, and recognizes as lawyers' letters, painful or pleasant, as the case may be; but more painful than pleasant generally. I read it, and you may judge of my astonishment to find that it ran thus:—

'DEAR MADAM,—We have the pleasure to inform you that our late client, Mr. John Babington, deceased on the 10th of May last, has appointed you by his will his residuary legatee. After all his special bequests are paid, including an annuity of a hundred a year to his mother, with remainder to Miss Babington, his only surviving sister, there will remain a sum of about £10,000, at present excellently invested on landed security, and bearing interest at four and a half per cent. By Mr. Babington's desire, precautions have been taken to bind it strictly to your separate use, so that you may dispose of it by will or otherwise, according to your pleasure, for which purpose we have accepted the office of your trustees, and will be happy to enter fully into the subject, and put you in possession of all details, as soon as you can favour us with a private interview.

'We are, madam,

'Your obedient servants,

'FOGEY, FEATHERHEAD & DOWN.'

'A temptation!' I cried; 'but, my dear, it is a fortune; and it is delightful: it will make you quite comfortable. Why, it will be nearly five hundred a year.'

I feel always safe in the way of calculating interest when it is anything approaching five per cent.; five per cent. is so easily counted. This great news took away my breath.

But Mrs. Merridew shook her head. 'It looks so at the first glance,' she said; 'but when you hear my story you will think differently.' And then she made a little uncomfortable pause. 'I don't know whether you ever guessed it,' she added, looking down, and doubling a new hem upon her handkerchief, 'but I was not Charles's equal when we married: perhaps you may have heard—?'

Of course I had heard: but the expression of her countenance was such that I put on a look of great amazement, and pretended to be much astonished, which I could see was a comfort to her mind.

'I am glad of that,' she said, 'for you know—I could not speak so plainly to you if I did not feel that, though you are so quiet now, you must have seen a great deal of the world—you know what a man is. He may be capable of marrying you, if he loves you, whatever your condition is—but afterwards he does not like people to know. I don't mean I was his inferior in education, or anything of that sort,' she added, looking up at me with a sudden uneasy blush.

'You need not tell me that,' I said; and then another uneasiness took possession of her, lest I should think less highly than was right of her husband.

'Poor Charles!' she said; 'it is scarcely fair to judge him as he is now. We have had so many cares and disappointments, and he has had to deny himself so many things—and you may say, Here is his wife, whom he has been so good to, plotting to take away from him what might give him a little ease. But oh, dear Mrs. Mulgrave, you must hear before you judge!'

'I do not judge,' I said; 'I am sure you must have some very good reason; tell me what it is.'

Then she paused, and gave a long sigh. She must have been about forty, I think, a comely, simple woman, not in any way a heroine of romance; and yet she was as interesting to me as if she had been only half the age, and deep in some pretty crisis of romantic distress. I don't object to the love stories either: but middle age has its romances too.

'When I was a girl,' said Mrs. Merridew, 'I went to the Babingtons as Ellen's governess. She was about fifteen and I was not more than twenty, and I believe people thought me pretty. You will laugh at me, but I declare I have always been so busy all my life, that I have never had any time to think whether it was true: but one thing I know, that I was a very good governess. I often wish,' she added, pausing, with a half comic look amid her trouble, 'that I could find as good a governess as I was for the girls. There was one brother, John, and one other sister, Matilda; and Mr. Merridew was one of the visitors at the house, and was supposed to be paying her attention. I never could see it, for my part, and Charles declares he never had any such idea; but they thought so, I know. It is quite a long story. John had just come home from the University, and was pretending to read for the bar, and was always about the house; and the end was that he fell in love with me.'

'Of course,' said I.

'I don't know that it was of course. I was so very shy, and dreaded the sound of my own voice; but he used to come after us everywhere by way of talking to Ellen, and so got to know me. Poor John! he was the nicest, faithful fellow—the sort of man one would trust everything to, and believe in and respect, and be fond of—but not love. Of course Charles was there too. It went on for about a year, such a curious, confused, pleasant, painful— I cannot describe it to you—but you know what I mean. The Babingtons had always been kind to me; of course they were angry when they found out about John, but then when they knew I would not marry him, they were kinder than ever, and said I had behaved so very well about it. I was a very lonely poor girl; my mother was dead, and I had nowhere to go; and instead of sending me away, Mrs. Babington sent him away—her own son, which was very good of her you know. To be sure I was a good governess, and they never suspected Charles of coming for me, nor did I. Suddenly, all at once, without the least warning, he found me by myself one day, and told me. I was a little shocked, thinking of Matilda Babington! but then he declared he had meant nothing. And so— When the Babingtons heard of it, they were all furious; even Ellen, my pupil, turned against me. They sent me away as if I had done something wicked. It was very, very hard upon me; but yet I scarcely wonder, now I think of it. That was why we married so early and so imprudently. Mrs. Mulgrave, I dare say you have often wondered why it was?'

I had to put on such looks of wonder and satisfied curiosity as I could; for the truth was, I had known the outlines of the story for years, just as every one knows the outlines of every one else's story; especially such parts of it as people might like to be concealed. I cannot understand how anybody, at least in society, or on the verge of society, can for a moment hope to have any secrets. Charles Merridew was a cousin of Mr. Justice Merridew, and very well connected, and of course it was known that he married a governess; which was one reason why people were so shy of them at first when they came to the Green.

'I begin to perceive now why this letter should be a temptation to you,' I said; 'you think Mr. Merridew would not like—'

'Oh, it is not that,' she said. 'Poor Charles! I don't think he would mind. The world is so hard, and one makes so little head against it. No, it is because of Mrs. Babington. I heard she lost all her money some years ago, and was dependent on her son. And what can she do on a hundred a year? A hundred a year! Only think of it, for an old lady always accustomed to have her own way. It is horribly unjust, you know, to take it from her, his mother, who was always so good to him; and to give it to me, whom he has not seen for nearly twenty years, and who gave him a sore heart when he did know me. I could not take advantage of it. It is a great temptation, but it would be a great sin. And that is why,' she added, with a sudden flush on her face, looking at me, 'I should rather—manage it myself—under cover of you—and— not let Charles know.'

She looked at me, and held me with her eye, demanding of me that I should understand her, and yet defying me to think any the worse of Charles. She was afraid of her husband—afraid that he would clutch at the money without any consideration of the wrong—afraid to trust him with the decision. She would have me understand her without words, and yet she would not have me blame Mr. Merridew. She insisted on the one and defied me to the other; an inconsistent, unreasonable woman! But I did my best to look as if I saw, and yet did not see.

'Then you want to see the lawyers?' I said.

'I want to see Mrs. Babington,' was her answer. 'I must go to them and explain. They are proud people, and probably would resist—or they may be otherwise provided for. If that was the case I should not hesitate to take it. Oh, Mrs. Mulgrave, when I look at all the children, and Janet there murmuring and grumbling, don't you think it wrings my heart to put away this chance of comfort? And poor Charles working himself out. But it could not bring a blessing. It would bring a curse; I cannot take the bread out of the mouth of the old woman who was good to me, even to put it into that of my own child.'

And here two tears fell out of Mrs. Merridew's eyes. At her age people do not weep abundantly. She gave a little start as they fell, and brushed them off her dress, with, I don't doubt, a sensation of shame. She to cry like a baby, who had so much to do! She left shortly after, with an engagement to meet me at the station for the twelve o'clock train next day. I was going to town on business, and had asked her to go with me—this was what was to be said to all the world. I explained myself elaborately that very evening to Mrs. Spencer and Lady Isabella, when I met them taking their walk after dinner.

'Mrs. Merridew is so kind as to go with me,' I said; 'she knows so much more about business than I do.' And I made up my mind that I would go to the Bank and leave my book to be made up, that it might not be quite untrue.

'Fancy Mrs. Mulgrave having any business!' said Lady Isabella. 'Why don't you write to some man, and make him do it, instead of all the trouble of going to town?'

'But Mrs. Merridew is going with me, my dear,' I said; and nobody doubted that the barrister's wife, with so much experience as she had, and so many things to do, would be an efficient help to me in my little affairs.

CHAPTER II

The house we went to was a house in St. John's Wood. Everybody knows the kind of place. A garden wall, with lilacs and laburnums, all out of blossom by this time, and beginning to look brown and dusty, waving over it; inside, a little bright suburban garden, full of scarlet geraniums, divided by a white line of pavement, dazzlingly clean, from the door in the wall to the door of the house; and a stand full of more scarlet geraniums in the little square hall. Mrs. Merridew became very much agitated as we approached. It was all that I could do to keep her up when we had rung the bell at the door. I think she would have turned and gone back even then had it been possible, but, fortunately, we were admitted without delay.

We were shown into a pretty shady drawing-room, full of old furniture, which looked like the remnants of something greater, and at which she gazed with eyes of almost wild recognition, unconsciously pressing my arm, which she still held. Everything surrounding her woke afresh the tumult of recollections. She was not able to speak when the maid asked our names, and I was about to give them simply, and had already named my own, when she pressed my arm closer to her, and interposed all at once—

'Say two ladies from the country anxious to speak with her about business. She might not—know—our names.'

'Is it business about the house, ma'am?' said the maid with some eagerness.

'Yes, yes; it is about the house,' said Mrs. Merridew, hastily. And then the door closed, and we sat waiting, listening to the soft, subdued sounds in the quiet house, and the rustle of the leaves in the garden. 'She must be going to let it,' my companion said hoarsely; and then rose from the chair on which she had placed herself, and began to move about the room with agitation, looking at everything, touching the things with her hands, with now and then a stifled exclamation. 'There is where we used to sit, Ellen and I,' she said, standing by a sofa, before which a small table was placed, 'when there was company in the evenings. And there Matilda—oh, what ghosts there are about! Matilda is married, thank Heaven! but if Ellen comes, I shall never be able to face her. Oh, Mrs. Mulgrave, if you would but speak for me!'

At this moment the door was opened. Mrs. Merridew shrank back instinctively, and sat down, resting her hand on the table she had just pointed out to me. The new-comer was a tall, full figure, in deep mourning, a handsome woman of five-and-thirty, or thereabouts, with bright hair, which looked all the brighter from comparison with the black depths of her dress, and a colourless, clear complexion. All the colour about her was in her hair. Though she had no appearance of unhealthiness, her very lips were pale, and she came in with a noiseless quiet dignity, and the air of one who felt she had pain to encounter, yet felt able to bear it.

'Pardon me for keeping you waiting,' she said; and then, with a somewhat startled glance, 'I understood you wanted to see—the house.'

My companion was trembling violently; and I cleared my throat, and tried to clear up my ideas (which was less easy) to say something in reply. But before I had stammered out half-a-dozen words Mrs. Merridew rose, and made one or two unsteady steps towards the stranger.

'Ellen,' she cried, 'don't you know me?' and stopped there, standing in the centre of the room, holding out appealing hands.

Miss Babington's face changed in the strangest way. I could see that she recognized her in a moment, and then that she pretended to herself not to recognize her. There was the first startled, vivid, indignant glance, and then a voluntary mist came over her eyes. She gazed at the agitated woman with an obstinately blank gaze, and then turned to me with a little bow.

'Your friend has the advantage of me,' she said; 'but you were saying something? I should be glad, if that was what you wanted, to show you over the house.'

It would be hard to imagine a more difficult position than that in which I found myself; seated between two people who were thus strangely connected with each other by bonds of mutual injury, and appealed to for something meaningless and tranquillizing, to make the intercourse possible. I did the best I could on the spur of the moment.

'It is not so much the house,' I said, 'though, if you wish to let it, I have a friend who is looking for a house; but I think there was some other business Mrs. Merridew had; something to say—'

'Mrs. Merridew!' said Miss Babington, suffering the light once more to come into her eyes; and then she gave her an indignant look. 'I think this might have been spared us at least.'

'Ellen,' said Mrs. Merridew, speaking very low and humbly—'Ellen, I have never done anything to you to make you so hard against me. If I injured your sister, it was unwittingly. She is better off than I am now. You were once fond of me, as I was of you. Why should you have turned so completely against me? I have come in desperation to ask a hearing from you, and from your mother, Ellen. God knows I mean nothing but good. And oh, what have I ever done?—what harm?'

Miss Babington had seated herself, still preserving her air of dignity, but without an invitation by look or gesture to her visitor to be seated; and in the silent room, all so dainty and so sweet with flowers, with the old furniture in it, which reminded her of the past, the culprit of twenty years ago stood pleading between one of those whom she was supposed to have wronged and myself, a most ignorant and uneasy spectator. Twenty years ago! In the meantime youth had passed, and the hard burdens of middle age had come doubled and manifold upon her shoulders. Had she done nothing in the meantime that would tell more heavily against her than that girlish inadvertence of the past? Yet here she stood— not knowing, I believe, for the moment, whether she was the young governess in her first trouble, or the mother of all those children, acquainted with troubles so much more bitter—among the ghosts of the past.

'I would much rather not discuss the question,' said Miss Babington, still seated, and struggling hard to preserve her calm. 'All the grief and vexation we have owed to you in this house cannot be summed up in a moment. The only policy, I think, is to be silent. Your very presence here is an offence to us. What else could it be?'

'I should never have come,' said Mrs. Merridew, moved by a natural prick of resentment, 'but for what I have just heard— I should never have returned to ask for pardon where I had done no wrong—had it not been for this—this that I feel to be unjust. Your poor brother John—'

'Stop!' cried the other, her reserve failing. 'Stop, oh! stop, you cruel woman! He was nothing to you but a toy to be played with—but he was my brother, my only brother; and you have made him an undutiful son in his very grave.'

The tears were in her eyes, her colourless face had flushed, her soft voice was raised; and Mrs. Merridew, still standing, listened to her with looks as agitated—when all at once the door was again opened softly. The aspect of affairs changed in a moment. To my utter amazement, Mrs. Merridew, who was standing with her face to the door, made a quick, imperative, familiar gesture to her antagonist, and looked towards an easy-chair which stood near the open window. Miss Babington rose quickly to her feet, and composed herself into a sudden appearance of calm.

'Mamma,' she said, going forward to meet the old lady, who came slowly in; 'here are some ladies come upon business. This is—Mrs. Merridew.' She said the name very low, as Mrs. Babington made her way to her chair, and Mrs. Merridew sank trembling into her seat, unable, I think, to bear up longer. The old lady seated herself before she spoke. She was a little old woman, with a pretty, softly-coloured old face, and had the air of having been petted and cared for all her life. The sudden change of her daughter's manner; the accumulation of every kind of convenience and prettiness, as I now remarked, round that chair; the careful way in which it had been placed out of the sun and the draught, yet in the air and in sight of the garden, told a whole history of themselves. And now Mrs. Merridew's passionate sense that the alienation of the son's fortune from the mother was a thing impossible, was made clear to me at once.

'Whom did you say, Ellen?' said the old lady, when she was comfortably settled in her chair. 'Mrs.—? I never catch names. I hope you have explained to the ladies that I am rather infirm, and can't stand. What did you say was your friend's name, my dear?'

Her friend's name! Ellen Babington's face lightened all over as with a pale light of indignation.

'I said—Mrs. Merridew,' she repeated, with a little emphasis on the name. Then there was a pause; and the culprit who was at the bar trembled visibly, and hid her face in her hands.

'Mrs. Merridew!— Do you mean—? Turn me round, Ellen, and let me look at her,' said the old lady with a curious catching of her breath.

It was a change which could not be done in a moment. While the daughter turned the mother's chair, poor Mrs. Merridew must have gone through the torture of an age; her hands trembled, in which she had hidden herself. But as the chair creaked and turned slowly round, and all was silent again, she raised her white face, and uncovered herself, as it were, to meet the inquisitor's eye. It might have been a different woman, so changed was she: her eyes withdrawn into caves, the lines of her mouth drawn down, two hollows clearly marked in her cheeks, and every particle of her usual colour gone. She looked up appalled and overcome, confronting, but not meeting, the keen, critical look which old Mrs. Babington fixed upon her; and then there was again a pause; and the leaves fluttered outside, and the white curtains within, and a gay child's voice, passing in the road without, suddenly fell among us like a bird.

'Ah!' said the old lady, 'that creature! Do you mean to tell me, Ellen, that she has had the assurance to come here? Now look at her and tell me what a man's sense is worth. That woman's face turned my poor boy's head, and drove Charles Merridew out of his wits. Only look at her: is there anything there to turn anybody's head now? She has lost her figure too; to be sure that is not so wonderful, for she is forty if she is a day. But there are you, my dear, as straight as a rush, and your sister Matilda as well. So that is Janet Singleton, our governess: I wonder what Charles thinks of his bargain now? I never saw a woman so gone off. Oh, Ellen, Ellen, why didn't she come and show herself, such a figure as she is, before my poor dear boy was taken from us? My poor boy! And to think he should have gone to his grave in such a delusion! Ellen, I would rather now that you sent her away.'

'Oh, mamma, don't speak like this,' cried Ellen, red with shame and distress; 'what does it matter about her figure? if that were all!—but she is going away.'

'Yes, yes, send her away,' said the old lady. 'You liked her once, but I don't suppose even you can think there could be any intercourse now. My son left all his money to her,' she added, turning to me—past his mother and his sister. You will admit that was a strange thing to do. I don't know who the other lady is, Ellen, but I conclude she is a friend of yours. He left everything past us, everything but some poor pittance. Perhaps you may know some one who wants a house in this neighbourhood? It is a very nice little house, and much better furnished than most. I should be very glad to let it, now that I can't afford to occupy it myself, by the year.'

'Mamma, the other lady is with Mrs. Merridew,' said Ellen; 'I do not know her—' and she cast a glance at me, almost appealing to my pity. I rose up, not knowing what to do.

'Perhaps, my dear,' I said, I confess with timidity, 'we had better go away.'

'Unless you will stay to luncheon,' said the old lady. 'But I forgot—I don't want to look at that woman any more, Ellen. She has done us enough of harm to satisfy any one. Turn me round again to my usual place, and send her away.'

Mrs. Merridew had risen to her feet too. She had regained her senses after the first frightful shock. She was still ghastly pale, but she was herself. She went up firmly and swiftly to the old lady, put Ellen aside by a movement which she was unconscious of in her agitation, and replaced the chair in its former place with the air of one to whom such an office was habitual. 'You used to say I always did it best,' she said. 'Oh, is it possible you can have forgotten everything! Did not I give him up when you asked me, and do you think I will take his money now? Oh, never, never! It ought to be yours, and it shall be. Oh, take it back, and forgive me, and say, "God bless you" once again.'

'Eh, what was that you said? Ellen, what does she say?' said the old woman. 'I have always heard the Merridews were very poor. Poor John's fortune will be a godsend to them. Go away! I suppose you mean to mock me after all the rest you have done. I don't understand what you say.'

Yet she looked up with a certain eagerness on her pretty old face—a certain sharp look of greed and longing came into the blue eyes, which retained their colour as pure as that of youth. Her daughter towered above her, pale with emotion, but still indignant, yielding not a jot.

'Mamma, pay no attention,' she said; 'Mrs. Merridew may pity us, but what is that? surely we can take back nothing from her hands.'

'Pity! I don't see how Janet Merridew can pity me. But I should like,' Mrs. Babington went on, with a little tremble of eagerness, 'to know at least what she means.'

'This is what I mean,' said Mrs. Merridew, sinking on her knees by the old lady's chair: 'that I will not take your money. It is your money. We are poor, as you say; but we can struggle on as we have done for twenty years; and poor John's money is yours, and not mine. It is not mine. I will not take it. It must have been some mistake. If he had known what he was doing he never would have left it to any one but you.'

'So I think myself,' said the old lady, musing; and then was silent, taking no notice of any one—looking into the air.

'Mamma,' said Ellen, behind her chair, 'I can work for you, and Matilda will help us. It cannot be. It may be kind of—her—but it cannot, cannot be. Are we to take charity?—to live on charity? Mamma, she has no right to disturb you.'

'She is not disturbing me, my dear,' said the old lady; 'on the contrary. Whatever I might think of her, she used to be a girl of sense. And Matilda always carried things with a very high hand, and I never was fond of her husband. But I am very fond of my house,' she added, after a pause; 'it is such a nice house, Ellen. I think I should die if we were to leave it. I shall die very soon, most likely, and be a burden on nobody; but still, Ellen, if she meant it, you know—'

'Mamma, what does it matter what she means? you never can think of accepting charity. It will break my heart.'

'That is all very well to say,' said Mrs. Babington. 'But I have lived a great deal longer than you have done, my dear, and I know that hearts are not broken so easily. It would break my heart to leave my nice house. Janet, come here, and look me in the face. I don't think you were true to us in the old times. Matilda did carry things with a very high hand. I told her so at the time, and I have often told her so since; but I don't think you were true to us, all the same.'

'I did not know—I did not mean—' faltered Mrs. Merridew, leaning her head on the arm of the old lady's chair.

It was clear to me that the story had two sides, and that my friend was perhaps not so innocent as she had made herself out to be. But there was something very pitiful in the comparison between the passion of anxiety in her half-hidden face, and the calm of the old woman who was thus deciding on her fate.

'My dear, I am afraid you knew,' said Mrs. Babington. 'You accepted my poor boy, and then, when I spoke to you, you gave him up, and took Charles Merridew instead. If I had not interfered, perhaps it would have been better; though, to be sure, I don't know what we should have done with a heap of children. And as for poor John's money, you know you have no more real right to it, no more than that other lady, who never saw him in her life.'

'She has the best possible right to it, mamma—he left it to her,' said Ellen anxiously, over her shoulder. 'Oh, why did you come here to vex us, when we were not interfering with you? I beg of you not to trouble my mother any more, but go away.'

Then there was a moment of hesitation. Mrs. Merridew rose slowly from her knees. She turned round to me, not looking me in the face. She said, in a hoarse voice, 'Let us go,' and made a step towards the door. She was shaking as if she had a fever; but she was glad. Was that possible? She had delivered her conscience—and now might not she go and keep the money which would make her children happy? But she could not look me in the face. She moved as slowly as a funeral. And yet she would have flown, if she could, to get safely away.

'Janet, my dear,' said the old lady, 'come back, and let us end our talk.'

Mrs. Merridew stopped short, with a start, as if a shot had arrested her. This time she looked me full in the face. Her momentary hope was over, and now she felt for the first time the poignancy of the sacrifice which it had been her own will to make.

'Come back, Janet,' said Mrs. Babington. 'As you say, it is not your money. Nothing could make it your money. You were always right-feeling when you were not aggravated. I am much obliged to you, my dear. Come and sit down here, and tell me all about yourself. Now poor John is dead,' she went on, falling suddenly into soft weeping, like a child, 'we ought to be friends. To think he should die before me, and I should be heir to my own boy—isn't it sad? And such a fine young fellow as he was! You remember when he came back from the University? What a nice colour he had! And always so straight and slim, like a rush. All my children have a good carriage. You have lost your figure, Janet; and you used to have a nice little figure. When a girl is so round and plump, she is apt to get stout as she gets older. Look at Ellen, how nice she is. But then, to be sure, children make a difference. Sit down by me here, and tell me how many you have. And, Ellen, send word to the house-agent, and tell him we don't want now to let the house; and tell Parker to get luncheon ready a little earlier. You must want something, if you have come from the country. Where are you living now? and how is Charles Merridew? Dear, dear, to think I should not have seen either of you for nearly twenty years!'

'But, mamma, surely, surely,' cried Ellen Babington, 'you don't think things can be settled like this?'

'Don't speak nonsense, Ellen; everything is settled,' said the old lady. 'You know I always had the greatest confidence in Janet's good sense. Now, my dear, hold your tongue. A girl like you has no right to meddle. I always manage my own business. Go and look after luncheon—that is your affair.'

I do not remember ever to have seen a more curious group in my life. There was the old lady in the centre, quite calm, and sweet, and pleasant. A tear was still lingering on her eyelash; but it represented nothing more than a child's transitory grief, and underneath there was nothing but smiles, and satisfaction, and content. She looked so pretty, so pleased, so glad to find that her comforts were not to be impaired, and yet took it all so lightly, as a matter of course, as completely unconscious of the struggle going on in the mind of her benefactress as if she had been a creature from a different world. As for Mrs. Merridew, she stood speechless, choked by feelings that were too bitter and conflicting for words. I am sure that all the advantages this money could have procured for her children were surging up before her as she stood and listened. She held her hands helplessly half stretched out, as if something had been taken out of them. Her eyes were blank with thinking, seeing nothing that we saw, but a whole world of the invisible. Her breast heaved with a breath half drawn, which seemed suspended half way, as if dismay and disappointment hindered its completion. It was all over then—her sacrifice made and accepted, and no more about it; and herself sent back to the monotonous struggle of life. On the other side of the pretty old lady stood Ellen Babington, pale and miserable, struggling with shame and pride, casting sudden glances at Mrs. Merridew, and then appealing looks at me, who had nothing to do with it.

'Tell her, oh, tell her it can't be!' she cried at last, coming to me. 'Tell her the lawyers will not permit it. It cannot be.'

And Mrs. Merridew, too, gave me one pitiful look—not repenting, but yet— Then she went forward, and laid her hand upon the old lady's hand, which was like ivory, with all the veins delicately carved upon it.

'Say, God bless us, at least. Say, "God bless you and your children," once before I go.'

'To be sure,' said the old lady cheerfully. 'God bless you, my dear, and all the children. Matilda has no children, you know. I should like to see them, if you think it would not be too much for me. But you are not going, Janet, when it is the first time we have met for nearly twenty years?'

'I must go,' said Mrs. Merridew.

She could not trust herself to speak, I could see. She put down her face and kissed the ivory hand, and then she turned and went past me to the door, without another word. I think she had forgotten my very existence. When she had reached the door she turned round suddenly, and fixed her eyes upon Ellen. She was going away, having given them back their living, without so much acknowledgment as if she had brought a nosegay. There was in her look a mute remonstrance and appeal and protest. Ellen Babington trembled all over; her lips quivered as if with words which pride or pain would not permit her to say; but she held, with both hands immovable, to the back of her mother's chair, who, for her part, was kissing her hand to the departing visitor. 'Good-bye; come and see us soon again,' the old lady was saying cheerfully. And Ellen gazed, and trembled, and said nothing. Thus this strangest of visits came to an end.

She had forgotten me, as I thought; but when I came to her side and my arm was within her reach, she clutched at it and tottered so that it was all I could do to support her. I was very thankful to get her into the cab, for I thought she would have fainted on the way. But yet she roused herself when I told the man to drive back to the station.

'We must go to the lawyer's first,' she said; and then we turned and drove through the busy London streets, towards the City. The clerks looked nearly baked in the office when we reached it, and the crowd crowded on, indiscriminate and monotonous. One feels one has no right to go to such a place and take any of the air away, of which they have so little. And to think of the sweet air blowing over our lawns and lanes, and all the unoccupied, silent, shady places we had left behind us! Such vain thoughts were not in Mrs. Merridew's head. She was turning over and over instead a very different kind of vision. She was counting up all she had sacrificed, and how little she had got by it; and yet was going to complete the sacrifice, unmoved even by her thoughts.

I confess I was surprised at the tone she took with the lawyer. She said 'Mr. Merridew and myself' with a composure which made me, who knew Mr. Merridew had no hand in it, absolutely speechless. The lawyer remonstrated as he was in duty bound, and spoke about his client's will; but Mrs. Merridew made very little account of the will. She quoted her husband with a confidence so assured that even I, though I knew better, began to be persuaded that she had communicated with him. And thus the business was finally settled. She had recovered herself by the time we got into the cab again. It is true that her face was worn and livid with the exertions of the day, but still, pale and weary as she was, she was herself.

'But, my dear,' I said, 'you quoted Mr. Merridew, as if he knew all about it; and what if he should not approve?'

'You must not think I have no confidence in my husband,' she said quickly; 'far from that. Perhaps he would not see as I do now. He would think of our own wants first. But if it comes to his ears afterwards, Charles is not the man to disown his wife's actions. Oh, no, no; we have gone through a great deal together, and he would no more bring shame upon me, as if I acted when I had no right to act—than—I would bring shame upon him; and I think that is as much as could be said.'

And then we made our way back to the station; but she said nothing more till we got into the railway-carriage, which was not quite so noisy as our cab.

'It would have been such a thing for us,' she said then, half to herself. 'Poor Charles! Oh, if I could but have said to him, "Don't be so anxious; here is so much a year for the children." And Jack should have gone to the University. And there would have been Will's premium at once' (i.e., to Mr. Willoughby, the engineer). 'The only thing that I am glad of is that they don't know. And then Janet; she breaks my heart when she talks. It is so bad for her, knowing the Fortises and all those girls who have everything that heart can desire. I never had that to worry me when I was young. I was only the governess. Janet's talk will be the worst of all. I could have made the house so nice too, and everything. Well!—but then I never should have had a moment's peace.'

'You don't regret?' I said.

'No,' said Mrs. Merridew with a long sigh. And then, 'Do you think I have been a traitor to the children?' she cried suddenly, 'taking away their money from them in the dark? Would Charles think me a traitor, as they do? Is it always to be my part?—always to be my part?'

'No, no,' I said, soothing her as best I could; but I was very glad to find my pony-carriage at the station, and to drive her home to my house and give her some tea, and strengthen her for her duties. Thus poor John Babington's fortune was disposed of, and no one was the wiser, except, indeed, the old lady and her daughter, who were not likely to talk much on the subject. And Mrs. Merridew walked calmly across to her house in the dusk as if this strange episode of agitation and passion had been nothing more solid than a dream.

CHAPTER III

We did not meet again for some days after this, and next time I saw her, which was on Sunday at church with her children, it seemed impossible to me to believe in the reality of the strange scene we had so recently passed through together. The calm curtain of ordinary decorums and ordinary friendliness had risen for a moment from Mrs. Merridew's unexcited existence, revealing a woman distracted by a primitive sense of justice, rending her own soul, as it were, in sunder, and doing, in spite of herself and all her best instincts, what she felt was right. That she should have any existence separate from her children had never occurred to anybody before. Yet, for one day, I had seen her resist and ignore the claims of her children, and act like an independent being. When I saw her again she was once more the mother and nothing more, casting her eyes over her little flock, cognizant, one could see, of the perfection or imperfection of every fold and line in their dresses, keeping her attention upon each, from little Matty, who was restless and could not be kept quiet, up to Janet, who sat demure, and already caught the eye of visitors as one of the prettiest girls of Dinglefield. Mrs. Merridew remarked all with a vigilant mother's eye, and as I gazed across at her in her pew, it was all but impossible for me to believe that this was the same woman who had clung so convulsively to my arm, whose face had been so worn and hollowed out with suffering. How could it be the same woman? She who had suffered poor John Babington to love her—and then had cast him off, and married her friend's lover instead; who had established so firm an empire over a man's heart, that, after twenty years, he had remembered her still with such intensity of feeling. How Janet would have opened her big eyes had it been suggested to her that her mother could have any power over men's hearts; or, indeed, could be occupied with anything more touching or important than her children's frocks or her butcher's bills! I fear I did not pay much attention to the service that morning. I could not but gaze at them, and wonder whether, for instance, Mr. Merridew himself, who had come back from circuit, and was seated respectably with his family in church, yawning discreetly over Mr. Damerel's sermon, remembered anything at all, for his part, of Matilda Babington or her brother. Probably he preferred to ignore the subject altogether—or, perhaps, would laugh with a sense of gratified vanity that there had been 'a row,' when the transference of his affections was discovered. And there she sat by his side, who had—had she betrayed his confidence? was she untrue to him in being this time true to her friends? The question bewildered me so that my mind went groping about it and about it. Once, I fear, she had been false to those whose bread she ate, and chosen love instead of friendship. Now was she false to the nearest of ties, the closest of all relationships, sitting calmly there beside him with a secret in her mind of which he knew nothing? 'Falsely true!'—was that what the woman was who looked to the outside world a mere pattern of all domestic virtues, without any special interest about her, a wife devoted to her husband's interest, a mother wrapped up, as people say, in her children? I could not make up my mind what to think.

'I hope you got through your business comfortably,' Mrs. Spencer said to me as we walked home from church.

'With Mrs. Merridew's assistance,' said Lady Isabella, who was rather satirical. And the Merridews heard their own name, and stopped to join in the conversation.

'What is that about my wife?' he said. 'Did Mrs. Mulgrave have Mrs. Merridew's assistance about something? I hope it was only shopping. When you have business you should consult me. She is a goose, and knows nothing about it.'

'I don't think she is a goose,' said I.

'No, perhaps not in her own way,' said the serene husband, laughing; 'but every woman is a goose about business—I beg your pardon, ladies, but I assure you I mean it as a compliment. I hate a woman of business. Shopping is quite a different matter,' he added, and laughed. Good heavens! if he had only known what a fool he looked, beside the silent woman, who gave me a little warning glance and coloured a little, and turned away her head to speak to little Matty, who was clinging to her skirts. A perfect mother! thinking more (you would have said) of Matty's little frills and Janet's bonnet-strings than of anything else in life.

And that was all about it. The summer went on and turned to autumn and to winter and to spring again, with that serene progression of nature which nothing obstructs; and the children grew, and the Merridews were as poor as ever, managing more or less to make both ends meet, but always just a little short somewhere, with their servants chosen on the same principle of supplementing each other's imperfect service as that which Janet had announced to me. For one thing, they kept their servants a long time, which I have noticed is characteristic of households not very rich nor very 'particular.' When you allow such pleas to tell in favour of an imperfect housemaid as that she is good to the children, or does not mind helping the cook, there is no reason why Mary, if she does not marry in the meantime, should not stay with you a hundred years. And the Merridews' servants accordingly stayed, and looked very friendly at you when you went to call, and did their work not very well, with much supervision and exasperation (respectively) on the part of the mother and daughter. But the family was no poorer, though it was no richer. The only evidence of our expedition to town which I could note was, that it had produced a new pucker on Mrs. Merridew's brow. She had looked sufficiently anxious by times before, but the new pucker had something more than anxiety in it. There was a sense of something better that might have been; a sense of something lost—a suspicion of bitterness. How all this could be expressed by one line on a smooth white forehead I cannot explain; but to me it was so.

Now and then, too, a chance allusion would be made which recalled what had happened still more plainly. For instance, I chanced to be calling one afternoon, when Mr. Merridew came home earlier than usual from town. We were sitting over our five-o'clock tea, with a few of the children scrambling about the floor and Janet working in the corner. He took up the ordinary position of a man who has just come home, with his back to the fire, and regarded us with that benevolent contempt which men generally think it right to exhibit for women over their tea; and everything was so ordinary and pleasant, that I for one was taken entirely by surprise, and nearly let fall the cup in my hand when he spoke.

'I don't know whether you saw John Babington's death in the Times three or four months ago, Janet,' he said, 'did you? Why did you never mention it? It is odd that I should not have heard. I met Ellen to-day coming out of the Amyotts, where I lunched, in such prodigious mourning that I was quite startled. All the world might have been dead to look at her. And do you know she gave me a look as if she would have spoken. All that is so long past that it's ridiculous keeping up malice. I wish you would call next time you are in town to ask for the old lady. Poor John's death must have been a sad loss to them. I hear there was some fear that he had left his property away from his mother and sister. But it turned out a false report.'

I did not dare to look at Mrs. Merridew to see how she bore it; but her voice replied quite calmly without any break, as if the conversation was on the most ordinary subject—

'Where did you manage to get so much news?'

'Oh, from the Amyotts,' he said, 'who knew all about it. Matilda, you know, poor girl' (with that half laugh of odious masculine vanity which I knew in my heart he would be guilty of), 'married a cousin of Amyott's, and is getting on very well, they say. But think over my suggestion, Janet. I think at this distance of time it would be graceful on your part to go and call.'

'I cannot think they would like to see me now,' she said in a low voice. Then I ventured to look at her. She was seated in an angular, rigid way, with her shoulders and elbows squared to her work, and the corners of her mouth pursed up, which would have given to any cursory observer the same impression it did to her husband.

'How hard you women are!' he said. 'Trust you for never forgiving or forgetting. Poor old lady, I should have thought anybody would have pitied her. But however it is none of my business. As for Ellen, she is a very handsome woman, though she is not so young as she once was. I should not wonder if she were to make a good marriage even now. Is it possible, Janet, after being so fond of her—or pretending to be, how can I tell?—that you would not like to say a kind word to Ellen now?'

'She would not think it kind from me,' said Mrs. Merridew, still rigid, never raising her eyes from her work.

'I think she would: but at all events you might try,' he said. All her answer was to shake her head, and he went away to his dressing-room shrugging his shoulders and nodding his head in bewildered comments to himself on what he considered the hard-heartedness of woman. As for me, I kept looking at her with sympathetic eyes, thinking that at least she would give herself the comfort of a confidential glance. But she did not. It seemed that she was determined to ignore the whole matter, even to me.

'I wish papa would take as much interest in us poor girls at home as he does in people that don't belong to him,' said Janet. 'Mamma, I never can piece this to make it long enough. It may do for Marian' (who was her next sister), 'but it will never do for me.'

'You are so easily discouraged,' said Mrs. Merridew. 'Let me look at it. You girls are always making difficulties. Under the flounce your piecing, as you call it, will never be seen. Those flounces,' she added, with a little laugh, which I knew was hysterical, 'are blessings to poor folks.'

'I am sure I don't think there is anything to laugh at,' said poor Janet, almost crying: 'when you think of Nelly Fortis and all the other girls, with their nice dresses all new and fresh from the dressmaker's, and no trouble; while I have only mamma's old gown, that she wore when she was twenty, to turn, and patch, and piece—and not long enough after all!'

'Then you should not grow so,' said her mother, 'and you ought to be thankful that the old fashion has come in again, and my old gown can be of use.' But as she spoke she turned round and gave me a look. The tears were in her eyes, and that pucker, oh, so deeply marked, in her forehead. I felt she would have sobbed had she dared. And then before my eyes, as, I am sure, before hers, there glided a vision of Ellen Babington in her profound mourning, rustling past Mr. Merridew on the stairs, with heaps of costly crape, no doubt, and that rich black silk with which people console themselves in their first mourning. How could they take it all without a word? The after-pang that comes almost inevitably at the back of a sacrifice, was tearing Mrs. Merridew's heart. I felt it go through my own, and so I knew. She had done it nobly, but she could not forget that she had done it. Does one ever forget?

And then as I went home I fell into a maze again. Had she a right to do it? To sit at table with that unsuspicious man, and put her arm in his, and be at his side continually, and all the time be false to him? Falsely true! I could not get the words out of my mind.

CHAPTER IV

I do not now remember how long it was before I saw in the Times the intimation of old Mrs. Babington's death. I think it must have been about two years: for Janet was eighteen, and less discontented with things in general, besides being a great deal more contented than either her friends or his desired, with the civilities of young Bischam from the Priory, who was always coming over to see his aunt, and always throwing himself in the girl's way. He had nothing except his commission and a hundred and fifty a year which his father allowed him, and she had nothing at all; and, naturally, they took to each other. It is this that makes me recollect what year it was. We had never referred to the matter in our frequent talks, Mrs. Merridew and I. But after the intimation in the Times, she herself broke the silence. She came to me the very next day. 'Did you see it in the papers?' she asked, plunging without preface into the heart of the subject: and I could not pretend not to understand.

'Yes,' I said, 'I saw it;' and then stopped short, not knowing what to say.

She had got a worn-out look in these two years, such as all the previous years in which I had known her had not given. The pucker was more developed on her forehead; she was less patient and more easily fretted. She had grown thin, and something of a sharp tone had come into her soft, motherly voice. By times she would be almost querulous; and nobody but myself knew in the least whence the drop of gall came that had so suddenly shown itself in her nature. She had fretted under her secret, and over her sacrifice—the sacrifice which had never been taken any notice of, but had been calmly accepted as a right. Now she came to me half wild, with the look of a creature driven to bay.

'It was for her I did it,' she said; 'she had always been so petted and cared for all her life. She did not know how to deny herself; I did it for her, not for Ellen. Oh, Mrs. Mulgrave, I cannot tell you how fond I was of that girl! And you saw how she looked at me. Never one word, never even a glance of response: and I suppose now—'

'My dear,' I said, 'you cannot tell yet; let us wait and see; now that her mother is gone her heart may be softened. Do not take any steps just yet.'

'Steps!' she cried. 'What steps can I take now? I have thrown altogether away from me what might have been of such use to the children. I have been false to my own children. Poor John meant it to be of use to us—'

And then she turned away, wrought to such a point that nothing but tears could relieve her. When she had cried she was better; and went home to all her little monotonous cares again, to think and think, and mingle that drop of gall more and more in the family cup. Mr. Merridew was again absent on circuit at this time, which was at once a relief and a trouble to his wife. And everybody remarked the change in her.

'She is going to have a bad illness,' Mrs. Spencer said. 'Poor thing, I don't wonder, with all those children, and inferior servants, and so much to do. I have seen it coming on for a long time. A serious illness is a dangerous thing at her age. All her strength has been drained out of her; and whether she will be able to resist—'

'Don't be so funereal,' said Lady Isabella; 'she has something on her mind.'

'I think it is her health' said Mrs. Spencer; and we all shook our heads over her altered looks.

I had a further fright, too, some days after, when Janet came to me, looking very pale. She crept in with an air of secrecy which was very strange to the girl. She looked scared, and her hair was pushed up wildly from her forehead, and her light summer dress all dusty and dragging, which was unlike Janet, for she had begun by this time to be tidy, and feel herself a woman. She came in by the window as usual, but closed it after her, though it was very hot. 'May I come and speak to you?' she said in a whisper, creeping quite close to my side.

'Of course, my dear; but why do you shut the window?' said I; 'we shall be suffocated if you shut out the air.'

'It is because it is a secret,' she said. 'Mrs. Mulgrave, tell me, is there anything wrong with mamma?'

'Wrong?' I said, turning upon her in dismay.

'I can't help it,' cried Janet, bursting into tears. 'I don't believe mamma ever did anything wrong. I can't believe it: but there has been a woman questioning me so, I don't know what to think.'

'A woman questioning you?'

'Listen,' said Janet hastily. 'This is how it was: I was walking down to the Dingle across the fields—oh! Mrs. Mulgrave, dear, don't say anything; it was only poor Willie Bischam, who wanted to say good-bye to me—and all at once I saw a tall lady in mourning looking at us as we passed. She came up to us just at the stile at Goodman's farm, and I thought she wanted to ask the way; but instead of that, she stopped me and looked at me. "I heard you called Janet," she said; "I had once a friend who was called Janet, and it is not a common name. Do you live here? is your mother living? and well? and how many children are there? I should like to know if you belong to my old friend."'

'And what did you say?'

'What could I say, Mrs. Mulgrave? She did not look cross or disagreeable, and she was a lady. I said who I was, and that mamma was not quite well, and that there were ten of us; and then she began to question me about mamma. Did she go out a great deal? and was she tall or short? and had she pretty eyes "like mine?" she said; and was her name Janet like mine? and then, when I had answered her as well as I could, she said, I was not to say a word to mamma; "perhaps it is not the Janet I once knew," she said; "don't say anything to her;" and then she went away. I was so frightened, I ran home directly all the way. I knew I might tell you, Mrs. Mulgrave; it is like something in a book, is it not, when people are trying to find out— oh, you don't think I can have done any harm to mamma?'

Janet was so much agitated that it was all I could do to quiet her down. 'And I never said good-bye to poor Willie, after all,' she said, with more tears when she had rallied a little. I thought it better she should not tell her mother, though one is very reluctant to say so to a girl; for Willie Bischam was a secret too. But he was going away, poor fellow, and probably nothing would ever come of it. I made a little compromise with my own sense of right.

'Forget it, Janet, and say nothing about it; perhaps it was some one else after all; and if you will promise not to meet Mr. Bischam again—'

'He goes to-night,' said Janet, with a rueful look; and thus it was evident that on that point there was nothing more to be said.

This was in the middle of the week, and on Saturday Mr. Merridew was expected home. His wife was ill, though she never had been ill before in her life; she had headaches, which were things unknown to her; she was out of temper, and irritable, and wretched. I think she had made certain that Ellen would write, and make some proposal to her; and as the days went on one by one, and no letter came— Besides, it was just the moment when they had decided against sending Jack to Oxford. To pay Willie's premium and do that at the same time was impossible. Mrs. Merridew had struggled long, but at last she was obliged to give in; and Jack was going to his father's chambers to read law with a heavy heart, poor boy; and his mother was half distracted. All might have been so different; and she had sacrificed her boys' interests, and her girls' interests, and her own happiness, all for the selfish comfort of Ellen Babington, who took no notice of her: I began to think she would have a brain fever if this went on.

She was not at church on Sunday morning, and I went with the children, as soon as service was over, to ask for her. She was lying on the sofa when I went in, and Mr. Merridew, who had arrived late on Saturday, was in his dressing-gown, walking about the room. He was tired and irritable with his journey, and his work, and perennial cares. And she, with her sacrifice, and her secret, and perennial cares, was like tinder, ready in a moment to catch fire. I know nothing more disagreeable than to go in upon married people when they are in this state of mind, which can neither be ignored nor concealed.

'I don't understand you, Janet,' he was saying, as I entered; 'women are vindictive, I know; but at least you may be sorry, as I am, that the poor old lady has died without a word of kindness passing between us: after all, we might be to blame. One changes one's opinions as one gets on in life. With our children growing up round us, I don't feel quite so sure that we were not to blame.'

'I have not been to blame,' she said, with an emphasis which sounded sullen, and which only I could understand.

'Oh no, of course; you never are,' he said, with masculine disdain. 'Catch a woman acknowledging herself to be in fault! The sun may go wrong in his course sooner than she. Mrs. Mulgrave, pray don't go away; you have seen my wife in an unreasonable mood before.'

'I am in no unreasonable mood,' she cried. 'Mrs. Mulgrave, stay. You know—oh, how am I to go on bearing this, and never answer a word?'

'My dear, don't deceive yourself,' he said, with a man's provoking calm, 'you answer a great many words. I don't call you at all a meek sufferer. Fortunately the children are out of the way. Confound it, Janet, what do you mean by talking of what you have to bear? I have not been such a harsh husband to you as all that; and when all I asked was that you should make the most innocent advances to a poor old woman who was once very kind to us both—'

'Charles!' said Mrs. Merridew, rising suddenly from her sofa, I can't bear it any longer. You think me hard, and vindictive, and I don't know what. You, who ought to know me. Look here! I got that letter, you will see by the date, more than two years ago; you were absent, and I went and saw her: there— there! now I have confessed it; Mrs. Mulgrave knows— I have had a secret from you for two years.'

It was not a moment for me to interfere. She sat, holding herself hysterically rigid and upright on the sofa. Whether she had intended to betray herself or not, I cannot tell. She had taken the letter out of her writing-desk, which stood close by; but I don't know whether she had resolved on this step or whether it was the impulse of the moment. Now that she had done it a dreadful calm of expectation took possession of her. She was afraid. He might turn upon her furious. He might upbraid her with despoiling her family, deceiving himself, being false, as she had been before. Such a thing was possible. Two souls may live side by side for years, and be as one, and yet have no notion how each will act in any sudden or unusual emergency. He was her husband, and they had no interest, scarcely any thought, that one did not share with the other; and yet she sat gazing at him rigid with terror, not knowing what he might do or say.

He read the letter without a word; then he tossed it upon the table; then he walked all the length of the room, up and down, with his hands thrust very deeply into his pockets; then he took up the letter again. He had a struggle with himself. If he was angry, if he was touched, I cannot tell. His first emotions, whatever they were, he gulped down without a word. Of all sounds to strike into the silence of such a moment, the first thing we heard in our intense listening was the abrupt ring of a short excited laugh.

'How did you venture to take any steps in it without consulting me?' he said.

'I thought—I thought—' she stammered under her breath.

'You thought I might have been tempted by the money,' he said, taking another walk through the room, while she sat erect in her terror, afraid of him. It was some time before he spoke again. No doubt he was vexed by her want of trust, and wounded by the long silence. But I have no clue to the thoughts that were passing through his mind. At last he came to a sudden pause before her. 'And perhaps you were right, Janet,' he said, drawing a long breath. 'I am glad now to have been free of the temptation. It was wrong not to tell me—and yet I think you did well.'

Mrs. Merridew gave a little choked cry, and then she fell back on the sofa—fell into my arms. I had felt she might do it, so strange was her look, and had placed myself there on purpose. But she had not fainted, as I expected. She lay silent for a moment, with her eyes closed, and then she burst into tears.

I had no right to be there; but they both detained me, both the husband and wife, and I could not get away until she had recovered herself, and it was evident that what had been a tragical barrier between them was now become a matter of business, to be discussed as affecting them both.

'It was quite right the old lady should have it,' Mr. Merridew said, as he went with me to the door, 'quite right. Janet did only what was right; but now I must take it into my own hands.'

'And annul what she has done?' I asked.

'We must consult over that,' he said. 'Ellen Babington, who has been so ungrateful to my wife, is quite a different person from her mother. But I will do nothing against Mrs. Merridew's will.'

And so I left them to consult over their own affairs. I had been thrust into it against my own will; but still it was entirely their affair, and no business of mine.

Mrs. Spencer and Lady Isabella called to me from their lawn as I went out to ask how Mrs. Merridew was, and shook their heads over her.

'She should have the doctor,' said Mrs. Spencer.

'But the doctor would not pay her bills for her,' said Lady Isabella.

And I had to answer meekly, as if I knew nothing about it, 'I don't think it is her bills.'

This conversation detained me some time from my own house; and when I reached my cottage, my maid stood by the gate, looking out for me, shading her eyes with her hands. It was to tell me there was a lady waiting for me in the drawing-room: 'A tall lady in mourning.' And in a moment my heart smote me for some hard thoughts, and I knew who my visitor was.

I found her seated by my table, very pale, but quite self-possessed. She rose when I went in, and began to explain.

'You don't know me,' she said. 'I have no right to come to you; but once you came to—us—with Mrs. Merridew. Perhaps you remember me now? I am Ellen Babington. I want to speak to you about—my brother's will. You may have heard that I have just lost—'

'Yes,' I said. 'I am very sorry. If there is anything I can do—'

'You can do all that I want from any one,' she said. 'Janet will never believe that I wanted to keep the money—now. I have seen all her children to-day at church; and I think, if she had been there, I should perhaps have been able—but never mind. Tell her I should like—if she would give her daughter Janet something out of the money—from me. She is a little like what her mother was. I am sure you are kind to them. I don't even know your name.'

'Mrs. Mulgrave,' I said; and she gave a little bow. She was very composed, very well-bred, terribly sad; with a look of a woman who had no more to do in the world, and who yet was, Heaven help her! in the middle of her life, full of vigour, and capability, and strength.

'Will you tell Janet, please, that it is all settled?' she said. 'I mean, not the girl Janet, but her mother. Tell her I have settled everything. I believe she will hear from the lawyers to-morrow; but I could not let it come only from the lawyers. I cannot forgive her, even now. She thinks it is Matilda she has wronged; but it is me she has wronged, taking my brother from me, my only brother, after all these years. But never mind. I kissed the little child instead to-day—the quiet little one, with the gold hair. I suppose she is the youngest. Tell her I came on purpose to see them before I went away.'

'But why send this message through me?' I said; 'come and see her. I will take you; it is close by. And the sight of you will do her more good—than the money. Come, and let her explain.'

I thought she hesitated for a moment, but her only answer was a shake of her head.

'What could she explain?' she cried, with strange impetuosity. 'He and I had been together all our lives, and yet all the while he cared nothing for his sister and everything for her. Do you think I can ever forgive her? but I never forgot her. I don't think I ever loved any one so well in my life.'

'Oh, come and tell her so,' said I.

Again she shook her head. 'I loved her as well as I loved him; and yet I hate her,' she said. 'But tell her I spoke to her Janet, and I kissed her baby; and that I have arranged everything with the lawyers about poor John's will. I am sure you are a good woman. Will you shake hands with me for the children's sake before I go?'

Her voice went to my heart. I had only seen her once in my life before, but I could not help it. I went up to her and took her two hands, and kissed her; and then she, the stranger, broke down, and put her head on my shoulder and wept. It was only for a moment, but it bound us as if for our lives.

'Where are you going?' I asked, when she went away.

'I am going abroad with some friends,' she said hurriedly.

'But you will come to us, my dear, when you come back?'

'Most likely I shall never come back,' she said hastily; and then went away alone out of my door, alone across the Green, with her veil over her face, and her black dress repulsing the sunshine. One's sympathies move and change about like the winds. I had been so sorry for Mrs. Merridew an hour ago; but it was not for her I was most sorry now.

And this was how it all ended. I was always glad that Mrs. Merridew had told her husband before the letter came next morning. And they got the money; and John went to the University, and Janet had new dresses and new pleasures, and a ring, of which she was intensely proud, according to Ellen's desire. I dare say Ellen's intention was that something much more important should have been given to the child in her name; but then Ellen Babington, being an unmarried woman, did not know how much a large family costs, nor what urgent occasion there is for every farthing, even with an addition so great as five hundred a year.

I am afraid it did not make Mrs. Merridew much happier just at first. She wrote letters wildly, far and near, to everybody who could be supposed to know anything about Ellen; and wanted to have her to live with them, and to share the money with her, and I don't know how many other wild fancies. But all that could be found out was that Ellen had gone abroad. And by degrees the signs of this strange tempest began to disappear—smoothed out and filled up as Nature smooths all traces of combat. The scars heal, new verdure covers the sudden precipice—the old gets assimilated with the new. By degrees an air of superior comfort stole over the house, which was very consolatory. Selina, the housemaid, married, and Richards retired to the inevitable greengrocery. And with a new man and new maids, and so much less difficulty about the bills, it is astonishing how the puckers died away from Mrs. Merridew's forehead—first one line went, and then another, and she grew younger in spite of herself. And with everything thus conspiring in her favour, and habit calmly settling to confirm all, is it wonderful if by and by she forgot that any accident had ever happened, and that all had not come in the most natural way, and with the most pleasant consequences in the world?

The other day I saw in a chance copy of Galignani, which came to me in a parcel from Paris, the marriage of Ellen Babington to a Frenchman there; but that is all we have ever heard of her. Whether it is a good marriage or a bad one I don't know; but I hope, at least, it is better for her than being all alone, as she was when she left my house that day in June, having made her sacrifice in her turn. If things had but taken their natural course, how much unnecessary suffering would have been spared: Mrs. Merridew is, perhaps, happier now than she would have been without that five hundred a year—but for two years she was wretched, sacrificing and grudging the sacrifice, and making herself very unhappy. And though I don't believe Ellen Babington cared for the money, her heart will never be healed of that pang of bitterness which her brother's desertion gave her. His companion for twenty years! and to think his best thoughts should have been given all that time to a woman who had only slighted him, and refused his love. Mrs. Merridew does not see the sting of this herself—she thinks it natural. And so I dare say would half the world beside.

THE BARLEY MOW

CHAPTER I

There was but one little harmless house of public entertainment at Dinglefield, a place not without its importance among us, with its little farm, and the fly with the old white horse which was an institution on the Green, and very serviceable when there was luggage to be carried to the railway, or any party going on in bad weather when our pony carriages could not be used.

This was the Barley Mow, a favourite and picturesque little village public-house, the most inoffensive article of the kind, perhaps, which was to be found for miles and miles around. The Green itself was not like the trim and daintily-kept greensward, with orderly posts and railings, which is to be seen in many suburban hamlets. It was long, irregular, and just wild enough to be thoroughly natural. The lower end, near the Barley Mow, was smooth and neat, the best cricket ground that you could find in the neighbourhood. But the upper part was still wild with gorse bushes, and bordered by a little thicket of rhododendrons, which had strayed thither from the adjacent park. Many a cricket match was played upon the lower Green, and on the bright summer Saturdays, when the cricket parties came, there was often quite a pretty little company from the surrounding houses to watch them, and a great traffic went on at the Barley Mow. It was an irregular old house, partly red brick, partly whitewashed, with a luxuriant old garden warm and sunny, opening through a green wicket set in a great hedge on the right hand. A signpost stood in the open space in front, where the road widened out, and by the open door you could see through a clean, red-tiled passage into the garden at the back, where the turf was like velvet, and the borders full of all kinds of bright and sweet old-fashioned flowers. There were neither standard rose-bushes nor red geraniums to be seen there, not that Widow Aikin, good woman, had any whim of taste that prompted her to despise these conventional inmates of the modern garden, but that the pinks and gilliflowers, the rockets and larkspurs, and great straggling rose-bushes were cheaper and gave less trouble, having established themselves there, and requiring no bedding out. The room which looked out upon this garden was where the strangers and gentlefolks who came from far were entertained, and there was a parlour, with a bow window in front, for humbler persons. But the favourite place in summer for that kind of 'company' was the bench outside the door, looking out upon the Green. There was little traffic of any kind in winter, but the summer aspect of the Barley Mow was a pleasant one. It had no air of stale dissipation about it, no heavy odour of spilt beer or coarse tobacco, but looked wholesome and sweet-smelling, a place of refreshment, not of indulgence. Anyhow, it was the fashion about the Green to think and say this of Widow Aikin's clean, honest, respectable house. She was a favourite with all the 'families.' She served them with milk as well as beer, and fresh eggs, and sometimes fruit. She had all sorts of little agencies in hand, found servants for the ladies on the Green, and executed little commissions of many kinds. She was a personage, privileged and petted: everybody had a smile and a kind word for her, and she for everybody. She was always about, never standing still, glancing in and out of the red-tiled passage, the bow-windowed parlour, the sunny garden, the noisy stable-yard. You saw her everywhere—now this side, now that—an ubiquitous being, so quick-footed that she was almost capable of being in two places at once.

It was a favourite subject with Mrs. Aikin to talk of her own loneliness, and incapacity to manage 'such a house as this.' She liked to dwell upon the responsibilities of the position and the likelihood that a lone woman would be imposed upon; and the Green generally considered this a very proper strain of observation, and felt it to be respectable that a widow should so feel and so express herself. But it was very well known that things had gone much better at the Barley Mow since Will Aikin managed very opportunely to be carried off by that vulgar gout which springs from beer, and has all the disadvantages with none of the distinctions belonging to its kindred ailment. There was no saying what might not have happened had he lived a year longer, for the creditors were urgent and the business paralyzed. It was this which made his death opportune, for the brewers were merciful to the widow, and gave her time to redeem herself; and when she was relieved from the necessity of nursing him and studying his 'ways,' which were as difficult as if the landlord of the Barley Mow had been a prince of the blood, the widow blossomed out into another woman. It is but a poor compliment to the lamented husband, but widows continually do this, it must be allowed, giving the lie practically to their own tears. Happily however Mrs. Aikin, like many others in her position, took her own desolation for granted, and attributed her increase of prosperity to luck or the blessing of God, which is the better way of stating it. 'Oh! that poor Will had but lived to see it!' she would say with kindly tears in her eyes, and never whispered even to herself that had poor Will lived it would never have been. She never missed an opportunity, good soul, of bringing him into her conversation, telling stories of his excellence, his good looks (he was one of the plainest men in the county), his good jokes (he was as dull as ditch-water) and his readiness in all encounters. She would stand in the doorway, with her apron lifted in her hand, ready to dry the tear which out of grief for his loss, or tremulous traditionary laughter over one of his pleasantries, was always ready to spring up in the corner of her eye. What did it matter to her that the poor old jokes were pointless? She never inquired into their claims, but accepted them as laughter-worthy by divine right.

Mrs. Aikin had but one child, Jane, a modest, dark-eyed girl, with pretty fair curling hair, which gave her a certain distinction among the rustic prettinesses about. Her mother professed to be annoyed by the mingling of two complexions, protesting that Jane was always 'contrary,' that such light hair should have gone with blue eyes, and that she was neither one sort nor another; but in her heart she was proud enough of her daughter's uncommon looks—and Jane was an uncommon girl. Next to the Barley Mow stood the smallest house on the Green, a little place half wooden, half brick, which would have been tumbledown and disreputable had it not been so exquisitely neat and well cared for. This was the poorest little place of all the gentry's houses, but it was not by any means the humblest of the inhabitants of the Green who lived at the Thatched Cottage. Old Mrs. Mowbray was a very great person, though she was a very small person. She was the tiniest woman on the Green, and she had the tiniest income, but she was related to half the peerage, and considered herself as great a lady as if she had been a grand duchess. Nor did any one dispute her claim. The greatest people in the county yielded the pas to old Mrs. Mowbray, partly no doubt because she was very old and her magnificent pretensions were amusing, but partly also because they were well founded. There was not one house on the Green that had such visitors as she had. She was grand-aunt to a duke, and nobody would have been surprised to hear that in her own person she had a far-away right to the Crown—a right, let us say, coming by some side-wind from the Plantagenets, leaping over the other families who are of yesterday. Many people at Dinglefield called her the fairy queen. She had the easy familiarity of royalty with all her surroundings. What could it matter to her what were the small gradations of social importance among her neighbours and friends? She could afford to be indifferent to such trifling distinctions of society. Widow Aikin was not appreciably further out of the reach of this splendid little old poor patrician than Lady Denzil. Education was in favour of the latter, it is true, but there was this against her, that it was possible for her to entertain some delusive idea of equality, of which Mrs. Aikin was guiltless. Mrs. Mowbray accordingly made no secret of the fact that she entertained a great friendship for the landlady of the Barley Mow, and was very fond of Jane. She had the girl with her a great deal, and taught her those pretty manners which were so unlike others of her class. When Jane was a growing girl of twelve or thirteen she used to wait upon the old lady's guests at tea as a maid of honour might have waited. It was done for love for one thing, which always confers a certain grace; and it was not possible to move awkwardly or act ungracefully under the eye of such a keen critic.

It was the general opinion of the ladies on the Green that this patronage might not be an advantage to Jane as she grew older, and it became necessary to choose what was to be her occupation in the world; but in this respect Mrs. Mowbray behaved with great wisdom. It was, indeed, against not only all her traditions, but all the habits of her mind to 'put nonsense in the girl's head,' and disgust her with her natural position, which was what the other ladies feared. It mattered nothing to Mrs. Mowbray whether the girl became a pupil-teacher; or pushed upward in the small scale of rank, as understood at the Barley Mow, to be a nursery governess and call herself a lady; or remained what she was by nature, her mother's right hand and chief assistant? Parties ran very high on the Green on this subject. It was fought over in many a drawing-room as hotly as if it had been a branch of the Eastern Question. Ought Jane Aikin to stay at the parish school with Mrs. Peters, whose favourite pupil she was, and become her aid and probable successor? Ought she, being so refined in her manners, and altogether such a nice-looking girl, to learn a little music and French, and become a governess? The ladies who were liberal, who believed in education, and that everybody should do their best to improve their position and better themselves, upheld the latter idea; but the strongest party was in favour of the pupil-teacher notion, which was considered a means of utilizing Jane's good manners and excellent qualities, without moving her out of 'her own sphere of life'—and this set was headed, by the Rector, who was very hot and decided on the subject. A third party, to which nobody paid much attention, and which consisted chiefly of Mrs. Aikin herself, the only real authority, intended Jane to remain where she was, head-waiter and superintendent at the Barley Mow. The question between the two first projects had already been warmly discussed in the drawing-rooms before it occurred to anybody that it could be Mrs. Aikin's intention to do such injustice to her daughter, or indeed that the good landlady had any particular say in the matter. What! make a barmaid of Jane! The Rector was, it is to be feared, very injudicious in his treatment of the question. He attempted to carry matters with a very high hand, and went so far as to say that no modest girl could be brought up in 'an alehouse,' as he was so foolish as to call it, an opprobrious epithet which Mrs. Aikin did not forgive for years. She was so desperately offended, indeed, that she went to chapel for four Sundays after she heard of it, walking straight past the church doors, and proclaiming her defection to the whole world. Mrs. Mowbray was the person who was employed to set this matter right. She was waited upon by representatives of the two different parties, both of them feeling secure of her sympathy, but both anxious at all events to bring that foolish woman, Jane's mother, to her senses. Mrs. Stoke was at the head of the governess set, and good Mr. Wigmore, our excellent church-warden, represented the Rector's views. They met at the gate of the Thatched Cottage upon this mission. 'I have not spoken to dear Mrs. Mowbray on the subject, because I feel so sure that she will be on our side—so fond as she is of Jane,' said Mrs. Stoke. 'Mrs. Mowbray is not the person to advocate any breaking up of the divisions which mark society,' said Mr. Wigmore. 'She knows the evil of all such revolutionary measures.' And thus they went in, each confident in his and her own cause.

Mrs. Mowbray sat by the fire in the big old carved ebony chair, which made her look more than ever a fairy queen. She had a handsome old ivory face, with a tinge of colour on the cheeks, which looked as if it might once have been rouge. Strangers considered that this peculiarity of complexion gave an artificial and even improper look to the old lady, but on the Green it was considered one of the evidences of that supreme aristocratism which would not take the trouble to disguise anything it pleased to do, but would rouge, if rouge was necessary, in a masterful and magnificent way, making no secret of it. However, as a matter of fact it was not rouge, but perfectly real, as was the fine ivory yellow of her old nose, a stately and prominent feature, evidently belonging to the highest rank. She would not have budged from her ebony chair to receive any one less than the Queen; but she permitted Mrs. Stoke to kiss her, and Mr. Wigmore to shake her hand, with serene graciousness. When they had both seated themselves she looked at them across her knitting with a smile. 'This looks likes a deputation,' she said. 'What do you want, good people? If it is to settle about my funeral there is no hurry—for my cold is much better, and I have a good many things to see after before I can think of such luxuries.' This distressed both her visitors, who did not like to hear an old lady speak of such serious matters in this light-minded way.

'Indeed, indeed, dear Mrs. Mowbray, it was nothing of the kind. When such a dreadful event occurs there will be weeping and wailing on the Green; and we all know very well that though you always talk so cheerfully, and so amusingly—'

'You regard such subjects with the melancholy which becomes right-thinking people,' said Mr. Wigmore; 'but we came—or to speak for myself, I came—'

'To speak of Jane Aikin,' cried Mrs. Stoke, feeling the importance of having the first word, 'and her mother's inconceivable foolishness in keeping her at home; and the still more foolish step she has taken in separating herself from all her true friends.'

'Frequenting the Dissenters' services,' said Mr. Wigmore. 'Few things more sad have come under my observation in this very distressing parish—which is really such a mixture of everything that is unsatisfactory—'

'The parish is just like other parishes,' said Mrs. Stoke, 'only much better, I should say—so many educated people in it, and so few poor comparatively. But I am sure our dear old friend will agree with me that Jane is quite out of place—'

'Now, my good people,' said the old lady, 'think a moment—what do you mean by out of place?— Everybody is out of place now-a-days. I see people in this room calmly sitting down by me whose fathers and mothers would have come to the kitchen door fifty years ago; but if I made a fuss what would any one say?'

This made Mr. Wigmore very uncomfortable, whose father had been a cheesemonger in a good way of business; but as for Mrs. Stoke she did not care, being very well born, as she supposed. Mrs. Mowbray, however, took them both in quite impartially. 'Unless people really belong to the old nobility,' she continued, 'I don't see that it matters about their place. It does not mean anything. Even in what we call the old nobility, you know, there's not above half-a-dozen families that are anything like pur sang. I know dukes that are just as much out of place as Jane Aikin would be at Windsor Castle. The only place any one has a right to is where their ancestors are born and bred—if they have any. And when you have not rank,' said the old lady, looking keenly at Mr. Wigmore, 'you had much better be peuple, as the French say. We haven't got an English word for it. No, it doesn't mean lower classes—it means peuple, neither less nor more. And Jane Aikin is pure peuple. She can't be out of place where she is.'

'But you forget her education, dear Mrs. Mowbray—and you yourself that have given her such a taste for beautiful manners, and spoiled her for her own common class.'

Mrs. Mowbray did not say anything, but she put on her spectacles and stared at her reprover. 'I never spoil any one,' she said; 'out of my own condition—I make no secret of it—one girl is very much like another to me. They should all be pretty-mannered—I never knew that to spoil any one, small or great.'

'Dear Mrs. Mowbray, no; but if we could raise her to a position in which she would be appreciated. She has taken such a step out of her own class in associating with you.'

'Associating—with me!' Mrs. Mowbray took off her spectacles again after she had gazed mildly with a wonder beyond speech in the speaker's face. Then she shrugged her shoulders slightly and shook her head. 'I can't recall at this moment any one in this neighbourhood who does that. I have a great many friends, if that is what you mean, and I am not so particular as most people about the little subdivisions—but associates! I don't know any. Yes, Mr. Wigmore? you were going to speak.'

'I am one of those who agree with you that the poor should be kept in their own place,' said Mr. Wigmore. As he spoke the old lady took up her spectacles again, and deliberately put them on, looking at him as if (Mrs. Stoke said) he was a natural curiosity, which somewhat discomfited the excellent man—'but, as our friend says, her manners and breeding are quite above her station.'

'Jane Aikin has no station,' said Mrs. Mowbray promptly. 'She is peuple, as I told you. I know nothing of your aboves and belows. Let her stay where she is, in her natural place, and do her duty. Do your duty in that condition to which God has called you: that's what the Catechism says. There's nothing about being above or below. Very lucky for her she's got a natural place and her duty plain before her. If one had not one's own rank, which of course one does not choose, that's what I should prefer for myself: a distinct place and a clear duty—and that's what Jane Aikin has.'

'In a public-house!' cried Mr. Wigmore, aghast.

'In her mother's house, sir,' said old Mrs. Mowbray.

Thus the Green was routed horse and foot; but the old lady on further talk accepted the position of mediatrix to bring back the Widow Aikin to her allegiance, and to show her her duty as a churchwoman. She sallied forth for that purpose the very next morning in her old quilted white satin bonnet and great furred cloak. She never changed the fashion of her garments, having had abundant time to discover what was most becoming to her, as she frankly said. Mrs. Aikin was standing at her front door, looking out upon the bright morning, when the old lady appeared. There was very little doing at the Barley Mow. The parlour with the bow window was full of a dazzling stock of household linen, which Jane and a maid were looking over, and putting in order. Jane herself had the task of darning the thin places, which she did so as to make darning into a fine art. This had been taught her by Mrs. Peters at the parish school. Perhaps it was not, after all, such a valuable accomplishment as it looked, but certainly Jane's darning had a beautiful appearance on the tablecloths, after they had passed their first perfection of being, at the Barley Mow.

'The sunshine's a pleasure,' said Mrs. Aikin, making her best curtsey, 'and I hope I see you well, ma'am, this bright morning. It shows us as how spring's coming. Might I be so bold as to ask you to step in and take a chair?'

'Not this morning,' said Mrs. Mowbray in her frank voice, not unduly subdued in tone, 'though I've come to scold you. They tell me you've gone off from your church, you that were born and bred in it, and Jane, though I taught her her Catechism myself. Do you mean to tell me you've got opinions—you?—with a nice child like Jane to thank God for, and everything going well—'

'Well, ma'am,' said Mrs. Aikin, growing red and smoothing her apron, 'I don't say as I'm one for opinions—more than doing your duty, and getting a bit of good out of a sermon when you can.'

'That's very pious and right,' said the old lady, 'but your church that you were christened in is more than a sermon. I don't pretend to get much good of them myself: but you'll not tell me that you have left your church for that.'

'Well, ma'am!' said Mrs. Aikin, reluctant to commit herself. She put out her foot, and began to trace patterns with her shoe in the sand on the doorstep, and fixed her eyes upon the process. She could not meet the little old lady's decided gaze. 'Mr. Short at the chapel do preach beautiful, he do. You should just hear him for yourself. He'll make you come all over in a tremble, when you're sitting quite quiet like, thinking of nothing; and then he's real comforting to poor folks and them as is put upon. It's almost a pleasure to feel as you've had your troubles with the quality too.'

'Quality! Where do you find any quality to have troubles with?' said Mrs. Mowbray. 'You and I have always been good friends. You don't consider that you're put upon, as you call it, because the Duke sent me my Christmas turkey. That was no offence to you.'

'No, ma'am, never—not you. There is them that shall be nameless—not but what they call names a plenty.'

'The woman's thinking of the Rector, I declare. Quality!' said Mrs. Mowbray with an accent of mingled amazement and amusement. 'No, my dear woman, he's not quality. But he meant no harm. He was thinking of the girl and her good. They think they know, these men; and we must submit, you know, to our clergy. It was because of his interest in Jane.'

'Interest in Jane!' said Widow Aikin (she pronounced the name something like Jeyeyn; but the peculiarities of Berkshire are too much for even phonetic spelling), 'if that shows an interest! telling her mother to her face as she wasn't fit to bring her up decent and respectable, and showing no more confidence than that in the girl herself.'

'It was his mistake,' said Mrs. Mowbray, 'he wants tact, that is what it is. He hasn't the right way of doing a thing, my dear woman. That is how these middling sort of people always break down. My nephew, the Duke, if he had to send you to prison, would do it as if it were the greatest kindness in the world. But the middling classes have no grace about them. That's not to say that you're to give up your church that you were christened in and married in. Who's to bury you, woman? Do you never think of that? Not your Mr. Short at the chapel, I hope. At least I know he would never do for me. There ought to be more in your church than a sermon, or even than a pleasant word.'

'Well, ma'am, I don't say but what that's true; and I never thought of the burying,' said the widow, hanging her head. She was subdued and awe-stricken at the turn which the discussion had taken, and, indeed, had never intended to forsake 'her church,' but only to make a demonstration of her independence. Jane had come out from the parlour, leaving her work to listen to this argument, with great anxiety and interest, for her heart was in it. She was hovering in the passage behind her mother, now and then giving her a little touch or pull to enforce something the old lady said. During the pause that followed she came forward very anxiously, and put forward a plea of her own, in which there did not seem much point or applicability.

'Oh, mother,' she said softly, pulling her sleeve, 'and Johnny in the choir!'

'Oh, go along with your Johnnys,' said the landlady of the Barley Mow. But it was clear enough that the victory was won.

CHAPTER II

It is full time that John should be spoken of, who was the other member of the family, and a very important one. He was Mrs. Aikin's nephew, the son of a brother who was very poorly off and had been taken in by his good aunt as a miserable stunted child when he was but six or seven. The brother was a soldier, who had been discharged, and whose character it is to be supposed did not recommend him sufficiently to get any interest made for him, or to establish him anywhere in one of the occupations which seem made for old soldiers. Instead of this he had fallen into a kind of vagabondism, wandering from place to place, and as his wife was dead this only child had been miserably neglected, and was in a bad way when Mrs. Aikin took him to her kindly care. He had never been a prepossessing boy, and he did not at all share with Jane in the interest of the Green. He was heavy and lowering in his looks, quiet to outward appearance, though tales were told of him which were not consistent with this subdued aspect. Both the women however were devoted to John, either because they had no one else to be fond of, or because he possessed some qualities at bottom which made up for his faults of exterior. He certainly did not seem at any time to give himself much trouble to secure their affections. All that he did seemed to be done unwillingly—the very sound of his voice was churlish—and except Mrs. Aikin and her daughter nobody cared for the boy. From his very first coming he had showed himself in an unfavourable light. He was then a boy of about eight years old, and little Jane, a delightful child, everybody's favourite, was a year younger. One summer evening he was standing with his hands in his pockets staring at the waggons with their big horses, when she came running up to him.

'Come and play, Johnny,' she said in her soft little voice.

'I won't,' he said, pushing her out of his way with his shoulder.

'Oh, Johnny, come and have tea in the garden,' said little Jane, 'mother says we may. I've got some cake and some gooseberries, and my own little tea-things, and all the best shall be for you. Oh, Johnny, come!'

'I won't,' he said again, though he faltered when he heard of the cake.

'Oh, Johnny, come to please me,' cried the poor little woman, already as foolish in her expectations as if she had been twenty years older.

'To please you! I'd a deal rather please myself,' cried the boy, once more thrusting her aside with a push of his shoulder. Little Jane was ready to cry, but the mother coming out full of business called to the children in her hasty way to go at once to the garden, and get out of her road. Upon which the boy shrugged his shoulders, and obeyed with brutish unwillingness and display of yielding to superior force. This was how he had been ever since. The little girl would coax and entreat, the kind mother give cheerful orders, never so much as seeing the lowering looks of rebellion.

'Poor boy!' Mrs. Aikin would say, 'he ain't got no mother, and I can see by his solemn face many a day as he's thinking and thinking of his poor father, which was never one as would settle down to anything. We has to do all we can to keep him cheerful, Jane and me.'

Thus from the very first they made up their minds to spoil the loutish, unpleasant boy. The widow was continually praising him, and holding him up to the admiration of her neighbours. When it was found that he had a good voice, this gave them as much delight and triumph as if they had inherited a fortune, and when he made his appearance for the first time with the choir in his white surplice, the faces of the two were a sight to see, so glowing were they with satisfaction and delight. In this way the two cousins had grown up—the boy always sullen and downlooking, resisting rather than responding to the kindnesses heaped upon him, the girl always ready to smooth away every cloud, to say the best for him, to explain his moodiness and backwardness.

'It is only his way,' Jane would say in her soft voice, and her way was so ingratiating and conciliatory that no one could stand against it. His aunt, too, was foolish in her affection for this unattractive hero. He was the son of the house, the young master, though he had not a penny. His opinion was always asked about everything, and his judgment constantly relied upon. It was true that the advice he gave was not always taken, for Mrs. Aikin was very active, and liked to manage everything her own way; but when it happened that he agreed with her, she would trumpet forth his praises and give him all the credit.

'I should never have thought of that but for Johnny. There's no telling the sense of him,' the good woman would say admiringly. All this special pleading however could not give the Green any interest in John. Nobody cared for him except the two who cared so much for him, and nobody believed in him, notwithstanding his imposing appearance in the choir and his beautiful voice. As he grew up this voice changed from its angelical soprano to a big melodious baritone. He was the chief singer at Dinglefield, and kept up the character of the place, which had always been noted for its choir, and indeed he was the only man in it to whom a solo could be entrusted. This made the Rector and Mr. Wigmore tolerant of the alehouse so far as he was concerned.

Thus the little family at the Barley Mow were happy enough when the difficulty was got over about Jane. Of course Mrs. Aikin had the best right to settle what her daughter was to do, and whatever they might advise, neither the clergy nor the ladies could interfere on their own account in the matter. So that when Mrs. Aikin gave up chapel and came back to her own pew all was forgiven and forgotten, and Jane, though the maid of the inn, became a greater favourite than ever. She was liked as much as her cousin was disliked. Even the contact which she could not be altogether saved from, in her position, with the roughest and coarsest class did not seem to affect her. She went about and served the beer, and waited on the summer visitors as softly and as neatly as she used to serve the ladies at tea in old Mrs. Mowbray's tiny drawing-room. She never took any notice of foolish things that might be said to her, and did not even seem to hear or see the squabbles and noisy talk that must always go on more or less about such places. In the cricketing time they were always very busy, and Jane no doubt had the additional temptation of the gentlemen who would have talked and flirted had she allowed them to do so: but she passed through everything like a humble Una, with a smile for everybody, but not a word that could have been objected to, had all the ladies in the Green sat in committee on her. Perhaps however her lout of a cousin did more for Jane than the ladies could have done. She was very modest and shy, and did not betray herself except to the keenest observation; but it was apparent enough to those who were chiefly interested that all her thoughts were for John. She was constantly doing his work for him in her quiet way, undertaking this and that to let him have a holiday, or go to a choral meeting, or have his innings at cricket.

'Girls don't want so much play as boys,' she would say with a smile. And he took her at her word, and accepted everything she did for him as if it had been the most natural thing in the world. Strangely enough, her mother did not object to this. She spoiled and petted the clumsy fellow just as much as Jane did, and took it for granted that he should have all kinds of indulgences as if he had been a favourite son. The great terror of both of them was his vagabond father, who appeared now and then, a scandal to their respectability, and a standing danger to John. The two women were always in a fright lest this undesirable relative should lead their darling astray.

'He is such a good boy now—he has always been such a good boy,' Mrs. Aikin said, with an uncomfortable sense that nobody accepted this statement as gospel, which made her more and more hot in giving it forth. And when old Mrs. Mowbray stopped in her walk to inquire after Jane and the poultry, the widow fairly wept over this one danger which threatened the family peace.

'Why do you let him come at all?' the old lady asked peremptorily. 'If I were in your place, I would order him off the premises. You have done too much for him already, my dear woman. When a man becomes a vagabond he has no more claim on his friends.'

This did not at all please the landlady of the Barley Mow. Her honest face flushed, and she dried her eyes indignantly.

'Nature is nature, ma'am,' she said; 'good or bad, you can't deny your own flesh and blood.'

'But I could keep my own flesh and blood at a distance,' said the old lady, 'especially if it has got more harm in it, and could do me an injury still.'

'That is all that troubles me,' said Mrs. Aikin. 'I'd be as happy a woman as steps the Green, but for that. Nature is nature, and a father's a father. And if so be as he was to put wild thoughts in our Johnny's head—what would me and Jane do? La, bless you, it would break that girl's heart.'

'And that is just what I am thinking of,' said Mrs. Mowbray briskly. 'You are a silly woman. What has Jane's heart got to do with it? You keep this boy by her side year after year. And now they're growing man and woman, and what's to come of it? What do you mean by it? That's what I say!'

'La, ma'am, what could come of it? They've been brought up like brother and sister,' the widow said with a laugh, and she went about with a smile on her face for the rest of the day. The other ladies made remonstrances of the same kind with equally little use. Of course it was very clear that this was what she had made up her mind to—that the two should marry and succeed her when she grew old, and carry on the business. It was all suitable enough and natural enough. And, of course, the fact that Jane was above her position made no difference. When a woman is above her position the best thing for her to do is to conceal it carefully, and make the best of the circumstances. And she herself was not conscious of the fact of her superiority. Whether Mrs. Aikin had been so foolish as to communicate her ideas to Jane no one knew, but there could be little doubt that the poor girl took the arrangement for granted as much as her mother did. It was so natural! She had been fond of her cousin all her life, loving him with that most powerful of all kinds of love, the close tie of tender habit, the affection one has for the being whom one has protected, excused, and been good to all one's life. If she had not pushed him softly through his work, coaxed him through his lessons, made the best of him to everybody, how could poor Johnny ever have got on at all? He wanted her backing up so perpetually, that it might be permitted to Jane to believe that he could not have got on without her. It is common to say that the love of a woman for a man has often a great deal that is motherly in it, and certainly this was the case here. It had been her duty to be kind to him, to make him feel himself at home, he who had no other home. All her own little pleasures, almost ever since she could remember, had been made secondary to Johnny—and what so natural as that this should go on? She took it for granted, poor girl. She scarcely expected to be courted as other girls were who 'fall in love' with strangers. It had not been necessary for her to fall in love. She had always been fond of her cousin. She had never thought of any other man.

And poor Jane was as delicate in her love as any lady of romance. She had none of the romping ways of country girls of her class. Neither was she sentimentally disposed. Her modest look dwelt upon him now and then with a tender pleasure, especially when he was singing, which was the only thing about him which seemed to justify that delusion. But even this look was so modest and so momentary that only careful observation surprised it now and then. She held her somewhat embarrassing position with a serious grace which was almost dignity—making no advances on her part, though she was the crown princess, and had everything to bestow, yet never doubting, I think, poor girl, what the course of affairs was to be. Was it not natural that he should love her best as she loved him best? and that their life should go on as it had always done, with something added but nothing taken away? Such was the simple, happy tenor of Jane's maiden thoughts.

Whether John divined what the women took for granted it would be difficult to say. Perhaps he saw the advantages of being master at the Barley Mow, and the homage he received no doubt increased his natural loutish self-complacency—that stolid vanity which so often dwells in the minds of those who have nothing in the world to be vain of. He took it for granted on his side that he was the sun of this little world, and accepted everything as a natural homage to his fine deservings. He thought the more of himself for all they did for him, not of them. As for Jane, her pretty looks, her superiority, her grace and good breeding were nothing to the lout. He would have liked her a great deal better had she been a noisy, laughing, romping girl. He accepted all the little sacrifices she made, and allowed her to do his work, with that satisfied consciousness that she liked it, which gave him the feeling of doing rather than receiving a favour. And very likely he might go on, and carry out the programme, and marry her in the same lordly way. For there could be no doubt that it was very much to his advantage, and that his position as Jane's husband would be much more assured than that of Mrs. Aikin's nephew. So things went on, day gliding into day, and summer into winter. They were both young—there was no hurry; and to quicken the settlement or alter anything from the pleasant footing on which it at present stood was not at all the widow's wish.

The picture would have been incomplete however had there not been something on the other side. When one man is indifferent to the goods the gods provide him it is almost certain there is another somewhere to whom these gifts would seem divine. Jane had always kept up her friendship with Mrs. Peters, the schoolmistress, who had trained her, and whose assistant the ladies on the Green had wished her to be. She was fond of going to see her in the winter afternoons when there was not much doing, and always found something to do among the girls, work to set right, or a class to look after which had wearied the schoolmistress: and she got on so well with them that it was clear the ladies on the Green had not been wrong in their idea of her powers. But while she thus came and went about the good schoolmistress whom she loved, another person had come into the little circle, of whom Jane took little notice. This was a brother-in-law of Mrs. Peters, who had been lately appointed schoolmaster, and was very highly thought of in the parish. He was ten years at least older than Jane, and appeared to her a middle-aged man, though he was scarcely over thirty. He was a good schoolmaster and a good man, a little precise in speech perhaps, and rigid in his ways, but true and honest and kind, anxious to be of real service to his pupils and everybody round him. It was not wonderful that his serious eye should be caught by the serious, gentle girl who was so sweet and so kind to his sister-in-law, so much at home in the school, so helpful, and so understanding. After he had taken tea half a dozen times in her company the good young man's head became full of Jane. And he was not so instructed in the ways of the place as to be aware of Mrs. Aikin's understood plans, or the kind of tacit arrangement by which everything seemed settled. He did not even know of John's existence at first—and when he did become aware of him there seemed nothing alarming in the loutish lad, whose appearance and manners were not attractive to the outward eye. Mr. Peters, though the very name of a public-house was obnoxious to him, began to come out in the evenings, when that first winter was over, and would sit down in the shade on a bench outside the door of the Barley Mow, sometimes for hours together, within reach of all the noises, and of the smoking and beer-drinking, which were a horror to him, and not respectable even, or becoming in his position. To see him seated there in his black coat, with that air of respectability half ashamed of itself, was both comical and touching. It was said that the Rector spoke to him about it, pointing out that the Barley Mow, however respectable in itself, was not a place where an instructor of youth ought to spend his evenings, a reproach which cut to the schoolmaster's very heart. But he was so far gone that he stood up in defence of the place where his beloved spent her life.

'Sir,' he stammered, reddening and faltering, 'I see a—person there: who is an example to—every one round.'

'You mean Mrs. Aikin,' the Rector said. 'Yes, yes, Peters, she is very respectable, I don't say anything against her; but it is not a place for you to be seen at, you know.'

And this was true, there could be no doubt. The schoolmaster after this would come late. He would be seen going out for a walk, passing the Barley Mow with wistful looks after his tea-time, casting glances aside at the cheerful bustle; and when the darkness was falling, and everything had grown indistinct in the twilight, some keen eye would see him steal to his accustomed seat and stay there, neither drinking nor talking, except to Jane when she passed him. He watched her taking the tray from her cousin's hand, letting him go free for his cricket or his practice, sometimes even sending him indoors to take a hand at whist, and had begun to be angry with the young man for letting her do his work for him before he surprised the gleam of soft love and kindness in Jane's pretty eyes which revealed the whole story. Was that what it meant? It was such a shock to him that the schoolmaster fell ill, and was not about the place for weeks. But at last he came back again, as people constantly do, to gaze at sights that break their hearts. The front of the Barley Mow was a cheerful place in these summer evenings. Mrs. Aikin allowed no rioting or excess of drinking on her benches, and she was as imperative as a little queen. And all the travellers who passed stopped there to get water for their horses and beverages not quite so innocent for themselves. The horses alone were a sight to see. The whole hierarchy of rank on four legs might be seen at the door. The beautiful riding-horses, slim and dainty, with their shy, supercilious looks; the carriage horses just a trifle less fine—the large, florid, highly-fed brutes in the drays, that made no stand on their quality, but looked calmly conscious of unlimited corn at home—the saucy little pony, ready for any impertinence—the shabby, poor gentleman in the fly who had seen better days, meek beast, broken-spirited, and unfortunate—the donkey, meeker still, but with a whole red revolution, if he could only but once get the upper hand, in his eye. It was curious to sit there in the darkening of the soft summer night, and see the indistinct vehicles gliding past, and all the dim figures of men, while the stars came out overhead, and the heat of the day sank into grateful coolness. And what a dramatic completeness the humble, bustling scene took, when one perceived the little human drama, tragedy or comedy, who could tell which, that was going on in the midst, Jane regarding the loutish cousin who was not her lover with those soft eyes of tenderness as the stars regarded the earth: he altogether indifferent, caring nothing, taking a vulgar advantage of her weakness to save himself trouble; and the spectator in the corner, hidden in the shadows, who did not lose a look or a word, whose very heart was burning to see the wasted affection, and made furious by the indifference. Mr. Peters would have given all he had in the world could he have purchased that soft look from Jane; but the lout thought nothing of it, except so far as it ministered to his own rude self-satisfaction. Perhaps he had his grievance too. He would have liked to escape from this propriety and quiet to the noisy revels on the other side of the Green, where there was always some nonsense going on at the Load-o'-Hay, a kind of rival, but much inferior place, which was the one place in the world which Mrs. Aikin regarded with feelings of hatred, and which moved even Jane to something like anger. He would have liked to have had 'a bit of fun' there, and left the steady business of the Barley Mow to take care of itself. How it was that neither Jane nor her mother perceived or guessed the discrepancy between his thoughts and theirs is past divining. The girl, at least, one would have thought, must have had some moments of distrust, some wondering doubts: but if so she never showed them, and as for Mrs. Aikin, she was too busy a woman to think of anything that did not come immediately under her eyes.

This state of calm, so full of explosive elements, could scarcely go on without some revelation, sooner or later, of the dangers below; and, again, the little old fairy queen, Mrs. Mowbray, had a hand in the revelation. Though she was so old, there was no more clear-sighted or keen observer in all the county; and, as her interest in Jane was great, it cannot be supposed that she had not seen through the complications about her. But as yet there had been no opening—nothing which could justify her in speaking particularly on this subject; and all that could be said in a general way had been already said. Her mind however was very much set upon it; and she had taken in with an eager ear all the gossip of her old maid about Mr. Peters, whose visits to the Barley Mow had been naturally much commented upon. Mrs. Mowbray, as has been already said, had a royal indifference to the particular grade of the people about her. They were all her inferiors; and, whether the difference seemed small or great to the common eye, it was one of kind, and therefore unalterable, in her impartial judgment. Acting on this principle, the loves of Jane and John at the Barley Mow were just as interesting as the loves of the young ladies and gentlemen on the Green, who thought much more highly of themselves.

This being the case, it will be less surprising to the reader to hear that, when Mrs. Mowbray in her walks encountered the schoolmaster, she managed to strike up an acquaintance with him; and ere long had so worked upon him with artful talk of Jane, that poor Mr. Peters opened his heart to the kind old lady, though he had never ventured to do so to the object of his love. The way in which this happened was as follows. It was summer—a lovely evening, such as tempted everybody out of doors. The schoolmaster, poor man, had gone out to walk the hour's walk which he imposed upon himself as a necessary preface to his foolish vigil in front of the Barley Mow, which had settled down into a regular routine. He made believe to himself, or tried to make believe, that when he sat down on that bench at the door it was only because he was tired after his long walk; it was not as if he went on purpose—to do that would be foolishness indeed. But he was no moth, scorching his wings in the flame—he was an honest, manly pedestrian, taking needful rest in the cool of the evening. This was the little delusion he had wrapped himself in. When he was setting out for his walk, he met Mrs. Mowbray, and took off his hat with that mixture of conscious respect and stiff propriety which became his somewhat doubtful position—that position which made him feel that more was expected from him than would be expected from the common people round. He was in his way a personage, a representative of education and civilization; but yet he did not belong to the sphere occupied by the ladies and gentlemen. This made poor Mr. Peters doubly precise. But as the old lady—whose lively mind was full of Jane, and of a little plan she had in her head—turned to look at him instead of looking where she stepped, she suddenly knocked her foot against a projecting root, and would have fallen had not the schoolmaster, almost too shy to touch her, and wondering much in his own mind what a gentleman would do in such an emergency, rushed forward to give his assistance. Mrs. Mowbray laid hold of him with a very decided clutch. She was not shy—she threw her whole weight (it was not much) upon his arm, which she grasped to save herself. 'I was nearly over,' she said, panting a little for breath, with a pretty flush rising into her pale old delicate cheeks. The shock stirred her old blood and made her heart beat, and brought a spark to her eyes. It did not frighten and trouble, but excited her not unpleasantly, so thorough-bred was this old woman. 'No, I am not hurt, not a bit hurt: it was nothing. I ought to look where I am going, at my age,' she said; and held Mr. Peters fast by the arm, and panted, and laughed. But even after she had recovered herself she still leant upon him. 'You must give me your arm to my house,' she said; 'there's the drawback of being old. I can't help trembling, as if I had been frightened or hurt. You must give me your arm to my house.'

'Certainly, madam,' said Mr. Peters. He did not like to dispense with any title of civility, though (oddly enough, and in England alone) the superior classes do so; but he would not say 'Ma'am,' like a servant. It seemed to him that 'Madam' was a kind of stately compromise; and he walked on, himself somewhat tremulous with embarrassment, supporting with the greatest care his unexpected companion; and though she trembled, the courageous old lady laughed and chattered.

'You were going the other way?' she said. 'I am wasting your time, I fear, and stopping your walk.'

'Oh, no, madam, not at all,' said Mr. Peters; 'I am very glad to be of use. I am very happy that I was there just at the moment—just at the fortunate moment—'

'Do you call it a fortunate moment when I hurt my foot—not that I have really hurt my foot—and got myself shaken and upset like this—an old woman at my age?'

'I meant—the unfortunate moment, madam,' said Mr. Peters, colouring high, and feeling that he had said something wrong, though what he scarcely knew.

'Oh, fie! that looks as if you were sorry that you have been compelled to help me,' said the old lady, laughing.

Poor Mr. Peters had not the least idea how to take this banter. He thought he had done or said something wrong. He coloured up to the respectable tall hat that shaded his sober brows; but she stopped his troubled explanations summarily.

'Where were you going? It does not matter? Well, you shall come in with me, and Morris will give you some tea. You can tell me about your school—I am always interested in my neighbours' concerns. You pass this way most evenings, don't you? I see you passing. You always take a walk after your day's work—a very wholesome custom. And then your evenings—where do you spend your evenings? Are there any nice people who give you a cup of tea? Do you go and see your friends? Yes, I am interested, always interested, to learn how my fellow-creatures get through their life; I don't do much myself but look on, now-a-days. And you know life's a strange sort of thing,' said the old lady. 'Nothing interests me so much. It isn't a line of great events, as we think in our youth—the intervals are more important than the events. Are you dull, eh? You are a stranger in this place. How do you spend your evenings after you go in?'

'Madam, there is always plenty to do,' said Mr. Peters; 'a master can never be said to have much leisure.' And then he unbent from that high seriousness and said, with a mixture of confused grandeur and wistfulness, 'In the circles to which I have admission there is not much that can be called society. I have to spend my evenings at home, or—'

'Or—?' said Mrs. Mowbray. 'Just so, that is the whole business; alone, or— But where is the 'or'? So am I. I am alone (which I generally like best), or—I have friends with me. Friends—I call them friends for want of a better word—the people on the Green. They bore me, but I like them sometimes. Now, you are a young man. Tell me what 'or' commends itself to you.'

Thus exhorted, Mr. Peters hung down his head; he stammered in his reply. 'I am afraid, madam, you would think but badly of me if you knew: without knowing why. I go and sit down there—in front of Mrs. Aikin's house.'

'In front of the Barley Mow! Dear me!' she said, with well-acted surprise; 'that is not the thing for a schoolmaster to do!'

'I know it, madam,' said Mr. Peters with a sigh.

'Ah!' said Mrs. Mowbray, with the air of one who is making an important discovery; 'ah! I divine you at last. It is a girl that beguiles you to the Barley Mow! Then it must be a good girl, for they allow no one else there. Bless me! I wonder if it should be Jane!'

'You know her, madam?'

'Ah, it is Jane then? Mr. Schoolmaster—I forget your name—you are a man of penetration and sense; I honour you. A man who chooses the best woman within his knowledge—that's the sort of man I approve of. It happens so seldom. Men are all such fools on that point. So it is Jane!'

Mr. Peters breathed a long sigh. 'She never looks at me, madam—she never knows I am there. You must not think she has anything to do with it.'

'Ay, ay, that's always the way. When the men show some sense the women are fools; or else it's the other thing. Now, listen to me. You say, Do I know Jane? Yes, I know her from her cradle. Why, I brought her up! Can't you see the girl has the manners of a lady? I gave them to her. There is nothing Jane will not do for me. And I like the looks of you. You're stiff, but you're a man. Do you think I should have come out of my way, and hurt my foot (oh, it is quite well now!) to speak to you, if I hadn't heard all about this? I want to help you to marry Jane.'

'Oh, madam, what can I say to you?' cried Mr. Peters, not knowing in his bewilderment what might be going to happen. He was shocked in his sense of propriety by being told that he was stiff, and by the old lady's frank avowal that she knew all about him after she had wormed his secret out of him; and he was excited by this promise of aid, and by the bold jump of his patroness to the last crown of success. To marry Jane! To get a word from her, or a kind look, seemed enough in the meantime; and he did not know on the spot whether he was ready to marry any one, even this queen of his affections.

He led Mrs. Mowbray to her door, and listened to her talk, divided between alarm and eagerness. She made everything so easy! She was willing to be his plenipotentiary—to explain everything. She would see no obstacle in the way—all he had to do was to put himself in her hands. The old lady herself got very much excited over it. She said more than she meant, as people have a way of doing when they are excited, and sent Mr. Peters away in the most curious muddle of hope and fear—hope that the way might be opened for him to Jane, fear lest he might be driven along that path at a pace much more rapid and urgent than he had meant to go.

Next morning Mrs. Mowbray had made up her mind to send for Jane and open the subject at once— merely to represent to her how much more satisfactory this man was than such a lout as John. What a suitable union it would be! just her own quiet tastes and ways. And a man able to sustain and help her, instead of a lad of her own age, whom she would have to carry on her shoulders, instead of being guided by. The pleas in his favour were so strong, that the old lady could not see what pretence Jane could find for declining to listen to the schoolmaster. But she was not so certain about it next morning— and she neither went to the Barley Mow nor sent for Jane—but gave herself, as she said, time to think.

And but for an accident that happened that very evening, prudence might have overcome the livelier impulse in her mind.

That evening however Mrs. Mowbray went out again to see the sunset, taking a short turn down the lane from her house. The lane ran between her house and the Barley Mow, and a back door from Mrs. Aikin's garden opened into it. It was a very green, very flowery bit of road, leading nowhere in particular except due west; and as the ground was high here—for Dinglefield stood on a gentle eminence raised above the rest of the valley—this lane of an evening, when the sun was setting, seemed to lead straight through into the sunset. It was an exceptional evening: the sunset glowed with all the colour that could be found in a tropical sky, and the whole world was glorified. It drew Mrs. Mowbray out in spite of herself; she had thrown a scarf over her cap and about her shoulders, being so near home, and was 'stepping westward,' like the poet, but with the meditative step of age which signifies leisure from everything urgent, and time to bestow upon this great pageant of Nature. To be so at leisure from everything in thought as well as in life is a privilege of the aged and solitary. And there is nobody who enjoys the beauty of such a scene or dwells upon it with the same delight. But the privilege has its drawbacks, like most human things. Those busy folks who give but a glance, and are gone, have perhaps a warmer, because accidental pleasure: the more deliberate enjoyment is a little sad. Mrs. Mowbray however was one to feel this as little as could well be. She walked briskly, and her mind, even in the midst of this spectacle, was full of her plans. She was half-way down the lane, with all the light in her face, when she suddenly perceived two figures black against the light in front of her, standing out like black silhouettes on the glow of lovely colour. She saw them dimly; but they, having their backs to the dazzling light, and being totally unmindful of the sunset, saw her very clearly, and were much alarmed by her appearance. They had been so much occupied with each other that the sound of the old lady's step upon some gravel was the first thing that roused them. The girl gave a frightened exclamation, and sprang apart from her companion, who for his part backed into the hedge, as if with the hope of concealing himself there. Though Mrs. Mowbray's attention and curiosity were immediately roused, she did not even then recognize them, and they might have escaped her if they had not been so consciously guilty. The girl was the first to be detected. She ran off after that startled look, with a half-laughing cry, leaving the other to bear the consequences.

'Bless me! Ellen Turner. The little flirt! She is after some mischief,' Mrs. Mowbray said to herself; and even then she thought nothing of the young man. But he was not aware of this. He did not know that her eyes, which had been fixed on the glow in the sky, were dazzled by it, and unable to see him; and feeling himself detected, it seemed to John safer to take the matter into his own hands. He made a step into the middle of the road, in front of her. He could not have done anything less wise. Mrs. Mowbray was thinking only of Ellen, and nothing at all of the man she was fooling. This was the way she put it to herself: What did it matter who the silly fellow was? If he put any dependence on such a little coquette as that, he was to be pitied, poor fellow. The old lady had half a mind to warn him. But she was much surprised to find him confront her like this, and even a little frightened. And it was only now that she recognized who he was.

He had forgotten what little manners he had, and all his awe of 'the quality' in the excitement of the moment. 'You'll go telling of us!' he cried, in sudden excitement, almost with a threat of his clenched hand.

A thrill of apprehension ran through the old lady's frame, but she stood still suddenly, confronting him with the courage of her nature. 'How dare you speak to me so, with your cap on your head?' she said.

John's hand stole to his hat in spite of himself. He fell back a step. 'I beg your pardon, my lady; but I was a-going to say—You won't say nothing to them?—It was a—accident—it wasn't done a-purpose. You won't tell—about her and me?'

'Whom am I to tell?' The old lady had seized the position already, and it made her herself again. She perceived in a moment the value of the incident. And he had taken his hat off by this time, and stood crushing it in his hands. 'I don't mean nothing,' he said. 'It's only a lark. I don't care nothing for her, nor I don't suppose she do for me.'

'That I'll answer for,' said Mrs. Mowbray briskly; 'neither for you nor any one else, you vain blockhead! But if it's only a lark, as you say, what are you frightened for? And what do you want of me?'

He stared at her for a moment with his mouth open, and then he said, 'Haunt and Jeyeyne thinks a deal of you.'

'I dare say they do,' said the old lady; 'but what of that? And they think a deal of you, you booby—more's the pity. If you have a fancy for Ellen Turner, why don't you let them know? Why don't you marry her, or some one like her, and have done with it? I don't say she's much of a girl, but she's good enough for you.'

His hand gripped his hat with rising fury; the very dullest of natures feels the keen edge of contempt. And then he laughed; he had a sharp point at his own command, and could make reprisals.

'They'd kill her,' he said, 'if they knew it. They're too sweet upon me to put up with it. They think as I don't see what they're after; but I see it fast enough.'

'And what are they after, if you are so clear-sighted?'

'They mean as I'm to settle down and marry Jeyeyne—that's what they mean. They think, 'cos I'm a quiet one, that I can't see an inch from my nose. They think a fellow is to be caught like that afore he's had his fling, and seen a bit of the world.'

'Oh,' said the old lady; 'so you want to have your fling, and see the world?'

'That is just about it, my lady,' said the lout, taking courage. 'I talks to her just to pass the time; but what I wants is to see the world. I won't say as I mightn't come back after, and settle down. Jeyeyne's a good sort of girl enough—I've nothing to say against her; and she knows my ways—but a man isn't like a set of women. I must have my fling—I must—afore I settle down.'

'And who is to do your work, Mr. John, while you have your fling? Or are you clever enough to see that you are not of the least use at the Barley Mow?'

'Oh, ain't I of use! See what a fuss there will be when they think I'm going! But Haunt can afford a good wage, and there's lots of fellows to be had.'

'You ungrateful cub!' cried the old lady; 'is this all your thanks for their kindness, taking you in, and making a man of you! You were glad enough to find a home here when you were a wretched, hungry little boy.'

'Begging your pardon, my lady, I never was,' said John, with a gleam of courage. 'I'd have been a deal better with father if they'd let me alone. He'd a got me into the regiment as a drummer, and I'd have been in the band afore this. And that's the sort of life to suit me. I ain't one of your dull sort—I likes life. This kind of a dismal old country place never was the place for me.'

'You ungrateful, unkind, impertinent'!—

Mrs. Mowbray stopped short. She could not get out all the words that poured from her lips, and the sight of him there opposite silenced her after all. Mrs. Aikin's goodness to this boy had been the wonder and admiration of everybody round. They had considered her foolishly generous—Quixotic, almost absurd, in her kindness; and now to hear his opinion of it! This bold ingratitude closes the spectator's mouth. Perhaps, after all, it is better to leave the bramble wild, and the street boy in the gutter, and give up all attempts to improve the one or the other. But there is nothing which so silences natural human sentiment and approval of charity and kindness. Mrs. Mowbray was struck dumb. Who could tell that he had not even some show of justice in his wrong—something that excused his doubt, if nothing to excuse his unkindness? This strange suggestion took away her breath.

'They've had their own way,' said John; 'they did it to please themselves; and that's what they'd like to do again—marry me right off—a fellow at my age, and stop my fun! But I'm not the sort to have a girl thrust down my throat. I'll have my fling first, or else I'll have nothing to say to it. Now, my lady,' he added, lowering his voice, and coming a step nearer,' if you'll stand my friend! There's nobody as Haunt and Jeyeyne thinks so much of as you. If you says it they won't oppose. I don't want to quarrel with nobody; but I will have my fling, and see the world!'

'And so you shall!' cried Mrs. Mowbray; 'if I can manage it. So you shall, my man! Get out of Jane's way—that's all I want of you. And I think better of you since you proposed it! Yes, yes! I'll take it all upon me! There's nothing I wish for more than that you should take yourself out of this. Have your fling! And I hope you'll fling yourself a hundred miles out of reach of the Barley Mow!'

John looked at her with dull amazement. What did she mean? His thanks were stopped upon his lips. For, after all, this was not a pleasant way of backing up. 'Get out of Jane's way!' His heavy self-complacency was ruffled for the moment. 'I don't mind how far I go,' he said, with a suspicious look.

'Nor I, I assure you,' cried Mrs. Mowbray briskly; 'I'll plead your cause;' and with that she turned round and went back again, forgetting all about the sunset. Nature is hardly treated by the best of us; we let her come in when we have nothing else in hand, but forget her as soon as a livelier human interest claims our attention. This was how even the old lady, who had been so meditatively occupied by Nature, treated the patient mother now.

Next day was Sunday, and of course Mrs. Mowbray could not enter upon the business which she had undertaken then. But when there is any undercurrent of feeling or complication of rival wishes in a family, Sunday is a very dangerous day, especially when the family belongs to the lower regions of society, and the Sunday quiet affords means of communication not always to be had on other days. This, of course, was scarcely the case among the household at the Barley Mow, but the habit of their class was upon them, and the natural fitness of Sunday for an important announcement, joined, it is to be supposed, with the fact that he had already unbosomed himself to one person, drew John's project out. When Mrs. Mowbray accordingly took her way to Mrs. Aikin's on the Monday morning, more and more pleased as she thought of it, with the idea of getting John out of the way, she saw at once by the aspect of both mother, and daughter that her news was no news. The two women had a look of agitation and seriousness which on Mrs. Aikin's part was mingled with resentment. She was discoursing upon her chickens when Mrs. Mowbray found her way into the barn-yard. 'They don't care what troubles folks has with them, not they,' she was saying with a flush on her cheek. 'The poor hen, as has sat on her nest all day, and never got off to pick a bit o' food. What's that to them, the little yellow senseless things? And them as we've brought up and cared for all our lives, and should know better, is just as bad.' Jane was putting up a setting of Brahmapootra eggs for somebody. She was very pale, and made no reply to her mother, but her hand trembled a little as she put them into the packet. 'What is the matter?' said the old lady as she came in. Jane gave her a silent look and said nothing. 'La, bless us, ma'am, what should be the matter?' said Mrs. Aikin. They were so disturbed that Mrs. Mowbray did a thing which she was not at all in the habit of doing. She departed from her original intention, and said nothing at all of her mission, concluding, as was the fact, that John himself had spoken. No later than that afternoon however her self-denial was rewarded, for Mrs. Aikin came to the Thatched Cottage, curtseying and apologetic. 'I saw as you didn't believe me, ma'am,' she said. 'There is nobody like you for seeing how things is. A deal has happened, and I don't know whether I'm most pleased or unhappy. For one thing it's all settled between Johnny and Jane.'

'All settled!' the old lady was so much surprised that she could scarcely speak.

'Yes, ma'am, thank you, the poor dears! I always said that as soon as he knew his own mind—There ain't a many lads as one can see through like our John.'

'You didn't wish it then?' said Mrs. Mowbray. 'I should have thought this morning that something bad had happened. You didn't wish it! Then we've all been doing you injustice, my dear woman, for I thought you had set your heart on this all along.'

'And so I have; and I'm as happy—that happy I don't know what to do with myself,' said Mrs. Aikin, putting her apron to her eyes.

'Happy! nobody would think it to look at you—nor Jane. I thought I knew you like my A, B, C, but now I can't tell a bit what you mean.'

'Jane, she's all of a flutter still, and she's that humble-minded, all her thought is, will she make him happy? But you don't suppose, ma'am, as I think any such nonsense—lucky to get her, I say, and so does everybody. It ain't that. But he's been seeing his father, and his father's put nonsense in the lad's head. I always said as he'd do it. Johnny's the best of boys; he'd never have thought of such a thing if it hadn't been put in his head. He says he wants to go out into the world and see a bit of life afore he settles down.'

'And that is what troubles you? If I were you I should let him go,' said the old lady. 'Lucky! I should think he was lucky. A young fellow like that! He is not half good enough for Jane.'

'Well, ma'am,' said Mrs. Aikin, half ruffled, half pleased, 'it is well known who was always your pet, and a great honour for her and me too—and I don't know how it is as folks do such injustice to our John. It's all the father, well I know; leave him to himself and a better boy couldn't be. But I've written him a letter and given him a piece of my mind. It's him as always puts fancies in the boy's head. See the world! Where could he see the world better than at the Barley Mow! Why there's a bit of everything at our place. There's them gentlemen cricketers in the summer, and the best quality in the kingdom coming and going at Ascot time, and London company in the best parlours most every Sunday through the season. All sorts there is. There was never a week, summer or winter, so long as I can remember, but something was going on at the Barley Mow. Summer, it's nothing but taking money from morning to night. I don't mean to say,' said Mrs. Aikin, suddenly recollecting that this sounded like a confession of large profits such as no woman in trade willingly acknowledges—'I don't mean to say as the expenses ain't great, or as it's all profit, far from it. But what I says to Johnny I don't deny anywhere—it's a living—and it's the amusingest living and the most variety of any I know.'

'And yet he wants to see the world; there's no accounting for men's depravity. Do you mean to let him go?'

Mrs. Aikin laughed. 'I ain't a good one to deceive,' she said; 'this morning I was all in a way, but now I've had time to think. You know yourself, ma'am, that to say "No" is the way to make a boy more determined than ever. Seemingly I'm a giving in, but I don't mean to take no steps one way or other. I'll let things take their course. And now that Jane and him understands one another, and the summer trade's so brisk, who can say? Maybe it'll go out of his head if he ain't opposed. I've give my consent—so far as words goes—but I tell him as there's no hurry. We can wait.'

She laughed again in thorough satisfaction with her own tactics. And Mrs. Mowbray, with a different sentiment, echoed the laugh. 'Yes, we can wait,' the old lady said; 'my poor little Jane!' That was all, but it made Mrs. Aikin angry, she could not tell why.

Mr. Peters at this period kept putting himself perpetually in Mrs. Mowbray's way. He went past her house for his walk, he came back again past the Thatched Cottage. She could scarcely go out in the evening that he did not turn up in her path: and for some days the old lady was cruel enough to say nothing to him. At last one evening she called the poor schoolmaster to her. 'You must make up your mind to it like a man,' she said, 'Jane is going to marry her cousin. It is all settled. The mother told me, like a fool.'

'All settled!' Poor Mr. Peters grew so pale that she thought he was going to faint. 'I saw him,' he gasped, 'only yesterday, with—'

'Never mind, yes; that's quite true,' said the old lady. 'That woman has settled it like a fool. They are going to throw the girl away among them. But we cannot do anything. You must make up your mind to it like a man.'

The schoolmaster's stiffness and embarrassment all melted away under the influence of strong feeling. He took off his hat unconsciously, showing a face that was like ashes. 'Then God bless her,' he said, 'and turn away the evil. If she is happy, what does it matter about me!'

'She will never be happy,' said the old lady, 'never, with that lout; and the thing for us to do is to wait. I tell you, what you've got to do is to wait. After all, the devil seldom gets things all his own way.'

Mr. Peters put on his hat again, and went away with a heavy heart. He did not go near the Barley Mow. He went home to his room, and sat there very desolate, reading poetry. He could bear it, he thought; but how could she bear it when she came to hear of Ellen Turner and those meetings in the lane?

At present however nothing was known of Ellen Turner at the Barley Mow. The very next Sunday after that the women had forgotten all the dangers of John's perversity, and remembered only the fact of the engagement, and that all doubt was over on the point which they thought so essential to their happiness. Mrs. Aikin had a new bonnet on, resplendent in red ribbons, and the happiness in Jane's face was better than any new bonnet. As it happened, there was a solo in the anthem that day which John sang standing up in his white surplice, and rolling out Handel's great notes so that they filled the church. He had a beautiful voice, and while he sang poor Jane's face was a sight to see: her countenance glowed with a kind of soft rapture. She clasped her hands unawares with the prayer-book held open in them, her eyes were raised, her lips apart, her nostrils slightly dilated. She had the look of a votary making a special offering. Poor simple Jane! There was no consciousness in her mind of any elevation above the rest, as she lifted that ineffable look, and praised God in a subdued ecstasy, offering to Him the voice of her beloved. For the moment Jane was as the prophets, as the poets, raised up above everything surrounding her, triumphing even over the doubt that was too ready to invade her mind at other times. She was but a country girl, the maid of the inn, occupying the most unelevated and most unelevating of positions, but yet no lady of romance could have stood on a higher altitude, for the time.

CHAPTER IV

This however was the last time that Jane's look of modest, silent happiness could touch any heart. Whether she caught sight of some private telegraphing which passed between her newly-betrothed and Ellen Turner in the very church that very day, is not known, but other people saw it with wonder and forebodings. Mr. Peters, who had seen the rapture in Jane's upturned face with a mingled pity and sympathy and pain which made him, too, heroic for the moment, perceived the nod and look of intelligence which passed between the baritone in the surplice and the little dressmaker in the free seats with an impulse of suppressed wrath which it took all the moral force he could command to resist. It was the first time the betrothed pair had appeared, as it were, in public, since it was known that 'all was settled.' And was it for this, for a vulgar reprobate who betrayed her at the moment of union, while the first happiness ought still to have been in delicate blossom, that she had overlooked altogether the far more worthy love of the other? He could not help wondering over that any more than Jane herself, a little while later, could help wondering. The best thrown aside, the worst chosen—is not this a far more poignant and wonderful evil than the tyrannies of parents or hindrances of fate which keep lovers apart? But no more from that day did Jane's celestial content wound any sufferer. She grew grave, pale, almost visibly older from that moment. She withdrew herself from everybody. Even the old lady at the Thatched Cottage, who depended upon her for so many things, did not see her for weeks together. And their next meeting was a chance one, and took place on an August evening, about a month after these events. How Jane could have kept out of sight for so long was a mystery which nobody could have explained; but she had managed it somehow, sending respectful messages of regret by her mother. This time they met face to face without warning, as Mrs. Mowbray was returning in the cool of the evening from Sir Thomas Denzil's, where she had been dining. The old lady sent her maid away instantly, so anxious was she to have a conversation with her favourite. Jane for her part would fain have escaped, but she could not be rude to her kind old patroness, and Mrs. Mowbray took her arm quite eagerly. 'You may go home, Morris,' she said; and almost without waiting till the maid was gone, 'What has become of you, Jane? Where have you been hiding? Is it because you are so happy, my dear, or for some other reason, that you run away from me?' A nervous quiver went over poor Jane; she said with a trembling voice, 'For another reason.' She did not even look her old friend in the face.

'Then what is it, my dear? Come, tell me. Don't you know, whatever it is, you can't hide it from me?'

To this Jane made answer by drooping her head and turning away her face; and then she pressed the old lady's hand, which was on her arm, to her side, and said hastily, 'I was coming—I wanted you to speak for me—oh! ma'am, if you would speak to mother! about—about—'

'What! my poor little Jane! What, dear? Tell me, tell me freely,' said the old lady, almost crying. There could be but one subject that could excite the poor girl so.

'About John's going away. Oh, he's sick of this quiet place! I can see it—and mother takes no notice. Men are not like us women. He's dying to get away, and mother she can't see it. She humours him in words, but she will not do anything. Oh, ma'am, speak for us! He's had all we have to give him, and he's tired of it, and he will never be happy till he gets away.'

'Do you wish him to go?—You, Jane?'

'Yes,' she cried passionately, 'I wish it too!—it will make me happier. I mean not so—miserable. Oh, ma'am, that's not what I mean. I am all confused like. I know—I know it's for his good to go away—'

'But it's your good I think of—and your mother, too,' said Mrs. Mowbray. 'We care for you, and not for him. You've avoided me, Jane, and never told me if you were happy—now that you're engaged, you and he.'

'It was a mistake,' she said, 'all a mistake! We didn't know our own minds. Don't you know, ma'am, that happens sometimes? I always felt it was a mistake: but mother deceived herself. It's so easy to believe what you wish. And he deceived himself. But now that he's done it it drives him wild— Oh, he must go— that's the only thing that will do any good. If she would only see it, and let him go!'

'Do you want to break it off, Jane?'

'Oh,' she cried, with a moan, 'break it off! Am I one to break it off? But he can't abide the place, and he wants to go.— If he has any true—respect—for me—he'll feel it when he's gone. That's what I think. Oh! ma'am, speak a word to mother, and tell her to let him go.'

'There is more in your mind,' said the old lady: 'but if it is as serious as this—I'll go there straight, my dear. I'll go straight and speak to your mother. I know you've got more in your mind.'

Jane did not make any reply, but quickened her steps to keep up with the active old woman as she hurried on. Poor Jane was past all make-believe. 'Think!' she said, almost under her breath, 'what it is when he comes and pretends to be fond of me— Oh, ma'am! pretends as if he loved me—after all I know!' She wrung her hands, and there was a suppressed anguish in her voice, such as only a tender creature outraged could have been driven to. Then Mrs. Mowbray, who knew all the gossip of the place, remembered to have heard that Ellen Turner, who was a dressmaker, had been working at Mrs. Aikin's—no doubt that was the cause. She went along quickly, almost dragging the girl with her. It was a beautiful evening, soft and cool after a hot day. The lights were beginning to twinkle about the Barley Mow. There were people sitting out on the bench, and people visible at the open windows with the lights behind them, and a murmur of cheerful voices. The scene was very homely, but the night was so soft, the shadows so grateful upon the refreshed earth, the dews so sweet, and nothing but rest and refreshment in the air. Overhead the sky was veiled, a few modest stars peeping from the edges of the clouds, nothing bright to jar upon the subdued quiet. All this went to Jane's heart. She began to cry softly, as she looked with wistful eyes at her home. The sensation subdued her. So peaceful and quiet, with the vague, half-dim figures about, the cheerful lights in the windows, was it possible that there could be such trouble there?

But all at once there came a jarring note into this tranquillity—the sound of a woman's voice raised in anger. They were going towards the garden door, but before they reached it somebody was pushed out violently, and, half falling forward, came stumbling against Jane, who was straight in the way. 'Get out of my sight, you little baggage, you treacherous, wicked, lying creature, you bad girl!' cried Mrs. Aikin in a furious voice. Jane clutched at Mrs. Mowbray's arm, and shrank back, while the girl who had stumbled against her gave a sudden scream of dismay. It was Ellen Turner, her cheeks blazing red with anger, though the sight of Jane cowed her. 'What have you been doing, you little flirt?' cried old Mrs. Mowbray. 'If a man speaks to me, ain't I to give him a civil answer?' cried the girl, standing still, and preparing to give battle. Jane did not say a word. She shook herself free of the old lady without knowing what she did, and went in to her mother, without as much as a look at the other. As soon as she had disappeared John showed himself out of the darkness like a spectre. 'Run, Nell, run,' he said. 'She's to-morrow. She's in Jane's hands, I'll see you safe now. Run. Nell, run.' And he darted back again among the guests, and threw himself into his work with devotion. Never before had John been seen so busy and so civil. Who could interfere with him in the middle of his work? He was as safe as if he had been at church.

What had happened was that Mrs. Aikin had found her nephew and the little dressmaker together, on very affectionate terms, and her outburst of sudden wrath was very hot and violent. But after the first moment it was entirely against Ellen that her anger was directed, and she was as little willing as before to listen to Mrs. Mowbray's suggestion that he should be sent away. She was, like most women of her class, perhaps like most women of all classes, furious against the girl, half sorry for, half contemptuous of, the man. 'Lord, what could Johnny do against one of them artful things?' she said, when she had calmed down. 'It's Jane's fault, as don't talk to him enough, nor keep him going. That minx shall never set foot in my house again.' Jane said very little while her mother talked thus. She was very pale, and her breath came quickly, but she betrayed no emotion either of grief or anger. She stood still by her mother's side while Mrs. Aikin cried and sobbed. Jane was past all that. She said, 'He don't know his own mind, mother. Let him go as he wishes.' They were both made incapable of work by this sudden incident. But John—John had turned into a model of industry and carefulness. While the two women retired into their little parlour with the door shut, he, safe from all interference, kept everything going. He ran about here and there, attending to everybody, civil and thoughtful. When he was asked what was the matter, he answered carelessly, 'Some row among the women,' as if that was too trifling and too everyday a matter for his notice. He had never shown so much cleverness in all his life before.

Even after this however the widow still temporized. Yes, she said in words, she would let him go, but after the bustle was over—after the summer work was done with. She gave a hundred excuses, and invented new reasons constantly for her delay. Jane said little, having said all she could. A new reserve crept over her, she talked to nobody—went no more to talk to Mrs. Peters, and never saw her old friend at the Thatched Cottage when she could help it. She was sick of her false position, as well as of those pangs which she told to nobody, which were all shut up in her own heart. No more in church or otherwise did the look of happiness come back to her face. When John sang she would stand with her eyes fixed on her book, or else would cover her face with her hand. The beautiful song was no longer hers to be offered up to God's praise. But sometimes during the sermon her eyes would turn unconsciously to that foolish pretty face in the free seats—the pink and white countenance of Ellen Turner, inferior in beauty as in everything else to herself. 'What is there in her that is better than me? Why should she be preferred to me?' was what Jane was asking herself, with a wondering pain that was half self-abasement and half indignation. Just so good Mr. Peters, in the school pew, gazed from her to the loutish baritone in his surplice and back again. Why should fate be so contradictory and hearts so bitterly deceived?

This state of affairs however could not go on very long—and it came to a conclusion quite suddenly at last. There was an agricultural show in the neighbourhood some twenty miles off from Dinglefield, to which all the rural people of the neighbourhood, and John among them, went at the end of August. In other circumstances Jane would have gone with her cousin; but she had no heart for shows of any kind. In the evening most of the Dinglefield people came home, but not John. Mrs. Aikin was evidently frightened by his non-appearance, but she made the best of it. 'He had gone off with some of his friends,' she said, 'and of course he had missed his train. He was always missing trains. He was the carelessest lad!' But when next day came, and the next, with no news of John, the mother and daughter could no longer disguise their alarm. The widow 'was in such a way' that her friends gathered round her full of condolence and encouragements; and Mrs. Mowbray herself put on her bonnet, and went to tell her not to be a fool, and to bid her remember that young men cannot be held in like girls. 'I know that, ma'am, I know that,' said Mrs. Aikin, soothed. The rest of her consolers had encouraged her by telling her they had always foreseen it, and that this was what over-indulgence always came to at last. The widow turned her back upon these Job's comforters, and clutched at Mrs. Mowbray's shawl. 'I've held him too tight, ma'am, and I should have taken your advice,' she said. They had sent expresses in all directions in search of him, and that very evening they had information that he had enlisted in the regiment to which his father had formerly belonged, and which was at the time quartered in the town where the show had been held. This is always, though it is hard to say why, terrible news for a decent family. "Listed!' do not all the vagabonds, the good-for-nothings, 'list? It was Mr. Peters who brought this news to the two anxious women. He had been in Castleville 'by accident,' he said; the truth being that he had given the children a holiday on purpose to offer this humble service to the woman who had his heart. It was good news, though it was such bad news, for the widow's imagination had begun to jump at all sorts of fatal accidents, and he was made kindly welcome, and allowed to remain with them until Mrs. Aikin's first fit of distress and relief, and shame and vexation, and content was over. 'It's his father, it's all his father,' she said. 'Such a thought would never, never have come into our Johnny's head.' Mr. Peters, with trembling anxiety, observed that Jane did not say a word. She was moving about with her usual quickness, preparing tea, that the kind visitor who had taken so much trouble should have some refreshment after his long walk. She was full of suppressed excitement, her cheek less pale than usual, her eyes shining. But she said nothing till her mother's outburst was over. Mrs. Aikin was a foolish, softhearted, sanguine woman. As soon as she knew the worst her mind leapt at a universal mending and making up. She had no sooner dried her eyes and swallowed a cup of tea, after protesting that she 'could not touch it,' than she began with a certain timidity in another tone.

'It's well known what most families do when such a thing happens,' she said with a sigh, 'folks as has more money than we have. And I've heard say as it was a foolish thing; but when you consider all things— lads is so silly, they never see what they're doing till after it's done, and past changing—past their changing I mean.'

Jane did not say anything, but she stood still suddenly in the middle of the room to listen, with a startled look.

'I dare to say he's repented long before this,' said the widow, 'him as never was put to hard work nor ordered about, him as had most things his own way, though he mightn't know it. It might have been better for Johnny if you and me hadn't been so fond of him, Jane—and it will all tell upon him now. We've spoiled him, and we're leaving him to bear it by himself! Oh! Jane! Jane!'

'What is it, mother? You are thinking of something,' said Jane with a harsh tone, quite unusual to her, in her voice.

'Oh, Jane, you're hard-hearted, you ain't forgiving, you're not like me,' cried the widow. 'If you were the girl folks think you, you would come to me on your knees, that's what you would do, to get me to buy him off.'

'Oh, mother, mother, I knew that was what you were coming to. Don't do it! I cannot bear it. I cannot go on with it. You may save him, but you'll kill me.'

'Kill you!—what has it got to do with you?' said Mrs. Aikin, drying her eyes. 'Thank the Lord, it ain't so bad but what it can be mended—when one comes to think of it! I'll write to the lawyer this very night.'

'If I can be of any use—' said Mr. Peters, faltering. The more he felt it was against himself, the more he was anxious to do it to show, if only to himself, that it was Jane and not his own interest that was nearest to his thoughts. But the poor man felt chilled to the heart as he made his offer. He did not understand Jane. It was only an impulse of anger, he thought, against the lover for whom, no doubt, she was longing in her heart.

'You're very kind, Mr. Peters—very kind. I'll never forget it—and you think it's the right thing, don't you now? He ain't fit for the army, isn't Johnny. He was always delicate in the chest, and needs to be taken a deal of notice of. And to give him up all for one thing—all for a minute's foolishness.'

'Mother!' said Jane, with a shrill tone of passion in her voice, 'he is not to come back here again; let him be!'

'No—no—no. You'll be the first to thank me, though you've lost your temper now. The fright will do him a deal of good,' Mrs. Aikin said, getting up with all her cheerfulness restored. 'We'll leave him a week or so just to see the error of his ways, and then we'll buy him off, and have him back, and settle everything. Poor lad! You may take my word he's miserable enough, thinking of you and me, and wondering what we are thinking of him. Poor John! We won't go on shilly-shallying any longer, but we'll have it all settled when he comes home.'

She was still speaking with the smile on her face which these pleasant anticipations had brought there when a sudden commotion got up outside—loud voices, and something like a scuffle. Sounds of this kind are not so rare or so alarming even at the best regulated of taverns as they are in a private house, and the widow paid but little attention. She went across the room and opened her big, old-fashioned chest. Her heart was warmed and her face brightened by her resolution. Jane gave a glance of despair at Mr. Peters (which he no more understood than if he had not seen it). She went across the room after her mother, and laid her hand on her shoulder. 'Mother,' she said, 'don't do it—don't do it; let him have his choice.'

'Ah! what was that?' cried Mrs. Aikin with a start.

The disturbance outside continued, and just at this moment the words became audible, along with the sound of steps rushing to the door. 'My 'usband, my 'usband!' cried the voice; 'what have you done with my 'usband?' The mother and daughter turned round by a common impulse, and looked at each other—then stood as if stiffened into stone, with their faces to the door. Without another word said they knew what it meant. They needed no further explanation, nor the sight of Ellen Turner, all in disorder, with her hair hanging about her neck, and her face swollen with tears, who suddenly dashed the door open and came wildly in. 'John, John! I want my 'usband!' the poor creature cried, half demented. Jane shrank back against her mother, leaning on her heavily, then cast a wondering gaze around, appealing, as it were, to earth and heaven. Could it be true? She put out one hand to the girl to silence her, and turned round and leant against the wall, with a gasp for breath and a low moan. This was all the demonstration she made. She was not even conscious of the altercation that followed, the crying, and questioning, and denying. Jane turned her face to the wall. People have died and broken their hearts with less pain. The world seemed to go round with her, and all truth and sense to fail.

When she was seen again, which indeed was next day, moving about her work as if nothing had happened, Jane was like a ghost in the first morning light. All the blood seemed to have been drained out of her. She was like a marble woman, moving unconsciously, not touched by anything she did. 'I am quite well,' she said when people asked, 'quite well, and quite right, there is nothing the matter.' As for the poor schoolmaster, he went home that night sobbing in the great pity of his heart. Though he loved her so, the good fellow felt that if anything could have brought back to her the wretched lout whom she had loved he would have done it had it cost him his life: but Mr. Peters had to go away helpless, unable to save her a single pang, as most of us one time or other have to do.

When and how John had found means and ways to make himself Ellen Turner's husband, or whether he had really done so at all, remained always a mystery to the Green. But she went off to him, and became a wretched hanger-on of the regiment, from which Mrs. Aikin no longer thought of buying him off. Nothing else could have settled the question so summarily, and but for Jane's stony face all the neighbourhood would have been glad. Her misery, which was so patient and sweet, and of which she talked to no one, lasted a great deal longer than it ought to have done, everybody felt. But it could not last for ever. Bad enough that such a girl should waste the first sweetness of her life on such a delusion, but the delusion must come to an end some time. After a longer interval than pleased the Green, an interval of which old Mrs. Mowbray was very impatient, declaring pettishly a hundred times that she would marry off the faithful Peters to some one if Jane did not mind, Jane came to herself. She is now the mistress of the school-room, if not the schoolmistress, with too many children of her own to be able to take charge of those of the parish, but so 'comfortable,' with what the Barley Mow affords, that the schoolmaster's income requires no eking out from her work. She is far better off, and in circumstances much more congenial to her than if she had been able to carry out the plan which had been her early dream, and which she and her mother had so passionately wished. And Jane is happy: but the scar of the old wound has never departed, and never will depart. It is unforgettable for the sake of the pain, more than for the sake of the love. As for the faithful Peters, he is as happy as ever schoolmaster was, and very proper and mindful of his position, and would not sit on a bench outside a village inn now-a-days night after night, as he once did, not for any inducement in the world.

Mrs. Aikin held out, and kept her place after Jane was married as long as that was practicable, but has sold the business now (and it brought in a pretty penny), and lives very happily with a cow of her own and a poultry yard, and half-a-dozen grandchildren. Happy woman! She has no scar upon her comfortable soul, and knows of no mistake she ever made: but she feeds the hungry mouths of her wretched nephew and his wretched family, and does not grumble, for, after all, she says, 'Nature is Nature, and it was all his father's fault.'

MY FAITHFUL JOHNNY

CHAPTER I

Everybody knows the charming song which is called by this name. I hear it sometimes in a young household full of life and kindness and music, where it is sung to me, with a tender indulgence for my weakness and limited apprehension of higher efforts, by the most sympathetic and softest of voices. A kind half-smile mingles in the music on these occasions. Those dear people think I like it because the translated 'words' have a semblance of being Scotch, and I am a Scot. But the words are not Scotch, nor is this their charm. I don't even know what they are. 'I will come again, my sweet and bonnie.' That, or indeed the name even is enough for me. I confess that I am not musical. When I hear anything that I like much, at least from an instrument, I instantly conceive a contempt for it, feeling that it must be inferior somehow to have commended itself to me. I wander vainly seeking an idea through fields and plains of sonatas. So do a great many other lowly people, like me, not gifted with taste or (fit) hearing; but, if you will only suggest an idea to me, I will thankfully accept that clue. I don't understand anything about dominant sevenths or any mathematical quantity. 'How much?' I feel inclined to say with the most vulgar. Therefore 'My Faithful Johnny' charms me because this is a suggestion of which my fancy is capable. I don't know who the faithful Johnny was, except that he is to come again, and that somebody, presumably, is looking for him; and, with this guide, the song takes a hundred tones, sorrowful, wistful and penetrating. I see the patient waiting, the doubt which is faith, the long vigil—and hear the soft cadence of sighs, and with them, through the distance, the far-off notes of the promise—never realized, always expected—'I will come again.' This is how I like to have my music. I am an ignorant person. They smile and humour me with just a tender touch of the faintest, kindest contempt. Stay—not contempt; the word is far too harsh; let us say indulgence—the meaning is very much the same.

I do not think I had ever heard the song when I first became acquainted with the appearance of a man with whom, later, this title became completely identified. He was young—under thirty—when I saw him first, passing my house every morning as regular as the clock on his way to his work, and coming home in the evening swinging his cane, with a book under his arm, his coat just a little rusty, his trousers clinging to his knees more closely than well-bred trousers cling, his hat pushed back a little from his forehead. It was unnecessary to ask what he was. He was a clerk in an office. This may be anything, the reader knows, from a lofty functionary managing public business, to numberless nobodies who toil in dusty offices and are in no way better than their fate. It was to this order that my clerk belonged. Every day of his life, except that blessed Sunday which sets such toilers free, he walked along the irregular pavement of the long suburban road in which I lived at nine o'clock in the morning were it wet or dry; and between five and six he would come back. After all, though it was monotonous, it was not a hard life, for he had the leisure of the whole long evening to make up for the bondage of the day. He was a pale man with light hair, and a face more worn than either his years or his labours warranted. But his air of physical weakness must have been due to his colourless complexion, or some other superficial cause, for his extreme and unbroken regularity was inconsistent with anything less than thoroughly good health. He carried his head slightly thrown back, and his step had a kind of irregularity in it which made it familiar to me among many others; at each half dozen steps or so his foot would drag upon the pavement, giving a kind of rhythm to his progress. All these particulars I became aware of, not suddenly, but by dint of long unconscious observation, day after day, day after day, for so many years. Never was there a clerk more respectable, more regular. I found out after a while that he lodged about half a mile further on in one of the little houses into which the road dwindled as it streamed out towards the chaos which on all sides surrounds London—and that when he passed my house he was on his way to or from the omnibus which started from a much-frequented corner about a quarter of a mile nearer town. All the far-off ends of the ways that lead into town and its bustle have interests of this kind. I am one of the people, I fear somewhat vulgar-minded, who love my window and to see people pass. I do not care for the dignity of seclusion. I would rather not, unless I were sure of being always a happy member of a large cheerful household, be divided from the common earth even by the trees and glades of the most beautiful park. I like to see the men go to their work, and the women to their marketing. But no; the latter occupation is out of date—the women go to their work too; slim, young daily governesses, hard-worked music-mistresses, with the invariable roll of music. How soon one gets to know them all, and have a glimmering perception of their individualities—though you may see them every day for years before you know their names!

After I had been acquainted (at a distance) with him for some time, and had got to know exactly what o'clock it was when he passed, a change came upon my clerk. One summer evening I saw him very much smartened up, his coat brushed, a pair of trousers on with which I was not familiar, and a rosebud in his button-hole, coming back. I was thunderstruck. It was a step so contrary to all traditions that my heart stopped beating while I looked at him. It was all I could do not to run down and ask what was the matter. Had something gone wrong in the City? Was there a panic, or a crisis, or something in the money-market? But no; that could not be. The spruceness of the man, the rose in his coat, contradicted this alarm; and as I watched disquieted, lo! he crossed the road before my eyes, and turning down Pleasant Place, which was opposite, disappeared, as I could faintly perceive in the distance, into one of the houses. This was the first of a long series of visits. And after a while I saw her, the object of these visits, the heroine of the romance. She also was one of those with whom I had made acquaintance at my window—a trim little figure in black, with a roll of music, going out and in two or three times a day, giving music lessons. I was quite glad to think that she had been one of my favourites too. My clerk went modestly at long intervals at first, then began to come oftener, and finally settled down as a nightly visitor. But this was a long and slow process, and I think it had lasted for years before I came into actual contact with the personages of this tranquil drama. It was only during the summer that I could see them from my window and observe what was going on. When at the end of a long winter I first became aware that he went to see her every evening, I confess to feeling a little excitement at the idea of a marriage shortly to follow; but that was altogether premature. It went on summer after summer, winter after winter, disappearing by intervals from my eyes, coming fresh with the spring flowers and the long evenings. Once passing down Pleasant Place towards some scorched fields that lay beyond—fields that began to be invaded by new houses and cut up by foundation digging, and roadmaking, and bricklaying, but where there was still room for the boys, and my boys, among others, to play cricket—I had a glimpse of a little interior which quickened my interest more and more. The houses in Pleasant Place were small and rather shabby, standing on one side only of the street. The other was formed by the high brick wall of the garden of a big old-fashioned house, still standing amid all the new invasions which had gradually changed the character of the district. There were trees visible over the top of this wall, and it was believed in the neighbourhood that the upper windows of the houses in Pleasant Place looked over it into the garden. In fact, I had myself not long before condoled with the proprietor of the said garden upon the inconvenience of being thus overlooked. For this hypocrisy my heart smote me when I went along the little street, and saw the little houses all gasping with open windows for a breath of the air which the high wall intercepted. They had little front gardens scorched with the fervid heat. At the open window of No. 7 sat my clerk with his colourless head standing out against the dark unknown of the room. His face was in profile. It was turned towards some one who was singing softly the song of which I have placed the name at the head of this story. The soft, pensive music came tender and low out of the unseen room. The musician evidently needed no light, for it was almost twilight, and the room was dark. The accompaniment was played in the truest taste, soft as the summer air that earned the sound to our ears. 'I know!' I cried to my companion with some excitement, 'that is what he is. I have always felt that was the name for him.' 'The name for whom?' she asked bewildered. 'My faithful Johnny,' I replied; which filled her with greater bewilderment still.

And all that summer long the faithful Johnny went and came as usual. Often he and she would take little walks in the evening, always at that same twilight hour. It seemed the moment of leisure, as if she had duties at home from which she was free just then. When we went away in August they were taking their modest little promenades together in the cool of the evening; and when we came back in October, as long as the daylight served to see them by, the same thing went on. As the days shortened he changed his habits so far as to go to Pleasant Place at once before going home, that there might still be light enough (I felt sure) for her walk. But by and by the advancing winter shut out this possibility: or rather, I could not see any longer what happened about six o'clock. One evening however, coming home to dinner from a late visit, I met them suddenly, walking along the lighted street. For the first time they were arm-in-arm, perhaps because it was night, though no later than usual. She was talking to him with a certain familiar ease of use and wont as if they had been married for years, smiling and chattering and lighting up his mild somewhat weary countenance with responsive smiles. 'I will come again, my sweet and bonnie—' I smiled at myself as these words came into my head, I could not tell why. How could he come again when, it was evident, no will of his would ever take him away? Was she fair enough to be the 'sweet and bonnie' of a man's heart? She was not a beauty; nobody would have distinguished her even as the prettiest girl in Pleasant Place. But her soft, bright face as she looked up to him: a smile on it of the sunniest kind; a little humorous twist about the corners of the mouth; a pair of clear, honest brown eyes; a round cheek with a dimple in it—caught my heart at once as they must have caught his. I could understand (I thought) what it must have been to the dry existence of the respectable clerk, the old-young and prematurely faded, to have this fresh spring of life, and talk, and smiles, and song welling up into it, transforming everything. He smiled back upon her as they walked along in the intermittent light of the shop windows. I could almost believe that I saw his lips forming the words as he looked at her, 'My sweet and bonnie.' Yes; she was good enough and fair enough to merit the description. 'But I wish they would marry,' I said to myself. Why did not they marry? He looked patient enough for anything; but even patience ought to come to an end. I chafed at the delay, though I had nothing to do with it. What was the meaning of it? I felt that it ought to come to an end.

CHAPTER II

It was some months after this, when I took the bold step of making acquaintance on my own account with this pair; not exactly with the pair, but with the one who was most accessible. It happened that a sudden need for music lessons arose in the family. One of the children, who had hitherto regarded that study with repugnance, and who had been accordingly left out in all the musical arrangements of her brothers and sisters, suddenly turned round by some freak of nature and demanded the instruction which she had previously resisted. How could we expect Fräulein Stimme, whose ministrations she had scorned, to descend to the beggarly elements, and take up again one who was so far behind the others? 'I cannot ask her,' I said; 'you may do it yourself, Chatty, if you are so much in earnest, but I cannot take it upon me;' and it was not until Chatty had declared with tears that to approach Fräulein Stimme on her own account was impossible, that a brilliant idea struck me. 'Ten o'clock!' I cried; which was an exclamation which would have gone far to prove me out of my senses had any severe critic been listening. This was the title which had been given to the little music-mistress in Pleasant Place, before she had become associated in our minds with the faithful clerk. And I confess that, without waiting to think, without more ado, I ran to get my hat, and was out of doors in a moment. It was very desirable, no doubt, that Chatty should make up lost ground and begin her lessons at once, but that was not my sole motive. When I found myself out of doors in a damp and foggy November morning, crossing the muddy road in the first impulse of eagerness, it suddenly dawned upon me that there were several obstacles in my way. In the first place I did not even know her name. I knew the house, having seen her, and especially him, enter it so often; but what to call her, who to ask for, I did not know. She might, I reflected, be only a lodger, not living with her parents, which up to this time I had taken for granted; or she might be too accomplished in her profession to teach Chatty the rudiments—a thing which, when I reflected upon the song I had heard, and other scraps of music which had dropped upon my ears in passing, seemed very likely. However I was launched, and could not go back. I felt very small, humble, and blamably impulsive however when I had knocked at the door of No. 7, and stood somewhat alarmed waiting a reply. The door was opened by a small maid-servant, with a very long dress and her apron folded over one arm, who stared, yet evidently recognized me, not without respect, as belonging to one of the great houses in the road. This is a kind of aristocratical position in the suburbs. One is raised to a kind of personage by all the denizens of the little streets and terraces. She made me a clumsy little curtsey, and grinned amicably. And I was encouraged by the little maid. She was about fifteen, rather grimy, in a gown much too long for her; but yet her foot was upon her native heath, and I was an intruder. She knew all about the family, no doubt, and who they were, and the name of my clerk, and the relations in which he stood to her young mistress, while I was only a stranger feebly guessing, and impertinently spying upon all these things.

'Is the young lady at home?' I asked, with much humility.

The girl stared at me with wide-open eyes; then she said with a broad smile, 'You mean Miss Ellen, don't ye, miss?' In these regions it is supposed to be complimentary to say 'Miss,' as creating a pleasant fiction of perpetual youth.

'To tell the truth,' I said, with a consciousness of doing my best to conciliate this creature, 'I don't know her name. It was about some music lessons.'

'Miss Ellen isn't in,' said the girl, 'but missus is sure to see you if you will step into the parlour, miss;' and she opened to me the door of the room in which I had seen my faithful Johnny at the window, and heard her singing to him, in the twilight, her soft song. It was a commonplace little parlour, with a faded carpet and those appalling mahogany and hair-cloth chairs which no decorative genius, however brilliant, could make anything of. What so easy as to say that good taste and care can make any house pretty? This little room was very neat, and I don't doubt that Miss Ellen's faithful lover found a little paradise in it; but it made my heart sink foolishly to see how commonplace it all was; a greenish-whitish woollen cover on the table, a few old photographic albums, terrible antimacassars in crochet work upon the backs of the chairs. I sat down and contemplated the little mirror on the mantelpiece and the cheap little vases with dismay. We are all prejudiced now-a-days on this question of furniture. My poor little music-mistress! how was she to change the chairs and tables she had been born to? But, to tell the truth, I wavered and doubted whether she was worthy of him when I looked round upon all the antimacassars, and the dried grasses in the green vase.

While I was struggling against this first impression the door opened, and the mistress of the house came in. She was a little woman, stout and roundabout, with a black cap decorated with flowers, but a fresh little cheerful face under this tremendous head-dress which neutralized it. She came up to me with a smile and would have shaken hands, had I been at all prepared for such a warmth of salutation, and then she began to apologize for keeping me waiting. 'When my daughter is out I have to do all the waiting upon him myself. He doesn't like to be left alone, and he can't bear anybody but me or Ellen in the room with him,' she said. Perhaps she had explained beforehand who he was, but in the confusion of the first greeting I had not made it out. Then I stated my business, and she brightened up still more.

'Oh, yes; I am sure Ellen will undertake it with great pleasure. In the Road at No. 16? Oh, it is no distance; it will be no trouble; and she is so glad to extend her connection. With private teaching it is such a great matter to extend your connection. It is very kind of you to have taken the trouble to come yourself. Perhaps one of Ellen's ladies, who are all so kind to her, mentioned our name?'

'That is just where I am at a loss,' I said uneasily. 'No; but I have seen her passing all these years, always so punctual, with her bright face. She has been a great favourite of mine for a long time, though I don't know her name.'

The mother's countenance brightened after a moment's doubt. 'Yes,' she said, 'she is a good girl— always a bright face. She is the life of the house.'

'And I have seen,' said I, hesitating more and more, 'a gentleman. I presume there is to be a marriage by and by. You must pardon my curiosity, I have taken so much interest in them.'

A good many changes passed over the mother's face. Evidently she was not at all sure about my curiosity, whether perhaps it might not be impertinent.

'Ah!' she said, with a little nod, 'you have remarked John. Yes, of course, it was sure to be remarked, so constantly as he comes. I need not make any secret of it. In one way I would rather he did not come so often; but it is a pleasure to Ellen. Yes; I may say they are engaged.'

Engaged? After all these years! But I remembered that I had no right, being an intruder, to say anything. 'I have seen them in the summer evenings—'

'Yes, yes,' she said; 'yes,' with again a nod of her head. 'Perhaps it was imprudent, for you never can tell whether these things will come to anything; but it was her only time for a little pleasure. Poor child, I always see that she gets that hour. They go out still, though you would not say it would do her much good in the dark; out there is nothing she enjoys so much. She is the best girl that ever was. I don't know what I should do without her;' and there was a glimmer of moisture in the mother's eyes.

'But,' I said, 'surely after a while they are going to be married?'

'I don't know. I don't see how her father can spare her.' The cheerful face lost all its brightness as she spoke, and she shook her head. 'He is so fond of Ellen, the only girl we have left now; he can't bear her out of his sight. She is such a good girl, and so devoted.' The mother faltered a little—perhaps my question made her think—at all events, it was apparent that everything was not so simple and straightforward for the young pair as I in my ignorance had thought.

But I had no excuse to say any more. It was no business of mine, as people say. I settled that Ellen was to come at a certain hour next day, which was all that remained to be done. When I glanced round the room again as I left, it had changed its aspect to me, and looked like a prison. Was the poor girl bound there, and unable to get free? As the mother opened the door for me, the sound of an imperious voice calling her came down-stairs. She called back, 'I am coming, James, I am coming;' then let me out hurriedly. And I went home feeling as if I had torn the covering from a mystery, and as if the house in Pleasant Place, so tranquil, so commonplace, was the scene of some tragic story, to end one could not tell how. But there was no mystery at all about it: When 'Miss Harwood' was announced to me next day, I was quite startled by the name, not associating it with any one; but the moment the little music-mistress appeared, with her little roll in her hand, her trim figure, her smiling face, and fresh look of health and happiness, my suspicions disappeared like the groundless fancies they were. She was delighted to have a new pupil, and one so near, whom it would be 'no trouble' to attend; and so pleased when I (with much timidity, I confess) ventured to tell her how long I had known her, and how I had watched for her at my window, and all the observations I had made. She brightened, and laughed and blushed, and declared it was very kind of me to take such an interest; then hung her head for a moment, and laughed and blushed still more, when my confessions went the length of the faithful lover. But this was nothing but a becoming girlish shyness, for next minute she looked me frankly in the face, with the prettiest colour dyeing her round cheek. 'I think he knows you too,' she said. 'We met you once out walking, and he told me, "There is the lady who lives in the Road, whom I always see at the window." We hoped you were better to see you out.' And then it was my turn to feel gratified, which I did unfeignedly. I had gone through a great deal of trouble, cheered by my spectatorship of life-out-of-doors from that window. And I was pleased that they had taken some friendly notice of me too.

'And I suppose,' I said, returning to my theme, 'that it will not be long now before you reward his faithfulness. Must Chatty leave you then? or will you go on, do you think, taking pupils after—?'

She gave me a little bewildered look. 'I don't think I know what you mean.'

'After you are married,' I said plumply. 'That must be coming soon now.'

Then she burst out with a genial, pretty laugh, blushing and shaking her head. 'Oh, no; we do not think of such a thing! Not yet. They couldn't spare me at home. John—I mean, Mr. Ridgway—knows that. My father has been ill so long; he wants attendance night and day, and I don't know what mother would do without me. Oh dear no; we are very happy as we are. We don't even think of that.'

'But you must think of it some time, surely, in justice to him,' I said, half indignant for my faithful Johnny's sake.

'Yes, I suppose so, some time,' she said, with a momentary gravity stealing over her face—gravity and perplexity too: and a little pucker came into her forehead. How to do it? A doubt, a question, seemed to enter her mind for a moment. Then she gave her head a shake, dismissing the clouds from her cheerful firmament, and with a smiling decision set down Chatty to the piano. Chatty had fallen in love with Miss Harwood, her own particular music-mistress, in whom no one else had any share, on the spot.

And after a while we all fell in love, one after another, with Miss Ellen. She was one of those cheerful people who never make a fuss about anything, never are put out, or make small troubles into great ones. We tried her in every way, as is not unusual with a large, somewhat careless, family, in whose minds it was a settled principle that, so long as you did a thing some time or other, it did not at all matter when you did it—and that times and seasons were of no particular importance to any one but Fräulein Stimme. She, of course—our natural disorderliness had to give way to her; but I am afraid it very soon came to be said in the house, 'Ellen will not mind.' And Ellen did not mind; if twelve o'clock proved inconvenient for the lesson, she only smiled and said, 'It is no matter; I will come in at three.' And if at three Fräulein Stimme's clutches upon Chatty were still unclosed, she would do anything that happened to be needed—gather the little ones round the piano and teach them songs, or go out with my eldest daughter for her walk, or talk to me. How many talks we had upon every subject imaginable! Ellen was not what is called clever. She had read very few books. My eldest daughter aforesaid despised her somewhat on this account, and spoke condescendingly of this or that as 'what Ellen says.' But it was astonishing, after all, how often 'what Ellen says' was quoted. There were many things which Ellen had not thought anything about; and on these points she was quite ignorant; for she had not read what other people had thought about them, and was unprepared with an opinion; but whenever the subject had touched her own intelligence, she knew very well what she thought. And by dint of being a little lower down in the social order than we were, she knew familiarly a great many things which we knew only theoretically and did not understand. For instance, that fine shade of difference which separates people with a hundred and fifty pounds a year from people with weekly wages was a thing which had always altogether eluded me. I had divined that a workman with three pounds a week was well off, and a clerk with the same, paid quarterly, was poor; but wherein lay the difference, and how it was that the latter occupied a superior position to the former, I have never been able to fathom. Ellen belonged, herself, to this class. Her father had been in one of the lower departments of a public office, and had retired with a pension of exactly this amount after some thirty years' service. There was a time in his life, to which she regretfully yet proudly referred as 'the time when we were well off,' in which his salary had risen to two hundred and fifty pounds a year. That was the time when she got her education and developed the taste for music which was now supplying her with work which she liked, and a little provision for herself. There was no scorn or hauteur in Ellen; but she talked of the working classes with as distinct a consciousness of being apart from and superior to them as if she had been a duchess. It was no virtue of hers; but still Providence had placed her on a different level, and she behaved herself accordingly. Servants and shopkeepers, of the minor kind at least, were within the same category to her—people to be perfectly civil to, and kind to, but, as a matter of course, not the kind of people whom in her position it would become her to associate with. When I asked myself why I should smile at this, or wherein it was more unreasonable than other traditions of social superiority, I could not give any answer. We are not ourselves, so far as I know, sons of the Crusaders, and it is very difficult to say what is the social figment of rank by which we hold so dearly. Ellen Harwood exhibited to us the instinct of aristocracy on one of its lower levels; and one learned a lesson while one smiled in one's sleeve. Never was anything more certain, more serious, than her sense of class distinctions, and the difference between one degree and another; and nobody, not a prince of the blood, would have less understood being laughed at. This serene consciousness of her position and its inherent right divine was a possession inalienable to our music-mistress. She would have comprehended or endured no trifling or jesting with it. One blushed while one laughed in an undertone. She was holding the mirror up to nature without being aware of it. And there were various fanciful particulars also in her code. The people next door who let lodgings were beneath her as much as the working people—all to be very nicely behaved to, need I say, and treated with the greatest politeness and civility, but not as if they were on the level of 'people like ourselves.' Lady Clara Vere de Vere could not have been more serenely unconscious of any possible equality between herself and her village surroundings than Ellen Harwood. Fortunately, Mr. John Ridgway was 'in our own position in life.'

These and many other vagaries of human sentiment I learned to see through Ellen's eyes with more edification and amusement, and also with more confusion and abashed consciousness, than had ever occurred to me before. These were precisely my own sentiments, you know, towards the rich linendraper next door; and no doubt my aristocratical repugnance to acknowledge myself the neighbour of that worthy person would have seemed just as funny to the Duke of Bayswater as Ellen's pretensions did to me. It must not be supposed however that Ellen Harwood was in a state of chronic resistance to the claims of her humbler neighbours. She was an active, bright, cheerful creature, full of interest in everything. Her father had been ill for years; and she had grown accustomed to his illness, as young people do to anything they have been acquainted with all their lives, and was not alarmed by it, nor oppressed, so far as we could tell, by the constant claims made upon her. She allowed that now and then he was cross—'which of us would not be cross, shut up in one room for ever and ever?' But she had not the least fear that he would ever die, or that she would grow tired of taking care of him. All the rest of her time after lessons she was in attendance upon him, excepting only that hour in the evening when John's visit was paid. She always looked forward to that, she confessed. 'To think of it makes everything smooth. He is so good. Though I say it that shouldn't,' she cried, laughing and blushing, 'you can't think how nice he is. And he knows so much; before he knew us he had nothing to do but read all the evenings—fancy! And I never met any one who had read so much; he knows simply everything. Ah!' with a little sigh, 'it makes such a difference to have him coming every night; it spirits one up for the whole day.'

'But, Ellen, I can't think how it is that he doesn't get tired—'

'Tired!' She reddened up to her very hair. 'Why should he get tired? If he is tired, he has my full permission to go when he likes,' she said, throwing back her proud little head. 'But nobody shall put such an idea into my mind. You don't know John. If you knew John that would be quite enough; such a thing would never come into your mind.'

'You should hear me out before you blame me. I was going to say, tired of waiting, which is a very different sentiment.'

Ellen laughed, and threw aside her little offence in a moment. 'I thought you could not mean that. Tired of waiting! But he has not waited so very long. We have not been years and years like some people—No; only eighteen months since it was all settled. We are not rich people like you, to do a thing the moment we have begun to think about it: and everything so dear!' she cried, half merry, half serious. 'Oh, no; he is not the least tired. What could we want more than to be together in the evening? All the day goes pleasantly for thinking of it,' she said, with a pretty blush. 'And my mother always manages to let me have that hour. She does not mind how tired she is. We are as happy as the day is long,' Ellen said.

I have always heard that a long engagement is the most miserable and wearing thing in the world. I have never believed it, it is true; but that does not matter. Here however was a witness against the popular belief. Ellen was not the victim of a long engagement, nor of a peevish invalid, though her days were spent in tendance upon one, and her youth gliding away in the long patience of the other. She was as merry and bright as if she were having everything her own way in life; and so I believe she really thought she was, with a mother so kind as, always, however tired she might be, to insist upon securing that evening hour for her, and a John who was better than any other John had ever been before him. The faithful Johnny! I wondered sometimes on his side what he thought.

CHAPTER III

One day Ellen came to me, on her arrival, with an air of suppressed excitement quite unusual to her. It was not, evidently, anything to be alarmed about, for she looked half way between laughing and crying, but not melancholy. 'May I speak to you after Chatty has had her lesson?' she asked. I felt sure that some new incident had happened in her courtship, about which I was so much more interested than about any other courtship I was acquainted with. So I arranged with all speed—not an easy thing when there are so many in a house, to be left alone, and free to hear whatever she might have to say. She was a little hurried with the lesson, almost losing patience over Chatty's fumbling—and how the child did fumble over the fingering, putting the third finger where the first should be, and losing count altogether of the thumb, which is too useful a member to be left without occupation! It appeared to me half a dozen times that Ellen was on the eve of taking the music off the piano, and garotting Chatty with the arm which rested nervously on the back of the child's chair. However she restrained these impulses, if she had them, and got through the hour tant bien que mal. It was even with an air of extreme deliberation, masking her excitement, that she stood by and watched her pupil putting away the music and closing the piano. Chatty, of course, took a longer time than usual to these little arrangements, and then lingered in the room. Generally she was too glad to hurry away.

'Go, Chatty, and see if the others are ready to go out for their walk.'

'They have gone already, mamma. They said they would not wait for me. They said I was always so long of getting my things on.'

'But why are you so long of getting your things on? Run away and see what nurse is about; or if Fräulein Stimme would like—'

'Fräulein isn't here to-day. How funny you are, mamma, not to remember that it's Saturday.'

'Go this moment!' I cried wildly, 'and tell nurse that you must go out for a walk. Do you think I will permit you to lose your walk, because the others think you are long of putting your things on? Nothing of the sort. Go at once, Chatty,' I cried, clapping my hands, as I have a way of doing, to rouse them when they are not paying attention, 'without a word!'

To see the child's astonished face! She seemed to stumble over herself in her haste to get out of the room. After the unusual force of this adjuration I had myself become quite excited. I waved my hand to Ellen, who had stood by listening, half frightened by my vehemence, pointing her to a chair close to me. 'Now, tell me all about it,' I said.

'Is it really for me that you have sent Chatty away in such a hurry? How good of you!' said Ellen. And then she made a pause, as if to bring herself into an appropriate frame of mind before making her announcement. 'I could not rest till I had told you. You have always taken such an interest. John has got a rise of fifty pounds a year.'

'I am very glad, very glad, Ellen.'

'I knew you would be pleased. He has been expecting it for some time back; but he would not say anything to me, in case I should be disappointed if it did not come. So I should, most likely, for I think he deserves a great deal more than that. But the best people never get so much as they deserve. Fifty pounds a year is a great rise all at once, don't you think? and he got a hint that perhaps about

Midsummer there might be a better post offered to him. Isn't it flattering? Of course I know he deserves it; but sometimes those who deserve the most don't get what they ought. That makes two hundred and twenty; an excellent income, don't you think? He will have to pay income-tax,' Ellen said, with a flush of mingled pride and gratification and grievance which it was amusing to see.

'I don't know that I think much of the income-tax; but it is very pleasant that he is so well thought of,' I said.

'And another rise at Midsummer! It seems more than one had any right to expect,' said Ellen. Her hands were clasped in her lap, her fingers twisting and untwisting unconsciously, her head raised, and her eyes fixed, without seeing anything, upon the blue sky outside. She was rapt in a pleasant dream of virtue rewarded and goodness triumphant. A smile went and came upon her face like sunshine. 'And yet,' she cried, 'to hear people speak, you would think that it was never the right men that got on. Even in sermons in church you always hear that it is rather a disadvantage to you if you are nice and good. I wonder how people can talk such nonsense; why, look at John!'

'But even John has had a long time to wait for his promotion,' said I, feeling myself the devil's advocate. I had just checked myself in time not to say that two hundred and twenty pounds a year was not a very gigantic promotion; which would have been both foolish and cruel.

'Oh, no, indeed!' cried Ellen; 'he looks a great deal older than he is. He lived so much alone, you know, before he knew us; and that gives a man an old look—but he is not a bit old. How much would you give him? No, indeed, thirty; he is only just thirty! His birthday was last week.'

'And you, Ellen?'

'I am twenty-four—six years younger than he is. Just the right difference, mother says. Of course I am really a dozen years older than he is; I have far more sense. He has read books and books till he has read all his brains away; but luckily as long as I am there to take care of him—' Then she made a pause, looked round the room with a half frightened look, then, drawing closer to me, she said in a hurried undertone, 'He said something about that other subject to-day.'

'Of course he did; how could he have done otherwise?' I said with a little momentary triumph.

'Please, please don't take his part, and make it all more difficult; for you know it is impossible, impossible, quite impossible; nobody could have two opinions. It was that, above all, that I wanted to tell you about.'

'Why is it impossible, Ellen?' I said. 'If you set up absurd obstacles, and keep up an unnatural state of things, you will be very sorry for it one day. He is quite right. I could not think how he consented to go on like this, without a word.'

'How strange that you should be so hot about it!' said Ellen, with a momentary smile; but at the bottom of her heart she was nervous and alarmed, and did not laugh with her usual confidence. 'He said something, but he was not half so stern as you are. Why should it be so dreadfully necessary to get married? I am quite happy as I am. I can do all my duties, and take care of him too; and John is quite happy—'

'There you falter,' I said; 'you dare not say that with the same intrepidity, you little deceiver. Poor John! he ought to have his life made comfortable and bright for him now. He ought to have his wife to be proud of, to come home to. So faithful as he is, never thinking of any other pleasure, of any amusement, but only you.'

Ellen blushed with pleasure, then grew pale with wonder and alarm. 'That is natural,' she said, faltering. 'What other amusement should he think of? He is most happy with me.'

'But very few men are like that,' I said. 'He is giving up everything else for you; he is shutting himself out of the world for you; and you—what are you giving up for him?'

Ellen grew paler and paler as I spoke. 'Giving up?' she said aghast. 'I—I would give up anything. But I have got nothing, except John,' she added, with an uneasy little laugh. 'And you say he is shutting himself out of the world. Oh, I know what you are thinking of—the kind of world one reads about in books, where gentlemen have clubs, and all that sort of thing. But these are only for you rich people. He is not giving up anything that I know of.'

'What do the other young men do, Ellen? Every one has his own kind of world.'

'The other young men!' she cried indignant. 'Now I see indeed you don't know anything about him (how could you? you have never even seen him), when you compare John to the other clerks. John! Oh, yes, I suppose they go and amuse themselves; they go to the theatres, and all those wrong places. But you don't suppose John would do that, even if I were not in existence! Why John! the fact is, you don't know him; that is the whole affair.'

'I humbly confess it,' said I; 'but it is not my fault. I should be very glad to know him, if I might.'

Ellen looked at me with a dazzled look of sudden happiness, as if this prospect of bliss was too much for her—which is always very flattering to the superior in such intercourse as existed between her and me. 'Oh! would you?' she said, with her heart in her mouth, and fixed her eyes eagerly upon me, as if with some project she did not like to unfold.

'Certainly I should.' Then, after a pause I said, 'Could not you bring him to-morrow to tea?'

Ellen's eyes sparkled. She gave a glance round upon the room, which was a great deal bigger and handsomer than the little parlour in Pleasant Place, taking in the pictures and the piano and myself in so many distinct perceptions, yet one look. Her face was so expressive that I recognized all these different details of her pleasure with the distinctest certainty. She wanted John to see it all, and to hear the piano, which was much better than her little piano at home; and also to behold how much at home she was, and how everybody liked her. Her eyes shone out upon me like two stars. And her big English 'Oh!' of delight had her whole breath in it, and left her speechless for the moment. 'There is nothing in the world I would like so much,' she cried at last: then paused, and, with a sobered tone, added, 'If mother can spare me'—a little cloud coming over her face.

'I am sure your mother will spare you. You never have any parties or amusements, my good little Ellen. You must tell her I will take no denial. You never go anywhere.'

'Where should I go?' said Ellen. 'I don't want to go anywhere, there is always so much to do at home. But for this once—And John would so like to come. He would like to thank you. He says, if you will not think him too bold, that you have been his friend for years.'

'It is quite true,' I said; 'I have looked for him almost every day for years. But it is not much of a friendship when one can do nothing for the other—'

'Oh, it is beautiful!' cried Ellen. 'He says always we are in such different ranks of life. We could never expect to have any intercourse, except to be sure by a kind of happy accident, like me. It would not do, of course, visiting or anything of that sort; but just to be friends for life, with a kind look, such as we might give to the angels if we could see them. If there only could be a window in heaven, here and there!' and she laughed with moisture in her eyes.

'Ah!' I said, 'but windows in heaven would be so crowded with those that are nearer to us than the angels.'

'Do you think they would want that?' said Ellen in a reverential low tone; 'don't you think they must see somehow? they would not be happy if they could not see. But the angels might come and sit down in an idle hour, when they had nothing to do. Perhaps it would grieve them, but it might amuse them too, to see all the crowds go by, and all the stories going on, like a play, and know that, whatever happened, it would all come right in the end. I should not wonder a bit if, afterwards, some one were to say, as you did about John, "I have seen you passing for years and years—"'

I need not repeat all the rest of our talk. When two women begin this kind of conversation, there is no telling where it may end. The conclusion however was that next evening John was to be brought to make my acquaintance; and Ellen went away very happy, feeling, I think, that a new chapter was about to begin in her life. And on our side we indulged in a great many anticipations. The male part of the household assured us that, 'depend upon it,' it would be a mistake; that John would be a mere clerk, and no more; a man, perhaps, not very sure about his h's; perhaps over-familiar, perhaps frightened; that most likely he would feel insulted by being asked to tea—and a great deal more, to all of which we, of course, paid no attention. But it was not till afterwards that even I realized the alarming business it must have been to John to walk into a room full of unknown people—dreadful critical children, girls and boys half grown up—and to put to the test a friendship of years, which had gone on without a word spoken, and now might turn out anything but what it had been expected to be. He was a little fluttered and red when Ellen, herself very nervous, brought him in, meeting all the expectant faces, which turned instinctively towards the door. Ellen herself had never come in the evening before, and the aspect of the house, with the lamps lighted, and the whole family assembled, was new to her. She came in without saying a word, and led her love, who for his part moved awkwardly and with shy hesitation, through the unknown place, threading his way among the tables and chairs, and the staring children, to where I sat. I have always said my little Chatty was the best bred of all my children. There was no one so much interested as she; but she kept her eyes upon her work, and never looked up till they were seated comfortably and beginning to look at their ease. John faltered forth what I felt sure was intended to be a very pretty speech to me, probably conned beforehand, and worthy of the occasion. But all that came forth was, 'I have seen you often at the window.' 'Yes, indeed,' I said hurriedly, 'for years; we are old friends: we don't require any introduction,' and so got over it. I am afraid he said 'ma'am.' I see no reason why he should not say ma'am; people used to do it; and excepting us rude English, everybody in the world does it. Why should not John have used that word of respect if he chose? You say ma'am yourself to princesses when you speak to them, if you ever have the honour of speaking to them; and he thought as much of me, knowing no better, as if I had been a princess. He had a soft, refined voice. I am sure I cannot tell whether his clothes were well made or not—a woman does not look at a man's clothes—but this I can tell you, that his face was well made. There was not a fine feature in it; but He who shaped them knew what He was about. Every line was good—truth and patience and a gentle soul shone through them. In five minutes he was at home, not saying much, but looking at us all with benevolent, tender eyes. When Chatty brought him his tea and gave him her small hand, he held it for a moment, saying, 'This is Ellen's pupil,' with a look which was a benediction. 'I should have known her anywhere,' he said. 'Ellen has a gift of description—and then, she is like you.'

'Ellen has a great many gifts, Mr. Ridgway—the house is sure to be a bright one that has her for its mistress.'

He assented with a smile that lit up his face like sunshine; then shook his head, and said, 'I wish I could see any prospect of that. The house has been built, and furnished, and set out ready for her so long. That is, alas! only in our thoughts. It is a great pleasure to imagine it; but it seems always to recede a little further—a little further. We have need of patience.' Then he paused, and added, brightening a little, 'Fortunately we are not impatient people, either of us.'

'Forgive me,' I said. 'It is a great deal to take upon me—a stranger as I am.'

'You forget,' he said, with a bow that would not have misbecome a courtier, 'that you were so kind as to say that we were not strangers but old friends.'

'It is quite true. Then I will venture to speak as an old friend. I wish you were not so patient. I wish you were a hot-headed person, and would declare once for all that you would not put up with it.'

He reddened, and turned to me with a look half of alarm, half, perhaps, of incipient, possible offence. 'You think I am too tame, too easy—not that I don't desire with my whole heart—'

'Not that you are not as true as the heavens themselves,' I said, with the enthusiasm of penitence. His face relaxed and shone again, though once more he shook his head.

'I think—I am sure—you are quite right. If I could insist I might carry my point, and it would be better. But what can I say? I understand her, and sympathize with her, and respect her. I cannot oppose her roughly, and set myself before everything. Who am I, that she should desert what she thinks her duty for me?'

'I feel like a prophet,' I said. 'In this case to be selfish is the best.'

He shook his head again. 'She could not be selfish if she tried,' he said.

Did he mean the words for himself, too? They were neither of them selfish. I don't want to say a word that is wicked, that may discourage the good—they were neither of them strong enough to be selfish. Sometimes there is wisdom and help in that quality which is so common. I will explain after what I mean. It does not sound true, I am well aware, but I think it is true: however in the meantime there was nothing more to be said. We began to talk of all sorts of things; of books, with which John seemed to be very well acquainted, and of pictures, which he knew too—as much, at least, as a man who had never been out of England, nor seen anything but the National Gallery, could know. He was acquainted with that by heart, knowing every picture and all that could be known about it, making me ashamed, though I had seen a great deal more than he had. I felt like one who knows other people's possessions, but not his own. He had never been, so to speak, out of his own house; but he knew every picture on the walls there. And he made just as much use of his h's as I do myself. If he was at first a little stiff in his demeanour, that wore off as he talked. Ellen left him entirely to me. She went off into the back drawing-room with the little ones, and made them sing standing round the piano. There was not much light, except the candles on the piano, which lighted up their small fresh faces and her own bright countenance; and this made the prettiest picture at the end of the room. While he was talking to me he looked that way, and a smile came suddenly over his face—which drew my attention also. 'Could any painter paint that?' he said softly, looking at them. As the children were mine, you may believe I gazed with as much admiration as he. The light seemed to come from those soft faces, not to be thrown upon them, and the depth of the room was illuminated by the rose-tints, and the whiteness, and the reflected light out of their eyes. 'Rembrandt, perhaps,' I said; but he shook his head, for he did not know much of Rembrandt. When they finished their little store of songs I called to Ellen to sing us something by herself. The children went away, for it was their bedtime; and all the time the good-nights were being said she played a little soft trill of prelude, very sweet, and low, and subdued. There was a harmonizing influence in her that made everything appropriate. She did things as they ought to be done by instinct, without knowing it; while he, with his gaze directed to her, felt it all more than she did—felt the softening of that undertone of harmonious accompaniment, the sweet filling up of the pause, the background of sound upon which all the little voices babbled out like the trickling of brooks. When this was over Ellen did not burst into her song all at once, as if to show how we had kept her waiting; but went on for a minute or two, hushing out the former little tumult. Then she chose another strain, and, while we all sat silent, began to sing—the song I had heard her sing to him when they were alone that summer evening. Was there a little breath in it of consciousness, a something shadowing from the life to come—'I will come again?' We all sat very silent and listened: he with his face turned to her, a tender smile upon it—a look of admiring pleasure. He beat time with his hand, without knowing it, rapt in the wistful, tender music, the longing sentiment, the pervading consciousness of her, in all. I believe they were both as happy as could be while this was going on. She singing to him, and knowing that she pleased him, while still conscious of the pleasure of all the rest of us, and glad to please us too; and he so proud of her, drinking it all in, and knowing it to be for him, yet feeling that he was giving us this gratification, making an offering to us of the very best that was his. Why was it, then, that we all, surrounding them, a voiceless band of spectators, felt the hidden meaning in it, and were sorry for them, with a strange impulse of pity—sorry for those two happy people, those two inseparables who had no thought but to pass their lives together? I cannot tell how it was; but so it was. We all listened with a little thrill of sympathy, as we might have looked at those whose doom we knew, but who themselves had not yet found out what was coming upon them. And at the end, Ellen too was affected in a curious sympathetic way by some mysterious invisible touch of our sympathy for her. She came out of the half-lit room behind, with trembling, hurried steps, and came close to my side, and took in both hers the hand I held out to her. 'How silly I am!' she cried, with a little laugh. 'I could have thought that some message was coming to say he must go and leave me. A kind of tremor came over me all at once.' 'You are tired,' I said. And no doubt that had something to do with it; but why should the same chill have crept over us all?

CHAPTER IV

The time passed on very quietly during these years. Nothing particular happened; so that looking back now—now that once more things have begun to happen, and all the peaceful children who cost me nothing but pleasant cares have grown up and are setting forth, each with his and her more serious complications, into individual life—it seems to me like a long flowery plain of peace. I did not think so then, and no doubt from time to time questions arose that were hard to answer and difficulties that cost me painful thought. But now all seems to me a sort of heavenly monotony and calm, turning years into days. In this gentle domestic quiet six months went by like an afternoon; for it was, I think, about six months after the first meeting I have just described when Ellen Harwood rushed in one morning with a scared face, to tell me of something which had occurred and which threatened to break up in a moment the quiet of her life. Mr. Ridgway had come again various times—we had daily intercourse at the window, where, when he passed, he always looked up now, and where I seldom failed to see him and give him a friendly greeting. This intercourse, though it was so slight, was also so constant that it made us very fast friends; and when Ellen, as I have said, rushed in very white and breathless one bright spring morning, full of something to tell, my first feeling was alarm. Had anything happened to John?

'Oh, no. Nothing has happened. At least, I don't suppose you would say anything had happened—that is, no harm—except to me,' said Ellen, wringing her hands, 'except to me! Oh, do you recollect that first night he came to see you, when you were so kind as to ask him, and I sang that song he is so fond of? I took fright then; I never could tell how—and now it looks as if it would all come true—'

'As if what would come true?'

'Somebody,' said Ellen, sitting down abruptly in the weariness of her dejection, 'somebody from the office is to go out directly to the Levant. Oh, Chatty, dear, you that are learning geography and everything, tell me where is the Levant? It is where the currants and raisins come from. The firm has got an establishment, and it is likely—oh, it is very likely: they all think that John, whom they trust so much—John—will be sent—'

She broke off with a sob—a gasp. She was too startled, too much excited and frightened, to have the relief of tears.

'But that would be a very good thing, surely—it would be the very best thing for him. I don't see any cause for alarm. My dear Ellen, he would do his work well; he would be promoted; he would be made a partner—'

'Ah!' She drew a long breath: a gleam of wavering light passed over her face. 'I said you would think it no harm,' she said mournfully, 'no harm—except to me.'

'It is on the Mediterranean Sea,' said Chatty over her atlas, with a great many big round 'Oh's' of admiration and wonder, 'where it is always summer, always beautiful. Oh, Ellen, I wish I were you! but you can send us some oranges,' the child added philosophically. Ellen gave her a rapid glance of mingled fondness and wrath.

'You think of nothing but oranges!' she cried (quite unjustly, I must say); then putting her hands together and fixing her wistful eyes upon me, 'I feel,' she said in the same breath, 'as if the world were coming to an end.'

'You mean it is just about beginning—for of course he will not go without you—and that is the very best thing that could happen.'

'Oh, how can you say so? it cannot happen; it is the end of everything,' Ellen cried, and I could not console her. She would do nothing but wring her hands and repeat her plaint, 'It is the end of everything.' Poor girl, apart from John her life was dreary enough, though she had never felt it dreary. Music lessons in the morning, and after that continual attendance upon an exacting fiery invalid. The only break in her round of duty had been her evening hours, her little walk and talk with John. No wonder that the thought of John's departure filled her with a terror for which she could scarcely find words. And she never took into account the other side of the question, the solution which seemed to me so certain, so inevitable. She knew better—that, at least, whatever other way might be found out of it, could not be.

Next day in the evening, when he was going home, John himself paused as he was passing the window, and looked up with a sort of appeal. I answered by beckoning to him to come in, and he obeyed the summons very rapidly and eagerly. The spring days had drawn out, and it was now quite light when John came home. He came in and sat down beside me, in the large square projecting window, which was my favourite place. There was a mingled air of eagerness and weariness about him, as if, though excited by the new prospect which was opening before him, he was yet alarmed by the obstacles in his way, and reluctant, as Ellen herself was, to disturb the present peaceful conditions of their life. 'I do not believe,' he said, 'that they will ever consent. I don't know how we are to struggle against them. People of their age have so much stronger wills than we have. They stand to what they want, and they have it, reason or no reason.'

'That is because you give in; you do not stand to what you want,' I said. He looked away beyond me into the evening light, over the heads of all the people who were going and coming so briskly in the road, and sighed.

'They have such strong wills. What can you say when people tell you that it is impossible, that they never can consent? Ellen and I have never said that, or even thought it. When we are opposed we try to think how we can compromise, how we can do with as little as possible of what we want, so as to satisfy the others. I always thought that was the good way, the nobler way,' he said with a flush coming over his pale face. 'Have we been making a mistake?'

'I fear so—I think so; yes, I am sure,' I cried. 'Yours would be the nobler way if—if there was nobody but yourself to think of.'

He looked at me with a wondering air. 'I think I must have expressed myself wrongly,' he said; 'it was not ourselves at all that we were thinking of.'

'I know; but that is just what I object to,' I said. 'You sacrifice yourselves, and you encourage the other people to be cruelly selfish, perhaps without knowing it. All that is virtue in you is evil in them. Don't you see that to accept this giving up of your life is barbarous, it is wicked, it is demoralizing to the others. Just in so much as people think well of you they will be forced to think badly of them.'

He was a little startled by this view, which, I confess, I struck out on the spur of the moment, not really seeing how much sense there was in it. I justified myself afterwards to myself, and became rather proud of my argument; but for a woman to argue, much less suggest, that self-sacrifice is not the chief of all virtues, is terrible. I was half frightened and disgusted with myself, as one is when one has brought forward in the heat of partisanship a thoroughly bad, yet, for the moment, effective argument. But he was staggered, and I felt the thrill of success which stirs one to higher effort.

'I never thought of that; perhaps there is some truth in it,' he said. Then, after a pause, 'I wonder if you, who have been so good to us all, who are fond of Ellen—I am sure you are fond of Ellen—and the children like her.'

'Very fond of Ellen, and the children all adore her,' I said with perhaps unnecessary emphasis.

'To me that seems natural,' he said, brightening. 'But yet what right have we to ask you to do more? You have been as kind as it is possible to be.'

'You want me to do something more? I will do whatever I can—only speak out.'

'It was this,' he said, 'if you would ask—you who are not an interested party—if you would find out what our prospects are. Ellen does not want to escape from her duty. There is nothing we are not capable of sacrificing rather than that she should shrink from her duty. I need not tell you how serious it is. If I don't take this—in case it is offered to me—I may never get another chance again; but, if I must part from Ellen, I cannot accept it. I cannot; it would be like parting one's soul from one's body. But I have no confidence in myself any more than Ellen has. They have such strong wills. If they say it must not and cannot be—what can I reply? I know myself. I will yield, and so will Ellen. How can one look them in the face and say, 'Though you are her father and mother, we prefer our own comfort to yours?'

'Do not say another word. I will do it,' I said, half exasperated, half sympathetic—oh, yes! more than half sympathetic. They were fools; but I understood it, and was not surprised, though I was exasperated. 'I will go and beard the lion in his den,' I said. 'Perhaps they will not let me see the lion, only his attendant. But remember this,' I said vindictively, 'if Ellen and you allow yourselves to be conquered, if you are weak and throw away all your hopes, never come to me again. I have made up my mind. You must give up me as well as all the rest. I will not put up with such weakness.' John stared at me with alarm in his eyes; he was not quite comfortable even when I laughed at my own little bit of tragedy. He shook his head with a melancholy perplexity.

'I don't see clearly,' he said; 'I don't seem able to judge. To give in is folly; and yet, when you think—supposing it were duty—suppose her father were to die when she was far away from him?'

'If we were to consider all these possibilities there never would be a marriage made—never an independent move in life,' I cried. 'Parents die far from their children, and children, alas! from their parents. How could it be otherwise? But God is near to us all. If we were each to think ourselves so all-important, life would stand still; there would be no more advance, no progress; everything would come to an end.'

John shook his head; partly it was in agreement with what I said, partly in doubt for himself. 'How am I to stand up to them and say, "Never mind what you want—we want something else?" There's the rub,' he said, still slowly shaking his head. He had no confidence in his own power of self-assertion. He had never, I believe, been able to answer satisfactorily the question, why should he have any special thing which some one else wished for? It was as natural to him to efface himself, to resign his claims, as it was to other men to assert them. And yet in this point he could not give up—he could not give Ellen up, come what might; but neither could he demand that he and she should be permitted to live their own life.

After long deliberation I decided that it would not be expedient to rush across to Pleasant Place at once and get it over while John and Ellen were taking their usual evening walk, which was my first impulse; but to wait till the morning, when all would be quiet, and the invalid and his wife in their best humour. It was not a pleasant errand; the more I thought of it, the less I liked it. If they were people who could demand such a sacrifice from their daughter, was it likely that they would be so far moved by my arguments as to change their nature? I went through the little smoky garden plot, where the familiar London 'blacks' lay thick on the grass, on the sweetest May morning, when it was a pleasure to be alive. The windows were open, the little white muslin curtains fluttering. Up-stairs I heard a gruff voice asking for something, and another, with a querulous tone in it, giving a reply. My heart began to beat louder at the sound. I tried to keep up my courage by all the arguments I could think of. Nevertheless, my heart sank down into my very shoes when the little maid, with her apron folded over her arm, and as grimy as ever, opened to me—with a curtsey and a 'La!' of delighted surprise—this door of fate.

CHAPTER V

I had a long time to wait before Mrs. Harwood came. The morning sun was shining into the room, making everything more dingy. No doubt it had been dusted that morning as well as the little maid could dust it; but nothing looked pure or fresh in the brightness of the light, which was full of motes, and seemed to find out dust in every corner. The dingy cover on the table, the old-fashioned Books of Beauty, the black horsehair chairs, stood out remorselessly shabby in the sunshine. I wondered what kind of house Ellen would have when she furnished one for herself. Would John and she show any 'taste' between them—would they 'pick up' pretty things at sales and old furniture shops, or would they buy a drawing-room suite for twenty-five pounds, such as the cheap upholsterers offer to the unwary? This question amused me while I waited, and I was sorry to think that the new household was to be planted in the Levant, and we should not see how it settled itself. There was a good deal of commotion going on overhead, but I did not pay any attention to it. I pleased myself arranging a little home for the new pair—making it pretty for them. Of her own self Ellen would never, I felt sure, choose the drawing-room suite in walnut and blue rep—not now, at least, after she had been so much with us. As for John, he would probably think any curtain tolerable so long as she sat under its shadow. I had been somewhat afraid of confronting the mother, and possibly the father; but these thoughts put my panic out of my head. These horsehair chairs! was there ever such an invention of the evil one? Ellen could not like them; it was impossible. When I had come this length my attention was suddenly attracted by the sounds up-stairs; for there came upon the floor over my head the sound of a foot stamped violently in apparent fury. There were voices too; but I could not make out what they said. As to this sound however it was easy enough to make out what it meant: nothing could be more suggestive. I trembled and listened, my thoughts taking an entirely new direction; a stamp of anger, of rage, and partially of impotence too. Then there was a woman's voice rising loud in remonstrance. The man seemed to exclaim and denounce violently; the woman protested, growing also louder and louder. I listened with all my might. It was not eavesdropping; for she, at least, knew that I was there; but, listen as I might, I could not make out what they said. After a while there was silence, and I heard Mrs. Harwood's step coming down the stairs. She paused to do something, perhaps to her cap or her eyes, before she opened the door. She was in a flutter of agitation, the flowers in her black cap quivering through all their wires, her eyes moist, though looking at me with a suspicious gaze. She was very much on her guard, very well aware of my motive, determined to give me no encouragement. All this I read in her vigilant eyes.

'Mrs. Harwood, I came to speak to you—I promised to come and speak to you—about Mr. Ridgway, who is a great friend of mine, as perhaps you know.'

The poor woman was in great agitation and trouble; but this only quickened her wits. 'I see John Ridgway every day of my life,' she said, not without a little dignity. 'He might say whatever he pleased to me without asking anybody to speak for him.'

'Won't you give your consent to this marriage?' I asked. It seemed wisest to plunge into it at once. 'It is my own anxiety that makes me speak. I have always been anxious about it, almost before I knew them.'

'There are other things in the world besides marriages,' she said. 'In this house we have a great deal to think of. My husband—no doubt you heard his voice just now—he is a great sufferer. For years he has been confined to that little room up-stairs. That is not a very cheerful life.'

Here she made a pause, which I did not attempt to interrupt; for she had disarmed me by this half-appeal to my sympathy. Then suddenly, with her voice a little shaken and unsteady, she burst forth: 'The only company he has is Ellen. What can I do to amuse him—to lead his thoughts off himself? I have as much need of comfort as he has. The only bright thing in the house is Ellen. What would become of us if we were left only the two together all these long days? They are long enough as it is. He has not a very good temper, and he is weary with trouble—who wouldn't be in his case? John Ridgway is a young man with all the world before him. Why can't he wait? Why should he want to take our only comfort away from us?'

Her voice grew shrill and broken; she began to cry. Poor soul! I believe she had been arguing with her husband on the other side; but it was a little comfort to her to pour out her own grievances, her alarm and distress, to me. I was silenced. How true it had been what John Ridgway said: How could he, so gentle a man, assert himself in the face of this, and claim Ellen as of chief importance to him? Had not they a prior claim?—was not her duty first to her father and mother? I was put to silence myself. I did not know what to say.

'The only thing is,' I said timidly at last, 'that I should think it would be a comfort to you to feel that Ellen was settled, that she had a home of her own, and a good husband who would take care of her when— She ought to outlive us all,' I added, not knowing how to put it. 'And if it were to be always as you say,' I went on, getting a little courage, 'there would be no marriages, no new homes. We have all had fathers and mothers who had claims upon us. What can it be but a heartbreak to bring up a girl for twenty years and more, and think everything of her, and then see her go away and give her whole heart to some one else, and leave us with a smile on her face?' The idea carried me away—it filled my own heart with a sort of sweet bitterness; for had not my own girl just passed that age and crisis? 'Oh! I understand you; I feel with you; I am not unsympathetic. But when one thinks—they must live longer than we; they must have children too, and love as we have loved. You would not like, neither you nor I, if no one cared—if our girls were left out when all the others are loved and courted. You like this good John to be fond of her—to ask you for her. You would not have been pleased if Ellen had just lived on and on here, your daughter and nothing more.'

This argument had some weight upon her. She felt the truth of what I said. However hard the after consequences may be, we still must have our 'bairn respectit like the lave.' But on this point Mrs. Harwood maintained her position on a height of superiority which few ordinary mortals, even when the mothers of attractive girls, can attain. 'I have never made any objection,' she said, 'to his coming in the evening. Sometimes it is rather inconvenient; but I do not oppose his being here every night.'

'And you expect him to be content with this all his life?'

'It would be better to say all my life,' she replied severely; 'no, not even that. As for me, it does not matter much. I am not one to put myself in anybody's way; but all her father's life—which can't be very long now,' she added, with a sudden gush of tears. They were so near the surface that they flowed at the slightest touch, and besides, they were a great help to her argument. 'I don't think it is too much,' she cried, 'that she should see her poor father out first. She has been the only one that has cheered him up. She is company to him, which I am not. All his troubles are mine, you see. I feel it when his rheumatism is bad; but Ellen is outside: she can talk and be bright. What should I do without her! What should I do without her! I should be nothing better than a slave! I am afraid to think of it; and her father—her poor father—it would break his heart; it would kill him. I know that it would kill him,' she said.

Here I must acknowledge that I was very wicked. I could not but think in my heart that it would not be at all a bad thing if Ellen's marriage did kill this unseen father of hers who had tired their patience so long, and who stamped his foot with rage at the idea that the poor girl might get out of his clutches. He was an old man, and he was a great sufferer. Why should he be so anxious to live? And if a sacrifice was necessary, old Mr. Harwood might just as well be the one to make it as those two good young people from whom he was willing to take all the pleasure of their lives. But this of course was a sentiment to which I dared not give utterance. We stood and looked at each other while these thoughts were going through my mind. She felt that she had produced an impression, and was too wise to say anything more to diminish it—while I, for my part, was silenced, and did not know what to say.

'Then they must give in again,' I said at last. 'They must part; and if she has to spend the rest of her life in giving music lessons, and he to go away, to lose heart and forget her, and be married by any one who will have him in his despair and loneliness—I hope you will think that a satisfactory conclusion—but I do not. I do not!'

Mrs. Harwood trembled as she looked at me. Was I hard upon her? She shrank aside as if I had given her a blow. 'It is not me that will part them,' she said. 'I have never objected. Often it is very inconvenient— you would not like it yourself if every evening, good or bad, there was a strange man in your house. But I never made any objection. He is welcome to come as long as he likes. It is not me that says a word—'

'Do you want him to throw up his appointment?' I cried, 'his means of life.'

She looked at me with her face set. I might have noticed, had I chosen, that all the flowers in her cap were shaking and quivering in the shadow cast upon the further wall by the sunshine, but did not care to remark, being angry, this sign of emotion. 'If he is so fond of Ellen, he will not mind giving up a chance,' she said; 'if some one must give in, why should it be Harwood and me?'

After this I left Pleasant Place hurriedly, with a great deal of indignation in my mind. Even then I was not quite sure of my right to be indignant; but I was so. 'If some one must give in, why should it be Harwood and me?' I said to myself that John had known what he would encounter, that he had been right in distrusting himself; but he had not been right in trusting me. I had made no stand against the other side. When you come to haggle about it, and to be uncertain which should give in, how painful the complications of life become! To be perfect, renunciation must be without a word; it must be done as if it were the most natural thing in the world. The moment it is discussed and shifted from one to another, it becomes vulgar, like most things in this universe. This was what I said to myself as I came out into the fresh air and sunshine, out of the little stuffy house. I began to hate it with its dingy carpets and curtains, its horsehair chairs, that shabby, shabby little parlour—how could anybody think of it as home? I can understand a bright little kitchen, with white hearth and floor, with the firelight shining in all the pans and dishes. But this dusty place with its antimacassars! These thoughts were in my mind when, turning the corner, I met Ellen full in the face, and felt like a traitor, as if I had been speaking ill of her. She looked at me, too, with some surprise. To see me there, coming out of Pleasant Place, startled her. She did not ask me, Where have you been? but her eyes did, with a bewildered gleam.

'Yes; I have been to see your mother,' I said; 'you are quite right, Ellen. And why? Because I am so much interested; and I wanted to see what mind she was in about your marriage.'

'My—marriage! there never was any question of that,' she said quickly, with a sudden flush.

'You are just as bad as the others,' said I, moved by this new contradiction. 'What! after taking that poor young man's devotion for so long, you will let him go away—go alone, break off everything.'

Ellen had grown pale as suddenly as she had blushed. 'Is that necessary?' she said, alarmed. 'Break off everything? I never thought of that. But, indeed, I think you are making a mistake. If he goes, we shall have to part, but only—only for a time.'

'How can you tell,' I cried, being highly excited, 'how long he may be there? He may linger out his life there, always thinking about you, and longing for you—unless he gets weary and disgusted, and asks himself what is the use, at the last. Such things have been; and you on your side will linger here, running out and in to your lessons with no longer any heart for them; unable to keep yourself from thinking that everybody is cruel, that life itself is cruel—all because you have not the courage, the spirit—'

She put her hand on mine and squeezed it suddenly, so that she hurt me. 'Don't!' she cried; 'you don't know; there is nothing, not a word to be said. It is you who are cruel—you who are so kind; so much as to speak of it, when it cannot be! It cannot be—that is the whole matter. It is out of the question. Supposing even that I get to think life cruel, and supposing he should get weary and disgusted. Oh! it was you that said it, you that are so kind. Supposing all that, yet it is impossible; it cannot be; there is nothing more to be said.'

'You will see him go away calmly, notwithstanding all?'

'Calmly,' she said, with a little laugh, 'calmly—yes, I suppose that is the word. I will see him go calmly. I shall not make any fuss if that is what you mean.'

'Ellen, I do not understand. I never heard you speak like this before.'

'You never saw me like this before,' she said with a gasp. She was breathless with a restrained excitement which looked like despair. But when I spoke further, when I would have discussed the matter, she put up her hand and stopped me. There was something in her face, in its fixed expression, which was like the countenance with which her mother had replied to me. It was a startling thought to me that Ellen's soft fresh face, with its pretty bloom, could ever be like that other face surmounted by the black cap and crown of shabby flowers. She turned and walked with me along the road to my own door, but nothing further was said. We went along side by side silent till we reached my house, when she put out her hand and touched mine suddenly, and said that she was in a hurry and must run away. I went in more disturbed than I can say. She had always been so ready to yield, so cheerful, so soft, independent indeed, but never harsh in her independence. What did this change mean? I felt as if some one to whom I had turned in kindness had met me with a blow. But by and by, when I thought better of it, I began to understand Ellen. Had not I said to myself, a few minutes before, that self-renunciation, when it had to be, must be done silently without a word? better perhaps that it should be done angrily than with self-demonstration, self-assertion. Ellen had comprehended this; she had perceived that it must not be asked or speculated upon, which was to yield. She had chosen her part, and she would not have it discussed or even remarked. I sat in my window pondering while the bright afternoon went by, looking out upon the distant depths of the blue spring atmosphere, just touched by haze, as the air, however bright, always is in London, seeing the people go by in an endless stream without noticing them, without thinking of them. How rare it is in human affairs that there is not some one who must give up to the others, some one who must sacrifice himself or be sacrificed! And the one to whom this lot falls is always the one who will do it; that is the rule so far as my observation goes. There are some whom nature moves that way, who cannot stand upon their rights, who are touched by the claims of others and can make no resistance on their own account. The tools are to him that can handle them, as our philosopher says; and likewise the sacrifices of life to him who will bear them. Refuse them, that is the only way; but if it is not in your nature to refuse them, what can you do? Alas! for sacrifice is seldom blessed. I am saying something which will sound almost impious to many. Human life is built upon it, and social order; yet personally in itself it is seldom blessed; it debases those who accept it; it harms even those who, without wilfully accepting it, have a dim perception that something is being done for them which has no right to be done. It may, perhaps—I cannot tell—bear fruit of happiness in the hearts of those who practise it. I cannot tell. Sacrifices are as often mistaken as other things. Their divineness does not make them wise. Sometimes, looking back, even the celebrant will perceive that his offering had better not have been made.

All this was going sadly through my mind when I perceived that some one was passing slowly, endeavouring to attract my attention. By this time it was getting towards evening—and as soon as I was fully roused I saw that it was John Ridgway. If I could have avoided him I should have done so, but now it was not possible; I made him a sign to come up-stairs. He came into the drawing-room slowly, with none of the eagerness that there had been in his air on the previous day, and it may easily be believed that on my side I was not eager to see him to tell him my story. He came and sat down by me, swinging his stick in his usual absent way, and for a minute neither of us spoke.

'You do not ask me if I have any news for you; you have seen Ellen!'

'No; it is only because I have news on my side. I am not going after all.'

'You are not going!'

'You are disappointed,' he said, looking at me with a face which was full of interest and sympathy. These are the only words I can use. The disappointment was his, not mine; yet he was more sympathetic with my feeling about it than impressed by his own. 'As for me, I don't seem to care. It is better in one way, if it is worse in another. It stops any rise in life; but what do I care for a rise in life? they would never have let me take Ellen. I knew that even before I saw it in your eyes.'

'Ellen ought to judge for herself,' I said, 'and you ought to judge for yourself; you are of full age; you are not boy and girl. No parents have a right to separate you now. And that old man may go on just the same for the next dozen years.'

'Did you see him?' John asked. He had a languid, wearied look, scarcely lifting his eyes.

'I saw only her; but I know perfectly well what kind of man he is. He may live for the next twenty years. There is no end to these tyrannical, ill-tempered people; they live for ever. You ought to judge for yourselves. If they had their daughter settled near, coming to them from her own pleasant little home, they would be a great deal happier. You may believe me or not, but I know it. Her visits would be events; they would be proud of her, and tell everybody about her family, and what a good husband she had got, and how he gave her everything she could desire.'

'Please God,' said John, devoutly; his countenance had brightened in spite of himself. But then he shook his head. 'If we had but got as far as that,' he said.

'You ought to take it into your own hands,' cried I in all the fervour of a revolutionary. 'If you sacrifice your happiness to them, it will not do them any good; it will rather do them harm. Are you going now to tell your news?'

He had got up on his feet, and stood vaguely hovering over me with a faint smile upon his face. 'She will be pleased,' he said; 'no advancement, but no separation. I have not much ambition; I think I am happy too.'

'Then, if you are all pleased,' I cried, with annoyance which I could not restrain, 'why did you send me on such an errand? I am the only one that seems to be impatient of the present state of affairs, and it is none of my business. Another time you need not say anything about it to me.'

'There will never be a time when we shall not be grateful to you,' said John; but even his mild look of appealing reproach did not move me. It is hard to interest yourself in people and find after all that they like their own way best.

CHAPTER VI

He was quite right in thinking Ellen would be pleased. And yet, after it was all over, she was a little wounded and disappointed, which was very natural. She did not want him to go away, but she wanted him to get the advancement all the same. This was foolish, but still it was natural, and just what a woman would feel. She took great pains to explain to us that it was not hesitation about John, nor even any hesitation on the part of John in going—for Ellen had a quick sense of what was desirable and heroic, and would not have wished her lover to appear indifferent about his own advancement, even though she was very thankful and happy that in reality he was so. The reason of the failure was that the firm had sent out a nephew, who was in the office, and had a prior claim. 'Of course he had the first chance,' Ellen said, with a countenance of great seriousness; 'what would be the good of being a relation if he did not have the first chance?' And I assented with all the gravity in the world. But she was disappointed, though she was so glad. There ought not to have been any one in the world who had the preference over John! She carried herself with great dignity for some time afterwards, and with the air of a person superior to the foolish and partial judgments of the world; and yet in her heart how thankful she was! from what an abyss of blank loneliness and weary exertion was her life saved! For now that I knew it a little better I could see how little that was happy was in her home. Her mother insisted that she should have that hour's leisure in the evening. That was all that any one thought of doing for her. It was enough to keep her happy, to keep her hopeful. But without that, how long would Ellen's brave spirit have kept up? Perhaps had she never known John, and that life of infinite tender communion, her natural happy temperament would have struggled on for a long time against all the depressing effects of circumstances, unaided. But to lose is worse than never to have had. If it is

Better to have loved and lost,
Than never to have loved at all,

yet it is at the same time harder to lose that bloom of existence out of your lot, than to have struggled on by mere help of nature without it. She had been so happy—making so little go such a long way!—that the loss of her little happiness would have been appalling to her. And yet she was dissatisfied that this heartbreak did not come. She had strung herself up to it. It would have been advancement, progress, all that a woman desires for those belonging to her, for John. Sacrificing him for the others, she was half angry not to have it in her power to sacrifice herself to his 'rise in life.' I think I understood her, though we never talked on the subject. She was dissatisfied, although she was relieved. We have all known these mingled feelings.

This happened at the beginning of summer; but all its agitations were over before the long sweet days and endless twilights of the happy season had fully expanded upon us. It seems to me as I grow older that a great deal of the comfort of our lives depends upon summer—upon the weather, let us say, taking it in its most prosaic form. Sometimes indeed to the sorrowful the brightness is oppressive; but to all the masses of ordinary mortals who are neither glad nor sad, it is a wonderful matter not to be chilled to the bone; to be able to do their work without thinking of a fire; without having a sensation of cold always in their lives never to be got rid of. Ellen and her lover enjoyed that summer as people who have been under sentence of banishment enjoy their native country and their home.

You may think there is not much beauty in a London suburb to tempt any one: and there is not for those who can retire to the beautiful fresh country when they will, and surround themselves with waving woods and green lawns, or taste the freshness of the mountains or the saltness of the sea. We, who go away every year in July, pined and longed for the moment of our removal; and my neighbour in the great house which shut out the air from Pleasant Place, panted in her great garden (which she was proud to think was almost unparalleled for growth and shade in London), and declared herself incapable of breathing any longer in such a close and shut up locality. But the dwellers in Pleasant Place were less exacting. They thought the long suburban road very pleasant. Where it streamed off into little dusty houses covered with brown ivy and dismal trellis work, and where every unfortunate flower was thick with dust, they gazed with a touch of envy at the 'gardens,' and felt it to be rural. When my pair of lovers went out for their walk they had not time to go further than to the 'Green Man,' a little tavern upon the roadside, where one big old elm tree, which had braved the dust and the frost for more years than any one could recollect, stood out at a corner at the junction of two roads, with a bench round it, where the passing carters and cabmen drank their beer, and a trough for the horses, which made it look 'quite in the country' to all the inhabitants of our district. Generally they got as far as that, passing the dusty cottages and the little terrace of new houses. A great and prolonged and most entertaining controversy went on between them as they walked, as to the kind of house in which they should eventually settle down. Ellen, who was not without a bit of romance in her, of the only kind practicable with her upbringing, entertained a longing for one of the dusty little cottages. She thought, like all inexperienced persons, that in her hands it would not be dusty. She would find means of keeping the ivy green. She would see that the flowers grew sweet and clean, and set blacks and dust alike at defiance. John, for his part, whose lodging was in one of those little houses, preferred the new terrace. It was very new—very like a row of ginger-bread houses—but it was very clean, and for the moment bright, not as yet penetrated by the dust. Sometimes I was made the confidante of these interminable, always renewed, always delightful discussions. 'They are not dusty yet,' Ellen would say, 'but how long will it be before they are dusty? whereas with the villas' (they had a great variety of names—Montpellier Villas, Funchal Villas, Mentone Mansions—for the district was supposed to be very mild) 'one knows what one has to expect; and if one could not keep the dust and the blacks out with the help of brushes and dusters, what would be the good of one? I should sow mignonette and Virginia stock,' she cried with a firm faith; 'low-growing flowers would be sure to thrive. It is only roses (poor roses!) and tall plants that come to harm.' John, for his part, dwelt much upon the fact that in the little front parlours of the terrace houses there were shelves for books fitted into a recess. This weighed quite as much with him as the cleanness of the new places. 'The villas are too dingy for her,' he said, looking admiringly at her fresh face. 'She could never endure the little gray, grimy rooms.' That was his romance, to think that everything should be shining and bright about her. He was unconscious of the dinginess of the parlour in Ellen's home. It was all irradiated with her presence to him. These discussions however all ended in a sigh and a laugh from Ellen herself. 'It is all very fine talking,' she would say.

And so the summer went on. Alas! and other summers after it. My eldest girl married. My boys went out into the world. Many changes came upon our house. The children began to think it a very undesirable locality. Even Chatty, always the sweetest, sighed for South Kensington, if not for a house in the country and a month in London in the season, which was what the other girls wished for. This common suburban road, far from fashion, far from society—what but their mother's inveterate old-fashionedness and indifference to appearances could have kept them there so long? The great house opposite with the garden had ceased to be. The high wall was gone from Pleasant Place, and instead of it stood a fresh row of little villakins like the terrace which had once been John Ridgway's admiration. Alas! Ellen's forebodings had been fully realized, and the terrace was as dingy as Montpellier Villas by this time. The whole neighbourhood was changing. Half the good houses in the road—the houses, so to speak, of the aristocracy, which to name was to command respect from all the neighbourhood—had been built out and adorned with large fronts of plate glass and made into shops. Omnibuses now rolled along the dusty way. The station where they used to stop had been pushed out beyond the 'Green Man,' which once we had felt to be 'quite in the country.' Everything was changing; but my pair of lovers did not change. Ellen got other pupils instead of Chatty and her contemporaries who were growing up and beyond her skill, and came out at ten o'clock every morning with as fresh a face as ever, and her little roll of music always in her hand. And every evening, though now he was set down at his lodgings from the omnibus, and no longer passed my window on his way home, John made his pilgrimage of love to Pleasant Place. She kept her youth—the sweet complexion, the dew in her eyes, and the bloom upon her cheek—in a way I could not understand. The long waiting did not seem to try her. She had always his evening visit to look for, and her days were full of occupation. But John, who had naturally a worn look, did not bear the probation so well as Ellen. He grew bald; a general rustiness came over him. He had looked older than he was to begin with: his light locks, his colourless countenance, faded into a look of age. He was very patient—almost more patient than Ellen, who, being of a more vivacious temper, had occasioned little outbursts of petulant despair, of which she was greatly ashamed afterwards; but at the same time this prolonged and hopeless waiting had more effect upon him than upon her. Sometimes he would come to see me by himself for the mere pleasure, it seemed to me, though we rarely spoke on the subject, of being understood.

'Is this to go on for ever?' I said. 'Is it never to come to an end?'

'It looks like it,' said John, somewhat drearily. 'We always talk about our little house. I have got three rises since then. I doubt if I shall ever have any more; but we don't seem a bit nearer—' and he ended with a sigh—not of impatience, like those quick sighs mixed up with indignant, abrupt little laughs in which Ellen often gave vent to her feelings—but of weariness and despondency much more hard to bear.

'And the father,' I said, 'seems not a day nearer the end of his trouble. Poor man, I don't wish him any harm.'

This, I fear, was a hypocritical speech, for in my heart I should not have been at all sorry to hear that his 'trouble' was coming to an end.

Then for the first time a gleam of humour lighted in John's eye. 'I am beginning to suspect that he is—better,' he said; 'stronger at least. I am pretty sure he has no thought of coming to an end.'

'All the better,' I said; 'if he gets well, Ellen will be free.'

'He will never get well,' said John, falling back into his dejection, 'and he will never die.'

'Then it will never come to anything. Can you consent to that?' I said.

He made me no reply. He shook his head; whether in dismal acceptance of the situation, whether in protest against it, I cannot tell. This interview filled me with dismay. I spent hours pondering whether, and how, I could interfere. My interference had not been of much use before. And my children began to laugh when this lingering, commonplace little romance was talked of. 'My mother's lovers,' the boys called them—'My mother's turtle-doves.'

The time had almost run on to the length of Jacob's wooing when one day Ellen came to me, not running in, eager and troubled with her secret as of old, but so much more quietly than usual, with such a still and fixed composure about her, that I knew something serious had happened. I sent away as quickly as I could the other people who were in the room, for I need not say that to find me alone was all but an impossibility. I gave Chatty, now a fine, tall girl of twenty, a look, which was enough for her; she always understood better than any one. And when at last we were free I turned to my visitor anxiously. 'What is it?' I said. It did not excite her so much as it did me.

She gave a little abstracted smile. 'You always see through me,' she said. 'I thought there was no meaning in my face. It has come at last. He is really going this time, directly, to the Levant. Oh, what a little thing Chatty was when I asked her to look in the atlas for the Levant; and now she is going to be married! What will you do,' she asked abruptly, stopping short to look at me, 'when they are all married and you are left alone?'

I had asked myself this question sometimes, and it was not one I liked. '"Sufficient unto the day is the evil thereof,"' I said; 'the two little ones of all have not so much as thought of marrying yet.'

Ellen answered me with a sigh, a quickly drawn impatient breath. 'He is to sail in a fortnight,' she said. 'Things have gone wrong with the nephew. I knew he never could be so good as John; and now John must go in a hurry to set things right. What a good thing that it is all in a hurry! We shall not have time to think.'

'You must go with him—you must go with him, Ellen!' I cried.

She turned upon me almost with severity in her tone. 'I thought you knew better. I—go with him! Look here,' she cried very hurriedly, 'don't think I don't face the full consequences—the whole matter. He is tired, tired to death. He will be glad to go—and after—after! If he should find some one else there, I shall never be the one to blame him.'

'Ellen! you ought to ask his pardon on your knees—he find some one else! What wrong you do to the faithfullest—the truest—'

'He is the faithfullest,' she said; then, after a moment, 'but I will never blame him. I tell you beforehand. He has been more patient than ever man was.'

Did she believe what she was saying? It was very hard to know. The fortnight flew by like a day. The days had been very long before in their monotony, but now these two weeks were like two hours. I never quite knew what passed. John had taken his courage in both hands, and had bearded the father himself in his den: but, so far as I could make out, it was not the father but the mother with her tears who vanquished him. 'When I saw what her life was,' he said to me when he took leave of me, 'such a life! my mouth was closed. Who am I that I should take away her only comfort from her? We love each other very dearly, it is our happiness, it is the one thing which makes everything else sweet: but perhaps, as Ellen says, there is no duty in it. It is all enjoyment. Her duty is to them; it is her pleasure, she says, her happiness to be with me.'

'But—but you have been engaged for years. No doubt it is your happiness—but surely there is duty too.'

'She says not. My mind is rather confused. I don't seem to know. Duty, you know, duty is a thing that it is rather hard to do; something one has to raise one's self up to, and carry through with it, whether we like it or whether we don't like it. That's her definition; and it seems right—don't you think it is right? But to say that of us would be absurd. It is all pleasure—all delight,' his tired eyelids rose a little to show a gleam of emotion, then dropped again with a sigh; 'that is her argument; I suppose it is true.'

'Then, do you mean to say—' I cried, and stopped short in sheer bewilderment of mind, not knowing what words to use.

'I don't think I mean to say anything. My head is all confused. I don't seem to know. Our feeling is all one wish to be together; only to see one another makes us happy. Can there be duty in that? she says. It seems right, yet sometimes I think it is wrong, though I can't tell how.'

I was confused too and silenced. I did not know what to say. 'It depends,' I said faltering, 'upon what you consider the object of life.'

'Some people say happiness; but that would not suit Ellen's theory,' he said. 'Duty—I had an idea myself that duty was easily defined; but it seems it is as difficult as everything is. So far as I can make out,' he added with a faint smile, 'I have got no duties at all.'

'To be faithful to her,' I said, recollecting the strange speech she had made to me.

He almost laughed outright. 'Faithful! that is no duty; it is my existence. Do you think I could be unfaithful if I were to try?'

These were almost the last words he said to me. I suppose he satisfied himself that his duty to his employer required him to go away. And Ellen had a feverish desire that he should go away, now that the matter had been broached a second time. I am not sure that when the possibility of sacrifice on his part dawned upon her, the chance that he might relinquish for her this renewed chance of rising in the world, there did not arise in her mind a hasty impatient wish that he might be unfaithful, and give her up altogether. Sometimes the impatience of a tired spirit will take this form. Ellen was very proud; by dint of having made sacrifices all her life, she had an impetuous terror of being in her turn the object for which sacrifices should be made. To accept them was bitterness to her. She was eager to hurry all his preparations, to get him despatched, if possible, a little earlier than the necessary time. She kept a cheerful face, making little jokes about the Levant and the people he would meet there, which surprised everybody. 'Is she glad that he is going? Chatty asked me, with eyes like two round lamps of alarmed surprise. The last night of all they spent with us—and it seemed a relief to Ellen that it should be thus spent, and not tête-à-tête as so many other evenings had been. It was the very height and flush of summer, an evening which would not sink into darkness and night as other evenings do. The moon was up long before the sun had gone reluctantly away. We sat without the lamp in the soft twilight, with the stream of wayfarers going past the windows, and all the familiar sounds, which were not vulgar to us, we were so used to them. They were both glad of the half light. When I told Ellen to go and sing to us, she refused at first with a look of reproach; then, with a little shake of her head, as if to throw off all weakness, changed her mind and went to the piano. It was Chatty who insisted upon Mr. Ridgway's favourite song, perhaps out of heedlessness, perhaps with that curious propensity the young often have to probe wounds and investigate how deep a sentiment may go. We sat in the larger room, John and myself, while behind, in the dim evening, in the distance, scarcely visible, Ellen sat at the piano and sang. What the effort cost her I would not venture to inquire. As for him, he sat with melancholy composure listening to every tone of her voice. She had a very sweet refined voice—not powerful, but tender, what people call sympathetic. I could not distinguish his face, but I saw his hand beat the measure accompanying every line, and when she came to the burden of the song he said it over softly to himself. Broken by all the babble outside, and by the music in the background, I yet heard him, all tuneless and low, murmuring this to himself: 'I will come again, I will come again, my sweet and bonnie.' Whether his eyes were dry I cannot tell, but mine were wet. He said them with no excitement, as if they were the words most simple, most natural—the very breathing of his heart. How often, I wonder, would he think of that dim room, the half-seen companions, the sweet and tender voice rising out of the twilight? I said to myself, 'Whoever may mistrust you, I will never mistrust you,' with fervour. But just as the words passed through my mind, as if Ellen had heard them, her song broke off all in a moment, died away in the last line, 'I will come a—' There was a sudden break, a jar on the piano—and she sprang up and came towards us, stumbling, with her hands put out, as it she could not see. The next sound I heard was an unsteady little laugh, as she threw herself down on a sofa in the corner where Chatty was sitting. 'I wonder why you are all so fond of that old-fashioned nonsense,' she said.

And next day the last farewells were said, and John went away.

CHAPTER VII

We left town directly after this for the autumn holidays. The holidays had not very much meaning now that all the boys had left school, and we might have gone away when we pleased. But the two youngest girls were still in the remorseless hands of Fräulein Stimme, and the habit of emancipation in the regular holiday season had clung to me. I tried very hard to get Ellen to go with us, for at least a day or two, but she resisted with a kind of passion. Her mother, I am sure, would have been glad had she gone; but Ellen would not. There was in her face a secret protestation, of which she was perhaps not even herself aware, that if her duty bound life itself from all expansion, it must also bind her in every day of her life. She would not accept the small alleviation, having, with her eyes open and with a full sense of what she was about, resigned everything else. She would have been more perfect, and her sacrifice more sweet, had she taken sweetly the little consolations of every day; but nobody is perfect, and Ellen would not come. I had gone to Pleasant Place to ask her, and the scene was a curious one. The mother and daughter both came to the parlour to receive me, and I saw them together for the first time. It was about a fortnight after John went away. Ellen had not been ill, though I had feared she would; but she was pale, with dark lines under her eyes, and a worn and nervous look. She was bearing her burden very bravely, but it was all the harder upon her that she was evidently determined not to complain. When I told my errand, Mrs. Harwood replied eagerly. 'You must go, Ellen. Oh, yes! I can do; I can do very well. It will only be for a week, and it will do you so much good; you must go.' Ellen took scarcely any notice of this address. She thanked me with her usual smile. 'It is very, very good of you—you are always good— but it is impossible.' 'Why impossible, why impossible?' cried her mother. 'When I tell you I can do very well—I can manage. Your father will not mind, when it is to do you good.' I saw that Ellen required a moment's interval of preparation before she looked round.

'Dear mother,' she said, 'we have not any make-believes between us, have we? How is it possible that I can go? Every moment is mapped out. No, no; I cannot do it. Thank you all the same. My mother wants to give me a pleasure, but it cannot be. Go away for a week! I have never done that in all my life.'

'But you think she can, you think she ought,' I said, turning to her mother. The poor woman looked at her child with a piteous look. I think it dawned upon her, then and there, for the first time, that perhaps she had made a mistake about Ellen. It had not occurred to her that there had been any selfishness in her tearful sense of the impossibility of parting with her daughter. All at once, in a moment, with a sudden gleam of that enlightenment which so often comes too late, she saw it. She saw it, and it went through her like an arrow. She turned to me with another piteous glance. What have I done? what have I done? her looks seemed to say.

'Two or three days,' the poor woman said, with a melancholy attempt at playfulness. 'Nothing can happen to us in that time. Her father is ill,' she said, turning to me as if I knew nothing, 'and we are always anxious, he thinks it will be too much for me by myself. But what does it matter for a few days? If I am overdone, I can rest when she comes back.'

Was it possible she could suppose that this was all I knew? I was afraid to catch Ellen's eye. I did not know what might come after such a speech. She might break forth with some sudden revelation of all that I felt sure must be in her heart. I closed my eyes instinctively, sick with terror. Next moment I heard Ellen's clear, agreeable voice.

'I don't want you to be overdone, mother. What is the use of all that is past and gone if I am to take holidays and run away when I like for two or three days? No, no; my place is here, and here I must stay. I don't want you to be overdone.'

And looking at her, I saw that she smiled. But her mother's face was full of trouble. She looked from Ellen to me, and from me to Ellen. For everything there is a beginning. Did she only then for the first time perceive what had been done?

However, after this there was nothing more to say. We did not see Ellen again till the days were short and the brilliant weather over. She changed very much during that winter. Her youth, which had bloomed on so long unaltered, seemed to leave her in a day. When we came back, from looking twenty she suddenly looked thirty-five. The bloom went from her cheeks. She was as trim as ever, and as lightfooted, going out alert and bright every morning to her lessons; but her pretty little figure had shrunk, and her very step on the pavement sounded different. Life and all its hopes and anticipations seemed to have ebbed away from her. I don't doubt that many of her neighbours had been going on in their dull routine of life without knowing even such hopes or prospects as hers, all this time by Ellen's side, fulfilling their round of duty without any diversions. Oh, the mystery of these myriads of humble lives, which are never enlivened even by a romance manqué, a story that might have been; that steal away from dull youth to dull age, never knowing anything but the day's work, never coming to anything! But Ellen had known a something different, a life that was her own; and now she had lost it. The effect was great: how could it be otherwise? She lost herself altogether for a little while, and when she came to again, as all worthy souls must come, she was another Ellen; older than her age as the other had been younger, and prepared for everything. No longer trying to evade suffering; rather desirous, if that might be, to forestall it, to discount it—if I may use the word—before it was due, and know the worst. She never told me this in words, but I felt that it was so. It is not only in a shipwreck that the unfortunate on the verge of death plunge in to get it over a few hours, a few minutes, sooner. In life there are many shipwrecks which we would forestall, if we could, in the same way, by a plunge—by a voluntary putting on of the decisive moment. Some, I suppose, will always put it off by every expedient that despair can suggest; but there are also those who can bear anything but to wait, until slowly, surely, the catastrophe comes. Ellen wanted to make the plunge, to get it over, partly for John's sake, whose infidelity she began to calculate upon—to (she believed) wish for. 'He will never be able to live without a home to go to, without a woman to speak to, now,' she said once, in a moment of incaution—for she was very guarded, very reticent, about all this part of her mind, and rarely betrayed herself. It is curious how little faith women in general, even the most tender, have in a man's constancy. Either it is because of an inherent want of trust in their own power to secure affection, which might be called humility; or else it is quite the reverse—a pride of sex too subtle to show, in any conscious way—overweening confidence in the power over a man of any other woman who happens to be near him, and want of confidence in any power on his part to resist these fascinations. Ellen had made up her mind that her lover when he was absent from her would be, as she would have said, 'like all the rest.' Perhaps, in a kind of wild generosity, she wished it, feeling that she herself never might be free to make him happy; but, anyhow, she was persuaded that this was how it would be. She looked out for signs of it in his very first letter. She wanted to have it over—to cut off remorselessly out of her altered being all the agitations of hope.

But I need not say that John's letters were everything a lover's, or rather a husband's letters should be. They were more like a husband's letters, with very few protestations in them, but a gentle continued reference to her, and to their past life together, which was more touching than any rhapsodies. She brought them to me often, folding down, with a blush which made her look like the blooming Ellen of old, some corner of especial tenderness, something that was too sacred for a stranger's eye, but always putting them back in her pocket with a word which sounded almost like a grudge, as who should say, 'For this once all is well, but next time you shall see.' Thus she held on to her happiness as by a strained thread, expecting every moment when it would snap, and defying it to do so, yet throbbing all the time with a passion of anxiety, as day after day it held out, proving her foreboding vain. That winter, though I constantly saw her, my mind was taken up by other things than Ellen. It was then that the children finally prevailed upon me to leave the Road. A row of cheap advertising shops had sprung up facing us where had been the great garden I have so often mentioned, and the noise and flaring lights were more than I could put up with, after all my resistance to their wishes. So that at last, to my great regret, but the exultation of the young ones, it was decided that we must go away.

The removal, and the bustle there was, the change of furniture—for our old things would not do for the new house, and Chatty, Heaven save us! had grown artistic, and even the little ones and Fräulein Stimme knew a great deal better than I did—occupied my mind and my time; and it took a still longer time to settle down than it did to tear up our old roots. So that there was a long interval during which we saw little of Ellen; and though we never forgot her, or ceased to take an interest in everything that concerned her, the distance of itself threw us apart. Now and then she paid us a visit, always with John's letter in her pocket, but her time was so limited that she never could stay long. And sometimes I, and sometimes Chatty, made a pilgrimage to the old district to see her. But we never could have an uninterrupted long talk in Pleasant Place. Either Ellen was called away, or Mrs. Harwood would come in and sit down with her work, always anxiously watching her daughter. This separation from the only people to whom she could talk of her own private and intimate concerns was a further narrowing and limitation of poor Ellen's life. But what could I do? I could not vex my children for her sake. She told us that she went and looked at the old house almost every day, and at the square window in which I used to sit and see John pass. John passed no longer, nor was I there to see. But Ellen remained bound in the same spot, seeing everything desert her—love, and friendship, and sympathy, and all her youth and her hope. Can you not fancy with what thoughts this poor girl (though she was a girl no longer) would pause, as she passed, to look at the abandoned place so woven in with the brightest episode of her life, feeling herself stranded there, impotent, unable to make a step—her breast still heaving with all the vigour of existence, yet her life bound down in the narrowest contracted circle? Her mother, who had got to watch her narrowly, told me afterwards that she always knew when Ellen had passed No. 16; and indeed I myself was rather glad to hear that at length No. 16 had shared the general fate, that my window existed no longer, and that a great shop with plate-glass windows was bulging out where our house had been. Better when a place is desecrated that it should be desecrated wholly, and leave no vestige of its old self at all.

Thus more than a year glided away, spring and winter, summer and autumn, and then winter again. Chatty came in one November morning, when London was half invisible, wrapped in mist and fog, with a very grave face, to tell me that she had met Ellen, and Ellen had told her there was bad news from John. 'I can't understand her,' Chatty said. 'I couldn't make out what it was; that business had been bad, and things had gone wrong; and then something with a sort of laugh that he had got other thoughts in his mind at last, as she knew all along he would, and that she was glad. What could she mean?' I did not know what she could mean, but I resolved to go and see Ellen to ascertain what the change was. It is easier however to say than to do when one is full of one's own affairs, and so it happened that for a full week, though intending to go every day, I never did so. It was partly my fault. The family affairs were many, and the family interests engrossing. It was not that I cared for Ellen less, but my own claimed me on every hand. When one afternoon, about a fortnight after, I was told that Miss Harwood was in the drawing-room and wished to speak to me, my heart upbraided me with my neglect. I hurried to her and led her away from that public place where everybody came and went, to my own little sitting-room, where we might be alone. Ellen was very pale; her eyes looked very dry and bright, not dewy and soft as they used to be. There was a feverish look of unrest and excitement about her. 'There is something wrong,' I cried. 'What is it? Chatty told me—something about John.'

'I don't know that it is anything wrong,' she said. The smile that had frightened Chatty came over her face—a smile that made one unhappy, the lip drawn tightly over the teeth in the most ghastly mockery of amusement. 'No; I don't know that it is anything wrong. You know I always expected—always from the moment he went away—that between him and me things would soon be at an end. Oh, yes, I expected it, and I did not wish it otherwise; for what good is it to me that a man should be engaged to me, and waste his life for me, when I never could do anything for him?'

Here she made a little breathless pause, and laughed. 'Oh, don't, Ellen, don't!' I cried. I could not bear the laugh; the smile was bad enough.

'Why not?' she said with a little defiance; 'would you have me cry? I expected it long ago. The wonder is that it should have been so long coming. That is,' she cried suddenly after a pause, 'that is if this is really what it means. I took it for granted at first; but I cannot be certain. I cannot be certain! Read it, you who know him, and tell me, tell me! Oh, I can bear it quite well. I should be rather glad if this is what it means.'

She thrust a letter into my hand, and going away with a rapid step to the window, stood there with her back to me, looking out. I saw her standing against the light, playing restlessly with the tassel of the blind. In her desire to seem composed, or else in the mere excitement which boiled in her veins, she began to hum a tune. I don't think she knew herself what it was.

The letter which she professed to have taken so easily was worn with much reading, and it had been carried about, folded and refolded a hundred times. There was no sign of indifference in all that—and this is what it said:—

'I got your last letter, dear Ellen, on Tuesday. I think you must have written in low spirits. Perhaps you had a feeling, such as we used to talk about, of what was happening here. As for me, nobody could be in lower spirits than this leaves me. I have lost heart altogether. Everything has gone wrong; the business is at an end: I shut up the office to-day. If it is in any way my fault, God forgive me! But the conflict in my heart has been so great that I sometimes fear it must be my fault. I had been low enough before, thinking and thinking how the end was to come between you and me. Everything has gone wrong inside and out. I had such confidence, and now it is all going. What I had most faith in has deceived me. I thought I never was the man to change or to fail, and that I could have trusted myself in any circumstances; but it does not seem so. And why should I keep you hanging on when all's wrong with me? I always thought I could redeem it; but it hasn't proved so. You must just give me up, Ellen, as a bad job. Sometimes I have thought you wished it. Where I am to drift to, I can't tell; but there's no prospect of drifting back, or, what I hoped for, sailing back in prosperity to you. You have seen it coming, I can see by your letters, and I think, perhaps, though it seems strange to say so, that you won't mind. I shall not stay here; but I have not made up my mind where to go. Forget a poor fellow that was never worthy to be yours.—JOHN RIDGWAY.'

My hands dropped with the letter in them. The rustle it made was the only sign she could have had that I had read it, or else instinct or inward vision. That instant she turned upon me from the window with a cry of wild suspense: 'Well?'

'I am confounded. I don't know what to think. Ellen, it looks more like guilt to the office than falsehood to you.'

'Guilt—to the office!' Her face blazed up at once in scorching colour. She looked at me in fierce resentment and excitement, stamping her foot. 'Guilt—to the office! How dare you? How dare you?' she cried like a fury. She clenched her hands at me, and looked as if she could have torn me in pieces. 'Whatever he has done,' she cried, 'he has done nothing he had not a right to do. Do you know who you are speaking of? John! You might as well tell me I had broken into your house at night and robbed you. He have anything to blame himself for with the office?—never! nor with any one. What he has done is what he had a right to do—I am the first to say so. He has been wearied out. You said it once yourself, long, long before my eyes were opened; and at last he has done it—and he had a good right!' She stood for one moment before me in the fervour of this fiery address; then, suddenly, she sank and dropped on her knees by my side. 'You think it means that? You see it—don't you see it? He has grown weary, as was so natural. He thought he could trust himself; but it proved different; and then he thought he could redeem it. What can that mean but one thing?—he has got some one else to care for him. There is nothing wrong in that. It is not I that will ever blame him. The only thing was that a horrible doubt came over me this morning—if it should not mean what I thought it did! That is folly, I know; but you, who know him—put away all that about wrong to the office, which is out of the question, and you will see it cannot be anything but one thing.'

'It is not that,' I said.

She clasped her hands, kneeling by my side. 'You always took his part,' she said in a low voice. 'You will not see it.' Why did she tremble so? Did she want to believe it, or not to believe it? I could not understand Ellen. Just then, from the room below, there came a voice singing. It was Chatty's voice, the child whom she had taught, who had been the witness of their wooing. She knew nothing about all this; she did not even know that Ellen was in the house. What so natural as that she should sing the song her mistress had taught her? It was that which Ellen herself had been humming as she stood at the window.

'Listen!' I said. 'You are answered in his own words—"I will come again."'

This was more than Ellen could bear. She made one effort to rise to her feet, to regain her composure; but the music was too much. At that moment I myself felt it to be too much. She fell down at my feet in a passion of sobs and tears.

Afterwards I knew the meaning of Ellen's passionate determination to admit no meaning but one to the letter. She had taken him at his word. In her certainty that this was to happen, she had seen no other interpretation to it, until it was too late. She had never sent any reply; and he had not written again. It was now a month since the letter had been received, and this sudden breaking off of the correspondence had been so far final on both sides. To satisfy myself, I sent to inquire at the office, and found that no blame was attached to John; but that he had been much depressed, unduly depressed, by his failure to remedy the faults of his predecessor, and had left as soon as his accounts were forwarded and all the business details carefully wound up: and had not been heard of more. I compelled, I may say,

Ellen to write, now that it was too late; but her letter was returned to her some time after. He had left the place, and nothing was known of him there; nor could we discover where he had gone.

CHAPTER VIII

This little tragedy, as it appeared to me at the time, made a great impression on my mind. It did not make me ill; that would have been absurd. But still it helped, I suppose, to depress me generally and enhance the effect of the cold that had hung about me so long, and for which the elder ones, taking counsel together, decided that the desire of the younger ones should be gratified, and I should be made to go to Italy for the spring. The girls were wild to go, and my long-continued lingering cold was such a good excuse. For my own part, I was not willing at all; but what can one woman, especially when she is their mother, do against so many? I had to give in and go. I went to see Ellen before we started, and it was a very painful visit. She was still keeping up with a certain defiance of everybody. But in the last two months she had changed wonderfully. For one thing, she had shrank into half her size. She was never anything but a little woman; but now she seemed to me no bigger than a child. And those cheerful, happy brown eyes, which had so triumphed over and smiled at all the privations of life, looked out from two hollow caverns, twice as large as they had ever been before, and with a woeful look that broke one's heart. It was not always that they had this woeful look. When she was conscious of inspection she played them about with an artificial activity as if they had been lanterns, forcing a smile into them which sometimes looked almost like a sneer; but when she forgot that any one was looking at her, then both smile and light went out, and there was in them a woeful doubt and question which nothing could solve. Had she been wrong? Had she misjudged him whom her heart could not forget or relinquish? Was it likely that she could give him up lightly even had he been proved unworthy? And oh, Heaven! was he proved unworthy, or had she done him wrong? This was what Ellen was asking herself, without intermission, for ever and ever; and her mother, on her side, watched Ellen piteously with much the same question in her eyes. Had she, too, made a mistake? Was it possible that she had exacted a sacrifice which she had no right to exact, and in mere cowardice, and fear of loneliness, and desire for love and succour on her own part, spoiled two lives? This question, which was almost identical in both, made the mother and daughter singularly like each other; except that Ellen kept asking her question of the air, which is so full of human sighs, and the sky, whither so many ungranted wishes go up, and the darkness of space, in which is no reply—and the mother asked hers of Ellen, interrogating her countenance mutely all day long, and of every friend of Ellen's who could throw any light upon the question. She stole into the room when Ellen left me for a moment, and whispered, coming close to me, lest the very walls should hear—

'How do you think she is looking? She will not say a word to me about him—not a word. Don't you think she has been too hasty? Oh! I would give everything I have if she would only go with you and look for John, and make it up with him again.'

'I thought you could not spare her,' I said with perhaps some cruelty in my intention. She wrung her hands, and looked piteously in my face.

'You think it is all my fault! I never thought it would come to this; I never thought he would go away. Oh, if I had only let them marry at first! I often think if she had been happy in her own home, coming to see her father every day, it would have been more of a change for him, more company than having her always. Oh! if one could only tell what is going to happen. She might have had a nice family by this time, and the eldest little girl big enough to run in and play at his feet and amuse her grandpa. He always was fond of children. But we'll never see Ellen's children now!' cried the poor woman. 'And you think it is my fault!'

I could not reproach her; her black cap with the flowers, her little woollen shawl about her shoulders, grew tragic as she poured forth her trouble. It was not so dignified as the poet's picture, but yet, like him, she

Saw the unborn faces shine
Beside the never lighted fire;

and with a groan of misery felt herself the slayer of those innocents that had never been. The tragic and the comic mingled in the vision of that 'eldest little girl,' the child who would have amused her grandpa had she been permitted to come into being; but it was all tragic to poor Mrs. Harwood. She saw no laugh, no smile, in the situation anywhere.

We went to Mentone, and stayed there till the bitterness of the winter was over, then moved along that delightful coast, and were in Genoa in April. To speak of that stately city as a commercial town seems insulting—and yet so it is now-a-days. I recognized at once the type I had known in other days when I sat at the window of the hotel and watched the people coming and going. It reminded me of my window in the Road, where, looking out, I saw the respectable City people—clerks like John Ridgway, and merchants of the same cut though of more substantial comfort—wending their way to their business in the morning, and to their suburban homes in the evening. I do not know that I love the commercial world; but I like to see that natural order of life—the man 'going forth unto his work and to his labour until the evening.' The fashion of it is different in a foreign town, but still the life is the same. We changed our quarters however after we had been for some time in that city, so-called of palaces, and were lodged in a suite of rooms very hard to get up to (though the staircase was marble), but very delightful when one was there; rooms which overlooked the high terrace which runs round a portion of the bay between the inns and the quays. I forget what it is called. It is a beautiful promenade, commanding the loveliest view of that most beautiful bay and all that is going on in it. At night, with all its twinkling semicircle of lights, it was a continual enchantment to me; but this or any of my private admirations are not much to the purpose of my story. Sitting at the window, always my favourite post, I became acquainted with various individual figures among those who haunted this terrace. Old gentlemen going out to sun themselves in the morning before the heat was too great; children and nursemaids, Genoese women with their pretty veils, invalids who had got up the stairs, I cannot tell now, and sat panting on the benches, enjoying the sea air and the sunshine. There was one however among this panorama of passing figures, which gave me a startled sense of familiarity. It was too far off to see the man's face. He was not an invalid; but he was bent, either with past sickness or with present care, and walked with a dropping head and a languid step. After watching him for a time, I concluded (having always a great weakness for making out other people's lives, how they flow) that he had some occupation in the town from which he escaped, whenever he had leisure, to rest a little and refresh himself upon the terrace. He came very regularly, just at the time when Italian shops and offices have a way of shutting up, in the middle of the day—very regularly, always, or almost always, at the same hour. He came up the steps slowly and languidly, stopped a little to take breath, and then walked half way round the terrace to a certain bench upon which he always seated himself. Sometimes he brought his luncheon with him and ate it there. At other times, having once gained that place, he sat quite still in a corner of it, not reading, nor taking any notice of the other passers-by. No one was with him, no one ever spoke to him. When I noticed him first he startled me. Who was he like? His bent figure, his languid step, resembled no one I could think of; but yet I said to myself, He is like somebody. I established a little friendship with him, though it was a friendship without any return; for though I could see him he could not see me, nor could I distinguish his face; and we never saw him anywhere else, neither at church, nor in the streets, not even on the festas when everybody was about; but always just there on that one spot. I looked for him as regularly as the day came. 'My mother's old gentleman,' Chatty called him. Everybody is old who is not young to these children; but though he was not young he did not seem to me to be old. And he puzzled as much as he interested me. Who was he like? I never even asked myself, Who was he? It would be no one I had any chance of acquaintance with. Some poor employé in a Genoa office; how should I know him? I could not feel at all sure, when I was cross-examined on the subject, whether I really remembered any one whom he was like; but yet he had startled me more than I can say.

Genoa, where we had friends and family reasons for staying, became very hot as the spring advanced into early summer, and we removed to one of the lovely little towns on the coast at a little distance, Santa Margherita. When we had been settled there for a few days, Chatty came in to me one evening with a pale face. 'I have just seen your old gentleman,' she said. 'I think he must live out here; but I saw by the expression of her eyes that there was more to say. She added after a moment, 'And I know who he is like.'

'Ah! you have seen his face,' I said; and then, before she had spoken, it suddenly flashed on myself in a moment, 'John Ridgway!' I cried.

'Mother,' said Chatty, quite pale, 'I think it is his ghost.'

I went out with her instantly to where she had seen him, and we made some inquiries, but with no success. When I began to think it over, he was not like John Ridgway. He was bent and stooping, whereas John was erect; his head drooped, whereas how well I recollected poor John's head thrown back a little, his hat upon the back of it, his visionary outlook rather to the skies than to the ground. No, no, not like him a bit; but yet it might be his ghost, as Chatty said. We made a great many inquiries, but for the moment with no success, and you may suppose that I watched the passers-by from my window with more devotion than ever. One evening in the sudden nightfall of the Italian skies, when darkness comes all at once, I was seated in my usual place, scarcely seeing however the moving figures outside, though all the population of the place seemed to be out, sitting round the doors, and strolling leisurely along enjoying the heavenly coolness and the breeze from the sea. At the further end of the room Chatty was at the piano, playing to me softly in the dark which she knows is what I like, and now and then striking into some old song such as I love. She was sure to arrive sooner or later at that one with which we now had so many associations; but I was not thinking of the song, nor for the moment of Ellen or her faithful (as I was sure he was still) lover at all. A woman with so many children has always plenty to think of. My mind was busy with my own affairs. The windows were open, and the babble of the voices outside—high pitched, resounding Italian voices, not like the murmur of English—came in to us as the music floated out. All at once, I suddenly woke up from my thinking and my family concerns. In the dusk one figure detached itself from among the others with a start, and came forward slowly with bent head and languid step. Had he never heard that song since he heard Ellen break off, choked with tears unshed, and a despair which had never been revealed? He came quite close under the window where I could see him no longer. I could not see him at all; it was too dark. I divined him. Who could it be but he? Not like John Ridgway, and yet John; his ghost, as Chatty had said.

I did not stop to think what I was to do, but rose up in the dark room where the child was singing, only a voice, herself invisible in the gloom. I don't know whether Chatty saw me go; but, if so, she was inspired unawares by the occasion, and went on with her song. I ran down-stairs and went out softly to the open door of the inn, where there were other people standing about. Then I saw him quite plainly by the light from a lower window. His head was slightly raised towards the place from which the song came. He was very pale in that pale, doubtful light, worn and old and sad; but as he looked up, a strange illumination was on his face. His hand beat the air softly, keeping time. As she came to the refrain his lips began to move as if he were repeating after his old habit those words, 'I will come again.' Then a sudden cloud of pain seemed to come over his face—he shook his head faintly, then bowed it upon his breast.

In a moment I had him by the arm. 'John,' I said in my excitement; 'John Ridgway! we have found you.' For the moment, I believe, he thought it was Ellen who had touched him; his white face seemed to leap into light; then paled again. He took off his hat with his old formal, somewhat shy politeness—'I thought it must be you, madame,' he said. He said 'madame' instead of the old English madam, which he had always used: this little concession to the changed scene was all the difference. He made no mystery about himself, and showed no reluctance to come in with me, to talk as of old. He told me he had a situation in an office in Genoa, and that his health was bad. 'After that fiasco in the Levant, I had not much heart for anything. I took the first thing that was offered,' he said, with his old vague smile; 'for a man must live—till he dies.' 'There must be no question of dying—at your age,' I cried. This time his smile almost came the length of a momentary laugh. He shook his head, but he did not continue the subject He was very silent for some time after. Indeed, he said nothing, except in reply to my questions, till Chatty left, the room and we were alone. Then all at once, in the middle of something I was saying—'Is she—married again?' he said.

'Married—again!'

'It is a foolish question. She was not married to me; but it felt much the same: we had been as one for so long. There must have been some—strong inducement—to make her cast me off so at the end.'

This he said in a musing tone, as if the fact were so certain, and had been turned over in his mind so often that all excitement was gone from it. But after it was said, a gleam of anxiety came into his half-veiled eyes. He raised his heavy, tired eyelids and looked at me. Though he seemed to know all about it, and to be resigned to it when he began to speak, yet it seemed to flash across him, before he ended, that there was an uncertainty—an answer to come from me which would settle it, after all. Then he leaned forward a little, in this sudden sense of suspense, and put his hand to his ear as if he had been deaf, and said 'What?' in an altered tone.

'There is some terrible mistake,' I said. 'I have felt there was a mistake all along. She has lost her hold on life altogether because she believes you to be changed.'

'Changed!' His voice was quite sharp and keen, and had lost its languid tone. 'In what way—in what way? how could I be changed?'

'In the only way that could matter between her and you. She thought, before you left the Levant, that you had got to care for some one else—that you had ceased to care for her. Your letter,' I said, 'your letter!'—half frightened by the way in which he rose, and his threatening, angry aspect—'would bear that interpretation.'

'My letter!' He stood before me for a moment with a sort of feverish, fierce energy; then he began to laugh, low and bitterly, and walk about as if unable to keep still. 'My letter!' The room was scarcely lighted—one lamp upon the table, and no more; and the half-darkness, as he paced about, made his appearance more threatening still. Then he suddenly came and stood before me as if it had been I that had wronged him. 'I am a likely man to be a gay Lothario,' he cried, with that laugh of mingled mockery and despair which was far more tragical than weeping. It was the only expression that such an extreme of feeling could find. He might have cried out to heaven and earth, and groaned and wept; but it would not have expressed to me the wild confusion, the overturn of everything, the despair of being so misunderstood, the miserable sum of suffering endured and life wasted for nothing, like this laugh. Then he dropped again into the chair opposite me, as if with the consciousness that even this excitement was vain.

'What can I say? What can I do? Has she never known me all along?—Ellen!' He had not named her till now. Was it a renewal of life in his heart that made him capable of uttering her name?

'Do not blame her,' I cried. 'She had made up her mind that nothing could ever come of it, and that you ought to be set free. She thought of nothing else but this; that for her all change was hopeless—that she was bound for life; and that you should be free. It became a fixed idea with her; and when your letter came, which was capable of being misread—'

'Then the wish was father to the thought,' he said, still bitterly. 'Did she show it to you? did you misread it also? Poor cheat of a letter! My heart had failed me altogether. Between my failure and her slavery— But I never thought she would take me at my word,' he went on piteously, 'never! I wrote, don't you know, as one writes longing to be comforted, to be told it did not matter so long as we loved each other, to be bidden come home. And there never came a word—not a word.'

'She wrote afterwards, but you were gone; and her letter was returned to her.'

'Ah!' he said, in a sort of desolate assent. 'Ah! was it so? then that was how it had to be, I suppose; things were so settled before ever we met each other. Can you understand that?—all settled that it was to end just so in misery, and confusion, and folly, before ever we met.'

'I do not believe it,' I cried. 'There is no need that it should end so, even now; if—if you are unchanged still.'

'I—changed?' He laughed at this once more, but not so tragically, with sham ridicule of the foolishness of the doubt. And then all of a sudden he began to sing—oh, it was not a beautiful performance! he had no voice, and not much ear; but never has the loveliest music moved me more—'I will come again, my sweet and bonnie: I will come—' Here he broke down as Ellen had done, and said, with a hysterical sob, 'I'm ill; I think I'm dying. How am I, a broken man, without a penny, to come again?'

Chatty and I walked with him to his room through the soft darkness of the Italian night. I found he had fever—the wasting, exhausting ague fever—which haunts the most beautiful coasts in the world. I did my best to reassure him, telling him that it was not deadly, and that at home he would soon be well; but I cannot say that I felt so cheerfully as I spoke, and all that John did was to shake his head. As we turned home again through all the groups of cheerful people, Chatty with her arm clasped in mine, we talked, it is needless to say, of nothing else. But not even to my child did I say what I meant to do. I am not rich, but still I can afford myself a luxury now and then. When the children were in bed I wrote a short letter, and put a cheque in it for twenty pounds. This was what I said. I was too much excited to write just in the ordinary way:—

'Ellen, I have found John, ill, heart-broken, but as faithful and unchanged as I always knew he was. If you have the heart of a mouse in you come out instantly—don't lose a day—and save him. It may be time yet. If he can be got home to English air and to happiness it will still be time.

'I have written to your mother. She will not oppose you, or I am much mistaken. Take my word for all the details. I will expect you by the earliest possibility. Don't write, but come.'

In less than a week after I went to Genoa, and met in the steamboat from Marseilles, which was the quickest way of travelling then, a trembling, large-eyed, worn-out creature, not knowing if she were dead or alive, confused with the strangeness of everything, and the wonderful change in her own life. It was one of John's bad days, and nobody who was not acquainted with the disease would have believed him other than dying. He was lying in a kind of half-conscious state when I took Ellen into his room. She stood behind me clinging to me, undistinguishable in the darkened place. The flush of the fever was going off; the paleness as of death and utter exhaustion stealing over him. His feeble fingers were moving faintly upon the white covering of his bed; his eyelids half shut, with the veins showing blue in them and under his eyes. But there was a faint smile on his face. Wherever he was wandering in those confused fever dreams, he was not unhappy. Ellen held by my arm to keep herself from falling. 'Hope! you said there was hope,' she moaned in my ear, with a reproach that was heart-rending. Then he began to murmur with his almost colourless yet smiling lips, 'I will come again, my sweet and bonnie; I will come—again.' And then the fingers faintly beating time were still.

But no, no! Do not take up a mistaken idea. He was not dead; and he did not die. We got him home after a while. In Switzerland, on our way to England, I had them married safe and fast under my own eye. I would allow no more shilly-shally. And, indeed, it appeared that Mrs. Harwood, frightened by all the results of her totally unconscious domestic despotism, was eager in hurrying Ellen off, and anxious that John should come home. He never quite regained his former health, but he got sufficiently well to take another situation, his former employers anxiously aiding him to recover his lost ground. And they took Montpellier Villa after all, to be near Pleasant Place, where Ellen goes every day, and is, Mrs. Harwood allows, far better company for her father, and a greater relief to the tedium of his life, than when she was more constantly his nurse and attendant. I am obliged to say however that the mother has had a price to pay for the emancipation of the daughter. There is nothing to be got for nought in this life. And sometimes Ellen has a compunction, and sometimes there is an unspoken reproach in the poor old lady's tired eyes. I hope for my own part that when that 'eldest little girl' is a little older Mrs. Harwood's life will be greatly sweetened and brightened. But yet it is she that has to pay the price; for no argument, not even the last severe winter, and many renewed 'attacks,' will persuade that old tyrant, invisible in his upper chamber, to die.

A song needs no story perhaps; but a story is always the better for a song: so that after all I need not perhaps apologize to Beethoven and his interpreters as I meant to do for taking their lovely music as a suggestion of the still greater harmonies of life.

Margaret Oliphant – A Short Biography

Margaret Oliphant Wilson was born on April 4th, 1828 to Francis W. Wilson, a clerk, and Margaret Oliphant, at Wallyford, near Musselburgh, East Lothian.

She spent her childhood at Lasswade, near Dalkeith, Glasgow before moving to Liverpool.

Her youth was spent in establishing a writing style so much so that, in 1849, she had her first novel published: Passages in the Life of Mrs. Margaret Maitland based on the Scottish Free Church movement. It met with some success and was a good start to her career.

Two years later, in 1851, her third book Caleb Field was published. It was also now that she met the publisher William Blackwood in Edinburgh and was asked to contribute to his well-received Blackwood's Magazine. It was to be a lifetimes endeavor. Over the course of the relationship she would have well over 100 articles published.

In May 1852, Margaret married her cousin, Frank Wilson Oliphant, at Birkenhead, and they settled at Harrington Square, Camden, London. He was an artist working primarily in stained glass. With the marriage she became Margaret Oliphant Wilson Oliphant.

Their marriage produced six children but three tragically died in infancy.

When her husband developed signs of the dreaded consumption (tuberculosis) they moved, on the advice of doctors, to warmer climes. In January 1859 it was to Florence, and then to Rome where, sadly, he died.

Margaret was naturally devastated but was also now left without support and only her income from her writing. She returned to England and took up the task of supporting her three remaining children by her literary activity.

By now she was being published both as an established novelist and regularly in Blackwood's Magazine, amongst others. Her incredible and prolific work rate increased both her commercial reputation and the size of her reading audience.

Against this her domestic life continued to be tragic, full of sorrow and disappointment.

In January 1864 her only remaining daughter Maggie died and was buried in her father's grave in Rome. Her brother, who had emigrated to Canada, was shortly afterwards involved in financial ruin. Margaret generously offered a home to him and his children, adding another demand to her already heavy responsibilities.

In 1866 she settled at Windsor to be closer to her sons, who were being educated at near-by Eton School. That year, her second cousin, Annie Louisa Walker, came to live with her as a companion-housekeeper. Windsor was now to be her home for the rest of her life.

Her literary career for three decades was one of constant delivery and success. Whether she wrote historical works or across several genres in fiction: domestic realism, historical, romance or supernatural she was successful.

For more than thirty years she pursued a varied literary career but family life continued to bring problems.

The literary ambitions she wished for her sons were unfulfilled. Cyril Francis, the eldest, died in 1890, leaving a Life of Alfred de Musset, incorporated in his mother's Foreign Classics for English Readers. The younger, Francis, who she nicknamed 'Cecco', collaborated with her in the Victorian Age of English Literature and won a position at the British Museum, but was rejected by Sir Andrew Clark, a famous physician. Cecco died in 1894.

With the last of her children now lost to her, she had but little further interest in life. Her health steadily and inexorably declined.

Margaret Oliphant Wilson Oliphant died at the age of 69 in Wimbledon on 20th June 1897. She is buried in Eton beside her sons.

At her death, Margaret was still working on Annals of a Publishing House, a record of Blackwood's Magazine with which she had enjoyed such a successful relationship.

Her Autobiography and Letters, which present a thoughtful picture of her domestic anxieties, was published in 1899. Only parts were written with a wider audience in mind: she had originally intended the Autobiography for her son, but he died before she could finish it.

Opinions on Oliphant's work are split, with some critics seeing her as a 'domestic novelist', while others recognize her work as influential and important to the Victorian literature canon. Critical reception from her contemporaries is also divided. John Skelton took the view that Oliphant wrote too much and too quickly. Writing a Blackwood's article called 'A Little Chat About Mrs. Oliphant', he asked, "Had Mrs. Oliphant concentrated her powers, what might she not have done? We might have had another Charlotte Brontë or another George Eliot." However not all of the contemporary reception was negative. The esteemed M. R. James admired Oliphant's supernatural fiction, concluding that "the religious ghost story, as it may be called, was never done better than by Mrs. Oliphant in 'The Open Door' and 'A Beleaguered City'. Mary Butts lavished praise on Oliphant's ghost story 'The Library Window', describing it as "one masterpiece of sober loveliness".

More modern critics of Oliphant's work include Virginia Woolf, who asked in Three Guineas whether Oliphant's autobiography does not lead the reader "to deplore the fact that Mrs. Oliphant sold her brain, her very admirable brain, prostituted her culture and enslaved her intellectual liberty in order that she might earn her living and educate her children."

Whatever the merits of their cases Margaret Oliphant has been shamefully neglected in modern years. She is now becoming more widely recognised as a leading writer of her day.

Margaret Oliphant – A Concise Bibliography

A canon of more than 120 works, including novels, travel books, histories, and volumes of literary criticism.

Novels

Margaret Maitland (1849)
Merkland (1850)
Caleb Field (1851)
John Drayton (1851)
Adam Graeme (1852)
The Melvilles (1852)
Katie Stewart (1852)
Harry Muir (1853)
Ailieford (1853)
The Quiet Heart (1854)
Magdalen Hepburn (1854)
Zaidee (1855)
Lilliesleaf (1855)
Christian Melville (1855)
The Athelings (1857)
The Days of My Life (1857)
Orphans (1858)
The Laird of Norlaw (1858)
Agnes Hopetoun's Schools and Holidays (1859)
Lucy Crofton (1860)
The House on the Moor (1861)
The Last of the Mortimers (1862)
Heart and Cross (1863)
Salem Chapel (1863)
The Rector (1863)
Doctor's Family (1863)
The Perpetual Curate (1864)
Miss Marjoribanks (1866)
Phoebe Junior (1876)
A Son of the Soil (1865)
Agnes (1866)
Madonna Mary (1867)
Brownlows (1868)
The Minister's Wife (1869)
The Three Brothers (1870)
John: A Love Story (1870)
Squire Arden (1871)
At his Gates (1872)
Ombra (1872
May (1873)
Innocent (1873)
The Story of Valentine and his Brother (1875)
A Rose in June (1874)
For Love and Life (1874)
Whiteladies (1875)
An Odd Couple (1875)

The Curate in Charge (1876)
Carità (1877)
Young Musgrave (1877)
Mrs. Arthur (1877)
The Primrose Path (1878)
Within the Precincts (1879)
The Fugitives (1879)
A Beleaguered City (1879)
The Greatest Heiress in England (1880)
He That Will Not When He May (1880)
In Trust (1881)
Harry Joscelyn (1881)
Lady Jane (1882)
A Little Pilgrim in the Unseen (1882)
The Lady Lindores (1883)
Sir Tom (1883)
Hester (1883)
It Was a Lover and his Lass (1883)
The Lady's Walk (1883)
The Wizard's Son (1884)
Madam (1884)
The Prodigals and their Inheritance (1885)
Oliver's Bride (1885)
A Country Gentleman and his Family (1886)
A House Divided Against Itself (1886)
Effie Ogilvie (1886)
A Poor Gentleman (1886)
The Son of his Father (1886)
Joyce (1888)
Cousin Mary (1888)
The Land of Darkness (1888)
Lady Car (1889)
Kirsteen (1890)
The Mystery of Mrs. Biencarrow (1890)
Sons and Daughters (1890)
The Railway Man and his Children (1891)
The Heir Presumptive and the Heir Apparent (1891)
The Marriage of Elinor (1891)
Janet (1891)
The Cuckoo in the Nest (1892)
Diana Trelawny (1892)
The Sorceress (1893)
A House in Bloomsbury (1894)
Sir Robert's Fortune (1894)
Who Was Lost and is Found (1894)
Lady William (1894)
Two Strangers (1895)
Old Mr. Tredgold (1895)

The Unjust Steward (1896)
The Ways of Life (1897)

Short stories
Neighbours on the Green (1889)
A Widow's Tale and Other Stories (1898)
That Little Cutty (1898)
The Open Door (1918)

Selected Articles

Mary Russel Mitford (Blackwood's Magazine, Vol. 75, 1854)
Evelin and Pepys (Blackwood's Magazine, Vol. 76, 1854)
The Holy Land (Blackwood's Magazine, Vol. 76, 1854)
Mr. Thackeray and his Novels (Blackwood's Magazine, Vol. 77, 1855)
Bulwer (Blackwood's Magazine, Vol. 77, 1855)
Charles Dickens (Blackwood's Magazine, Vol. 77, 1855)
Modern Novelists—Great and Small (Blackwood's Magazine, Vol. 77, 1855)
Modern Light Literature: Poetry (Blackwood's Magazine, Vol. 79, 1856)
Religion in Common Life (Blackwood's Magazine, Vol. 79, 1856)
Sydney Smith (Blackwood's Magazine, Vol. 79, 1856)
The Laws Concerning Women (Blackwood's Magazine, Vol. 79, 1856)
The Art of Caviling (Blackwood's Magazine, Vol. 80, 1856)
Béranger (Blackwood's Magazine, Vol. 83, 1858)
The Condition of Women (Blackwood's Magazine, Vol. 83, 1858)
The Missionary Explorer (Blackwood's Magazine, Vol. 83, 1858)
Religious Memoirs (Blackwood's Magazine, Vol. 83, 1858)
Social Science (Blackwood's Magazine, Vol. 88, 1860)
Scotland and her Accusers (Blackwood's Magazine, Vol. 90, 1861)
The Chronicles of Carlingford (Blackwood's Magazine 1862–1865)
Girolamo Savonarola (Blackwood's Magazine, Vol. 93, 1863)
The Life of Jesus (Blackwood's Magazine, Vol. 96, 1864)
Giacomo Leopardi (Blackwood's Magazine, Vol. 98, 1865)
The Great Unrepresented (Blackwood's Magazine, Vol. 100, 1866)
Mill on the Subjection of Women (The Edinburgh Review, Vol. 130, 1869)
The Opium-Eater (Blackwood's Magazine, Vol. 122, 1877)
Russian and Nihilism in the Novels of I. Tourgeniéf (Blackwood's Magazine, Vol. 127, 1880)
School and College (Blackwood's Magazine, Vol. 128, 1880)
The Grievances of Women (Fraser's Magazine, New Series, Vol. 21, 1880)
Mrs. Carlyle (The Contemporary Review, Vol. 43, May 1883)
The Ethics of Biography (The Contemporary Review, July 1883)
Victor Hugo (The Contemporary Review, Vol. 48, July/December 1885)
A Venetian Dynasty (The Contemporary Review, Vol. 50, August 1886)
Laurence Oliphant (Blackwood's Magazine, Vol. 145, 1889)
Tennyson (Blackwood's Magazine, Vol. 152, 1892)
Addison, the Humorist (Century Magazine, Vol. 48, 1894)

The Anti-Marriage League (Blackwood's Magazine, Vol. 159, 1896)

Biographies

Edward Irving (1862)
Francis of Assisi (1871)
Count de Montalembert (1872)
Dante (1877)
Cervantes (1880)
Life of Sheridan in the English Men of Letters series (1883)
John Tulloch (1888)
Laurence Oliphant (1892)

Historical & Critical Works

Historical Sketches of the Reign of George II (1869)
The Makers of Florence (1876)
A Literary History of England from 1760 to 1825 (1882)
The Makers of Venice (1887)
Royal Edinburgh (1890)
Jerusalem (1891)
The Makers of Modern Rome (1895)
William Blackwood and his Sons (1897)
The Sisters Brontë. In: Women Novelists of Queen Victoria's Reign (1897)

Made in United States
North Haven, CT
13 March 2023

34015754R00143